CRASH INTO ME

FLYNN & BRIGHTEN

KNOX COUNTY
BOOK 4

RACHAEL OGLE

CONTENTS

Author's Note   vii

PART 1
HIGH SCHOOL, END OF SENIOR YEAR
17 YEARS AGO

Chapter 1   3
Flynn

Chapter 2   11
Brighten

Chapter 3   22
Flynn

Chapter 4   35
Brighten

Chapter 5   49
Flynn

Chapter 6   59
Flynn

Chapter 7   66
Flynn

Chapter 8   72
Brighten

Chapter 9   81
Flynn

Chapter 10   89
Brighten

Chapter 11   100
Flynn

Chapter 12   109
Flynn

Chapter 13   116
Brighten

PART 2
COLLEGE, JUNIOR YEAR
14 YEARS AGO

Chapter 14   131
Flynn

Chapter 15   141
Brighten

Chapter 16   154
Flynn

Chapter 17   161
Brighten

Chapter 18   169
Flynn

Chapter 19   178
Brighten

Chapter 20   187
Brighten

Chapter 21   199
Flynn

Chapter 22   206
Brighten

PART 3
COLLEGE, SENIOR YEAR
14 YEARS AGO

Chapter 23   215
Brighten

Chapter 24   224
Brighten

Chapter 25   233
Flynn

Chapter 26   246
Flynn — Six Months Later

Chapter 27   252
Brighten

Chapter 28   261
Flynn

Chapter 29   274
Brighten

PART 4
THE DARK DAYS
3-13 YEARS AGO

Chapter 30   287
Flynn

PART 5
PRESENT DAY

Chapter 31   299
Brighten

Chapter 32   310
Flynn

Chapter 33   319
Brighten

Chapter 34   329
Flynn

Chapter 35   343
Brighten

Chapter 36   350
Flynn

Chapter 37   361
Brighten

Chapter 38   369
Flynn

Chapter 39   381
Brighten

Chapter 40   394
Flynn

Chapter 41   405
Brighten

Epilogue   412

Also by Rachael Ogle   417
About the Author   419

AUTHOR'S NOTE

Dear Reader,

As with my other books, I will try to be as transparent as possible about the contents of these pages. **YOUR MENTAL HEALTH MATTERS!**

Just because a book has a happy ending doesn't always mean that it's a fun, fluffy, happy journey all the way through. Flynn and Brighten's story is no exception. To date, this story is one that has stuck with me the most and I'm not going to lie, it came close to breaking me a few times. **Emotional damage ahead. You've been warned.**

This story contains themes relating to **chronic/terminal illness of a parent**, **death of a parent** (off-page), **cancer** (not MC), **death of a spouse** (off-page), **alcoholism** (not MC), **car accident** (not MC, historical, off-page), **gore**, **pregnancy**, **forced birth**, **depression**, and **suicidal ideation**.

Please protect your peace. No book is worth your mental health; not even mine.

Much love, Rach

Playlist

Dress | Taylor Swift	03:50
Hands to Myself | Selena Gomez	03:21
18 | One Direction	04:08
Everything has Changed (Taylor's Version) | Taylor Swift, Ed Sheeran	04:05
Not In The Same Way | 5 Seconds of Summer	03:41
Foolish One (Taylor's Version) | Taylor Swift	05:12
Love You Goodbye | One Direction	03:17
Love in the Dark | Adele	04:46
Right Where You Left Me | Taylor Swift	04:05
Tin Man | Miranda Lambert	04:19
Every Little Thing | Carly Pearce	03:00
She Used to Be Mine | Sara Bareilles	04:10
Favorite Crime | Olivia Rodrigo	02:33
That Way | Tate McRae	02:55
1000 Times | Sara Bareilles	04:30
Power Over Me | Dermot Kennedy	03:27
Gravity | Sara Bareilles	03:53
Last Kiss (Taylor's Version) | Taylor Swift	06:09
What a Time | Julia Michaels, Niall Horan	02:53
Someone You Loved | Lewis Capaldi	03:02
How Do I Say Goodbye | Dean Lewis	02:44
Sad Beautiful Tragic (Taylor's Version) | Taylor Swift	04:45
I Miss My Friend | Darryl Worley	04:03
See You Later (Ten Years) | Jenna Raine	03:08
Moonlight Sonata | Ludwig von Beethoven	07:27

PART 1

HIGH SCHOOL, END OF SENIOR YEAR

17 YEARS AGO

CHAPTER ONE

FLYNN

Surely, I must be dreaming. Or maybe I'm in a coma and this is the way my brain is attempting to heal itself. Or more likely, I'm dead and this is my heaven. It's the only legitimate explanation for the question Brighten just asked me.

"I'm sorry, what?" My voice cracks as I say the words, I'm so caught off guard. I know there's no way she just asked me what she did, because that would be impossible. I clear my throat and repeat my question.

She rolls her eyes. "Don't be so dramatic. It's just sex."

Except that it's not. It would be sex. With *Brighten*. It would be doing what I've been firmly convincing myself would never happen between the two of us. What I'd convinced myself *could* never happen. Not with her.

It would be a line we can't uncross. It would jeopardize a six-year friendship. I'm not sure I could do it. Not because I don't want to, but because I do. I just never thought Brighten saw me that way. Not Brighten Dawes of the perfect hair and body and face and personality variety. Not when it's me of the none of those things.

I'm not Jess. My twin brother—who, although identical to me, *isn't*. Jess, who doesn't need braces or glasses or Accutane for terrible acne. Jess, who can eat whatever the fuck he wants and, as long as he plays a game of pickup basketball, never has to worry about losing his six-pack. Jess, who has worked his way through the entire girls' volleyball team in the past year. Jess, who has *game*. I'm just me, who has none.

When I don't say anything, she puts her hand on my arm. Her hand with those long, slender fingers that play piano better than anyone I've ever known. The hand that she uses to ruffle my messy hair and push my glasses back up my nose and fist bump me with when we play *Mario Kart* and ace math tests. "Are you telling me you want to graduate high school a virgin?"

I blush. "No, of course not. But did you have to come out and say it like that?"

Brighten frowns, her auburn brows drawing down over those huge green eyes that I could pick out of lineup of thousands of other green eyes. "Like what?"

I lower my voice, even though everyone else in the cafeteria is caught up in their own conversations. "You said, 'I think we should fuck' like you would've said, 'The sky is blue.' Like it wouldn't be a big fucking deal, Crash."

"Why? Like I said, it's just sex. I'd rather lose my virginity to my best friend than some guy who doesn't know me or wouldn't actually take his time. I'd rather it be with someone I trust than some frat guy in college who will be too set on adding a notch to his bed post to make my experience enjoyable. I'd rather it be with someone who won't flinch when they see my scar."

Her last sentence makes me angry. "Who would flinch if they saw it? Your scar's badass."

She rolls her eyes. "I know you think so but it freaks a lot of people out. And you haven't even seen all of it, so you might flinch, too."

"No, I wouldn't." I'd probably be too busy looking at her tits to even notice the scar I know runs from her sternum across to her right armpit.

"See? It has to be you. You're one of the only people who doesn't try to kiss up to me in the hopes that they can meet my mom."

I shrug. "Your mom's a bitch."

She laughs. "See. You also don't sugarcoat with me."

"Because I'm an asshole."

She narrows her eyes. "We both know you're not. You just have a very low tolerance for bullshit. Good thing I don't bullshit."

I look down at my untouched lunch, my glasses sliding down my nose. I don't know how to tell her no because I don't want to. I also don't know how to tell her yes since if I do this, it will be the final thing that pushes me over the edge for her.

For the past three years, I've had feelings for her, but she doesn't feel the same way about me. It really is just friends for her and I accept that. And I get wanting to be comfortable with the first person you have sex with; I really do. But this isn't like us practicing kissing when we were fifteen. Although, to be fair, I'd say that's what did it for me.

This is sex.

It's a big fucking deal.

"Flynn, are you really going to make me beg? Don't let my first time be terrible, please?" she pleads. And that voice she uses when she really wants to get her way kills me because I always end up doing whatever she wants. It's my fucking kryptonite.

I look back over at her, my heart pounding, and push my glasses back up. "How would we even do this? When? Where?

Because neither of us has a big enough car for something like this. Jess said it's a pain in the ass to navigate."

She laughs. "He would know." Thinking for a moment, she plucks at her bottom lip. Those lips that I know the feel and taste and fullness of and think about regularly when I'm alone. Thoughts like, what they'd feel like other places on my body. What they'd look like wrapped around—. "My mom will be gone this weekend on a shoot; we could do it Saturday."

Her tone is so nonchalant, I have no clue how I'm even supposed to react. That only gives me two days to prepare myself. *Shit*. Should I be truthful and explain why this is a terrible fucking idea for me? Or, can I simply be her friend in this and fulfill a need for her? Could I do that without leaving her house completely in love with her? Probably not, but I also don't want her to have a shit first time. I'm not so much worried about me because I'm a guy and any sex would be fantastic, I'm sure. But her first time should be as perfect as possible.

And at least, if it's me, I can make sure it is, right?

I level her with a gaze. "Are you sure you want to do this? With me, I mean?" I hope she doesn't hear the vulnerability in my voice. I can't help but add, "You don't think it might make things weird between us?"

She frowns. "Why would it be weird? You're my best friend, Flynn. You know me better than anyone. Hell, we've kissed. That was okay, right? It hasn't been weird since then."

It was fucking amazing.

"Yeah, of course. I—I don't want you to have any regrets."

"Why would I have regrets?"

I shrug, unable to tell her that as hung up as she is about her scar, I'm self-conscious about my entire body. When you have a twin who's body is the ideal and yours isn't, it tends to fuck with your mind. And if she saw me naked and didn't like what she saw, I'm not sure I'd be able to handle it.

Instead, I swallow thickly and ask, "What if you fall in love someday? Don't you want that guy to be your first?"

She snorts. "Yeah, I think not. You know I don't believe in love. On the off chance I do, by the time I meet the guy, I will be a sex goddess and be able to wow him with my skills."

Tamping down that sliver of hope she could've ever said anything remotely resembling, "But I'm already in love with *you*, Flynn." I know, I know. It does me no good to play out scenarios in my head.

Nerves already twisting in my gut, I blow out a breath. "So, Saturday?"

Her eyes widen in shocked delight. "So, is that a yes?"

Even knowing I'll probably regret this, I nod. Not physically. Physically, it will probably be amazing. Emotionally, I will definitely regret this. Because for her, it will be nothing. For me, it will be...*everything*.

"Okay, well I guess, here's to Saturday," she says excitedly, holding up her bottle of Mountain Dew like a toast. I clink my glass of tea to her soda and smile back at her.

Later at home, I'm staring at the same passage from my assigned English reading that I've been trying to read for an hour—but have been imagining what having sex with Brighten will be like—when I feel a sharp pain in my arm. I look up and see Jess standing, annoyed, by my bed. "What the hell, dude?" I yell and rub the ache out of my bicep.

"I called your name a ton. What's up with you?"

I shut my book and toss it onto the bed and push my glasses up my nose. "Nothing."

"You sure? You look like you did before you took your ACTs. You're not redoing them again, are you? You've already scored high enough to get into any school you want, man."

"I'm not taking them again."

"So, what's up?"

I shake my head. "Like I said, nothing. Just thinking about graduation. Was there something you needed?"

"Oh, right. Dad said supper's almost done."

"Okay."

I slide off the bed and start toward the door and Jess grabs my arm. "Is it a girl?"

"What?"

He heaves an exasperated sigh. "What's got you all twisted? Is it a girl?"

"There is no girl, you know that."

"Just because you don't have one doesn't mean there isn't one you want. There are plenty I want," he says with a smirk.

"There are plenty you get, too, Jess," I reply, annoyed.

"Don't get all pissy with me just because you won't put yourself out there a little more. Maybe if you didn't look like you had a giant stick up your ass most of the time, people might like you, you know. You're not half bad sometimes. I'm sure there's a girl who'd want you when you're having five good minutes." He laughs. "Five minutes would probably be about all you need."

"Is that what it was like for you the first time? Five minutes?" The words are out of my mouth before I can stop them, but oh, well.

He blinks, surprised by my question. "Oh, uh, yeah, I guess. First time's pretty shit. Especially if the girl's a virgin, too. It hurts her and you're trying not to pop off in thirty seconds."

"So, it was bad?"

One brow lifts in curiosity. "Why are you so curious all of a sudden? Are you thinking about finally cashing in your V-card? It's about time."

I roll my eyes. "I'm eighteen. Statistically, I will live until I'm at least in my seventies. I'm still in my infancy. Being a virgin isn't a huge thing."

"Let's talk again after you're no longer a virgin." His tone is amused, but then he sobers. "Is there someone?" I shrug. "So, that's a yes. Anyone I know?"

"Jess, we know all the same people."

"So, that's a yes, too. Okay. Who? And does Brighten approve, because if she doesn't get along with her, it'll never work out. I mean, if you want it to work out. If you're only looking to get down and get gone, I guess it doesn't matter what Brighten thinks." I swallow at the mention of Brighten's name and look at my feet. "Holy shit. It's Brighten? When did this happen? I didn't even know you guys were like that."

"We're not," I say with a sigh and drag my hands through my hair. "She wants to get things over with, so to speak, and would rather it be with someone she knows and trusts than some frat guy when she goes to college in the fall. She's worried about her scar and being self-conscious."

"But y'all are just friends?" he confirms.

"Yeah."

"Would you worry she's going to fall for you and it be weird?"

"No," I reply pointedly. "She is just a friend."

That's all she'll ever be, unfortunately.

His brow furrows. "But is this what you want?"

"I don't want her to have a shitty first time if I can help it. She's my best friend."

"Hate to break it to you, but it will probably still be shit." I drop back onto the bed and take my glasses off and put my head in my hands. Jess chuckles and sits next to me. "Probably doesn't mean definitely, dude. I'm sure you'll be fine. Have y'all fooled around?"

"No, we kissed a few years ago, but that's it. And that was only so we'd know what to do. I guess I shouldn't be surprised by this, but I don't want to fuck it up."

"Has she fooled around with anyone?"

I shake my head. "Not that I know of. We talk about everything, so I can't imagine she would've and didn't tell me."

"And there hasn't been anyone else for you?"

I sigh. "Who would there have been, Jess?"

He splays his arms in an exaggerated shrug. "Fuck if I know. I'm just trying to get a frame of reference so I can gauge what you know."

I give my brother my full attention. "I know nothing, Jess. There's been no one else. Brighten is about the only person I'm able to put up with. I don't want things to be weird between us after, but she asked me for this, so I want to do it for her. She's my best friend."

My twin examines my face and finally nods. "Okay. Then there are some things you need to know."

CHAPTER TWO

BRIGHTEN

I stand at the mirror, taking stock. Is this really what I'm going to wear when I lose my virginity? Jeans and a T-shirt? I mean, it's not like this is an actual date. It's Flynn. And it's the checking of a box. Still, is this something I feel sexy in? Does it matter? Seems like Flynn wouldn't care. He wasn't too enthusiastic about the whole thing anyway.

I don't think he'll back down simply because I put on *the voice*. The voice that always makes him cave. Because in spite of his sullen exterior, he's really a big teddy bear. And Flynn is my best friend and would do anything for me.

Even this though?

He acted like it was a big deal, but I'm not sure why. If we were in a relationship, it might be, but that's not us. He's great, but I'm not sure I feel that way about anyone, not just him. Still, I couldn't think of anyone other than Flynn who I'd prefer to take this step with. If nothing else, he'll be gentle and caring, because that's him.

Scowling at my appearance, I drag off the T-shirt and jeans. For a split second, I imagine what would happen if I answered the door in my underwear. It would be a shock, for sure, but probably too much, right? Rehanging my discarded clothes, I flip through my closet one last time until I come across a black sundress. I won't be able to wear a bra with it, but I guess that doesn't matter.

Pulling the dress off the hanger, I bring it over to the bed and lay it out before unhooking my bra. My left hand reflexively comes to cover my right breast, the scar tissue puckered under my fingers. Flynn knows I have it. He's seen some of it, but not all of it. He won't flinch. He said so. And if he said so, I believe him.

I think back on our six years of friendship. And truthfully, if I didn't have this scar, we might not even be friends. Despite attending the same school since kindergarten, we didn't hang out. Flynn's always been pretty quiet. Jess was always the life of the party; the sweet to Flynn's sour.

But that all changed the day I crashed my bike and was impaled on a piece of steel at a construction site. Flynn happened to be walking by and he stayed with me until the ambulance got there. He visited me every day at the hospital and I realized there was more to Flynn than what everyone else saw. We bonded over *Mario Kart* and he snuck me Mountain Dew into my hospital room. We've been inseparable ever since.

I know I'm probably what most people would consider "conventionally attractive". I'm average height and weight, even though Vanessa thinks I can stand to lose ten pounds. I tend to eat another slice of pizza when she says this. She also thinks I should go blonde, but I love my red hair. How can I not; I got it from my dad. I wish it wasn't one of the only things I got from him. I look like my mother. Well, at least my mother before the Botox and implants and all the things she felt were necessary to compete with women younger than her.

Not wanting to think about her, I take a moment to pull on

the dress and give myself one last look, unwilling to change clothes again. Scanning my room—God, I can't wait to escape this princess pink hell. Seriously, a canopy bed, Vanessa? What am I, seven? And still, I ensure everything is in place and check my nightstand one last time, even though I know there are condoms in the drawer, since they gave them to me at the health department when I got my prescription for birth control pills last year.

I thought by now, I would've been able to put those suckers to use, but no takers, unfortunately. I'm not sure why neither Flynn nor I have dated anyone during high school. Well, I think he hasn't because he can't stand a lot of the people we go to school with; he's smarter than most of them. And if we were in the same grade as Cole Campbell, he and Flynn would've probably vied for valedictorian. But Cole and his twin brother, Silas, graduated last year, and now it's our turn. And Flynn is the valedictorian.

And not that Flynn is pretentious, but he likes to be around people who can keep his interest intellectually. As it were, he bores easily. Well, except for *Mario Kart*. With that, he's a big 'ol kid.

I'm not sure why Flynn doesn't have a girlfriend. Granted, Jess has made quite a splash in the dating pool at our school since his breakup with Josie Campbell—Cole and Silas's younger sister—last year, but Flynn is an amazing guy. He's my favorite person. And no, he's not ripped like Jess, but he's definitely still handsome. In truth, I like that he's not so muscle-bound. I like that he's soft. He's my teddy bear.

The doorbell rings and my heart lurches. Showtime, I guess. I head down the steps and smooth my dress one last time before I check the peephole and open the door. Flynn stands on the porch with a smile, his braces peeking out, his black-framed glasses already sliding down his nose and covering the green eyes I could identify by their shade alone. They're this great mossy green with golden-honey around the pupil. He pushes his glasses back up and steps inside and shoves his hands in the pockets of his jeans. "Hey," I say, feeling like tension enters the house the same time he does.

"Hey, Crash."

I relax a bit with his pet name for me. I used to hate the nickname he gave me, since it reminded me of my accident. But now, I don't know what I'd do if he didn't call me that and I give him a smile.

"I ordered pizza, so it should be here any minute. I made some tea for you, too."

He nods. "Thanks. By the way, you look really nice."

"Thanks, Flynn; so do you." And he does. His longish, dark hair looks to be behaving for once. Or, more likely, he's not dragged his fingers through it to the point of making it a disheveled mess. His Yale T-shirt is clean and he's ditched his standard hoodie. I turn to walk toward the living room and I don't have to look to see if he's following. "I'm thinking I need a Rainbow Road rematch. I swear, I'm *this* close to whipping your ass."

Flynn huffs a laugh. "Keep dreaming."

"Want to boot up the GameCube and I'll get our drinks?"

"Sure."

I leave him in front of the TV and go into the kitchen to pour our drinks. Adding ice to the glasses, my eyes slide to the liquor cabinet and for a brief moment, I debate downing a shot of something to take the edge off. It is what my mother would do, after all. Hell, she'd probably down half the bottle in three long gulps. But that's not how I want to lose my virginity. I want to be sharp and remember everything. And God knows the last thing I ever want to be is like my mother.

Returning to the living room, I set our drinks on the coffee table, along with some plates and paper towels. The doorbell rings again and Flynn takes off to retrieve the pizza. I follow to pay, but he's already got his wallet out. When he turns, pizza in hand, I frown. "I was getting my purse."

"I got it. It's fine." We start back toward the living room and he drops the box onto the coffee table.

"I'll pay you back before you leave."

"I said it's fine. Don't think twenty bucks is going to break me."

I drop to my knees and fold my legs under me. "You're saving for a new car, so yeah, it might."

He shrugs and opens the box and pulls out a slice for each of us. "You pay all the time. It makes me feel like a mooch."

"Correction," I say around a mouth full of food, "my mother pays for everything. Might as well accept her financial love since lord knows I'll probably never get her emotional love. Besides, it brings me great joy for her to know I bought carbs and dairy with her money. I'm sure, if she could move her face, she'd have so many wrinkles from simply frowning at me so much. So, yes, you will let me pay you back. When you are some big shot and making six figures a year, you can buy me dinner to repay me."

"*If* I'm ever a big shot. I have to graduate, finish college, find a job, *and* be good at it before I can ever be considered a big shot."

I roll my eyes and give his statement a dismissive wave. "Details. You'll get there. You're the smartest and most driven person I know. I mean, do you know anyone else who got accepted to Harvard, Yale, Princeton, and Dartmouth? And yet, you chose to stay home and go to UT."

He shrugs. "Even though I plan on making a shit-ton of money, I don't want to have to spend it all on student loans."

"Yeah, I think we both know there's more to it than that.

You could probably get any scholarship you wanted. You want to stay close to your dad. And that makes you a good son and terribly sweet."

My statement affords me a glare from him. "I'm not sweet."

"Sure you are. You just don't want people to know. Because then, they'd see what a big softie you are and not the broody asshole you project. And then everyone would want to be your friend and you'd become Mr. Popular and leave me behind."

Flynn snorts and takes a sip of his tea, working his tongue behind his lips to try to clear his braces of pizza. When he's finished, he shakes his head. "For starters, you're delusional. Seems to me you have your mom's flair for the dramatic, Crash. I don't want more friends. You are more than enough energy for me most of the time. Secondly, I could never leave you behind; you're the only person I actually like."

"So you say, but what will you do in the fall?"

"Oh, you mean when you're off at NYU becoming the next big political mind? I'll probably still be a broody asshole."

"I'll be home to visit, so you'll have to drop the scaly armor when we get together."

He takes a deep breath and lets it out. "I will." Tossing his uneaten crust onto his plate, he dusts off his hands, signaling— as is his custom—that he's finished. As usual, he also rises to go brush his teeth. Braces are a bitch and one thing about Flynn is, he's fastidious about his personal hygiene.

But knowing he's going to have minty breath and I'm going to have pizza breath, I realize I should probably brush my teeth, too. I jump up to dump our scraps in the trash and set the dishes in the sink before running up the stairs to my room and my bathroom.

When I return, he's still not back, so I retake my seat on the floor and get *Mario Kart* going. Doing a practice run of Rainbow Road so I can hopefully—finally—beat him, he rejoins me. "You always take those curves too fast and you get too close to the edge."

I scoff. "You ride the edge, too."

He smirks. "Yeah, but I'm better at it than you."

I narrow my eyes at him. "Put up or shut up, Tate."

Flynn's smirk morphs into a full-blown grin. It's rare that he smiles big because he hates his braces, but occasionally, he'll give me that huge, lopsided smile that makes him look more carefree and I love it. "Fine, but no crying like a baby when I beat your ass." He scoots closer to me and picks up his controller.

"Best two out of three," I supply.

"So, only two then?" he quips.

"So cocky. But one of these days, I will beat you. I will stand over your decimated corpse and plant my foot on your chest and have my moment of victory."

He laughs as we choose our characters. "Wow, you really are your mother's daughter. That was quite the theatrical answer. Speaking of your mother, where is 'ol Vanessa this weekend?"

"Shooting a commercial for some face cream, I think. Like her lack of wrinkles is the product of a ten-dollar moisturizer. It's such a joke. She's got a project this summer, too."

"Do you have to go?"

"Have to? No, probably not. But it's in Ireland, so that might be cool."

"Oh. Well, kiss the Blarney Stone for me."

"You could come with me."

He falters his controller and hits pause. "What?"

I shrug and look at him. "What? You could come. My mom wouldn't care. She'd pay, you know that."

"I can't go to Ireland."

"Why not? It'd be fun. We could see all the castles. The

legal drinking age over there is eighteen, so we could bar hop and have one last hurrah before we have to be adults and shit."

"I have that internship with Intuition. It starts the first week of June. I'll be in Nashville all summer."

"Oh, right." For some reason, although I knew about his internship, him coming with me to Ireland was the only thing that sounded right. I nod. "And you're going to be great at it. You'll wear a suit every day. No more hoodies? Whatever will you do with yourself?"

He rolls his eyes. "Don't remind me."

"You're going to get a lot of tail dressed in a suit, you know. The ladies love that."

He shakes his head. "I'm an asshole, remember? Jess is the one who got all the game genes, not me."

Sighing, I turn my body to face his. "I think you just need some confidence." I take the controller from his hand and set them both down and pat his knee. "Turn around here and face me."

His dark brows draw down in confusion but he obeys. I fold my legs to mirror his, but tuck my dress under me so I don't flash anything. Although, that thought almost makes me want to laugh, because isn't that what we're doing tonight? I shake the thoughts away and scoot a bit closer to him until our knees touch.

"You act like you're this horrible troll, Flynn. Are you prickly to almost everyone? Yeah. Can you be a know-it-all? Yeah. Are you so competitive you'd trip your own mother in a footrace in order to win? Also, yes. But you're also compassionate and kind and so brilliant it blows my mind. You're usually five steps ahead of your opponent and it's going to make you a shark when you get a job."

He swallows and rakes his teeth over his bottom lip. "It's easy for you and Jess and Josie and Hensley. Y'all are likable.

You guys are all good looking and have great taste. I don't know how to ingratiate myself to people. Hell, I'll probably flame out of this internship because I'm not a people person."

"So, learn. You think everyone doesn't have confidence issues about something? We all do. At least yours is something you can change. You can learn to play the part you have to in order to succeed." I reflexively bring my hand to my chest. "Some of us aren't so lucky."

Flynn's expression softens and his eyes fall to where my hand rests before bringing his gaze back to mine. "Anyone who is worth your time won't care about your scar, Crash."

"Yeah, and anyone worth your time will be able to see past that façade you put in place. Because deep down, you're a sweet guy, Flynn. I won't always be the only one who knows that."

I reach up to take off his glasses and he startles. "What are you doing?"

"I want to see your eyes without them."

He huffs a laugh but doesn't stop me from sliding them off his face. I fold them up and set them on the coffee table. "They look the same. The glasses don't change them, they just correct my vision."

"Not up close. You'll still be able to see me. I think sometimes, you hide behind these, too."

"Without my glasses, who would be able to tell I'm Flynn and not Jess? Oh, right. Jess is shredded and has the good skin and perfect hair. No worries about getting us mixed up," he says bitterly.

"Flynn, shut up. You're perfect."

He snorts. "Most definitely not. Perfect people don't have craters on their face or such bad teeth they require braces for their entire high school career or fifty pounds to lose."

I shake my head. "You know none of that stuff is what

makes you great, right? Although there's nothing wrong with you. Your skin is a lot better than it used to be, and you're getting your braces off in a month. And some girls like guys who are not all hard and chiseled. I like your body. But I like the guy underneath even better. Any girl who is only going to look at your face or hair or anything physical isn't going to be the right girl for you anyway."

His eyes slide away, but he's not really looking at anything, just considering my words. I bring my hands up to his face and turn him to look at me. "There's a reason you're my best friend, Flynn. I have great taste, remember? And for you to disparage yourself insults my good taste and I won't have it. You're the best guy I know. I get that all the girls are enamored with Jess. He's the life of the party and flashes his cocky grin and they all drop their panties.

"Don't get me wrong, your brother is a great guy, but I'm lucky because I'm fortunate enough to get to know how deep and insightful you are. All people see is his shiny exterior; they don't even look deeper; he doesn't ask them to. You make people work for it and only the ones who are willing to do the work are worth your time. It just makes me better than the rest of them."

"You are better than the rest of them. You're the best of all of them."

His words make warmth bloom in my chest and in this moment, there's nowhere else I'd rather be. Flynn truly is my best friend. His green eyes, lighter than my own *see* me; better than anyone else. And he's getting ready to do this great thing for me.

My hands are still on his face and his lips part on an exhale, his tongue darting out to wet them. I drop my eyes for a split second before rising to my knees and leaning in. Flynn's breath catches and he brings his hands up to grip my wrists. "Are you sure you want to do this?"

I freeze and search his eyes. "Why? Did you change your mind?"

His mouth opens and closes and he shakes his head and I let my hands fall from his face. "No, I just wanted to make sure." His throat bobs with a swallow. "It's something we can't take back."

"I know. But you're my best friend, Flynn. I don't want to do this with anyone else."

His chest rises and falls and he nods and lifts his hand to my face, his touch gentle. "If you change your mind, we stop, okay? If you get uncomfortable or anything at all, don't let me keep going. I don't want to hurt you."

"You won't hurt me."

"Promise me, Crash. I'm not willing to fuck up our friendship because you asked for this and I agreed and then you get cold feet and don't say anything until all over. I'd never forgive myself."

"I won't get cold feet. I promise." I stand, and with anticipatory butterflies swarming in my belly, I tilt my head in the direction of the stairs. Flynn's eyes widen ever so slightly and he swallows thickly before standing and grabbing his glasses from the table.

CHAPTER THREE

FLYNN

Holy. Fucking. Shit. Is this really happening? I know she was going to kiss me a minute ago, but now she's walking up the stairs to her room and I'm following, unable to take my eyes off her ass.

Although I excused myself earlier to brush my teeth and rub one out in the hopes I last longer than thirty seconds, this is so surreal now that it's actually go time.

I'm always caught off guard when I walk into Brighten's room. It's *so* not her. It's pink and ultra-feminine and looks like something a little girl obsessed with unicorns and fairytales would envy. That's not Brighten. I know Vanessa won't let her change it, so I'm interested to see what her own place will look like someday when she's able to make her own decor choices.

As it currently stands, there are about twenty frilly pink and white lace pillows on Brighten's huge white canopy bed. The walls are a soft pink and the floors are a bright white, high-pile carpet. Even as I lean against the door frame, unable to fully enter the room just yet, I marvel at how un-Brightenlike this space is.

"Your room is like something out of Wednesday Addams's nightmares. You realize that, right?"

Her lip curls up in disgust as she looks around. The white feminine furniture, girly floral paintings on the walls, the ornate bookshelf full of books that denote the only touches she's been allowed to add to this room. Tomes of non-fiction, political history books, thrillers, sci-fi, and mystery-suspense novels line the shelves.

"I cannot wait to get out of this Pepto Bismol hell. You don't get to rag me about it; you know how much I hate it."

I can't help but smile. Despite my nerves and apprehension about doing this, giving Brighten shit is fun. "I know. Let me guess, your NYU dorm room will be decked out in about fifty shades of black?"

"All I know is, if I ever have any pink in my future decor, feel free to take me out back and shoot me."

"I'll remember that."

While she shoves all the pillows off the bed into the floor on the other side, I take the opportunity to look at her without fear of her catching me. Starting at her feet, I lazily drag my eyes up her toned calves to what I can see of her thighs as she bends to continue tossing pillows. Although the dress she wears flows over her hips, you'd have to be blind to miss how fantastic her ass is. It's well honed from the years Vanessa made her do dance, even though she hated it. But in the year since she stopped, her body is still just as strong and graceful as it was.

As my eyes travel higher and higher, her long red hair tumbles over her shoulder in a thick sheet of copper, gold, and crimson. She turns her head to switch on the bedside lamp and I catch a glimpse of the elegant curve of her neck and jaw, her high cheekbones and big green eyes. I take a mental snapshot of her exactly like this because I never want to forget this moment. Or what's about to happen.

"Going to be hard for you to get me naked if you're standing way over there."

She sits on the edge of the bed and pats the spot beside her, and my heart lurches. And hard is an understatement. I'm not sure I'll be able to walk over to her and not draw attention to exactly how hard I am already. Just watching her and being in this room is enough to have my body thinking it's go time. I guess it is.

Toeing off my shoes and leaving them by the door, I shut it behind me before crossing the room, my heart hammering in my chest. Dropping onto the bed beside her, I will myself to calm down, knowing she may change her mind or decide halfway through she's not having a good time. I already gave her that out and at this point, I'm not sure whether I should hope she takes it.

Is it absurd to hope that she puts a stop to all of this? To want her to tell me she's changed her mind so we don't cross this line? To save me from what I know will happen if we do this. Because regardless of how badly I want this now that the option has been presented to me, I'm terrified that I'll lose her as my friend even more than I'm dying to know what it might be like to kiss and touch and feel her.

She might take the out when she sees me naked, for all I know; what with my chest hair and stretch marks and soft middle. I'm strong; I know that. I lift my dad from his wheelchair when his MS is particularly bad and his mobility suffers. I haul countless numbers of sacks of mulch and fertilizer at the garden shop where I work after school. But I'm not my brother with his rippling muscles and six-pack.

"Are you okay?" Brighten's hand squeezing mine brings me out of my thoughts and when I look at her, her expression is a bit apprehensive as well. "I know you asked me if I was sure, but are you? I know you said you haven't changed your mind, but I don't want you to feel pressured, either."

Am I sure? Sure that I want Brighten? I've never wanted anything more in my life. I know for her this is no big deal; something she simply wants out of the way. For me, it's so much more. But I can't tell her that. I don't have any delusions about the way she feels about me. And me telling her how I feel will only make this awkward. She'll be forced to tell me she only loves me as a friend and I'll be forced to continue to push my feelings down anyway, so what's the point?

I nod and hope the expression I give her looks reassuring. "I'm good, Crash." Relief flits through her gaze and her smile softens as I bring my free hand up to tuck her hair behind her ear. "Sorry if my hands are rough."

"Your hands are fine, Flynn. As long as they're clean, you'll hear no complaints from me."

I huff a laugh at her pragmatism. "They are."

"I know. You always have clean hands and fingernails in spite of working with all that dirt."

"I try." I let my fingertips trail down the side of her neck and jaw until her chin rests on my index finger. I can't resist running my thumb over her full bottom lip and her breath hitches.

"Flynn." I bring my eyes to hers, worried I'll see doubt, but all I see is her pupils blown wide and her breaths coming a bit short. "Kiss me?"

Instead of answering, I lean in until our lips meet. And it's different from last time, because I didn't have braces before, so I try to be mindful of that, but it's also different because I actually have feelings for her. Yep, I definitely have feelings for her. Her lips are soft and perfect and for several seconds, I simply give her these soft, gentle kisses, feeling her lips against mine.

Soon though, I need more and even though she's the one who wants this—has asked for this—she seems to be content to let me lead. I'm not sure what to do with that, but my body seems to know, so I go with it. Sliding my hand to the back of her neck and letting my fingers thread through the hair at her nape, I capture her bottom lip between mine and suck it gently and Brighten lets out a soft gasp that goes straight to my dick.

I tentatively swipe my tongue against the seam of her mouth and am met with no resistance. And even though we've done this before, the gravity of what's coming makes it feel all the more monumental. Brighten winds her arms around my neck and pulls me closer and I smile inwardly at the thought that she might also think this is good. Because it's really, *really* good. She tastes like mint and smells like that Victoria's Secret lotion she always wears and her tits rise and fall as her chest expands with each of her labored breaths.

After a long moment, I have to come up for air and I rest my forehead against hers as I try to collect myself. "Okay?" she asks.

"Yeah. You?"

"Yeah. I don't remember us kissing being like this last time."

I shake my head, unable to meet her gaze out of fear that she'll see my feelings in my eyes. "I don't think it was. It's alright, though, right?"

She smiles. "It's good, Flynn. Really good. You can touch me, you know."

Even hearing her say it makes my heart kick over. Touching will make it feel even more real and will be one more nail in the coffin that houses my "strictly platonic" feelings for Brighten. But God, how I want her. I want to know what she feels like and sounds like and smells like and tastes like. I want to be able to know that I was the first guy who was ever with her like this.

I'm not some kind of dreamer who thinks I'll be the only guy she's ever with. But I can be her first and I can make it memorable—and hopefully pleasurable—for her.

Tilting my head to claim her mouth again, she smiles against my lips and runs her fingers down my arm to my hand, where it's still planted on the mattress and lifts it, bringing it to her waist. I can't resist giving it a squeeze before wrapping my arm around her and pulling her closer.

Brighten shifts, never breaking our kiss, to straddle my lap. I'm so shocked by her movement, I pull back. "What?" she asks, her chest heaving.

I swallow, nerves knotting my guts. "Nothing, just surprised is all."

"Is this okay?"

I huff a laugh. "Everything is okay. Anything you want is okay."

She gives me a soft smile and slides my glasses off my face and sets them on the nightstand. "Anything you want is okay, too." She shifts in my lap and I know there's no way in hell she can miss how hard I am. Her grin turns a bit wicked, and my heart kicks over and my dick twitches. "I mean, it seems like you want something."

I have to grab her hips to stop her writhing against me. "You have to stop that," I say, nearly breathless.

She leans in and trails kisses up my jaw and my eyes fall closed and I can't stop myself from letting my hands roam over her hips and up her back and waist. Her lips brush down my neck and I almost shiver. "I like your hands on me."

"I like my hands on you, too, Crash." Dropping my hands to her ass, I give it a squeeze. "You've got a great ass."

She huffs a laugh against the side of my neck. "Well, thanks."

"You've got great everything."

"Not everything, but it's okay."

I pull back and return my hands to her face and force her to look me in the eye. "You're perfect. All of you." Keeping my gaze locked on hers, I slide my hands down to her hips and hold her in place as I grind myself against her. Her eyes widen slightly and her mouth falls open. "As cool and great as you are, if I wasn't attracted to you, I wouldn't have agreed to this. You're beautiful."

Covering her hand with my own, I bring them up to her right breast, where her scar is. "Every part of you is beautiful." She blinks rapidly and swallows and worries her bottom lip. Unable to not kiss that lip, I claim her mouth and Brighten lets out a soft moan into our kiss and God, I never want to hear another sound for the rest of my life.

I let my hands fall to her thighs, where they bracket my hips and run my fingertips up the outsides of them, feeling her soft skin under my fingers. She startles when I inch my hands under the hem of her dress and I freeze. I begin to pull back and she holds me in place. "I'm fine. It just tickled. Don't stop. Please."

Fuck, how can I stop when she pleads like that? Shit, I'm such a goner. Her skin is silky under my callused fingertips, and when I reach her hips and feel the elastic of her panties, I can't bite back a groan as I slide my thumbs under the sides and around to her ass. Her bare ass because she's wearing a thong. Sweet Jesus.

I grip those perfect globes and pull her into me, needing her closer and she gasps. "Oh God, Flynn."

My name on her lips like *that*? Fucking hell, I'm done for. Sliding my hands farther up her waist, I'm hindered by the top of her dress as it has no stretch. "Zipper," she supplies between kisses.

Yanking my hands out from under the dress and up to her back, I feel around until I find the fastener in question. Pulling my mouth from hers, I look into her eyes before I slide it down. "You're sure?"

She nods and returns to kissing me, her lips seeking and giving and making me forget why I had any reservations about this in the first place. The zipper descends, almost silently, exposing her back to my fingers. When it's completely down, she leans back and climbs off my lap to stand in front of me.

I try to prepare myself, but I'm not sure how I could ever prepare myself for this moment. Dragging her fingers over her shoulders, the straps slide down her arms, the dress following suit, revealing inch after inch of her breasts, stomach, hips, thighs, and the triangle of fabric covering her pussy.

Stepping out of the pool of black cotton at her feet, I can only stare in awe and release a slow *fuck* nearly under my breath as she closes the distance between us. I drag my eyes back up her body and hope she can see exactly how much I want her.

When she's within arm's reach I pull her in by her hips and look up at her. "You're so fucking perfect." She blushes but as her eyes fall to her scar, her confidence wanes. I shake my head. "Did I stutter?" She frowns and I bring my left hand up to trace her scar, starting at her sternum. "This scar?" I ignore the ache in my balls as I drag my fingertip across her breast, marveling at the softness of the swell. "This scar means you survived. This scar is the reason we're friends. This scar makes you my Crash. Don't hate on something that means so much to me."

I lean in to press my lips to her scar and Brighten's breath catches. And yes, her nipple is only a couple inches below the scar and I don't miss how hard it is, but I need her to know how much this scar changed not only her life, but mine.

She threads her fingers through my hair and arches her

back, her nipple dragging up my chin and against my lips. I can't resist sucking it into my mouth, swirling the tight peak with my tongue. "Shit," she breathes, her grasp on my hair stinging my scalp. I bring my hand up to her other breast and rub my thumb across the nipple, feeling it harden under my touch.

With my free hand, I tug her closer and into my lap as I kiss my way back up to her lips. When I cover her mouth with mine again, I can't keep the hunger out of the kiss; the need to claim her, make her mine. If only this once.

Wrapping my arms tight around her, I lift her and lay her on her back. She lets out a surprised yelp, but I don't stop kissing her as I run my hands down her body, memorizing her by touch. I slide my hand up her inner thigh and she shudders when my fingers brush the edge of the crotch of her panties. Pausing, I look down at her. "Do you want me to stop?"

"No. Please touch me, Flynn." Again, my heart kicks over hearing her ask me for what she wants; hearing my name on her lips. I bend to kiss her again and she puts her hand on my chest and I freeze.

"What?"

She doesn't say anything, but simply runs her hands down my sides and tugs up the hem of my shirt. I nearly yank it back down, but knowing how vulnerable she's been with me, I fight the urge. "Take this off?" I search her eyes and see nothing but encouragement. Taking a deep breath, I rise to my knees to pull off my shirt. Brighten smiles and when I start to lie down, she opens her mouth again. "And your pants?"

I huff a laugh and climb off the bed. With her eyes on me, I undo my belt and button and zipper of my jeans and let them fall down my hips, pushing them off with my feet before reaching down to tug off my socks and dropping them next to my pants.

Her eyes travel down my body as I rejoin her on the bed in only my boxers and she pulls me between her legs. Suddenly aware of how little is actually left between us, my heart rate picks up considerably. With her knees bracketing my hips and my chest pressed against her tits, it's all I can do to not bust from this alone.

"Your skin feels good against mine," she says softly, running her hand up my arm and over my shoulder.

"Yeah," I agree as her hand grips the back of my neck to pull my mouth back to hers. She rolls her hips against me and I feel the heat from her pussy radiate through the thin fabric of our underwear and I groan with the sensation and the thought of how close I am to her.

"Flynn, please touch me," she pleads in that voice that would make be happily jump off a fucking cliff if she asked. Even as I slide my hand back up her thigh, I can't stop myself from grinding into her, and her head falls back as she moans. "Shit."

"God, Crash."

"Sorry."

I freeze. "For what?"

"The noises. Sorry. I'll stop."

A bark of a laugh escapes me. "The fuck you will." She laughs and I claim her mouth as I push her panties to the side and nearly die with how wet she is. "Holy fuck," I breathe into our kiss.

Sweeping my fingers up her silky center, she moans when the tip of my finger brushes over a small, swollen pad of skin I know must be her clit. Inwardly, I'm pleased—ecstatic—that I've discovered it, but try to remember what Jess said. *Steady rhythm and pressure. Don't change things up once she starts moaning or grinding her hips. Don't fuck her until she's gotten off at least once, because that's what separates the boys from the men. A man takes care of her first.*

I follow his advice and sure enough, Brighten writhes her hips. "Oh God," she moans, making my cock jerk. "Oh, shit."

Dragging my mouth up her jaw, I whisper in her ear. "You feel so fucking good, Crash."

"Flynn, please. I need more."

Moving only on instinct—God knows it's not skill; not yet—I replace my finger with my thumb and slide one finger into her pussy and groan into her neck as she gasps. "Fuck, you're perfect."

Brighten pulls my face to hers and kisses me, a whine working its way up her throat as she grinds against my hand. I break my lips from hers to watch her face as I add another finger. Her mouth falls open on a moan and I never want to forget what her face looks like in this moment.

Her pussy pulses around my fingers and her breaths grow more and more short. I watch as her brows pinch together and a flush travels down her face and chest. "Oh God, Flynn, I'm coming. Oh, fuck."

My heart seems to stop beating altogether as she cries out, her hands gripping my shoulders, and I don't take a full breath until she does. I slowly withdraw my hand and she sits up and opens the drawer of her nightstand and fishes out a condom and extends it to me. Seeing the foil packet makes everything feel even more real and I take it, my chest heaving. Brighten shimmies her panties down her hips and lies down.

Heart thudding behind my ribs, I rise to shuck my boxers. I'm about to rip the wrapper, and she sits up. "Can I touch you?"

"Crash, if you touch me, I will probably blow my load. I'm barely hanging on by a thread here."

She doesn't touch, but looks on with curiosity. "Does it hurt? Being hard for so long?"

I shrug as I clumsily roll down the condom. "It aches a little."

"It's nice."

I huff a laugh and return to the bed. "It's nice that it aches? Thanks, that's sweet."

"No, smart ass. Your dick, it's nice. Pretty even."

I snort a laugh. "Dicks are not pretty. Pussies are pretty." I look down at hers in appreciation. "Like yours. That's pretty. Dicks are dicks."

We both sober as I settle between her legs, my cock pressing against her inner thigh. I grip her hip and bring my free hand up to her face. "Are you sure?"

"Yeah."

"I don't want to hurt you."

She gives me a reassuring smile. "I'll be fine. Kiss me?"

I nod and lower my mouth to hers for a hard kiss as I shift my hips forward. Groaning as I slide inside her, she gasps and bites down on her bottom lip. "You want me to stop?" My words come out between labored breaths because she's so tight and I'm trying not to move so I don't hurt her.

"No, I'm okay. It's just a lot." Her eyes meet mine and her cheeks are flushed. "Go slow?"

Giving her a jerky nod, I try to do just that, even though it feels like my dick is in a vice. I withdraw as slowly as I can before pushing back in. Although I already feel like I'm about to come, I try to hold off, my breaths turning into pants after only about a minute. Brighten tilts her hips and I groan through gritted teeth. "Fuck."

She touches my face. "Okay?"

I huff a laugh, trying with all my might to stave off what I know is coming way sooner than I'd like. "Yeah. Fuck. You feel too good. I'm going to come. I'm sorry."

She smiles up at me. "It's okay. I already got mine. Kiss me, Flynn."

Bending to press my lips to hers, she rocks her hips, encouraging my movements and with one embarrassing final thrust, I gasp and spill into the condom, knowing without a doubt, my world is forever changed.

CHAPTER FOUR

BRIGHTEN

As Flynn's breathing levels back out, he pulls out and climbs from the bed. "Be right back."

I nod. "Okay." He grabs his clothes and heads into the bathroom and I sit up and pull on my panties and dress as I evaluate what we did. I'm glad it was Flynn. He made it a definite positive experience and although I hoped it would be good and it totally was, it was more fun than I expected. I don't think I expected to laugh.

When he reenters the room, he's dressed and comes to sit next to me on the bed and searches my face. "Are you alright?"

I huff a laugh. "Perfect." I wrap my arms around him for a hug. "Thank you, Flynn."

Returning my embrace after a beat, he sputters, "Oh, uh, you're welcome. I should be thanking you."

Pulling back, I ask, "Was it okay for you?"

His eyes widen. "Okay? It was great."

"Yeah. Fun, right?"

Nodding, he reaches over me to pick up his glasses and slides them up his nose. "Definitely fun."

"Want to go play some more *Mario Kart*?"

"Sure. We still have pizza left, right? I'm starving."

I snort a laugh. "Worked up an appetite there, did you?"

"Looks that way."

My phone rings on my nightstand and I squint as bright beams of sunlight stream in through my obnoxious pink curtains, casting the room in a peachy sort of glow. The phone continues to ring, and I sit up, wincing at the residual soreness from last night. Looking at the screen, I roll my eyes when I see it's my mother. "Hello?"

"Darling, are you still in bed? You should be practicing your piece for your audition."

I sigh. "Mom, we talked about this. I'm not auditioning for Juilliard. I'm going to NYU. I've already been accepted. Don't you have a commercial to shoot? Shouldn't *you* be the one rehearsing?"

"Don't change the subject. I pulled a lot of strings to get you that audition. The least you can do is pretend like you want to go to a prestigious school. You shouldn't let your music die like you did dance."

"I'm not. I already told you I might minor in music simply to appease you, but I'm majoring in political science. We've talked about this. And for the record, NYU *is* a prestigious school. Can we discuss this some other time? I need my sleep."

"Do not take that tone with me, young lady. I'm just trying to help you secure the best future possible."

"Mom, you realize most people would be thrilled their child wanted to be a lawyer with political ambitions, right?"

"Politicians are so boring. Musicians lead much more exciting lives."

"Do you hear yourself? To me, the idea of drafting public policy in the hopes it gets passed *is* exciting. We're not the same people, Mom. Please do not try to highjack my youth because you feel yours slipping away. And don't insult Dad by saying politicians are boring. He was a politician and I can think of no greater way to honor him than by following in his footsteps and completing the journey he started."

My phone beeps and I pull it away to see an incoming call from Flynn. "Mom, I have to go. Flynn's calling."

"That's another thing. Can't you find a cuter boy to associate with? Why not his twin? He's the better looking brother."

It's way too early for this shit, and I clench my jaw. "Mom, don't insult my best friend. Goodbye." I answer the other line. "Hey."

"Hey. Did I wake you up?"

"No," I say with a sigh. "Vanessa did."

"Eww. I'm sure that was a nice wake up call."

"Not really. She's on her shit about Juilliard again."

"Are you going to do the audition?"

I settle back against the pillows. "No. What's the point?"

He huffs a laugh. "I don't know; to be able to say you got into the best music school in the country and turned it down."

"Oh, so like you with the *four* ivy league schools you turned down."

"Exactly," he says with a smile in his voice. After a beat, he asks, "How are you feeling? Okay?"

"Fine. You?"

"Good. Plans for today? You know, besides avoiding your mother? Is she coming home today?"

"Tomorrow. Nothing much. Are you working today?"

"Yeah. Until five."

"Want to come over after?"

He's quiet for a minute and I'm about to ask him if he's okay when he answers, "Sure. Want me to bring a movie?"

"Okay. Can you also bring your calculus notes?"

Flynn huffs a laugh. "I see. You only want me for my math prowess."

I almost say something like, *the dick's pretty good, too*, but I keep it in. "Definitely. Your brain is one of my favorite things about you, you know that."

"Even now?" I can almost picture his grin as he asks the question and I blush.

"Well, you know, it's hard to say. For all I know, that was beginner's luck." The words are out before I can even think about biting them back and I clamp my mouth shut. He coughs softly through the line and we're both quiet for a beat. "Sorry."

"Why are you sorry?" His voice is quiet and I'm wondering if things have somehow changed between us. I mean, other than knowing that sex is something I want to do again—in the very near future, if I have any say in the matter—I don't feel any different about Flynn. He's still my best friend; still the person who knows me better than anyone.

"Sorry if I made it weird just then," I admit. "With my joke."

"Nah. We're good."

"We didn't talk about this part of stuff before yesterday."

"What do you mean?"

His belt buckle jangles through the phone and I imagine him taking his belt off and what came after that. How nice it was. How good he made me feel. Desire blooms low in my belly, hot and needy, so fast I nearly gasp. I clear my throat. "Um, about if yesterday was a onetime thing."

"Oh. I guess we didn't. We probably should've. Want to talk about it tonight? I'm getting ready to head to brunch with my parents and then work."

"Yeah, we should. Okay. Tonight. Want me to cook?"

"That's okay. I'll have to swing by the house to shower after work. I can stop and get some burgers. Barbecue bacon for you?"

"Sure. And—."

"I know. Chocolate shake."

"And—."

"Crash, I got it. Cheese fries. I know what you like."

"Yeah, I guess you do." My tone comes off a bit more flirty than I plan, and I cringe. Have I always been like this with Flynn? Surely not.

"I'll see you around six, okay? I've gotta go."

He disconnects the call and I toss the phone onto the bed and drag my hand down my face. Making a mental pro-con list in my head, I weigh the merits of continuing a physical relationship with my favorite person on the planet.

Pro: It was a lot of fun. Con: It could get messy if one of us develops feelings. Pro: Flynn apparently has some skills I would like to have him use on me again. Con: We would only be able to do this for a few more weeks since he's leaving for Nashville and I'm going to Ireland. Pro: That's enough time to experiment and find out what I like. Con: It could get messy.

Granted, I don't have *those* types of feelings for Flynn. He's funny and kind and my best friend and apparently we have good chemistry. But I don't feel all ooey-gooey about him. I don't picture a white picket fence and two-point-five kids and a dopey dog. To be honest, I don't picture that with anyone. I picture myself as a member of a presidential cabinet making real change. Nowhere in my plan does a family fit. Good sex? Sure. More than that? Nah.

Right at six, Flynn sweeps into the house with a brown paper sack and two shakes. He's dressed in basketball shorts and a T-shirt and sneakers, his dark hair still damp from a shower. I, too, am freshly showered, my hair in a thick braid over my shoulder. I've gone for more casual and am dressed almost the same way as him, except my shorts are considerably shorter and I've got on a tank top.

We drop into chairs at the kitchen table since the burgers are messy and he divvies out the food. "How was work?"

He shrugs. "Fine. Same as always. Cole stopped by and asked if I might want a summer job. He's going to be doing some landscaping. Says by next summer he'll hopefully have his business fully off the ground. I hated to turn him down, because the money would be better than what I'm making now, but with the internship, I can't take it."

"That was nice of him to offer, though."

Flynn nods and takes a bite of an onion ring. "Yeah. Maybe next summer, unless the internship goes well and that turns into something, I guess."

"Maybe."

He examines my face. "Are you really feeling okay today? Are you sore?" Concern is clear in his expression and his tone and I shake my head.

"I was a little this morning. I'm good. What about you? Sore?"

He laughs. "It doesn't work that way, Crash."

I roll my eyes. "I know. I just wanted to show you the same kind of courtesy."

He nods. "I am also good." He sips his shake and drops an onion ring onto my burger wrapper with a grin.

Twenty minutes later, we're lying on my bed watching a movie because this is where the DVD player is. And because it's one we've seen before, I'm not really paying attention.

We're on our stomachs, but I keep glancing at Flynn out of the corner of my eye and getting whiffs of his aftershave. It's a familiar smell, but I now have a sense memory to go with it, so it's making me have the urge to grab his face and kiss him.

Unable to stand not knowing if or how this is going to play out, I roll onto my side. He immediately mirrors me. This is nothing new, except it is, and I want to run my hand up his shirt and feel the soft hairs on his stomach. *Focus, Brighten. With your brain, not your vagina.* "What are your thoughts about yesterday?"

He's quiet for a long moment before giving me that lopsided grin that's my favorite one. "Um, I'm a guy. It was sex. Ergo, it was pretty fucking awesome."

I laugh and swat his chest. "Seriously. Do you feel weird about it? Because it was us?"

After another pause, he shakes his head. "No. I'm honored you asked me. I wanted to make sure you had a good experience. I hope I succeeded."

I worry my bottom lip and nod. "You did. It was an amazing first time, Flynn. Really." His smile widens, a slight blush coloring his cheeks. "Do you want it to be a onetime thing?"

He picks up my braid and rubs the end between his thumb and index finger. "Crash, I'm not going to lie and say I'd hate it if I got laid again; I'm a dude. It was a lot of fun. It was a lot of fun with you. But I don't want you to feel like I ever expect it again just because we did it once. If that's not something you'd want, I'd never feel cheated or anything."

"If we did it again, or kept doing it, how would it work? We're not dating, so what, it's friends with benefits?"

He looks at the end of my braid and nods. "Well, we are friends. It would be some pretty excellent benefits."

"With an end date," I supply.

He nods again, still fidgeting with my braid. I pull it out of his grasp and lift his chin. "Is that something you're okay with? You leave for Nashville in three weeks. I leave for Ireland right after that."

"So, you decided for sure to go?"

"Might as well. After this summer, I'm grinding till I reach Congress. I will be a busy, busy girl. One last summer of fun sounds good to me."

"It does. I hope you do have fun."

I grin. "It's no internship at a big market research firm, but I'll try my best. I'm really proud of you, you know that?"

"Thanks. I'm proud of me, too."

"So, are we decided about this?"

Flynn searches my face and drags his teeth over his bottom lip. "I'm game."

"Rules?"

He lifts a brow. "Rules? What rules?"

I shrug. "Well, I can't do sleepovers."

"I have a curfew anyway," he interjects.

"Right. Dating other people?"

"I haven't exactly had anyone banging down my door in the past eighteen years, so it's not likely to happen in the next three weeks."

"Me neither, but I'm just trying to cover all the bases."

He smirks. "Pretty sure we rounded all the bases and slid across home plate yesterday, Crash."

I blush. "You are correct. How about, if we have a potential date in the next three weeks, we revisit things?"

Flynn considers. "Sounds like a mature solution."

I nod. "And what about after the next three weeks? Like, breaks and stuff or times when we might visit each other? Do we just go back to not having sex?"

He's quiet for a long moment. "How about we play things

by ear? I mean, if we're together and not exclusively seeing anyone else, I don't see why this can't be a regular thing."

I can't deny I'm a bit surprised by his suggestion. Of course, it might all stop if Flynn gets a girlfriend. Especially if he meets someone at his internship and they find out how great he is. Although the idea of being able to hookup with Flynn when I come home for visits doesn't sound like a horrible idea in the least. Especially with as good as it's been between us already. Surely, it would only get better with time, right? "You'd be okay with that?"

"I mean, it was a lot of fun, right?" When I nod, he smiles. "Then I don't see why not."

Nodding, I run my fingertip down his chest and tug up the hem of his shirt, dragging the backs of my fingers up his stomach. He tenses and I bring my eyes to his. "What?"

He shrugs. "Sorry. It's a me problem, not a you problem."

Saddened by how hung up he is on shit with his body that are nonissues, I simply nod, because I get it and I tell him so. "I get it. If you don't want me to touch you there, I won't."

He shakes his head. "You can touch me wherever you want. I'll be fine."

I pull his glasses off and lay them on the bench at the end of my bed and lean in until our lips touch and, just like yesterday, heat explodes in my middle. But unlike yesterday, the kisses aren't tiny pecks. They start hungry and needy and after only minutes, we're both gasping for breath. I'm not sure if I remember kissing Flynn being like this when we practiced kissing all those years ago. And even with his braces, he's a great kisser.

He rolls me on my back and wedges himself between my legs as he kisses down my neck, goosebumps scattering down my arms. When he grinds himself against me, he's already hard and through the thin fabric of both of our clothes, I feel everything and can't bite back a moan as I sink my fingers into his hair. "God, you smell good," Flynn says against my neck.

"So do you."

He braces on one arm and runs his hand up my shirt. It should feel strange knowing Flynn and I were nothing just over twenty-four hours ago, and now we're *this*. It's a bit surreal how good it feels to have his hands on me, but God, they do. His thumb brushes my nipple through the fabric of my sports bra and I reflexively arch my back into his touch, my hips rolling against him. "Oh, God, Flynn."

He huffs a breath against my chest as kisses his way down my sternum. Raising up, he yanks up the tail of my shirt. "Off." The word comes out husky and not a request, and my skin prickles with the command and I scramble to obey. For good measure, I shuck the bra too and he groans as my breasts pops free. "Jesus Christ, you've got great tits, Crash."

Heat climbs up my neck with his compliment and as I lie back down, he bends to brush kisses over the swell of each breast, before flicking his tongue over my nipple and I exhale sharply. He focuses his oral attention on my nipples and breasts, while his free hand skims over my side and around to my butt to knead the flesh through my shorts.

Needing to touch some part of him, I run my toes up his bare calves as I writhe my hips, needing more friction. Flynn groans against my breast and I moan with the vibration.

"Do you want me to touch you, Crash?"

"Yes. Please," I breathe.

He smiles and begins kissing down my stomach, his eyes raising to mine. "What if I wanted to taste you instead?"

Somewhat surprised, I ask, "Do you want to?"

Flynn gives me that crooked grin and laughs. "Fuck yes, I do. If I could've stood to wait any longer yesterday, I would've eaten you out until you screamed."

My mouth falls open with the image his words conjure and I huff a breath. "You sound awful sure of yourself there, Tate."

He smirks. "Confidence is half the battle, right?"

I snort a laugh. "Not sure that translates to oral sex, but sure."

"Is that a challenge?"

"Do you want it to be?"

He hooks his fingers in the waistband of my shorts and panties and drags them over my hips. "I do like a goal to work toward." He kisses and licks below my belly button as he scoots his way down the bed to lie on his stomach.

When his lips brush over my inner thigh, I reflexively squeeze my legs together. Flynn splays his large hand over the inside of my knee. "Open up for me. God, you smell good." He grins up at me. "I bet you taste even better; you going to let me see?"

I lean back on my elbows and try to relax, letting my knees fall open. "Where'd you get that dirty mouth from?"

"Not real sure. Do you like it? Or do you want me to stop talking? Is it distracting?"

I laugh. "No. It's hot. Don't stop."

Pleased, he nods. "Yes, ma'am." His breath ghosts over my sensitive flesh and he bends his head down, but then it pops back up. "If you don't like what I'm doing, tell me. Or, if what I'm doing isn't doing anything, let me know?"

I nod. "Okay. Although, you seem to be able to read my body pretty well."

He blushes with my compliment. "I aim to please."

"Then stop teasing and *please* me."

He chuckles. "So bossy."

"I prefer asser—." The word dies in my mouth as his tongue sweeps up my pussy to flick over my clit. "Shit." He groans and the vibration makes my hips buck involuntarily. "Fuck." I don't take my eyes off his face, even when his own eyes close as he gets lost in his task. A task which he is also apparently skilled at. I've always known Flynn is good at everything he sets his mind to. I guess that means sex, too.

He sucks my clit into his mouth and I scream with the intense sensation, my heart threatening to burst from my chest. "Oh God, Flynn. Shit." I sink my fingers into his hair and he lets out a low growl and I watch as he grinds his hips into the mattress. Seeing him needing to find relief because of either what he's doing to me or the sounds I'm making or just because it feels good for him, sends an extra jolt of pleasure through me and my orgasm hits me suddenly and my head falls back and I moan, my legs shaking with the force.

My breathing is ragged as Flynn kisses his way back up my body and I sit up and yank up his shirt. He laughs at my enthusiasm, but complies and pulls his shirt over his head. I press my hand into his chest and he lies back, his expression curious, although he doesn't say anything.

When I straddle his waist, curiosity gives way to hunger and he brings his hands up to cup my breasts, his thumbs brushing my nipples. "You going to ride me?"

Despite my orgasm from only seconds ago, I would happily come again. But I didn't get to touch him yesterday and I'm dying to know what he feels like under my hands and in my mouth. "Not yet." I bend to kiss my way down his chest and stomach and his breaths come short as I scoot down his body.

"Crash, if you get anywhere near my dick with your mouth, I will probably come."

I bring my eyes to his and give him a slow smile. "Isn't that the point? I didn't get to touch you yesterday. You're not taking that away from me today. If we can't have actual sex or whatever today, that's fine. This is still pretty fantastic."

I skim my fingers under the waistband of his shorts and he

huffs a breath. Tugging his shorts and boxers down his hips, my eyes fly to his cock as it pops free. Dropping his clothes on the floor, I eye his dick, my mouth nearly watering. My original assessment stands. It's...pretty. Thick and veined with a slight downward curve. He's also long, and I know there's no way I'll be able to fit all of him in my mouth.

Glancing back up at him, my own confidence begins to fade. "Can you show me how you like it?"

His brows rise in surprise at my question. "What?"

"Show me. I want to make you feel good, but I don't want to mess up."

He smiles. "Pretty sure you could just touch me and I'd pop off." I level him with a gaze, and he chuckles. "Give me your hand." I do, and he covers mine with his and wraps it around his shaft.

It jerks in my hand and I look back up at him. "Does it do that a lot?"

He grins. "Sometimes." He blows out a breath, seeming to concentrate. Sliding our hands up his length, he adds pressure at the tip and exhales sharply. "Fuck, Crash. Seriously, just your hand on me is enough to make me want to come."

Liquid beads at the tip and I drag my teeth over my bottom lip. "Can I taste you, Flynn?"

He groans. "Jesus Christ. I'll take 'Questions I never thought Crash would ever ask me' for two hundred, Alex."

I huff a laugh. "Is that a yes?"

His breathing is ragged and his chest heaves and I watch as his Adam's apple bobs in his throat as he swallows. "I'm really close. You don't have to."

"I want to. You can come in my mouth, just warn me, okay?"

His brow furrows, and he groans again. "Fuck, Crash, are you trying to kill me?"

"Maybe a little," I tease and drag my fingertip up the underside of his dick and his intake of breath is sharp. "Do you want me to suck your cock, Flynn?"

"Fucking hell, woman. You're either going to have to suck me or ride me because I'm about to die here."

I keep my eyes on his as I lower my mouth and when my lips close around the head of his dick, I breathe in the smell that's simply him—clean and a bit musky—and his hips buck as he mutters a curse through gritted teeth and I gag.

"Sorry," he says, his breath more a pant than anything at this moment. I huff a laugh as I slide my mouth up and down his length, focusing suction on the tip, and his head rolls back. "Fuck, Crash. That's good. Shit."

His hands are fisted in the covers and I pry his fingers loose and bring his hand to the back of my neck and his head snaps up, eyes going wide and locking onto mine. He threads his fingers into my braid and although he doesn't push me down, he holds me in place as he slowly thrusts and I moan, some part of me liking that he's controlling this.

"I'm close. Like, really close," he warns. "If you don't want me to come in your mouth, I won't. But, fuck, you're going to have to decide." I have no intentions of stopping because I'm enjoying the knowledge that I'm the one bringing him pleasure. I keep going until his hips buck a final time.

"Shit, Crash. Oh God, I'm coming," he grits out as his dick swells just before a spurt of hot, salty liquid spills into my mouth as he lets out a low grunt, his grip on my hair nearly painful. I don't move until his cock stops pulsing and then I pull off and swallow.

CHAPTER FIVE

FLYNN

I am *so* going to regret these few weeks. Well, not *regret*, because that would imply I'd want to take it all back, and I'd rather die than take it back. But knowing how I already feel about Brighten, the idea of having to give her up at the end of three weeks hurts like a motherfucker.

Still trying to catch my breath, I lie on my back and look at the sheer white canopy above me. Brighten huffs a laugh and crawls up the bed to lie next to me and I roll toward her and take in her face. It's a face I've committed to memory and can recall in perfect detail. But her like this? All naked and smiling and her hair disheveled from me holding her in place as I fucked her mouth? This is a whole different face I want to memorize.

Sweeping a stray hair off her forehead, I lean in to kiss her. A small part of me expects her to pull away and tell me our business is complete. We both got off; it's time for me to leave. But she scoots closer to me and accepts my kiss, her hand coming to rest on my jaw. And I'll be damned if I not going to soak up every minute I'm allowed to have her.

Throwing her leg around my hip, she tugs me closer, her kiss turning greedy, her hands roaming over my arms and chest and sides and down to my ass. I let my fingers explore her body as well, unsure if I'll ever get enough of her. Her curves and softness and how perfect she feels under my hands and under me.

After a moment, Brighten pulls her mouth from mine, her brows rising in surprise when my cock presses into her hip, already ready for round two. "You're hard again? Already? Is that normal?"

I huff a laugh. "I don't know that I'd get used to it all the time. Pretty sure my dick is just excited to get more action than my own hand."

She chuckles and reaches over me, nearly rolling me onto my back as she grabs a condom from the drawer. Holding it in front of my face, she asks, "Do you have time, or do you have to get home?"

I snatch it from her. "Shit, I'll make fucking time." I rip the wrapper with my teeth and roll the latex down before grabbing Brighten's face for a kiss as I roll us and shift to settle between her legs. Trailing my mouth down her cheek and jaw, I ask, "You're not sore? You're sure."

"I'm fine. Fuck me. Please?" She pulls my mouth back to hers and as I enter her, she inhales sharply. "Shit."

I huff out a breath, my heart thundering behind my ribs as her pussy pulses around me. "No kidding. Fuck."

She brings her hand to my face and smiles up at me as I begin to move. And God help me, I love her. I'm so fucked. Rocking her hips, she pulls me in deeper with a moan, and I can't bite back a low groan.

Dropping my forehead to her chest, I brush kisses over her breast and flick the nipple with my tongue, trying to keep up a steady rhythm with my thrusts. Brighten gasps and digs her fingers into my hair. "Flynn. Fuck. God, don't stop."

So I don't. I keep working her tits while trying to hold off until she lets out this choked rasp, her pussy clenching so tight around me, I can't hold back my release and I pump my hips one final time with a deep grunt.

Trying not to collapse on top of her, I pull out with a groan and shift my body so I'm beside her. "I can't move. Just tell my family I died happy."

Brighten laughs and rolls her eyes. "I'll remember that."

When my heart rate has nearly returned to normal, I finally rise and go clean up and when I get back, Brighten has pulled on her panties and tank top, not bothering with her bra or shorts. I redress and sit on the bed to pull on my socks. "Is that what you wear to bed?"

She looks down at herself and shrugs. "Maybe. Why?"

I smirk. "Just trying to get a visual for when I go home."

"Don't tell me you think you'll be able to go again? Damn."

"Probably not. I'm wiped. I'll go home and crash, and Jess will make fun of me for going to bed so early."

She worries her bottom lip. "Did you tell him?"

"I talked to him before yesterday, told him what we'd planned. I wanted to pick his brain, make sure I could give you the best first time possible."

She blushes, a small smile pulling at the corners of her mouth. "You did. You think he suspects it's only a onetime thing, or what?"

"I don't know, honestly. He just asked me how it went and I told him." I add quickly, "I didn't give him details, of course. Have you told anyone?"

She shakes her head. "No, Hensley had a party last night, so no way I was going to be able to stay up and talk to her. Although, I don't guess it's anyone's business but ours, right?"

"Right." I glance down at my watch. "Shit, I've gotta go. I need to finish the final draft for my English paper."

"Sure. But you do realize you're already valedictorian, right? You could coast for the next few weeks if you wanted."

"Nah, might as well finish strong." I lean over and give her a quick kiss. "See you tomorrow."

Knowing we're up against the clock, the next three weeks fly by and Brighten and I spend almost every evening together. Normally, by the time I get off work, her mom is already past drunk and verging on passed out and doesn't even acknowledge my presence. And because Vanessa doesn't really give a shit what Brighten does, we always meet at her house.

Two days before I'm scheduled to leave for Nashville and my internship—and the day after my braces finally come off, thank God—my parents insist on having a family dinner as my going away celebration. And because Brighten has been my best friend for the past six years, she got an automatic invite, along with my grandparents.

I would've preferred to spend my last night with only Brighten, but it's probably a good thing we're not since I'd probably be too sad. Knowing I'm leaving at six in the morning to make it to my orientation and I won't get to say goodbye to her after tonight, my heart feels heavy.

Still, I manage to put on a brave face and have a good time, but I long to take Brighten's hand in mine or lean over to kiss her cheek or tuck her hair behind her ear. But I can't do any of that because we aren't dating. We were only fucking. At least, that's the way Brighten views it.

I've known for almost as long as I've known her that she has big goals and ambitions. She wants to be President someday, but would settle for being a senator or governor. She's said numerous times that a relationship would only complicate her dreams. She's also said she's pretty sure never wants to get married or have kids. Not that I'm a hundred percent sold on having kids myself, but if they were with Brighten, I might entertain the idea.

A tapping on my window jars me out of a dead sleep. Thinking it's rain, I simply roll back over, knowing my alarm isn't scheduled to go off for hours. But when it becomes more insistent, I get up and turn on the bedside lamp and shove my glasses on my face. I nearly scream when I open the blinds and see Brighten standing at the window with a flashlight poised under her chin like someone telling ghost stories at camp.

After I can breathe again, I open the window as quietly as possible and help her climb inside before shutting it and lowering the blinds. Once I jog over to lock my bedroom door, I return to stand in front of her. "What are you doing here?" I ask in a whisper.

"I wanted to tell you goodbye. Properly." She drags off her T-shirt and grips the back of my neck and pulls me down for a kiss. And even knowing how much more it's going to hurt to leave after this, I wrap my arms around her and shuffle us over to my bed and toss my glasses back onto the nightstand.

Only wearing boxers, it's mere seconds before I'm hard as a fucking rock and I'm unhooking her bra and shoving her shorts and panties over her hips, needing to put my hands on her one last time.

Although we've only been doing this song and dance for a few weeks, I've learned her body and she's learned mine. We've made it work in beds and cars and even the shower. It's been the best three weeks of my life and I'm nearly bereft that it's ending. Even if it is with a bang.

Slipping my hand between her legs, I marvel once again at how soft and silky she feels on my fingers. The soft moans and puffs of air that leave her mouth. The way she rides my hand as she gets close to coming. "God, Flynn; that's good." Her words are hushed, as we've grown accustomed to having to sneak around.

"You feel so fucking good. Come for me. Fuck. Please."

I bring my free hand up to her breast and roll the nipple between my fingers and she drags my mouth to hers as she orgasms, her cry muffled by our kiss.

Wasting no time, I reach over into my nightstand and pull out a condom, ripping the wrapper as I shuck my boxers. Two seconds later, I've rolled it down and I'm pushing inside her, clamping my mouth closed to stifle my groan.

Giving in to my frantic need for her, I set a brutal pace and Brighten gasps so loud, I cover her mouth with my hand, for fear my parents hear and interrupt. Because I'll be damned if I stop. I can't. She drags my hand from her mouth and intertwines our fingers, putting them above her head.

My movements falter for a beat in my surprise and I check in with her. "You want me to pin your hands?"

She nods, excitement flashing in her eyes. "I think so."

I run my free hand down her other arm and bring her hand to my lips and press a kiss to her palm before placing both her hands above her head, clasped in one of mine.

As I deepen my thrusts, Brighten's eyes fall closed and her mouth falls open in a near silent sigh. It's a sight I never want to forget. Hooking my forearm under her thigh, I press it back, needing to go deeper, harder; needing to make this last time *more* somehow.

She gasps, even with her lips pressed tightly together, and I claim her mouth to muffle her cries. Dropping my forehead to hers, I breathe in her scent and listen to her sounds and focus on the way she feels; the way we move together. "Flynn, please. So close."

"I've got you. I promise," is what I say just before we both let go at almost the exact same time. But what I wanted to say is, *I love you. Always.*

When my alarm sounds, I feel for Brighten on the other side of the bed, but it's cold. I sit bolt upright and wonder briefly if it was a dream, but as I roll over and smell her shampoo on my pillow, I know it wasn't. A heavy weight sinks like lead into my guts and I blink back tears.

Twenty minutes later, I'm driving west on I-75 and although I tried to tell my parents I could make the drive all by myself, they insisted on coming to make sure my apartment is up to their standards. Dad requested to ride with me, so I drive the wheelchair-accessible van that is outfitted to make it easier for him to get around without having to get out of his wheelchair. Mom follows behind in my car.

Diagnosed with multiple sclerosis at twenty-five, right after Jess and I were born, his MS has advanced rapidly over the last couple of years, although he refuses to admit it. He chooses to live in denial and, while Mom and Jess coddle him and try to do everything for him, Dad and I have an understanding. I don't ask him if he needs help, and he actually asks for it when it's needed.

"So, how did you and Brighten leave things?" His question catches me off guard since, for the last two hours, we've talked about everything but Brighten. My hopes for college, the internship, Jess's constant rotation of girls, Mom's plans for turning the basement at home into an apartment.

I shove my glasses up my nose and grip the steering wheel tighter. "What do you mean?"

My dad drills me with a *don't bullshit me* stare in the rearview mirror. "Oh, was that not her sneaking in your window around midnight last night?" I blink rapidly, my mouth opening and closing as I scramble to find some plausible excuse. "Flynn, I don't sleep much these days. When I can't sleep, I read. So I don't disturb your mother, I read in the sunroom. Which, as you know, looks out onto the back of the house. I was just rolling into the sunroom with my new Grisham when I saw a pretty redhead tiptoeing through our backyard. I hadn't even turned on the lamp yet. How long have y'all been seeing each other? I didn't know you guys were dating."

"We're not."

"So, what? Y'all were hanging out and there were sparks? Kinda romantic to think you two were friends all those years, and it became more."

I sigh. "You sound like Mom."

"Your mother is a smart woman. I could do a lot worse than sound like her. Did she spend the night?"

"She left before I got up," I admit. "I'm not sure when."

"So, what's going to happen?"

"Nothing. We had an end date. It was supposed to be before last night."

"You don't sound too happy about that. I don't pretend to know what things are like for you boys. I've loved your mom since I was seventeen, so all this casual stuff isn't something I understand. But it sounds like it's not very casual for you."

Dad opens and closes his left hand, rubbing his fingertips with his thumb, and I know the tingling must be bad today.

Some days are better than others, but thankfully, his mind is still good. I know it might not be in coming years.

"It doesn't matter what I want. It's over now."

"So you didn't tell her how you felt?"

"No," I reply, resigned.

"Do you love her?"

"Like I said, it doesn't matter."

He huffs a laugh. "Sure it does. Y'all would be great together. Brighten is the one person you actually like. She doesn't let you be so prickly all the time. She's the only person you actually smile for."

"No, it doesn't, Dad. She doesn't like me that way."

He frowns, his dark brows almost meeting in the middle. "Then why did you guys sleep together? I assume last night wasn't the first time."

I could be embarrassed to talk to my dad about things, but aside from Brighten, he's the person I'm closest to in the world. Even closer than I am with Jess. Maybe it's because we're a lot alike, I don't know.

I blow out a breath. "She didn't want to graduate high school a virgin. She asked me to do it and I knew if it was me, she'd be taken care of because I care about her. It was fun, and we agreed it was only until I left for my internship. I've had feelings for her for a while. She doesn't have feelings for me.

"She's focused on her goals and her political aspirations. She never wants to get married or have kids. And not that I necessarily want those things now, but I do someday. She doesn't. I've always known that. She says she's not built that way.

"I knew if I told her how I felt, things would be awkward. And I would've rather had her for what little time I did and push my feelings down than make her uncomfortable and feel like she had to end our friendship or lie to me. I'd rather have her as a friend than nothing."

My father gives me a sad smile. "I'm sorry, Flynn. I'm sure that's hard knowing you love someone you might never have. But if you know she's never going to be able to offer you more than her friendship, it might be best if you try to move on. Use this time in Nashville to learn who you are without her. You and Brighten have been in a vacuum for the last six years. It's going to be a real shock to your system to be around people who aren't her. Y'all might even drift apart. I hope that's not the case. But in situations like this, where the feelings are one-sided, it can be difficult on a friendship. Especially if there's been a physical aspect to things."

"Dad, you don't need to put on your guidance counselor hat for me. I'll be okay. She'll be in Ireland all summer and I'll be in Nashville and other than emails and occasional calls, we probably won't even be able to be in touch much."

The thought of not speaking to her every day makes my chest ache. In the past six years, I've never gone more than twenty-four hours without talking to her.

"Well, whatever you do, don't sit in your apartment and mope. Nashville's a pretty hopping city from what I remember from college. I know you probably won't even want to look at any girl who's not Brighten, but it might actually do you some good. See what else is out there. Make some friends. I know that's not the easiest for you, but you're worth the effort. If someone tries to get past your walls, maybe you should let them."

CHAPTER SIX

FLYNN

Dad's advice about making friends swirls through my mind as I sit in my orientation with all my fellow interns. I'd also be lying if I said Brighten's advice about playing a part didn't sit front and center, either. I know I'll have to play a part here; especially if I want to get in good with the partners and work toward the future I want.

Unaccustomed to wearing a suit, I can't help but fidget with my tie as my new peers stream into the conference room at Intuition. My phone vibrates in my pocket and I pull it out to see a text from Brighten.

> Crash: Good luck today. Remember not to be
> an asshole all the time.

My fingers are poised to respond, a smile on my face, when a voice next to me catches my attention. "Girlfriend or boyfriend?"

I snap my head in the direction of the words and blink as I push my glasses up my face. "Excuse me?"

The person from whom the voice originates is a tall, slim

guy with dark olive skin, blue eyes, and black hair styled perfectly. His suit screams Brooks Brothers and not JC Penney like mine. He gives me a warm grin and jerks his chin down at my phone. "Girlfriend or boyfriend? I'm guessing a good luck text? First day and all."

I shake my head. "Neither. Best friend."

He nods, frowning thoughtfully, before extending his hand. "Sullivan Sanchez. Or, Sully. Whichever."

I glance down at his hand before accepting the handshake. "Flynn Tate."

"Nice to meet you."

I simply nod and sip my coffee, before Brighten's words shoot through my brain. *Be nice, Flynn. Make friends.* "You, too."

I turn my attention back to my phone and he asks, "So, where are you from?"

Annoyed, but trying to make my dad and Brighten proud, I return my phone to my pocket and give Sully my full attention. "Knoxville. You?"

"Miami."

"So you gave up the beach for this?"

He shrugs, sipping a cup of coffee. "I gave up the pretty girls in bikinis for the chance at a good future. I can have those again once I'm rolling in the big bucks. Knoxville's only a few hours from here, right?"

"Yeah."

"What about after this; college-wise?"

"University of Tennessee. Statistics."

"You like numbers, huh? Cool. I'll be giving up even more pretty girls in bikinis at Harvard. Not exactly looking forward to the cold, but grad schools see Harvard and tend to give you a second look."

"I'm sure. I got accepted there, but decided to stay closer to home."

His brows rise. "You got in at Harvard and you're not going? Why the hell not? They only have, like, a three percent acceptance rate and you turned them down? Damn. You got some pretty girl back home swaying your decision? You know they have those in Cambridge, right?"

I shrug. "Probably, but no. Not a girl."

"Or, boy?"

I huff a laugh. "Not a guy, either. I'm straight. Just sticking around."

"Hmm. A mystery. I like mysteries. I'll figure you out, Flynn Tate."

"There is nothing to figure out."

He opens his mouth, but a door on the far end of the conference room opens and a petite woman with dark brown skin looking to be in her early thirties with hair twisted into a knot at the base of her skull and tight curls falling over her forehead, dressed in a leather pencil skirt, white silk blouse, and black stilettos enters and plants her hands on the end of the table.

"Good morning. My name is Sharice Carter and I'll be your internship coordinator for the duration of your time here at Intuition. I'm sure, whatever high school you come from, you were the best and brightest. That will not be the case here. You may be used to being the smartest person in the room in your hometown. Here, you may not even be the tenth smartest. Intuition is home to some of the most brilliant minds in market research. We spot trends five years ahead of time and we make things happen.

"I'm sure all of you have curious minds and substantial intellect, but without the proper tools, that'll only take you so far. We hope to help equip you with some tools for you to use in the future and maybe, if some of you—and us—are lucky, a few of you may even be back as members of the Intuition team.

"This year's internship group has twelve participants, and you'll be paired up with a fellow intern to be assigned to an account. For the most part, your day-to-day will consist of grunt work; fetching coffee and copies, and pretty much any cliche thing you can think an intern would do. But at the end of your time here, you will have learned invaluable skills that will carry over to your future.

"I'll go ahead and announce the partnerships and your assigned team member. The remainder of the information you need regarding your responsibilities and expectations are in the folder in front of you. My business card is in there and if you need me, I'm here for you. Get to know your partner. Who knows, they may be a valuable resource in the future."

Miss Carter gestures out a glass door and six people enter. "These will be your mentors during your time here. They will push you and may even make you want to give up by the end of the first week." The mentors all share a collective laugh and she smiles. "But they will also be a tremendous fount of knowledge for you during this time. Use it wisely. Out of the hundreds of applications we receive for this internship every year, you are the twelve we've chosen. Don't make our decision have been in error.

"When you hear your name, you'll follow your mentor and it's off to the races. I hope you've hydrated and carboloaded. This is a marathon, people, not a sprint. Terri Chavez, you have Abbott and Canton. Jackie Wong, you have Jones and Howard." Two by two, pairs leave with their assigned mentors until it's only down to Sully and me.

Miss Carter's eyes fall on the two of us. "And last, but certainly not least, Elias Washington, you have Tate and Sanchez. Good luck, gentleman."

Sully and I share a glance and follow our mentor—a stocky man in his late fifties who's about six feet tall with medium-brown skin and a shaved head in an expensive suit—out of the conference room, folders tucked under our arms. Mr. Washington doesn't say anything until he leads us to a door with his name engraved on a placard. He ushers us in and gestures for us to take seats in the chairs across from his desk.

Looking around the room, there's no way to miss all the framed degrees and certificates, photos with politicians and celebrities, and multiple award plaques and trophies lined up on shelves. Expensive leather couches line two walls of the sleek metal and glass office and Washington stands with his back to a large picture window that looks out onto the impressive Nashville skyline.

"As Sharice said, I will be your mentor during this internship. I've been in market research for almost thirty-five years, and there are still things I don't know. So don't think as soon as you enter the game you'll have all the answers. The market is a fickle mistress sometimes. If you learn nothing else this summer, learn that even the predictable can be unpredictable. All of your expectations can be subverted."

He walks around to the front of his desk and leans against the large dark wood structure. "You can call me Elias or Mr. Washington; I'll answer to either. I'm not a hard ass. I don't believe in making interns shine my shoes or fetch my coffee. No one's coffee beats my wife's, so I'll bring that from home. But I also expect you to put in the work."

His eyes travel from Sully to me and back. "Of course, I have your transcripts and essays and shit, but I want to know why you're here. What is it about market research that fascinates you?" Looking at Sully, he scratches his chin. "Sullivan, right?" When Sully nods, he says, "Harvard bound in the fall. Valedictorian of your graduating class. Entrance essay was about wanting to honor both your Puerto Rican and Irish heritage, but struggling to find your place sometimes, correct?"

Sully swallows and nods. "Yes, sir."

"Why market research?"

He blows out a breath and smirks. "I like forecasting, but weather trends never really appealed to me. I enjoy predicting in all facets of life. What my football team will do in the next season, what the next big drink Starbucks will sling, who the next big star will be. Most of the things that turn into trends have indicators. I like to spot them."

Elias nods. "Okay." Turning his gaze on me, he tilts his head in curiosity and I push my glasses up my nose and prepare to answer the same question Sully did. "Flynn. Also valedictorian of your class while maintaining perfect attendance and a near full-time job. Accepted to Harvard, Yale, Princeton, and Dartmouth." Sully's head snaps my direction as our mentor continues. "But you've committed to attending the University of Tennessee in the fall, is that right?"

"Yes, sir."

"Why?"

I blink at his demand for an explanation. "Excuse me?"

"What is it UT has that those ivy league schools don't? Besides the SEC, I mean," he says with a small, amused smile.

The only person who knows my real reasons for staying close to home is Brighten, but I get the feeling if I lie, Elias will know and besides, I'm not a liar. Even if I lie to myself about how I feel about Brighten. I swallow and lick my lips and hold my mentor's gaze. "My father has advanced progressive multiple sclerosis. I don't want to be that far away from him if he gets worse."

"And statistically, you believe that is a high likelihood." It's not a question. It's as if he somehow knows how many hours I've spent going over data and my father's records and have weighed the risk versus reward of leaving home simply to get an education.

"Yes, sir," I admit.

He nods and folds his arms across his broad chest. "As one of the senior associates here at Intuition, I get my pick of interns. I chose the two of you. My gut is never wrong. You two," he says, gesturing between Sully and me, "have something most other interns don't have. Heart. And as much as statistics and forecasting play a role in market predictions, so do heart and gut. This industry tries to focus on the tangible things —numbers, past performance, cyclical trends—but some things aren't tangible. You just feel them. I think both of you will. Don't lose that part of yourself in your journey to predict 'the next big thing'."

Standing to travel back around to the other side of his desk and drop into his chair, he picks up a pair of reading glasses and hands over a sheaf of papers to each of us. "Let's get started, gentleman."

CHAPTER SEVEN

FLYNN

"No, I think you're cracked. Who does this shit for fun?" I ask, huffing breaths, bent over with my hands on my knees, as we ride the elevator up to our apartments.

Sully laughs, barely even winded. "Lots of people. It'll get easier and you might actually crave it."

"I call bullshit."

"Well, at least now, we can enjoy our burgers, guilt-free."

I down some water. "Trust me, my burgers have always been guilt-free."

The elevator dings and we step off. "I just need ten minutes to shower and we can—." I freeze when I see the top of a familiar redhead sitting, knees pulled up, at my door. My heart does this flip-flop thing in my chest and my breath catches at the sight of Brighten. Her head snaps up when she hears my voice, a huge smile creasing her face.

Fatigue forgotten, I jog to close the distance between us. She stands and throws her arms around me. "What are you doing here? You're supposed to be in Ireland."

She steps back and nods. "I am. I leave in the morning from

here. I wanted to surprise you." Her eyes taken in my sweaty appearance. "Were you running? You don't run."

"Apparently, it's good for me or some shit. I hate it. Sully makes me do it."

The man himself steps up. "This must be the infamous Brighten."

"Sorry. Sully, this is Brighten. Brighten, Sully."

Brighten gives Sully a warm smile and they shake hands. "I've heard a lot about you, Sully. Good to put a face with a name." She looks back up at me. "Glad to see you made a friend. I would've worried about you."

Sully returns her smile. "Heard a lot about you, too." He looks from her to me. "Do we need to take a raincheck on burgers?"

Brighten's eyes light up. "Burgers? I'm starving."

I'm torn between wanting to keep her to myself until I have to say goodbye to her and fostering this growing friendship I've got with Sully. He's actually a really cool guy and in a lot of ways, reminds me of Brighten in that he's easy to talk to, somehow makes me want to talk to him, and doesn't seem to mind when I'm quiet and surly. And by some strange chance, we actually live in the same building—on the same floor, no less. I shake my head at Sully. "Nah, we can all go, if it's cool. Like I said, I just need a quick shower."

"Okay. Meet you downstairs in a half-hour?"

"Sounds good." I dig my keys out of my pocket and, for the first time, notice Brighten's bags. She has a large suitcase and smaller carry-on and rolls them in with her as she follows me inside.

"Running, really?"

"Elias—our mentor—has all of his mentees run a half-marathon at the end of their internship; provided they don't have any physical limitations preventing them from doing so.

Sully ran cross country in high school. He's training me. It sucks ass."

"He seems nice."

"Yeah. He's friendly. Kinda hard not to like him. He's like Jess, in that he's a big people person."

I toe off my shoes at my closet door and tug off my socks and toss them in the hamper. "So, you leave in the morning?" I don't want to get my hopes up that I'll get to have her all night, but I still find them rising.

"Yeah. Okay if I crash here?"

I huff a laugh. "Are you joking?"

"No. I can get a hotel room if I need to."

"Crash, you're staying here."

She looks up at me from her seat on my bed. My apartment is a tiny studio with barely enough room for a double bed and tiny kitchen table that serves as both eating space and desk. "Does that mean you'll give me a proper goodbye?" she asks, a brow lifted and a wicked smile on her face.

I wish I could tell her I never want to say goodbye to her, but I know I won't. I simply nod. "Absolutely."

An hour later, we're parking a few blocks from The Pharmacy, arguably the best burgers in Nashville, and by some miracle, we get seated almost immediately. Brighten takes the seat next to mine and I can't resist draping my arm over the back of her chair as we look over our menus.

"Order me a chocolate shake? I have to use the bathroom," Brighten says after a moment.

I nod. "Sure, Crash." Our server shows up seconds after Brighten departs and I order a tea and Brighten's shake and Sully orders a soda.

Once she's gone, Sully eyes me. "I thought y'all were just friends."

"We are."

"Friends who fuck?"

"As of late," I admit.

"Well, good for you. I could do with some friends like that. She's beautiful."

"Yes, she is," I reply, my voice sounding wistful, even to myself.

"Oh, it's like that, huh?"

I shrug, frowning. "Like what?"

"You like her. And not just because you get to fuck her. You liked her before that. How bad is it?"

"Who are you?" I ask with narrowed eyes.

He shrugs. "I'm perceptive. You're not exactly subtle. Well, except that she doesn't seem to see it."

"She also doesn't feel the same way, so I'd appreciate it if you keep your mouth shut."

Sully sips his soda as it's delivered. "I got you. You'll take what you can get versus nothing at all, am I right?"

"When it's her? Yeah."

His eyes dart toward the restrooms and he sits up straighter. "Gotcha."

Brighten retakes her seat and dives into her shake as she and Sully get to know one another. I'm content to let them chat since I can simply look at her and run my fingers down her long ponytail.

When our food arrives, as is our custom, we share our meals, taking bites of one another's food, and Sully looks on in curiosity. "So, how long have you guys been friends?"

"Since we were twelve," I answer.

"And why does he call you Crash?" he asks Brighten.

"Because I crashed my bike and impaled my right boob on a

chunk of steel. It's how we got to know each other. Flynn stayed with me until the ambulance got there. We've sorta been inseparable since." I laugh at her simplified explanation of events and she smiles up at me. "Well, inseparable until this week."

Outwardly, my smile stays in place, but inwardly, that part of me that knows nothing will be the same anymore after this summer hopes for just five more minutes of time with her. Time all to myself where I can pretend she's only mine. Time I can pretend there's a future that exists where I get to fall asleep with her in my arms and wake up beside her. I wouldn't even need kids as long as I had her.

"And are you going to UT in the fall?" Sully asks.

Brighten pops a fry into her mouth. "No. NYU."

"Wow, why there?"

She huffs a laugh. "To spite my mother and not go to Juilliard."

Sully shakes his head, eyes wide. "Okay, I get why Flynn would turn down ivy, but Juilliard? For real? What is with you people? You get accepted to schools people would kill to attend and you say no?"

Brighten shrugs. "What can I say, I'd rather be a public servant than a concert pianist."

"Public servant?"

She nods. "Yep. Hopefully, you're looking a future president."

His smile is wide and at first he thinks she's joking, but when he sees she's not, he gives her a thoughtful frown. "Well, future Madam President, think you can do something about the rising cost of healthcare?"

She gives me a soft smile before returning her gaze to Sully. "First thing on my agenda. Free healthcare for those suffering chronic illnesses or conditions. We'll work up to the rest of the country."

Again, my heart does that stupid flip-flop I can't control. Some would say that Brighten's whole goal of fixing healthcare is simply to pander, but I know she's one hundred percent serious. Between my father's MS and her own father's death from cancer when she was young, healthcare is something she is genuinely passionate about.

"And what takes you to Ireland this summer? Wouldn't you rather kick around Nashville with Flynn?"

I blink. Fuck, why didn't I think of that? Why didn't I ask her to spend the summer with me? Regret for not thinking of that sooner burns through my middle. Of course, it might be better if we didn't play house all summer. All I would do is fall deeper in love with her and yeah, the sex would be amazing, but she'll still only be my friend.

Brighten shrugs. "My mom has a project that's filming in County Cork. I've always wanted to go see all the castles. If I have to put up with my mother to get to do it, I will." She nudges me. "If it weren't for this great internship, Flynn would be going with me."

"Is your mother in entertainment?"

Brighten grimaces. "Yeah. Vanessa Eldridge."

Sully's eyes go wide and his mouth falls open. "Your mom is Vanessa fucking Eldridge? Holy shit. What's that like?"

"She's a bitch," Brighten says flatly.

"But she's so—."

"Fake? Vapid? Opportunistic? Shallow? A drunk?"

Sully glances at me to see if I'll contradict her and I don't. Instead, I give the back of her neck a supportive squeeze and a small smile when her eyes meet mine.

CHAPTER EIGHT

BRIGHTEN

Seeing Flynn actually make a friend reassures me that he'll be okay without me. Seeing him after a run caught me off guard. Although, seeing him sweaty and panting made me want to drag him into his apartment and fuck him.

When I went to say goodbye to him the night before he left for Nashville, I didn't mean to fall asleep with him. That isn't what we do. Even knowing that, I know that's what I'm doing tonight, and it verges on something different from just Flynn and me having a good time. But knowing I won't see him for at least two months, I couldn't stop myself from coming.

Even getting to email with him and talk and text, it's not the same as getting to see him and spend time with him and I'm going to miss him. I know this is a great opportunity for him, but I'd be lying if I said I wouldn't rather have him in Ireland with me, internship be damned.

Exiting the elevator, I learned Sully lives in the same building and on the same floor as Flynn and I feel even better about leaving him. Sully seems like a great guy and even though I just met him, I give him a quick hug as we say our goodbyes. "Take care of him for me?" I ask in a whisper.

"You got it." When we part, he gives me a final nod. "Say hello to my ancestors for me?"

"Sure thing," I reply with a smile.

"Later, Sully," Flynn calls as we head toward his apartment door. He tugs me inside and locks the door behind us. "What time is your flight?"

"Eleven."

He smiles. "So, can I take you to breakfast in the morning?"

"I'd love that." I look around his small space with its dingy beige walls and double bed, single nightstand, and smaller dinette table, and not even enough room for a sofa. The single burner hot plate, dorm-size fridge, microwave, and coffeemaker are his only appliances. The small television mounted on the wall. "Who would've thought you'd be the first one of us to have their own place? Do you like it?" I ask, dropping onto the end of his bed.

He toes off his shoes and stores them in the tiny closet before joining me. "I'm really only here to sleep for the most part. Elias has us on the same schedule as him. The man is a workaholic. Sully and I are dragging ass at six and Elias is alert. Most days, we're in the office until seven, eating from takeout containers. Today, we got out early because he had to go with his wife to some appointment. We've been doing our runs after we get off and then I come in and crash. I've never been so happy to sleep in on a Saturday in my life." His expression and tone are excited and I can tell how much he's loving the work, even only after a week.

"So, you like your mentor?"

"He's amazing. He's a veteran in the industry and actually handpicked Sully and me as his mentees. Talk about humbling."

"That's awesome, Flynn. You look happy here; doing this."

My best friend nods. "I am. I feel like I'm exactly where I'm supposed to be. I'm with people who speak the same language as me, if that makes sense."

Even though I love that he's finally found something that makes him shine, I can't help but give him shit. "And what do I speak, Latin?"

He rolls his eyes. "No, you're pretty fluent in asshole, Crash. It's why you're good at talking to me." His eyes search mine. "I can't believe you're here."

I bite my lip and shrug. "It might be the last time we're together for who knows when. I had the opportunity, and I wasn't going to pass it up."

"It means a lot that you'd come."

"You're my best friend, Flynn."

"I know. And you're mine." He looks away and stands. "Can I get you something to drink? I don't have any Mountain Dew, but I have some bottles of water."

"Sure, water's fine." Walking over to his little fridge, he squats to pull out two bottles of water and a realization hits me. "Where are your glasses?"

His head snaps up and he laughs. "You just now noticed I'm not wearing my glasses?"

"Yeah. I'm so used to you wearing them, I guess I see them even when they aren't there. Where are they?"

"Got some contacts. I'm trying them out. I'd ordered them a couple of weeks before I left, but they just came in. Mom mailed them to me."

"You keep changing and you're not going to look like you," I warn. "First you lose the braces, you start running, and now you're wearing contacts? I'm not going to recognize you the next time I see you." He returns to the bed and extends a bottle in my direction. Instead of accepting it, I turn and reach to grip his face and look him in the eye. "Don't change too much on me, huh? I won't know what to do with you."

"Everyone changes, Crash. It's part of life. I'll just look more like Jess's actual twin now."

"There's nothing wrong with the way you are. You look good in your glasses."

He gives my wrists a light squeeze. "Yeah, and they're also a pain in the ass. They irritate my acne and slide down my face all the time. Contacts are a piece of cake."

"Promise you won't change too much?"

He gives me that lopsided grin. "What constitutes too much change?"

"Losing all those parts of yourself that make you who you are. Next thing you'll tell me is that you're the popular guy and life of the party."

He snorts and lets his forehead drop to mine. "I don't think you have anything to worry about there. I'm definitely not the life of the party. Not sure that will ever be the case."

I breathe in his familiar scent and for as long as I live, this clean laundry smell and whatever body wash or deodorant he's always used will forever be the one that I automatically associate with Flynn. He inhales deeply and for a long moment, we stay exactly like this. We don't move. We don't speak.

We both know that after tonight, it all changes. We'll go our separate ways and hope we'll still be okay. It's the thought of Flynn and me drifting or possibly going days or weeks or months or years without speaking or seeing one another that has a tear rolling down my face. I sniff involuntarily and it's congested with all the tears I'm holding back.

Flynn pulls back and I open my eyes to see his are worried. "What's wrong?"

"We're grownups, Flynn."

He huffs a laugh and swipes my tears away with the pad of his thumb. I don't cry in front of Flynn often, but he doesn't seem to mind in this moment and for that, I'm thankful. "Well, yeah. That's what happens. Why are you crying?"

"I don't want things to change. I don't want you to not be the Flynn I know anymore. I don't want us to go weeks or months without seeing one another." He opens his mouth and I push forward. "I'm not talking about college because there will be breaks and I'll come home. I'm talking about after. When I'm in D.C. and you're who knows where predicting what the next big toothpaste trend will be or whatever."

He chuckles and I start to cry harder and he sobers. "I could be halfway around the world and you'd still be my best friend. We could go five years without speaking—not that that could happen because I'd track your ass down before I'd ever go that long without seeing you. But even then, you'd still be the person I'd want to tell everything to. You'd still be *my* Crash. No matter what. Okay?"

"Promise?"

He swallows thickly, his own eyes shiny. "Promise. No matter what, if you call, I come running. I'm there. Got it? No matter what, you're always going to be my best friend. No amount of time or space is ever going to change that."

I throw my arms around his shoulders and sob into his neck. Flynn pulls me into his lap and simply holds me. He rubs my back and presses kisses into my hair and if I'm not mistaken, he sniffles some, too, and I don't feel so bad about getting emotional.

When my tears finally subside, I pull back and wipe my face and sigh. "Sorry."

He huffs a laugh. "Why are you sorry? Not every day someone breaks down over the thought of going months without seeing me. It's liable to give me a big head."

I swat his arm. "Asshole. I was having a moment. I'm allowed."

He snatches my hand and brings it to his chest. "I know."

I swallow, my tears threatening again. "I'm just really going to miss you."

He nods and looks up at the ceiling and blinks rapidly and clears his throat. "Fuck. This is harder than I though it would be. I thought I already survived saying goodbye to you."

I bring my free hand to his face and he drops his eyes back to mine. "Say goodbye to me again?" Tears roll down his cheeks and mine start again as I press my lips to his. The kiss is sweet and tender and sad and my chest aches with how much I'm going to miss my best friend.

Even through our tears, we slowly get undressed and crawl into bed and Flynn pulls the covers up around us. We lie facing one another and for a long time, he simply runs a knuckle along my jaw. "We'll still be us, right?" I can't help but ask.

He considers my question for a moment and nods. "We're still us now, right?"

"Yeah."

"So, see, we'll be fine." He drags his fingertips down the side of my neck and down my bare back to my waist and over my hip to give it a tight squeeze and pull me closer. I come willingly, tangling my legs with his, loving how his leg hairs feel against my smooth skin. I trail my hand down his chest and stomach and try to memorize the way he feels under my fingers.

I stare down at his chest as I contemplate the next part of my life and Flynn nudges my forehead with the tip of his nose and I lift my face to look at him. His eyes roam over my features. "You're beautiful, Crash. Thank you for being my best friend."

Nodding, I slide my hand back up his chest and around to the back of his neck to pull his mouth to mine. The touch of my lips to his seems to break whatever spell had us stalling, because within only seconds, our kiss turns hungry and desperate and I feel like I'm drowning and the only air in the room comes from him.

I moan into our kiss and he slides his hand down to my butt to knead the flesh and pulls me into him. He's hard against my belly and between his kisses and his hands seeming to touch every inch of my body, I'm already wet and pressing my thighs together.

He licks a hot line down the column of my throat and I tilt my head to give him better access. "Fuck, Flynn. God, please."

Rolling me onto my back, he looks down at me, his expression sincere, even with his eyes hooded with lust. "What do you need?"

I don't know how to answer him in this moment. I need him to make me forget I'm leaving. I need him to take this pain away. I need to know we're going to be okay. I need to sear this moment in my memory since it might be the last time we're ever like this. Another tear rolls out of my eyes and into the hair at my temple. "Right now, I just need you. Please?"

He nods and reaches over to open his nightstand and pulls out a condom. I close my eyes and try not to cry, even as my lashes grow wet with my efforts. He shifts his hips and his cock notches at my entrance. "Look at me." I obey and his eyes shine with wetness and he presses a soft kiss to my lips. "I've got you." Our gazes stay locked as he pistons his hips forward, a gasp falling from my lips as he enters me.

For a while—ten minutes, two hours, I have no clue—we don't look away. Even when our movements grow more frantic, our breathing more clipped, our sounds dissolving into a cacophony of murmured words, curses, and moans. Even when he guides my hand between us to my clit and I come with his name on my lips. Even only moments later, when his own release explodes with a grunt, we never stop looking into each other's eyes.

Flynn is gone when I wake up and a quick check of my phone says it's a little after six. Smelling coffee, I rise from the bed, still dressed in the T-shirt he took off last night that smells like him. I shuffle toward the scent of my lifeblood and spot a note next to the coffeemaker.

> Crash,
> Went for a run. Back soon.
> -F

    I pour myself a cup of coffee and dig through the small basket of takeout sugar packets and creamer pods behind the one other mug he has sitting next to the machine. After doctoring my coffee, I climb back into bed and lean against the headboard.

    I could turn on the TV or read or take a shower. There are a lot of things I could do. I could burrow back under the covers and wait for Flynn to return and pull him back under the covers with me. I know I won't do that, though. We won't have sex again before I leave. I'm still too emotionally raw from last night. Knowing I have to say goodbye to him is already too much.

    For the briefest of moments, I contemplate leaving before he gets back so I won't have to tell him goodbye in person, but I also know I won't do that, either. He's my best friend and I can't not say goodbye to him; as much as it's going to hurt.

Sure enough, it hurts like a bitch. By some unspoken agreement, we don't kiss goodbye. Maybe that would feel too relationship-y? Flynn does pull me into his arms for a long hug and I manage to hold the tears at bay long enough to round the corner and be out of his sight after going through security at the airport. For better or worse, everything is different now.

CHAPTER NINE

FLYNN

"Dude, if you don't get your ass out here, I'm getting the super. We're going to be late and Elias is going to kick our asses. Is this really how you want to play it on the second week? Sack up, Tate."

I'm moving slower than I'd like and skipped my run this morning. I am dressed, though, so there's that. I open the door. "Fuck, can't a guy just be having an off morning?"

Sully scoffs. "Not when your mentor is Elias Washington. Get your ass in gear. I know you're bummed about Brighten, but you've gotta get your head in the game. You know we have that meeting with the client this morning."

I blink and tie my shoes. "Fuck. I forgot. You've got the notes, right?"

"Yes, I have the notes that will save our asses. You're lucky I didn't have a piece of tail to occupy my time and make me all surly when she left. We both would've been fucked."

Grabbing my bag and shoving my laptop inside, I snatch my cup of coffee, keys, and phone as we head out the door. "What can I say, I excel at surly. Ask Brighten; it's my default."

We run onto the elevator, and he breathes a sigh of relief and checks his watch. "We're cutting it close this morning. Next time, I leave your ass."

I lean against the wall and let my head fall back. "Thanks, Sully," I mumble. "Sorry about making us late. It won't happen again."

He sticks his fist out for me to bump it. "No big, dude. I get it. You miss your girl."

I tap his fist with my own. "Yeah, except she's not. She'll never be *my* girl."

"You don't know that; she cares about you. She even asked me to keep an eye on you."

I nod, not looking at him. "She does care about me, just not like that. She doesn't want a relationship. Not just with me, with anyone."

The elevator doors open at the parking garage level and we head toward Sully's Lexus. "Never?"

"Nope. She's got plans. Big ones."

He huffs a laugh as he starts the car. "Yeah, I heard. President."

"She'd also settle for senator or governor."

"You never know, dreams change. Plans change."

———

Thankfully, Sully really does save our asses with his notes and when Elias asks for input about the forecasted predictions about increases in hybrid car purchases for the next five years, he's ready with an answer. And even though we both receive credit for our work, I don't feel right taking all the praise and make sure to let Elias know Sully did most of the research when I pop into his office later in the day.

"And why is that?" Elias asks after gesturing for me to close the door and take a seat. He leans his large bulk against the desk, arms folded across his chest, brown eyes expectant.

"I'm sorry to say I had an off weekend. It won't happen again. I've assured Sully of this as well."

He nods and scratches his chin. "Flynn, this is only your second week. The work is only going to increase. If the pressure is too much, there's no shame in admitting this field may not be right for you. And honestly, it's better you find out now before you spend four plus years on your education with the intent of entering this industry."

I'm shaking my head before he's even done speaking. "No, sir. It's not the work. I love the work. It was a personal issue. Like I said, it won't happen again."

He examines my face. "Is it your father? Everything okay?"

Surprised he'd show concern about my dad, I blink. "No, sir. He's fine. Thank you for asking."

He lifts a brow. "So, a girl then. I see. Well, not that I condemn you for sowing your wild oats or whatever you young people do these days, but you're going to have to get a better hold on keeping those kinds of things from bleeding into your professional life. I'm sure it's exciting to be in a new city and be on your own with a plethora of beautiful young women to occupy your time."

I huff a laugh, the idea of being with anyone besides Brighten nearly comical. "No, sir. No plethora for me. It's just my best friend. She left for Ireland for the summer, and I won't see her for at least a couple of months. We've never spent this much time apart. That's all. Like I said, just an off weekend. I'll be back on my game tomorrow. You have my word."

"I trust that's true, Flynn. For what it's worth, having a heart isn't a weakness. It's one of the things I think will take you the farthest. There will be times you have to be ruthless, no doubt, but it's important you don't lose those things that make you a good man, not just a good asset to a company."

I nod. "Thank you, Elias."

As we finish our normal Friday night run—and Sully was totally right, it is getting a little easier—I'm finally not feeling as though my heart's been ripped out with Brighten's absence.

"So, plans this weekend?" he asks as we take the steps as up to our floor as our cooldown.

"Going home to visit. Jess and I have to go to a birthday party for a friend of ours tomorrow."

He nods. "What kind of friend? One like Brighten?" He wiggles his eyebrows and I huff a laugh.

"No. Not like Brighten. Not to me, anyway. Jess dated her while we were in high school, but they're just friends now. You got shit to do? You're welcome to come. Josie's pretty cool. The party is at our friend Hensley's house. Her parents are loaded and there's a pool."

Sully considers. "Where would we stay?"

"There will probably be booze, so most likely at Hensley's. Her place is giant, so there's plenty of space. Should be a lot of fun. We'd have to leave by three."

"I'm in."

As we pull in at Hensley's parents' estate, Sully gapes. "You know, I make no apologies for my parents having money, but fuck, this is...shit, dude."

I snort. "Right? Hensley's pretty down to earth, though. And her parties are always kick ass."

"Is she hot? Single?"

"Yes, she's hot. I assume she's single. I've not seen her with anyone since Josie's older brother, Silas, a couple of years ago. He and her other brother, Cole, and Cole's girl-friend, Ada, will probably be here, too. Cole and Silas are twins, too."

"Is there just something in the water here? Did you go to school with a lot of other twins?"

I shake my head as we exit the car. "No, just us. And if you're looking for tail, I should've warned you, I don't think you'll find it here. You're welcome to try with Hens or Josie, but they don't usually show up alone."

We let ourselves into the house and I lead the way out toward the blaring music and sounds of splashing and squealing feminine voices. Stepping out onto the back patio, a collective yell of greeting emanates from around the pool. I make the rounds, introducing Sully to everyone, and we grab a drink.

Josie climbs out of the pool and runs over, and I pull her in for a hug, not even caring that she's soaking wet. "And how is my other favorite Tate twin?"

"I'm good. Happy birthday, by the way. This is my friend, Sully."

She eyes me, impressed. "And here I thought Brighten was the only friend you claim. Nice to meet you, Sully."

"You, too. Great party."

"That's all Hensley's doing." Josie gestures to Hensley across the patio, where she chats with Jess. "She's a great host-ess. I'll see y'all later. Thanks for coming," she calls just before jumping back into the pool.

Sully nods appreciatively and sips his beer. "I think I'm definitely going to need more face time with her. Damn, you've got hot friends." He jerks his chin in the direction of the snack table where a tall brunette in a bikini fills a plate. "And what about her?"

"That's Ada. Way off limits."

"Like, how off limits?"

"Like, if her boyfriend doesn't kick your ass, his twin brother will. I'm pretty sure he's also got a thing for her."

He frowns and lowers his voice. "So they, what, share?"

I choke on my beer. "Fuck, no. Not like that. I just meant Silas has always had a crush on her. He'd never do that to Cole, though. They're good people. Brothers don't do that to each other."

He shrugs. "Wouldn't know. Only child. But, just so I'm clear, Josie and Hensley are fair game?"

"Best of my knowledge. Have at 'em."

Sully grins, rubbing his hands together as if he's scheming. "Don't mind if I do. Catch you later, man."

"Sure." I make my way over to Hensley and Jess and greet my brother with a fist bump and Hensley with a hug. "Hens, looking gorgeous as always."

"Thanks, Flynn. Who's your friend?"

"Sully. We're in an internship together. He's good people."

Jess rises from his chair. "Going to get a refill. Y'all need anything?"

"I'm good," I reply and drop into his vacated seat. Once he's gone, Hensley slugs my shoulder and I wince. "What the fuck, Hens? Shit, I told you I was bringing a friend. Don't act like you don't always plan accordingly."

"It's not that, asshole." She lowers her voice. "You and Brighten? Really? What the hell were you thinking?"

I take a long pull of my beer and sigh. "So, I guess she finally told you?"

"Yeah. Before she went to Nashville last weekend. Are you

insane? You're going to end up getting your heart broken, Flynn."

"Why do you say that?" I ask, even though I already know the answer.

Hensley rolls her blue eyes and drags her fingers through her blonde hair. "Because you've been in love with her for years. I don't know why everyone thinks I'm a fucking idiot. I can sniff out unrequited love like a bloodhound. You know she's never going to settle down or want anything long term. She's never going to want kids or get married, right?"

"Yes, I fucking know that. I know better than anyone what her plans are. They're all we've talked about for years."

Her expression softens. "Then why would you do this to yourself?"

"What was I supposed to say? No? She asked me to do it. If there was someone you had feelings for and they asked you to take their virginity, what would you do? Would you let someone who doesn't care about them do it? Some cheese-dick frat guy with dirty hands who wouldn't make sure it was good for her? Fuck that," I spit out, the thought of it being anyone but me making me want to commit murder.

She sighs. "Okay, I get that. But why continue to do it? Is that really the best thing for you?"

"It doesn't matter; it's over now." I down what's left of my beer and toss the empty into the recycle bin fifteen feet away, sinking the shot easily.

"So, y'all are just going to go back to not fucking?"

"She'll be in New York. I'll be here. It's not like we'll see each other."

Hensley drags a tray of shots over. "And what about breaks?" she asks, downing a shot of tequila. "Just playing devil's advocate here, but what if she brings someone home with her next summer? What if she meets someone? What will you do then? Will you tell her how you feel?"

Something in my gut knots painfully at the thought of her with anyone who isn't me, even though I know the likelihood that she doesn't meet someone else to at least occupy her time—even while she's in Ireland—is slim to none. She likes sex. She'll be around guys better looking than me who will have Irish accents and who can probably do sexy Irish things in bed that I have no clue about. And I'll just be...here.

"Earth to Flynn," she says, snapping her fingers in front of my face. "Where did you go? What will you do? You didn't say."

"I don't know what I'll do," I admit, downing a shot, the tequila burning all the way down.

CHAPTER TEN

BRIGHTEN

After six weeks in Ireland, I haven't seen nearly as much as I would like in terms of pubs, castles, or really anything except my mother. She's insistent on me hanging around and as I don't currently have her rental car keys or access to her driver without her permission, I am held hostage by Vanessa and her ever-present cloud of Chanel No. 5 to cover the smell of the cheap vodka.

So, what have I been doing with myself, one might ask? Zilch. Zip. Nada. Fuck all. If I do get out, it's with Vanessa in tow; in which case we're always accosted by fans and paparazzi and I hate the limelight since Vanessa only trots me out to pretend to be an actual human and not an attention-seeking clout chaser.

To top it off, I've only gotten to actually speak to Flynn twice the entire time I've been here. I miss his voice and being able to bitch about Vanessa with him. Our email chain, on the other hand, is quite lengthy.

He and Sully are forming a great friendship and his internship seems to be working out exactly like he hoped it would.

The photos he sends me catch me off guard because without his glasses and braces, I'm not sure if it's actually him. Pair that with the weight he seems to have dropped overnight and his acne almost completely gone, he's not the Flynn I know anymore. Physically, anyway. In everything else, he's very much still the same surly goofball I know and love.

Determined to at least see *something* before I leave in a week, I have websites for several local tourist spots pulled up when I get an alert that I have an email. And since I obviously have nothing better to do, I click over to check it.

From: Flynn Tate (flynn_tate@yahoo.com)
To: Brighten Dawes (b.dawes@hotmail.com)
Subject: Re: we might be apart, but you're still stuck with me

Crash,

What do you mean, you still haven't gone to see the castles?! You are running out of time. I swear, if you get back to the States and you tell me you did nothing but watch Vanessa get her face caked up every day, I will chop off all of your hair. Please don't make me have to do that. You have really great hair.

How goes the prep for your dorm? Have you decided on your 47th shade of black? I know you keep waffling between smoke and ebony. I say, shoot for ebony. Let's hope your room-mate isn't overly fond of pink.

As for the Sully-Josie saga, I can report she was leaving his apartment on Monday morning as we were leaving for the office. Pretty sure he's in love. Josie is predictably tightlipped. You know her. I think they've only lasted as long as they have since it's long-distance. If she saw him more than once a week, they would've been done weeks ago. I'm waiting for the fallout and will update as I know more.

Should I expect you to have picked up an accent in the four weeks since we last spoke? Are you sounding like Madonna when she moved to England and started sounding a bit British?

Dad sends his love, of course. He keeps saying the numbness in his hands/arms is getting better, but it's not. The vision in his right eye is also getting worse. He tries to be stoic but I know he's only brave for Mom. Have I mentioned lately how much I fucking hate MS?

Sorry, didn't mean to get morbid.

Do you need a ride home from the airport when you get back? I know you're only going to have a few days to pack all your stuff before you have to be at NYU, so I was going to see if you needed help.

Hope to get to hear your voice soon. I bet Ireland is loving you, but Tennessee misses you.

-Flynn

I smile reading Flynn's email until I get to the stuff about his dad. I was a lot younger than him when I lost my own father and most days, I don't remember his voice or specifics about his appearance unless I look at a photo. I was only seven when the pancreatic cancer took him. I honestly don't remember much at all.

Hearing the fear and anger—even through email—in Flynn's words, sometimes I wonder if I got the easy end of things. I miss my dad, but it's nothing like he and Jess will miss Jude Tate when complications from his MS most likely claim his life. He's a sweet man and has always treated me kindly. He's offered me fatherly advice when I needed it most and I admire his spirit and fighting nature.

I'd be lying if I said Ione probably won't be more crushed by his passing than my own father's. I've almost had Jude in my life longer, and I'll remember him better. I will also hurt because my best friend will be hurting. I dread that day and know it's probably closer than anyone would prefer to admit.

Checking the clock on my laptop, I see I have about ten minutes to respond to Flynn's email before I have to get ready, so I hit reply.

From:Brighten Dawes (b.dawes@hotmail.com)
To: Flynn Tate (flynn_tate@yahoo.com)
Subject: Re: we might be apart, but you're still stuck with me

Flynn,

The castle situation will be remedied, so help me, no later than tomorrow. I was actually looking at the closest castles to me when I received your email, so there. There will be no hair chopping necessary. I'd like to see you try, anyway. I think we both know you'd come back with a nub before you ever got near my hair, buddy.

I believe ebony would be a fine choice. I've actually been in email contact with my roommate. She seems pretty cool. Said she hates pink. Sounds like a winner to me.

Vanessa has continued to surprise no one with her boozy antics. I swear, I thought the director was going to have a coronary yesterday. Pretty sure there will be another stay for "exhaustion" in her future. I know I don't remember much of what she was like before Dad died, but surely this can't be the same woman he fell for, right?

I'll send an inevitable consolation fruit basket to Sully when Josie no doubt jumps ship. Hopefully, she can someday find someone she doesn't want to shake. Not likely knowing her, but I guess only time will tell.

As far as I can tell, I still very much sound like myself. At least, that's the impression I get from the locals who tell me I sound like Dolly Parton. I'll take it as a compliment. I guess you'll have to tell me yourself.

A ride would be great. Thank God I'm leaving a few days ahead of Vanessa and she's not driving with me to New York. I'll update you when I have more concrete travel plans. And if you want to help me pack, I will so buy you pizza and make sure you get the slice with the most pepperoni.

Tell your dad when I come into town, to make sure to have his Yahtzee skills brushed up. I'm going to take him down. I, too, fucking hate MS, Tate. You're allowed to be morbid. If you can't be morbid and angry and your best friend be there to commiserate, who else can you do it with?

Ireland has nothing on Tennessee. My favorite people are there and I miss them.

See you soon,

B.

No sooner have I hit send, than the door to Vanessa's trailer opens and she shambles up the few steps and falls onto the couch across the table where I'm currently setup. "Darling, let's go hit the town. We've only got a few days left. I won't be able to go out with you for drinks when we get back to the States. I've been looking forward to having a drink with my daughter for as long as I can remember."

I roll my eyes. "You realize it's not normal to fantasize about taking your daughter to get hammered, right? Besides, it seems like you've already had enough to drink for the both of us. I'm good. I'm going out later with Saoirse. She's been begging me the entire time I've been here."

"So you're not going to spend any time with me? Isn't that why you came here? I have an evening free, darling. Please?"

That's actually the opposite of why I came here.

"Sorry, we already made plans. I don't want to blow her off. We'll have a last hurrah before I have to leave." I check my watch. "I've gotta get ready. Don't you have another call time today? You don't want to be late. Stop by craft service and have some coffee, okay?"

"So, what are American boys like?" Saoirse, one of the locals who's acting as a gofer for the production team, asks. She's around my age, petite and slim and fair skinned with jet black hair and blue eyes.

I look around the pub that must be at least two hundred years old. We don't have places like this in Tennessee with all this history. Warm wooden floors that are dinged and scuffed and waxed are juxtaposed against the exposed brick walls that were probably made by hand. The pub is warm and dim, adding to the cozy ambiance. It's lively, though, and quite crowded from where I stand toward the back of the main room.

Shrugging, I sip my Guinness. "Probably the same as they are here. Most of my friends are guys. They're cool."

"Do you have a boyfriend?"

I huff a laugh. "No. No boyfriend for me."

She raises a brow. "Well then, I won't have to beat them off you while you're here. And for sure, there're a few giving you a look or two."

"Anyone interesting?" I ask with a smile. I can't deny that

I'm wound so tight I could probably come from a stiff breeze. Who knew I was such a sex fiend?

Saoirse grins. "Yeah, over your right shoulder. There's a guy coming over. Tall, big, nice smile."

I glance coyly over my shoulder to try to spot the guy she was referring to. Sure enough, there's one who looks like the epitome of what I picture rugby players must be built like in real life is striding our way. He's white and probably mid-twenties, at least six-three and as wide as the table we're currently standing at, and solid. She's right, he's got a nice smile, too. Complete with dirty blonde hair cropped short and brown eyes, his massive arms are sleeved in colorful tattoos.

"Well, hello," tall and giant grins down at me. "Saoirse, who's your friend?"

I glance at her. "You know this guy?"

"Oh, and American, too? Well, well." His voice is deep and I have to admit, the Irish accent is definitely doing it for me. He leans his forearms on the table and his grin widens. "How are you enjoying fair Ireland, darlin'?"

"It's lovely, from what I've seen."

Saoirse pipes up. "She hasn't seen anything, Sean. Been here six weeks, and this is the first night she's even been out."

His—Sean, apparently—brows draw down in feigned concern. "That's a shame. Anything special you're hoping to see—?" He trails off, expectant, and I realize he doesn't know my name.

"Brighten," I supply.

"Brighten, eh? That's different. Common name in the States?"

I snort. "No. Sean is definitely more common than Brighten."

"Well, Brighten, good to meet you. Buy you a pint?"

I hold up my nearly full beer. "How about just a conversation?"

He nods. "Fine."

Saoirse spots something or someone on the other side of the pub and hops up and yells, "Cillian, what're you doing here with Rosie?" She runs away and Sean and I share a surprised laugh.

"So, what brings you to Ireland?"

I sigh. "It was supposed to be my last big adventure before college."

"And has it been?"

"Not really. I'm hoping to see a few things before I leave next week."

"And what if I wanted to see you before you leave?"

"A bit forward to assume I'd be interested, don't you think?"

"Nah. You said you're looking for adventure. Look no further," he quips with a wink and wicked grin.

"And what are you offering on this *adventure*?" I ask with a lifted brow. I don't hate the idea of this big guy possibly showing me a good time.

Sean leans in and whispers in my ear. "You have a boyfriend?" I look up at him and shake my head. "Husband?"

I laugh. "No. I'm only eighteen. Damn." He nods, thoughtful. "How old are you?" I ask.

"Twenty-six."

I motion up and down his body. "And are all these muscles just for looks, or are they functional, too?"

He chuckles and sips his beer. "Sweetheart, I could toss you over my shoulder as easy as I can breathe."

I bite my lip. "Care to prove it?"

"Happy to." He downs his beer and takes my hand. It's warm and large and callused, and I immediately think of

Flynn's hand and a pang of guilt hits me square in the chest. Flynn and I aren't together. We don't have any kind of arrangement. He's probably living it up in Nashville as we speak and has fucked ten—or fifty—girls since I left. I push away thoughts of Flynn and let Sean pull me toward a back hall and into a bathroom.

He slams the door and flips the lock before pulling me to him, his mouth covering mine in a kiss. It's so different from kissing Flynn, it's a shock to my system. Not bad, just different. Sean lifts me easily and sets me on the sink and steps between my knees. "Are you a virgin?" he asks as he kisses his way down my jaw and neck.

"No," I answer, tugging up the hem of the T-shirt he wears. Sean's solid under my fingers and he doesn't have as much chest hair as Flynn.

Stop thinking about Flynn, Brighten.

"You smell good," he breathes against my chest. I let my head fall back against the mirror and moan as he yanks me flush against him, his dick already hard in his jeans. He continues kissing down my chest, tugging my tank top and bra lower until he freezes.

It takes me a beat to realize he's stopped kissing me or moving. "What?" I ask, almost breathless. But when I open my eyes, I see. He's looking at my scar, something like pity in his gaze, and my desire instantly cools.

He blinks, his expression neutralizing. "Nothing." He attempts to resume kissing me, and I put my hand on his chest.

"I don't think this is going to work for me." He opens his mouth to say something, his face a mask of contrition, and I shake my head. "It's not you. It's me. Thank you though, Sean." I hop down from the sink and leave the bathroom as shame and embarrassment have my stomach roiling. Thankfully, he doesn't come after me. I spot Saoirse across the pub and make my way over to her. "I need to go. Can you take me back to my hotel?"

She examines my face and nods. "Alright. Everything okay?"

I nod. "Yeah, just not feeling great. Too much Guinness, I think. I'm not a big drinker."

Giving me a smile, she bids farewell to the guy she's speaking with and we make our way outside. "Did something happen?" she asks as she pulls out of the parking lot. "Did Sean do something wrong?"

"No. I'm okay."

"Are you sure?"

"Yes. And thank you for taking me out. I had a good time; I'm just not feeling well."

I make it to my room and shut the door before the tears start. Thankfully, Vanessa is nowhere in sight and I fall onto my bed and roll onto my side and pull my knees up to my chest and when I close my eyes, all I can see is that look of pity.

Bringing my left hand up, I slip it into the top of my shirt and cover my scar, fat tears rolling off my nose. I wish it were gone and I was normal. I know it's not a moral failing or short-coming, but when the first guy aside from Flynn sees it and freezes up, it makes me see I was right to ask him to be my first. God, I hate this scar.

Don't hate on something that means so much to me.

Flynn's words spoken the first time he saw me naked replay in my mind and, in this moment, I want nothing more than to hear his voice. Picking up the room phone—overseas call costs be damned—I follow the instructions to place an international call.

It rings as I grab a tissue and dab my eyes. "Flynn's phone," a female voice answers. She's breathing hard and my stomach drops. For a long moment, I can't say anything, the vivid images of Flynn fucking another girl the only thing I can see and I'm not sure how to feel. "Hello? Is someone there?"

There's some muffled words in the background as Flynn's voice drifts down the line, the sound getting louder by the second. "Who is it?"

"I don't know; the number's weird." The phone changes hands, but I still hear her—whoever this *her* is—say, "I'm going to grab a shower."

CHAPTER ELEVEN

FLYNN

As I reenter the bedroom, Nina has my phone pressed to her ear. "Hello? Is someone there?" She looks at me and extends the device toward me.

"Who is it?" I ask, swiping the towel over my wet hair.

She shrugs. "I don't know; the number's weird." Passing me as she hands it over, she says, "I'm going to grab a shower."

I nod and bring the phone to my ear. "Hello?" No one says anything, but I hear soft breathing. Pulling it back away from my face, I look at the number. Realizing it has to be an international call, my heart kicks over. "Crash? Is that you?" Hope and longing vie for top emotion in this moment as I pray it's her.

"Uh, yeah. Hey. Sorry to just call. I didn't mean to interrupt your day."

A surprised bark of laughter falls from my mouth. "Crash, what the hell are you talking about? You're not an interruption. Are you okay? You sound off."

She clears her throat. "I'm fine. Just a little homesick, I guess."

But knowing Brighten the way I do, it has to be more than that. "You sure?"

"Yeah, just needed to hear a friendly voice." After a beat, when she speaks again, she sounds more upbeat. "So, who's the girl? You finally tap into the bottomless well of Nashville snatch?"

Having this kind of conversation with Brighten isn't something I ever anticipated and to hear her be so casual makes something twist in my chest, but I modulate my tone to match hers. "Who, Nina? No. Her shower is acting up and the super can't get to it for a few days, so I offered to let her use mine so she doesn't have to go to work smelling like a gym sock. We just got done with a run."

"Oh, so she's a neighbor?"

"Yeah." I lounge back on the bed to settle into a conversation with her. I've missed her voice as much as I've missed her body and emails just don't cut it, so I'll talk to her for as long as she'll let me. "So, did you finally decide which castles you were going to hit? I'm going to be so mad at you if you haven't seen any. It was one of the biggest reasons you wanted to go to Ireland in the first place."

"Yeah, I think so. I went out tonight with a girl from the production. She's a local."

"So, to a pub? Was it weird not having to worry about needing a fake ID?"

"Kinda. But there were a lot of people our age there."

"Did you have fun?" It's unusual I have to draw her out like this. Normally, she's pretty chatty, and even though her voice sounds normal, something is off.

"It was great."

"What is it, Crash? Are you sure you're okay? Did something happen?" A sniffle on the other end of the line lets me know I was right and I sigh, my chest aching with the thought of her being in pain and me not being able to be there for her. I have a terrifying thought that someone came on to her while she was out and wouldn't take no for an answer. "Are you hurt? Did someone hurt you? At the pub? Talk to me. You're scaring me. Please?"

"No, nothing like that. I'm okay." Except she's in full-blown tears and I drag my hand down my face knowing there's not a damn thing I can do for her right now.

"What the hell happened? You've got me thinking I need to hop a plane and kick some guy's ass, Crash."

"I'm okay, Flynn. I promise. It's just..."

I heave a relieved sigh. "It's just what?"

"He flinched."

Confused, I blink. "Who flinched? Why?"

Brighten clears her throat. "This guy at the pub." Even knowing we don't have any kind of agreement about not sleeping with other people, and even knowing there was always a good chance she would, it hurts. It hurts so much more than I ever imagined it would to hear about her with another guy.

But I signed up for this, right? To keep being her best friend? Because I'd rather have her in my life in that capacity than none at all. She's still speaking, so I refocus on her words so I can be her friend and not the guy who's in love with her.

"We were making out and when he saw my scar, he froze. God, you should've seen his face. It was like this...pity. He tried to hide it, but I didn't stick around to see if he did."

Although I'm relieved she didn't sleep with someone else, knowing how self-conscious she is about her scar, I hate this for her. "I'm sorry."

She laughs, but it's dejected. "I'm going to have to only have sex with the lights off in the future. That way, I don't have to see them look at my scar."

"Fuck that," I can't help but say, even though we don't ever talk about us having sex. Our emails, texts, and calls thus far have all been strongly platonic. But I'll be damned if she ever thinks there's anything wrong with her. And since I can't show her, in this moment, how much I love her body, words will have to suffice. "You're gorgeous with the lights on. Watching you fuck is one of the best things ever, Crash. Any guy who doesn't see how amazing your scar makes you isn't worth it. I love your scar. You know that, right?"

"Yeah," she replies softly.

"Then you remember that. Any guy who deserves the opportunity to even be in the vicinity of that stellar pussy should know and acknowledge exactly how beautiful you are. And they can't do that with the lights off."

"Stellar, huh?" Amusement laces her tone and my heart lifts hearing it.

"Definitely stellar. I mean, not that I have anything to compare it to, but in my expert opinion, it's exceptional."

"So you're not sleeping with the neighbor?"

Her tone sounds casual, and I shouldn't want her to sound pleased that I'm not sleeping with Nina, but would it kill her to be a little territorial?

She's not territorial, Flynn. She doesn't see you as hers. So, no territory to piss on.

"No, I'm not sleeping with the neighbor, Crash. I barely have time or energy to train for the race after work, let alone get it up. Besides, Nina's gay, so I don't think I'm her type."

"Pretty sure you're everyone's type, Flynn."

I only want to be your type.

"Careful now, you'll give me a big head."

"Are you going to be able to finish the race? How's training going?

Taking her cue to change the subject away from sex, I nod even though she can't see. "It's good. My pace is good. I almost don't hate it now."

"I wish I could be there when you cross the finish line. I bet it will be amazing."

"So, come," I reply before I can stop myself. The idea of having her there as I do this huge thing—at least, it's pretty huge for me—is a thought I can't be anything but excited about. "I can pick you up at the airport and you can ride home with me since I go back to Knoxville the day after the race. You can come to the internship wrap party with me and meet Elias. It might even rival an Irish pub. There won't be any Guinness, but I'll be in a suit if that's any sort of incentive." My tone sounds more pleading than I intend and I adjust my voice. "I mean, if you wanted to. I get it if you can't."

"A suit, huh? Well, how am I supposed to say no to that?"

Excitement spikes through my chest. "You'll come? I promise, it wasn't a guilt trip or anything, but I'd be lying if I said I haven't missed you."

Best friends tell each other they miss them, right? That doesn't sound like, "Hey, I'm in love with you. Come home and let me kiss your face off." Right? Right.

"Ireland hasn't been what I expected. I think if you'd been able to come, it would've been so much better. I should've taken Sully's suggestion and stayed in Nashville. At least then, I wouldn't have been subjected to Vanessa on a daily basis."

I close my eyes and imagine what it would have been like with her here all summer. God, it would have been a dream. Something nudges my toe and I pop my eyes open to see Nina waving as she leaves. I give her a nod and wave.

"I'm sorry I couldn't come. We would have ruled Ireland by the time it was over."

"But your internship has been really good for you. I can tell. You've made friends and are this big market research expert now."

I snort at her appraisal of me. "Yeah, I don't think so. Sully's been a great friend and intern partner. Elias is an amazing mentor. I really have enjoyed this summer. But your absence has been felt, Crash. A lot."

"Yours, too," she replies. "So, do I need a dress for this party? I can't have you showing me up."

"Not possible. But yes, it's formal. Or, formal adjacent, I guess."

She blows out a breath. "Okay. Let me move some stuff around. I'll email you with my flight details?"

I *so* didn't expect today to turn out like this. "So, you're coming? Really?" I couldn't hide the excitement in my voice if I tried.

"Yeah. It's three days from now, right?"

"Yeah, Saturday morning is the race and the party is that night."

"Okay. I'll be there." After a beat, she mutters a curse. "Shit. I've gotta go. Vanessa's here. I'll see you in a few days." She doesn't wait for a response before disconnecting the call.

I can't keep the goofy grin off my face. I'm still sitting and smiling into my empty apartment when my door opens. Sully doesn't even bother knocking anymore. He knows I don't bring girls here; knows there aren't any girls I want in spite of his efforts to get me to partake in the "bottomless well of Nashville snatch", as Brighten put it.

"What's with your face? You look like you found out Santa is, in fact, real." He squats to pull some waters from my fridge and tosses one to me. I catch it and twisting the top, down a few gulps.

"Brighten's coming to the race."

His eyes widen. "What? How'd you swing that?"

I shrug. "Good timing, I guess? She was having a bad day, we got to talking. She's homesick. I mentioned the race and the party. I'm not complaining."

"So, how's Ireland?"

"Irish, I guess. Some asshole made her feel like shit, so for a second, I thought I was going to have to hop a plane."

"She's okay, though, right? What happened?"

I clench my jaw in annoyance. "That bike wreck when we were kids?" He nods. "She's got this huge scar." I hold my thumb and index finger a couple of inches apart and run it across my chest to indicate the size and width of her scar. "Dude flinched when he saw it and it upset her."

He drops onto the end of my bed, his expression pained. "That sucks."

I nod. "Yeah. That's always been a big fear for her. It was one of the reasons we slept together in the first place. She worried if it was someone who didn't know her well and saw her without knowing her history, they'd react. She didn't want to have that as her first sexual memory and it give her some kind of complex. Sucks to know her fears have now been confirmed."

"How do you feel about her hooking up with someone else?"

"She didn't hook up with him. But I don't know. Jealous as fuck," I answer honestly. "But she's not mine and we don't have any kind of arrangement or whatever. I fucking hate it that someone made her feel less than beautiful, because she is. I hate that someone—even inadvertently—made her think there's anything wrong with her. She said something about how she'll only ever be able to have sex with the lights off from now on. I wanted to put my fist through the wall."

He claps a hand on my shoulder. "Well, if she's coming, you can reassure her, right?" he asks and wiggles his eyebrows.

I shrug. "Who knows? Our conversations this whole summer, with the exception of today, have all stayed completely G-rated. I don't know."

Sully lifts a brow and gives me a knowing smile. "You can't tell me you don't want to, though. You've gotta be dying."

"Of course I want to. But she'll leave again in a couple of weeks. She'll be in New York and I'll be here."

He nods. "Want me to keep tabs on her? Be your hype man? You know I will. Harvard's only a few hours from NYU."

I shake my head. "Nah. Thanks, though. If I knew there was any chance she wanted a future with anyone at all, I might throw my hat in the ring, but she doesn't. That's never going to change."

"So, what, you'll just survive off crumbs for the rest of your life? What kind of life is that? I know I'm not Mister Monogamy or anything, but you're in love with her, Flynn. Is this going to be enough for you?" I open my mouth and he presses forward. "I know you'll take what you can get with her *because* you love her, but at what point would it be too hard for you? You need to think about that because if you get to that line and what she can give you isn't enough, you might need to rethink things. Otherwise, it's like Elias says, you lose that part that makes you a good man, not just a good asset. And you are, dude."

I give him an appreciative smile, and he extends his fist for me to bump and I do. "You're a good friend, Sully."

"So are you. Even when you're an asshole and whining about running." He sips his water. "I don't think Josie's coming back," he says, his tone resigned.

I nod. "Sorry, dude. I tried to warn you."

"I know. She was really hot, though. And damn, that ass. Fuck."

I huff a laugh. "If you say so."

"Yeah, I know, you've only got eyes for Brighten, but I'm telling you, the pool is deep, my friend. Someday, you might have to jump in."

"Thankfully, that day is not today."

CHAPTER TWELVE

FLYNN

Having not seen Brighten in almost two months, I'm nervous to see her now and feel as though I'm about to crawl out of my skin as I wait by baggage claim the night before the half marathon. A flash of red hair has my heart kicking over as she comes into view. When she spots me, her grin grows exponentially, and she starts jogging. I take off at a sprint and nearly collide with her.

Taking her face in my hands, I almost kiss her, but that's not what we are. We don't do public displays of affection because that's what couples do and we are not a couple. And even knowing I won't kiss her, I let my forehead drop to hers and I breathe her in. She smells like travel, but also that distinct scent that only belongs to her. "Fuck, I've missed you." My words sound wistful even to my own ears, and I school my features into a wide smile and adjust my tone. "Good flight?"

She nods and goes up on her toes to press a kiss to my cheek. "So glad to be home, though. Take me for some real biscuits and gravy, please?"

I huff a laugh and drape my arm around her shoulder and drop a kiss on the top of her head as we make our way back to baggage claim. Her arm snakes around my waist and she squeezes my side. She looks up at me, her eyes wide. "You're so skinny. What did you do?"

"Ran my fucking my ass off," I say with a laugh. "You can blame Sully."

"Oh, I will. Don't you worry. He will face my wrath. After you feed me."

I nod. "Can do," I answer and lift her bag off the belt. "Any other requests?"

She gives me a slow smile. "Yes, but nothing I can say in the vicinity of other people."

My breath catches and although I hoped I'd be able to kiss and touch and fuck her enough to slake my thirst for her, I didn't dare consider it a given. Heart beating triple time, I take her hand in mine. "Well, I look forward to hearing what those requests are."

After what might be the longest hour of my life as we go eat, even though I relish any time with her, my dick is screaming with Brighten's proximity and it's all I can do not to fuck her right this second in my car as I make the drive back to my apartment.

And as much as I love Sully, I almost want to rage when we pass him as we exit the elevator. But Brighten and Sully, both being the people they are, have to spend ten minutes catching up. It's not until he catches the murderous look in my eyes that he makes a hasty escape. "We'll catch up more tomorrow. I've gotta pick up my suit at the cleaners for the party. Welcome home, Brighten."

"Thanks, Sully. See you later."

"Much later," I say in way of a warning to let him know

that under no circumstances is he allowed to so much as look in the direction of my apartment door for the foreseeable future.

Laughing, he climbs onto the elevator and I unlock and turn my doorknob in one quick move, tugging Brighten inside behind me. Unable to not have her right the fuck now, I pivot and grab her face, claiming her mouth in a deep, hungry kiss, backing her against the wall.

She's quick to respond and drops her bags to the floor and wraps her arms around my waist, her hands skimming under my T-shirt. Goosebumps scatter up my torso as her nails scrape over my ribs. She moans into our kiss and yanks me toward her, and I know there's no way she can miss how hard I am for her already.

As I drag my mouth down her jaw and neck, she gasps and I let out a groan. "Fuck, I've missed that."

"I've missed your mouth. Shit, Flynn." Working my hands under the thin cardigan she wears, I shove it down her arms as I continue trailing kisses down her chest. I tug the straps of her camisole and bra off her shoulder until her right breast is exposed and I kiss and lick over the swell, slowing my kisses over her scar. She lets out a deep breath and sinks her fingers into my hair. "God, that's good," she whines.

Cupping her breast, I swirl my tongue over the nipple before sucking it into my mouth. A long moan falls from her mouth as she writhes against me. "You miss that, Crash?"

"Fuck, yes."

I bring my face level with hers. "No more missing." I cover her mouth with mine and run my hands down her waist and hips and over her ass. Gripping it firmly in both hands, I lift her off the floor and she wraps her legs around my waist as I ferry her over to the bed.

Laying her down, I yank my shirt off and her eyes travel down my torso. "You don't even look like you."

I make quick work of ridding myself of my remaining layers as she does the same. "I promise, I'm still me," I counter and open my nightstand drawer to pull out a condom. Tossing it on the mattress, I drop to my knees at the edge of the bed and hook my arms under her thighs and yank her toward me.

Letting out a soft yelp of surprise, she laughs. "Except stronger maybe."

Running my tongue up the inside of her thigh, I shake my head. "Still the same amount of strong. Just horny as fuck."

She snorts and starts to say something, but when I slide my thumbs up her folds to spread her open for me, she inhales sharply. I almost growl with primal need as I take in how wet and slick she is for me already. And in this moment, she is wholly mine and I fucking act like it.

After taking a beat to lap up every bit of her sweetness, I settle in at her clit and she gasps, her hips already grinding against my face. I laugh against her, knowing how horny she must be, too. "Fuck," she breathes and grips my hair. I flatten my tongue against her clit and she holds me in place and rides my face, and I grope her thighs and hips and tits as she takes her pleasure. "Oh, God, Flynn. Fuck. Fuck. *Fuck*. Just like that. Sweet Jesus."

Pushing away the ache in my balls and needing to feel exactly how close she is, I sink two fingers into her and groan with how wet she is and how her pussy is already pulsing. Crooking my fingers against her g-spot, her hips buck and she nearly screams and I know I've hit it. Satisfaction floods my chest as she comes undone seconds later, a raspy sigh falling from her lips and her legs shaking on my shoulders.

Kissing my way back up her body as I withdraw my fingers, she grabs my face and pulls me to her for a frantic kiss. I join her on the bed and she writhes against me, nearly animalistic in her hunger. And fuck if I'm not here for it.

I grope around for the condom on the mattress and finally locate it, pulling my mouth from hers just long enough to rip it open with my teeth. Two seconds later, it's rolled down. "I want on top," she says, chest heaving.

Getting into position in the middle of the bed, I laugh. "You ain't gotta convince me. Have at it."

For a beat, she looks apprehensive. "We haven't done that before."

I sit up and take her face in my hands. "It's just like everything else; we'll learn together."

Nodding, she straddles me and I grip my cock, watching as her pussy swallows it as she sinks down with a gasp. Holy fuck, it's enough to make me come almost immediately. She shifts from side to side and I grab her hips. "Wait. Fuck."

Alarm written on her face, she blinks. "What?"

I huff a breath. "Feels too good. Fuck. Just give me a second. Shit."

A blush creeps into her face and she smiles. "Is it different like this? For you?"

I take some deep breaths and lie back. "Just watching you slide down nearly made me nut. Your pussy's too pretty, Crash."

Giving an experimental roll of her hips, her mouth falls open on a sigh. "You feel bigger like this."

Huffing a laugh, I slide my hands up her thighs and over her hips. "Good to know. Your tits look fantastic from this angle."

"Good to know," she echoes with a grin. For several moments, she seems to simply find what works for her and closes her eyes as she gets into a rhythm. And I just watch. For as long as I live, I'll always know I was the one she learned with. I'm the one who had her first. I'm the one who loved her first and most. It won't matter who comes after; you never forget your first, right? I know I'll never be able to forget her; any part of her.

Soon though, my body is demanding I move and I grip her hips, my fingertips digging into the soft flesh, and thrust up into her. "Fuck," she gasps. I do it again and she reaches for the headboard. "Shit, Flynn. Oh, God."

Her pussy pulses around me and I groan. "Fuck, Crash. Get there. Please. I'm not going to last. Shit."

She reaches down and works her clit and I hold off just long enough for her to finish a second time before I'm grunting through gritted teeth, lightning shooting down my spine and into my balls, my head falling back as I spill into the condom.

Brighten lets her head fall forward, her face coming to rest in the crook of my neck. "Now that's a proper welcome home." I can't help but laugh and turn my face to capture her mouth in a kiss.

For the rest of the night we vacillate between talking and fucking and by midnight, I'm pretty sure all of my energy stores are completely zapped. Brighten's not faring much better, what with the time change and all. She lies facing me and I watch her fall asleep and her breathing level out. "Crash," I whisper. She doesn't acknowledge me or stir. "Brighten?" I keep my voice barely audible. And I never call her by her actual name to her directly and it almost feels strange to do it now. "Are you awake?"

She doesn't move, and I trace the lines and curves of her face with my eyes. "I love you." The words are bittersweet as they leave my mouth and tears burn my eyes. It would be so much easier if I didn't love her. If all this was for me was fun and sexy. If it didn't feel like half my heart left whenever she does.

I'm quick to remind myself that I chose this because if the choice is to keep this to myself and still have her any way I can or not at all, I'll endure this ache knowing she doesn't feel the same way. For how long, I can't say. But for now, I will.

CHAPTER THIRTEEN

BRIGHTEN

Even fatigued, jet-lagged, and sexed out as I am, I stand here, waiting anxiously for Flynn and Sully to cross the finish line in the heat of the late July morning. Seeing him yesterday was a shock to my system. He's lost so much weight and he's all lean muscles and long sinews and tendons. He has actual abs. I'm not sure how I feel about it.

To imagine the boy he was only a few months ago seems like a different person than who he is now. His shaggy hair, his braces and acne, his glasses and softness. His constant wardrobe of baggy jeans and hoodies. He now gets actual hair cuts and his acne is all but gone. So are all the other things that outwardly separated him from his twin. Now? He's more like Jess than ever before.

Thankfully, inside, he's still my Flynn. Except not *mine*. Because I don't do that. I don't have romantic feelings for him. Sometimes, I think it would be nice if I did. It would make my life infinitely easier if I did. But I don't. And if I don't feel it for him, who I love, but not like *that*, could I ever feel it for anyone? Probably not.

I grow antsy when the first runners cross the finish line. Looking at the clock above, I know from what Flynn told me his average time was, he probably won't cross it himself for about another ten minutes. Even so, I stand on tiptoe to peer above the crowd, my heart thundering when I see his dark head bobbing as he runs alongside Sully a few minutes later.

To say I'm proud of him as he crosses the finish line and beats his best time would be the understatement of the century. His eyes lock with mine, his grin wide, even as he bends at the waist, his hands on his knees before popping back upright and lacing his fingers on top of his head as he attempts to catch his breath.

We both weave through the crowd and when he pulls me into his arms, I don't even notice how absolutely drenched with sweat he is. "Oh my God, you were amazing. You beat your time, Flynn."

He nods, still huffing. "I blame Sully."

I turn to the man in question and give him a hug as well. "Fair warning," he says returning my embrace, "I'm even sweatier than Flynn." I laugh as I congratulate them both and as they accept their medals, I take a picture with my phone, as they smile into the camera. Sully holds out his hand. "Now one of just the two of you."

I happily stand next to Flynn who drapes his arm around my shoulder and pulls me closer and I loop my arms around his waist, my head on his chest. Sully snaps the photo and hands my phone back to me.

"I need food," Flynn announces. "Carbs. Fat. Protein."

"So, pancakes and bacon?" I supply.

"Fuck, yes," Flynn and Sully say in unison and we all share a laugh.

"So, is it going to be all shop talk at this thing? Will I even know how to converse with these people?" I ask as I slip my dress over my hips and pull the straps up my arms.

Flynn automatically steps up behind me to zip me up and drop a kiss on my bare shoulder. "Crash, you're the smartest person I know. You'll be fine. You talk to Sully and me without any problems."

"Yeah, because you don't talk about work. I know almost nothing about market research. And *you* are the smartest person you know. Don't pretend otherwise," I reply with a lifted brow, waiting to see if he challenges me.

He gives my hand a squeeze. "I'm trying to be more humble; less arrogant asshole."

I turn to face him and straighten his tie. "Well, tonight you're a handsome, humble asshole; I'll give you that."

That lopsided grin that's my favorite makes an appearance. "Such a way with words, Dawes." He searches my face and sweeps a stray hair off my forehead. "You look beautiful." His voice is soft and I blush.

"I sorta feel like we're going to prom."

He laughs. "We didn't go to prom."

I roll my eyes. "I know that. I said it *sorta* felt like prom. We're dressed up, going out; it feels like prom."

Flynn considers. "I wouldn't have looked anywhere near this good at our prom."

"You would have to me," I say, my tone serious. "You've always looked good to me."

His smile softens and his eyes light with affection. "Thanks, Crash. Are we ready?"

I give myself one last look in the tiny mirror over the bathroom sink. My hair is in a loose chignon with a few tendrils falling over my shoulders and the black cocktail dress I've chosen has a scoop neck that hides my scar and my black stilettos make me only a few inches shorter than Flynn, who looks downright sexy in a charcoal gray suit. I know, with the weight he's lost, he was forced to have all of his suits tailored. And damn, did it make a difference. He looks so much more mature than when he came to Nashville; like an actual man instead of the boy I grew up with.

"One second," I supply, swiping on some red lipstick and dropping the tube into my clutch purse. "Ready."

"Let's do it."

Twenty minutes later, we're pulling into the parking lot of a large glass office building. "Is this the office?"

"Yeah," he replies, helping me from the vehicle. "This is Intuition. They've converted the meeting space on the top floor to accommodate the party. Should be really pretty with the skyline at night." Flynn opens the door to the building after swiping a badge.

"Fancy," I supply.

He chuckles. "I have to give it back after tonight, so there's that."

Leading me to a bank of elevators, I look around at the sleek glass and marble expanse of the office. It screams top-tier professional opulence without being gaudy. The partners have shelled out quite the pretty penny to make a good impression on clients.

"So, aside from Elias, are there any people of note I should be aware of?"

He considers as the elevator ascends. "Sharice Carter is the internship coordinator, but I didn't really deal with her much. The partners are all supposed to make an appearance, but it's mainly just the interns and mentors."

"Have you spent much time with the partners?"

Flynn shakes his head. "I know who they are, of course, just from being here every day and some meetings Sully and I sat in on with Elias, but I've never interacted with them personally."

"Will you still point them out and tell me who they are so I'll know and not look like an idiot?"

He smiles as the doors open and takes my hand. "Crash, you could never look like an idiot. Ever. It's impossible. But, yes; I will tell you."

"I'm really proud of you, Flynn. You've grown so much over this summer."

His grin widens, and he pats his now flat stomach. "Not all of me. Parts of me got smaller."

"You know what I mean," I say, squeezing his hand so he can see I'm serious. "You are not the same surly boy who left Knoxville. You are becoming a legit man, my friend."

His eyes scan mine. "And you are a beautiful young woman, Brighten Dawes. NYU isn't going to know what hit it. And neither will Washington, D.C. Someday, I'm going to be able to say, 'I knew President Dawes when she was this scrawny little girl. Now look at her. She is incomparable.'"

I can't remember the last time he called me by my name. He only ever uses it when introducing me to other people or sometimes pulls out my last name. I'm never "Brighten" to him. And hearing him say it now, when it's just us, feels different and I'm not sure what to think.

"There he is." A booming male voice breaks us out of our locked gaze. Our heads snap forward and a large, older man with medium-brown skin who I know must be Elias, Flynn and Sully's mentor, just based on their description of him.

Flynn smiles and extends his hand. "Elias, hey." They shake and his mentor gives him a fond nod before Flynn gestures to me. "Elias, this is Brighten Dawes, my best friend. Brighten, this is Elias Washington, the smartest man in any room he's in."

I give Elias a warm smile and shake his extended hand. "That must be saying something, Flynn. You're usually the smartest one in any room you're in. Well, unless your dad's there," I say with a wink.

Elias laughs, and it's deep and genuine, and he nods at Flynn. "You were right; she's good people. Y'all come on into the party, now. The partners will be here soon and we'll be presenting the awards."

Flynn's eyebrows rise. "Awards? I wasn't aware there were any awards."

"Now, why would I tell you there were awards? You're supposed to work hard for hard work's sake. You shouldn't need extra incentive. Have I taught you nothing? Let's go. Sullivan's already at our table."

We follow Elias into the party space and the feeling we're at a prom only gets stronger with the decor of shiny silver satin table linens, string lights, and a dedicated dance space. I lean over to Flynn as we take our seats and whisper in his ear. "Remember what I said about—."

"Prom?" he finishes and we share a light laugh. "Definite prom vibes. You think I'll be king?"

I nod. "If anyone could be, it's you."

He bends to brush a kiss across my cheek and turns to greet Sully and his date, who he must just be getting to know since before now, he's been seeing Josie pretty regularly and Flynn mentioned last night she's stopped coming to visit and stopped returning his calls.

I sip my water and look from table to table. There are people our age spread throughout the room; along with nearly as many a lot older. From what Flynn said, hundreds of people applied for this internship and he and eleven others were chosen. It makes me that much more proud of him for this huge accomplishment.

He drapes his arm over the back of my chair and leans close so he can keep his voice low. "The partners are seated at that table in front of the window." I let my eyes travel to where he's directed. He names them off, left to right, and they all have one thing in common except for the one on the far right: they're all much older and he's definitely not.

Even seated, the man is tall and stocky with olive skin and light brown hair. I can't see what color his eyes are from where I sit, but they look dark. An expensive watch hangs off his wrist and as he scans the room, his eyes lock on mine and he gives me a subtle nod and his lips pull up at the corners in a slight smile. He's handsome in the way powerful men who exude money and bravado usually are.

"And the last guy, his name is Baker Roberts."

I bring my eyes back to Flynn. "He a lot younger than the rest."

He nods. "Yeah, his parents started the firm. He's the senior partner. Thirty-one and has a net worth of three hundred million." My mouth falls open and Flynn nods, an amused smile on his face, and brings his finger up to touch under my chin so I'll close it again. "I know, right?"

"I can't even fathom that kind of wealth."

"Says the girl who has a healthy trust of her own and a mom who's worth fifty mil."

"For one, I don't have access to my trust until I'm twenty-one. And Vanessa will probably drink away what's left of her money," I retort.

He sighs. "Probably."

As the evening progresses, we enjoy a catered meal of beef Wellington and smashed potatoes, caramelized brussels

sprouts, and crème brûlée. And just like a prom, there is dancing. Flynn and I dance for a few songs, but neither of us are big
dancers, so we retake our seats and simply watch the party
unfold.

Shortly before ten PM, the senior partner, Baker Roberts,
rises with two plaques in hand and comes to stand at a podium
near the head of the partners' table. A hush falls over the small
crowd and everyone gives him their undivided attention.

"It is our habit here at Intuition to award ingenuity, hard
work, and perseverance. And to our internship class of this
year, I say you have all proven yourselves in that regard in
spades. Simply by making it to this program proves that you
are some of the best and brightest stars to watch in this
industry in the coming years. We can't wait to see what
you do.

"Over these past several weeks, the mentors have moni-
tored the progress of all the interns. They were not only looking
for who had the grit and determination to make it in this industry, but also those who wouldn't be afraid to take risks, but also
admit their own weaknesses and accept criticism with grace.

"This industry can be both exciting and, at times, tedious.
Sometimes, our entire goal is to figure out what sort of flavor
profile our clients should add to their ranch dressing. I mean,
that's nice and all, but not always the glamorous side of things."

Everyone shares a collective chuckle as he continues. "But
know that it's the mundane clients and their needs that fund
our ability to chase the bigger, shinier ones. The ones that make
this job worth doing. Don't lose heart when you're missing out
on the fun and exciting jobs; they'll be around the next corner.

"Not too many years ago, I sat in those same seats as you
interns. I remember feeling as if, even though this company is
my family's legacy, I'd found my calling. I hope you've discovered that same calling during your time with us this summer.

And in the future, maybe some of you will be here as team members and not simply interns.

"Without further ado, this year's recipients of Intuition's Intern Achiever award are Sullivan Sanchez and Flynn Tate."

My gasp is audible and Flynn and Sully share shocked looks as the room erupts in polite applause. Elias practically has to usher them up to the podium himself, but soon, they're both walking, still stunned, to accept their award from Baker Roberts, who gives them both congratulatory hand shakes. They fist bump as they make their way back to the table.

Flynn is beaming and I can't resist grabbing his face for a kiss. "I'm so proud of you. Seriously."

He flushes with pride and elation and gives me a tight hug. He brushes a kiss under my ear and goosebumps scatter down my arms. "Proud enough to let me fuck you in this dress? Here at this party where I've just been crowned prom king, Crash?"

My breath catches, and when I pull back, my cheeks are hot. His eyes are green fire and his smile is wicked. And although, by some unspoken agreement since we started doing this thing, we don't do public displays of affection, I suddenly want nothing more than to celebrate Flynn's big achievement. Right here. Right now. I nod and his lips pull into that lopsided grin I love.

He leans over to whisper something in Sully's ear and he nods and gives us both a knowing smile. I should care that Sully knows, but I don't. The thrill of what Flynn and I are about to do spreads under my skin like electricity.

We bid goodbye to Elias, and Flynn tugs me out of the party room. "Where are we going?" I whisper, the clicking of my heels echoing off the marble floors and glass walls.

"In there." Tugging me toward a door, he glances around before opening it and guiding me inside. I don't realize it's a private bathroom until he flips on the light and locks the door. I immediately have a flashback of just a couple of days ago when I was in the bathroom at the pub with Sean.

Flynn doesn't give me time to consider where we are before stepping toward me, his hand coming up to cup my jaw, his eyes no longer only heated, but full of affection. "You know there's no one else I would've rather shared tonight with than you, right?"

I nod. "I'm glad I got to see you win. You should've seen your face," I say with a grin.

He smiles and slides his hand to the back of my neck. "I got to see yours. It was pretty epic." Lowering his mouth to mine, he captures my bottom lip between both of his and gently suckles, making a soft moan work its way up my throat.

Slipping my hands inside Flynn's suit jacket, I wrap my arms around his waist and pull him closer as his tongue sweeps into my mouth. He deepens and controls the kiss and shuffles me toward the sink.

We're both panting by the time he kisses his way down my neck and I gasp as his teeth scrape over my collarbone. My ass hits the edge of the sink and I lean back to allow him better access to my chest, my breasts, any part of me he wants as I thread my fingers through his hair.

He gently tugs the shoulder straps of my dress down my arms until my breasts pops free. His eyes come to mine as he swirls his tongue over my right nipple and then my left, and I clamp my teeth down on my bottom lip to muffle my moans. "Oh God, Flynn. Shit." Mindful of where we are, I keep my words whispered, despite wanting to scream.

He gives me a wicked grin before yanking up the hem of my dress. "Are you wet for me, Crash? Going to let me pound that pussy?" His words settle in, as though some sort of haze sinks over me and heat shoots through my middle and has me pressing my thighs together, seeking friction. "Let's find out," he says and slips his hand into my panties and I release a shuddery breath as his fingers slide through my folds and brush over my clit. "Fucking soaked."

Flynn reclaims my mouth in a punishing kiss as he works my clit. "Open up for me. Let me feel this sweet cunt," he commands into my mouth, nudging my legs farther apart with his knee.

"Fuck," I whine. "Flynn, Jesus."

I frantically work the belt and fastenings of his pants, needing to put my hands on him, give him some fraction of the pleasure he's currently offering me. Dipping my hand inside his boxers, I wrap my fingers around his cock and give him a rough stroke and he lets out a low groan. "Fuck, Crash. Shit, baby."

He drags his mouth back down to my breast and flicks the nipple and I let my head fall back as I moan, my orgasm beginning to overtake me. "Oh God. Flynn, shit. I'm coming. Jesus. Don't stop."

He chuckles against my skin and I let go with a muffled cry behind lips clamped tightly closed. Flynn withdraws his hand and snatches mine away from his dick. "Turn around." His voice is husky and his breaths come in ragged puffs. I quickly obey and face the sink.

Taking out his wallet, he plucks a condom from inside and rips it with his teeth, taking a few seconds to roll the latex down before shoving my dress up my waist and tugging my panties down my hips. "Step out of these." I gingerly step out of my underwear and he shoves them in his pocket and gives me a slow smile in the mirror as he steps up behind me. "Those are mine, now."

My cheeks flame with the knowledge that Flynn just stole my panties and I'm going to have to walk out of here without any on. He chuckles as though he can read my mind. "Don't pretend you don't like the idea."

"I do," I admit. "Are you going to talk to me or fuck me, Tate?"

He pushes my feet wider with his shoes and grabs my hips and yanks them back. "So mouthy. Let's see if I can make you stop talking." He drops a kiss onto my shoulder blade. "Better hold on to something."

Even gripping the side of the sink, I'm not prepared for him to slam inside my pussy with enough force to nearly steal my breath. "Fuck," I gasp.

He withdraws nearly to the tip and drives back in and groans. "Fuck is right, Crash. Shit, your pussy feels so fucking good." Setting a brutal rhythm, I can only hold on as he fucks me hard and thoroughly enough that I'm not sure I won't be sore tomorrow. And fuck, do I welcome it.

As he reaches around to grab and knead my breast, I let my head fall forward as my body seems to give itself over to him completely. I lose all thought, all sense of time, all feeling except *this*. This connection between our two bodies that I'm not sure will ever be met or exceeded by anyone else.

A hand clamps over my mouth and my eyes pop open, locking with Flynn's in the mirror. "You're going to get us caught," he says through gritted teeth. "Fuck."

I reach between my thighs and work my clit, moaning against his hand as he continues his relentless pace. The orgasm builds quickly and overtakes me so suddenly, tears spring to my eyes and a sob is wrenched from my chest.

"Oh, Fuck. Sweet Jesus, you're going to make me come. This fucking pussy, Crash. Shit."

His forehead drops to my shoulder blade as his hips buck one final time and he lets out a guttural groan, his breath coming out in hot puffs against my back.

It's several moments before either of us can actually stand

upright and I lift his hand from where he's dropped it to the sink and press a kiss to his palm.

His phone vibrates in his pocket and he finally pulls out with a groan and digs it from his pants and checks the screen. "Fuck. We've gotta go. The party's wrapping up."

We hurriedly clean up and I attempt to fix my hair and makeup. "Do I look like I was just fucked within an inch of my life, because I'm pretty sure I was."

Flynn blushes and gives me one last kiss before sticking his head out of the bathroom to ensure the coast is clear. He glances back at me, his eyes roaming over my face. "You look like the best thing I've ever seen."

PART 2

COLLEGE, JUNIOR YEAR

14 YEARS AGO

CHAPTER FOURTEEN

FLYNN

I wish I could say that once Brighten and I were in two different states, I wouldn't think about her constantly or dream about us having sex or that I might finally get desperate enough to break down and pursue one of the many girls who seem to think I'm hot shit. Fuck if I know why. But the truth is, even if Brighten isn't mine, I'm hers. And with the visits she makes home and us hooking up when she's here, it gives me just enough of a taste of her to keep me on the hook until the next time.

On the plus side, my grades are phenomenal. Unlike my brother, I am not elbow deep in a different pussy every week. For all I know, he assumes I am, but since I live at the dorms and he's got his own place, we don't cross paths very often, except on the weekends.

The two summers between my summer in Nashville and now were spent doing more internships with almost no physical contact with Brighten, since she was also interning with different members of Congress. I'm pretty sure my dick is ready to commit a mutiny with the lack of action I get these days.

Now that I'm nearly in the spring semester of my junior year, I've all but accepted that I will be celibate for months, if not years, at a time. Thankfully, though, our texts, calls, and emails remain the same as they've always been. We don't talk about the men she sees or the women I don't. She asks about my marathon pacing times and I ask about Vanessa, who seems to be spiraling and hasn't worked since the movie she shot in Ireland. Part of me thinks Vanessa not working and being back in Knoxville is one of the reasons Brighten doesn't come home much. Can't say I blame her.

This weekend, though, we're throwing Dad a huge birthday party. His MS has progressed more rapidly over the past couple of years and he's now completely blind in his right eye. We all know he's going downhill, even if none of us are willing to admit it.

Wanting to confirm with Brighten she's coming to the party, since I haven't heard from her in a few days, I shoot off a text.

> Flynn: Haven't heard from you in a few days, wanted to check and see if you'll be able to come to Dad's party. He's been asking about you a lot lately.

And it's true. He misses Brighten and asks about her constantly. I think secretly—or, not so secretly—he keeps hoping she and I will get together for real and she'll be the daughter he's always seen her as.

> Crash: Wouldn't miss it. New Year's Eve, right?

Flynn: Yeah. Mom said you're welcome to stay at the house if you didn't want to see Vanessa. The basement apartment is all ready for company.

I'm hoping she takes Mom up on the offer of a stay. The idea of her being over thirty seconds away from me if I only get her for one night is too much.

Crash: Would that be weird?

Flynn: I mean, you can stay in my room and I'll stay in the basement if you'd be more comfortable. Not like you haven't slept in my bed before.

Crash: Yeah, but not without you in it... I'm not sure I'd know how.

Flynn: I'm pretty good at sleeping. I'll be happy to give you a lesson.

Crash: Would there be a test? Perhaps an oral or hands-on evaluation?

Flynn: Look at you, learning all those different methods of evaluation up in New York.

Crash: I love it here, but I miss Tennessee and all my favorite people.

Flynn: Your favorite people miss you, too. So, is that a yes on the stay?

Crash: That's a hell yes. Tell Jude I'll be there will bells on. Possibly literally. It is New Year's, after all. You think he'll make it to midnight?

Crash: Reading that back, I realize how bad that sounds. Sorry. I only meant, do you think he'll be able to stay awake?

I can't help but laugh.

Flynn: I knew what you meant. It's a coin toss, honestly. He tires really easily these days. I'm glad you'll get to see him.

Crash: Me, too. Would you be upset with me if I gave your dad my kiss at midnight if he's still awake? After your mom, of course.

Flynn: I think he'd be upset if you didn't. Can't wait to see you.

Crash: Me, too.

"Son, stop fidgeting with your tie and come tell me how good I look."

I tear my eyes away from the driveway and walk over to where my father has just rolled into the living room. I bend down and straighten his bowtie. "You look great, Dad."

He reaches his hand up to squeeze my wrist and his fingers tremble badly, but I try not to look at them. "So, our girl is staying here tonight, huh?"

"That's the plan. She's riding over with us to the hotel," I supply, continuing to fuss over his clothes. "Mom and Jess said they'd meet us there."

"And is she staying with you or *with* you?" Dad wiggles his eyebrows suggestively and I laugh. He touches my cheek, almost like a pat, his expression sobering. "You should tell her, Flynn."

My smile falls. "I can't."

"Can't never could, as my daddy would've said."

I huff a laugh. "I've never understood that saying, Dad."

"It's sorta like that old saying, 'whether you think you can or you can't, you're right'. What's the worst thing that happens if you tell her?"

"I'll lose her altogether. It'll get weird and we'll drift and it'll be worse than the way things are right now. Because at least right now, I have part of her."

"Sometimes. *Sometimes* you have part of her. Meanwhile, she has all of you, son. Do you know how sad that makes me for you? You're too young to be fully invested in someone who's not fully invested in you."

I scoff. "Says the man who's been in love with the same woman since he was seventeen."

He gives me a shaky nod. "Yeah, and she's been in love with me, too. I'm a lucky bastard, Flynn. I've loved the same woman for almost thirty years. But I've also been loved. You need to be good to yourself; not just to her. As much as I love Brighten—and you know I do—if she can't love you the way you deserve, you should stop this thing y'all have going on. It'll only get worse for you." He looks over my shoulder. "Ah, speak of the devil. There's our girl now."

I stand up straighter and feel as though my heart is back in its rightful place when she walks through the door. Her hair is shorter, nearly to her shoulders, and cut in a sleek bob, and she wears a beautiful high-necked green cocktail dress with black stilettos.

Rushing over to take her bag, I pull her in for a hug and breathe in her familiar aroma. Even under whatever new perfume she wears, there's an underlying scent that's just *her*.

"Miss me, Tate?" she asks in a whisper and brushes a kiss across my cheek.

"You have no clue."

Loathe as I am to let her go, my father clears his throat and reminds us we're not alone. Her face is flushed when we part and she immediately steps to my father and drops a kiss onto the top of his head and bends down until they're eye level and I drop her bag next to the basement steps. She takes his hands in hers, ignoring his worsening tremor, and gives him a big smile. "Hey, Jude."

"Oh, so now you fancy yourself not only some future politician but a Beatles impersonator?"

She laughs. "Never. Only the politician."

He nods. "Promise me something?"

"Anything," she says, her tone sincere.

His eyes flit to me and my stomach drops, thinking he's going to reveal something I can't take back. "Make sure Flynn's okay when I'm gone?"

"Dad," I scold. "Don't be so damn morbid. You're probably still going to be kicking when I'm pushing up daisies. You're too stubborn to die, old man."

But they both ignore me, locked in some sort of stare down and my chest aches knowing he's asking her this for me because I'm too chicken shit to ask her for any kind of commitment. But apparently, Dad's not.

Brighten's eyes glitter with unshed tears and she nods. "You have my word, Jude."

He gives her a jerky nod and finally looks at me. "What is the kids say? Let's ride, bitches."

Brighten and I both snort a laugh and I'm thankful the tense moment is broken.

Dad spends the entire evening dancing with my mother and many of their friends share toasts in his honor. Brighten laughs with my parents and even steals Jess away for a dance.

I watch her as I sip my beer and marvel at her ease with people. She laughs and makes friends as easily as breathing. People flock to her like a moth drawn to a flame. Maybe that's why her parents named her Brighten, since she lights up any room she's in. All I know is, she's the brightest spot in my life.

Maybe this is what obsession is. And maybe it truly is like Einstein said and it's insanity, since I keep doing the same thing over and over. But am I expecting different results? Or am I simply hoping for them? My phone vibrates in my pocket and I pull it out.

> Sully: I know it's early, but I'm getting ready to be too wasted to type correctly anymore. Happy New Year. See you this summer. Hope your dad had a great birthday.

> Flynn: Thanks, Sul. Happy New Year to you, too. See you in Atlanta.

As the party winds down, and the clock strikes midnight, so many thoughts bombard my mind. Is this the year things change between Brighten and me even more? Is this the year I lose my dad? Am I really graduating college in eighteen months? Will I be ready? Will I land somewhere close to Brighten? Would that matter?

A warm breath on my neck breaks me out of my spiraling. "Your mom said she got a room for her and your dad here at the hotel as a surprise. Take me home?"

Images of a future where, when she asks a question like that, it's with the understanding that "home" is a place we share on a permanent basis. But there will probably never be that kind of home for Brighten and me.

Downing the rest of my beer, I stand and smile down at her and offer her my arm. "Gladly."

We say our goodbyes to my parents and she holds out the keys to my mom's car and asks, "You need me to drive?"

I huff a laugh and take the keys as we begin walking. "I think we both know who has a better driving record."

She scoffs. "For one, I was twelve. For two, they should've had that pile of debris corded off or something. For three, I was just checking to make sure you hadn't had too much to drink. Don't be an asshole this early in the evening."

"I'm good. I promise. I'd never do anything to hurt you, you know that."

She smiles up at me. "I know."

We barely make it in my bedroom door before Brighten's pushing my jacket off my shoulders and crashing her lips to mine. I toe off my shoes and reach around to unzip her dress as she steps out of her heels. She yanks my shirt from my dress pants and makes quick work of pulling my tie free and undoing the buttons.

As we undress, our mouths never part and soon, we're standing naked and it's all I can do to not simply bend her over my bed and fuck her into the mattress. I step back from her to take her in. God, I've missed this body, but she now has something she didn't have before and I feel like I've been slapped. She has a tattoo that completely covers her scar. It's an intricate feather with splashes of watercolor. And while it's beautiful, I instantly hate it.

"Why?" is all I can ask, tears burning my eyes. "Why would you do that? Why didn't you tell me?"

She blinks, shocked by my reaction. "I wanted to surprise

you. Now, instead of being self-conscious, I don't have to worry about it."

I drag my thumb along my lash line to dry my tears. I guess this also answers the question I refuse to ask, even to myself. *Does she sleep with other men?* "You're not self-conscious with me. You know I love your body exactly the way it was. Why would you think I'd ever be excited that you'd cover up the thing responsible for why we met?"

Her expression hardens. "I don't need your permission to do something to make myself feel more comfortable in my own skin. To make it so I don't have to endure strange looks or stares of pity."

I nod, instantly feeling like a total shit for what I've said. Even if I love her scar because of what it represents, it's never been something she's comfortable with. I try to calm down and be a bit more rational, even if I'm not rational when it comes to Brighten.

If I were, we probably wouldn't both be here. I would've ended this after the first time. Or that first weekend. Or anytime in the last three years. I swallow. "You're right; you don't need my permission. I didn't mean to imply that. You don't need my permission to do anything. I know it's always bothered you, and if you're happy with it, I'm happy for you. I was just shocked and I'm sorry I reacted badly."

I take a step closer to her and drag my finger along where her scar now sits under layers of ink, hidden from view. "I'll always know it's there and I get why you wanted to do it. But I wish you loved it as much as I do and see what I do when I look at it.

"I see a little girl who was terrified and bleeding, who was still so brave. I see *Mario Kart* and algebra and a thousand school lunches. I see the person who is one of the only people on this planet I can tolerate for more than five minutes. I see the first girl I kissed and I see the person who, despite my own hangups, made me feel wanted. I see the first and only woman I've ever made love to."

I know as soon as the words leave my mouth, I've fucked up. We don't talk about things like exclusivity. We don't talk about rules. When we're together, we're together and when we're not, we're back to simply being platonic. And we most certainly don't talk about how she's the only woman I ever want to know the feel of.

CHAPTER FIFTEEN

BRIGHTEN

I see the first and only woman I've ever made love to.

I blink, trying to understand his words. *Only?* Surely Flynn hasn't been *only* sleeping with me. It's absurd. Since Nashville almost two-and-a-half years ago, we've only been together a handful of times. We're not in an exclusive relationship. That's not what we do.

God knows I haven't only been sleeping with him. I've very much been enjoying myself. And while none of the guys I've been with besides Flynn satisfy me the way sex with him does, I refuse to not partake simply because it's not as good.

Flynn picks his boxers up and slips them back on. "What are you doing?"

He sighs and drops onto the edge of the bed. "I can't have a serious conversation while I'm naked. It's distracting."

I snatch his dress shirt off the floor and slip it on and fasten a few of the buttons. "What do you mean *only*, Flynn?"

"Nothing. Forget it."

I plant my hands on my hips. "Flynn Maverick Tate, I will

not forget it. What the fuck did you mean when you said only? Are you telling me you haven't slept with anyone else?"

He looks up at me, his expression resigned. "No, I haven't slept with anyone else."

Shocked, I close the distance between us and sit on the bed beside him. "Why?"

He swallows thickly. "You're the only one I want. I'm sorry. I know we don't have any kind of rules or arrangement and we're not exclusive. I know when we're together, we're together and when we're not, it's understood there will be other people."

He looks down at his hands and his eyes well with tears and my chest aches seeing him be in any pain, but I don't understand why he's hurting. I open my mouth, but he continues speaking. "I know you don't do relationships. I know you never want to get married or have kids or settle down. I know you don't plan on ever falling in love. I know you love me, but not like *that*. These are things I've always known. I accept them as truths in my life. These are things I don't expect will change about you."

His eyes come to mine and the emotion I see in his isn't one I'm accustomed to. It's raw and vulnerable and I don't know how to feel about it. "I know you will never be all mine because you're not built that way. I know as long as we do this thing, I will always have to share you. It's what I signed up for. I don't expect you to change. But just because you're not all mine doesn't mean I don't want to be all yours.

"I'd rather have you any way you can give yourself to me than not at all. For however long you're willing to share yourself with me. And even if you never share yourself with me physically again, you'll still be my best friend. I meant what I said in Nashville. No matter what, we're still us. When you need me, I will be there, no matter what. Please know that. Regardless of how I feel for you or how you don't feel for me, you're still my favorite person and my best friend."

As his words sink in, my eyes fill with tears. I ache for my best friend who wants things he can't have. I feel guilty because he wants things I can't give him. I feel about an inch tall knowing what Flynn is willing to accept, when it's obvious he deserves so much more.

Seeing my tears, he takes my face in his hands. "I didn't say any of that so you'd feel bad. Please don't. I'm okay with the way things are."

I shake my head. "You deserve more, Flynn. If I was able to see having a relationship—a future—with anyone, it would be you. You deserve so much more than I can give you."

He presses his forehead to mine. "Why don't you let me worry about what I deserve? I deserve you, any way you're willing to share yourself with me. I will be content if this is my life for the rest of my life. If that ever changes for me, I will tell you."

"Flynn—."

He prevents any further words from escaping by pressing his lips to mine. As his best friend, I shouldn't let him accept only these crumbs I can give him. I should and do want more for him.

Selfishly, though, I don't want to give up any part of how our relationship has evolved. I love having him as my best friend and I love sex with him. I also can't deny I don't want to be tied down to anyone, not even Flynn. And knowing that someday, there is a real possibility that Flynn does find someone who can give him the things he wants, I will take what I can get for as long as I can and give in to his kiss.

Although I can't stand my mother, after last night and my conversation with Flynn, I find myself needing something I haven't had in a while: my father. Bracing myself for whatever I find as I open the door, I blow out a long breath. It's only nine AM, so I should be surprised to find my mother mixing a pitcher of bloody marys in the kitchen. The sad thing is, I'm not. If anything, I'm surprised she's diluting her liquor with any mixers.

As the daughter of an alcoholic, I know I'm at a higher risk of developing alcoholism myself. And although I drink, I have a strict set of rules for myself. So to see her not even blink when someone walks in while she's pouring a half gallon of vodka into a pitcher, it makes me irrationally angry.

I constantly have to remind myself that addiction is a disease. But when the person suffering won't let themselves get better when they have the means and opportunity to do so, it's more difficult to be sympathetic. Especially in my mother's case, because it's apparent she only lacks the motivation to take the steps necessary to get better. I've never been enough motivation for her to stay sober. To be honest, I'm not sure she's ever been sober a day in my life.

"Brighten, darling, can I pour you a drink? You're legal now," she says with a grin that's been filled to the point that her lips no longer resemble anything close to mine. I used to marvel at how much my mother and I look alike. We no longer do as she has spent years and countless fortunes chasing her idea of what perfection is.

"Mother, it's nine o'clock in the morning. I'll pass."

She glances up at me from where she's stirring the pitcher. Her eyes are still clear and the exact shade of green as mine. I wonder if she sees her younger self when she looks at me. Before the fillers and injections and plastic surgery. As if I'm Norma Jean and she's Marilyn. "I didn't know you'd be coming into town. I wish I had; we could've gone for brunch. We still could."

"I only came in for Jude's party. I have a flight this afternoon. I just stopped by for something."

"So, not to see your mother then. I suppose I should be used to that by now. You'll do things for that family you'd never do for me. You'll fly in for one night to see them when you won't even return my calls. You left Ireland during my last film just so you could see that awful boy. You moved all the way to New York and wouldn't even audition for Juilliard simply because it was something I wanted for you." Her tone is bitter and her lips curl into a snarl, itching for a fight I refuse to give her.

I hold up my hands in mock surrender. "I'm not going to fight with you. I'll be gone soon." Turning to head toward the stairs, my heart lurches when the glass pitcher my mother's been stirring shatters against the wall next to me. The proximity is so close, shards of glass and a fair amount of red liquid hit my arm and clothes, the sharp and spicy tang of the tomato juice, hot sauce, and vodka landing on my lip.

I pivot and stare at my mother in disbelief as I grab a nearby kitchen towel and mop my skin. "What the fuck?"

"You will not walk away from me, Brighten. I was not done speaking with you."

I huff a disgusted laugh. "It's laughable that you think you have any power in this situation. You've never acted like a mother to me. I'm not sure why you think I'd suddenly want to have some sappy heart-to-heart with you."

"You are my daughter and you will act like it."

"No, what I am is a grown woman who is no longer going to parent my parent. Just because we share DNA doesn't mean shit to me. You never wanted kids, and you got me. But you sure as hell didn't raise me; Dad did. And then, once he was gone, you had staff. I'm not your daughter. I'm the publicity token you drag out when you need good will. But I guess you don't have any more of that these days, do you?

"You've ruined your career and now, no studio will touch you with a ten-foot pole. I bet even your agent has stopped returning your calls. I refuse to be dragged into your toxic bubble."

I turn away and remembering something else she said, I pivot and stalk toward her, my head held high. "And that family is the only real family I've ever had. And that 'awful boy', as you called him, is the best man I know. And maybe if you hadn't fucked me up so bad, I could love him the way he deserves. But I don't know how to love. So, with no respect whatsoever, fuck you. You don't get to talk about *my* family. I'll be leaving as soon as I get what I came for, so you'll soon be able to continue to dull whatever of your senses are left."

I back away, not trusting to turn my back on her again until I'm far out of throwing range. She watches me with narrowed, angry eyes. "You are an ungrateful little bitch, you know that? I gave you everything. Everything. Every opportunity to live the life I set before you and what do you do? You treat it like it's shit on your shoe. What did I do to deserve this?"

I stop in my retreat and nearly want to laugh. "Do you hear yourself? You gave me the things *you* wanted. You never asked what *I* wanted for my life. I never wanted to be a musician. And simply because I was good at piano doesn't mean I give a shit to pursue that as a career. I have goals and ambitions that have nothing to do with you.

"You thought when you had a daughter who looked so much like you, I'd act like you, too. But guess what, I'm not you, Vanessa. I'm my father's daughter. And like him, I'd rather serve the people than myself. How he ever thought you were worth marrying, I'll never understand. He was twice the person you'll ever be."

She bangs her fist on the granite countertop. "You know nothing about your father. You think because he was this beloved pillar of the community that he was perfect? He wasn't a saint, Brighten, contrary to what you believe. And trust me, he served himself plenty. You're right; I never wanted kids. And by the time I found out I was pregnant with you, it was too late to do anything about it. But I've done the best I can with you and I've sacrificed plenty. You think I wanted to live in this shit hole of a town? Fuck no. But your father was tied to this place, and he chained me to him with you, so here I am.

"Someday, you'll see. You mark my words. You think because you're 'grown', you know everything? You don't know shit. I look forward to the day I can see you eat every word you've just spit at me. You will face impossible decisions in your life and sometimes, no matter what you do, there is no good option.

"So, go. Go on and be the people's champion you've claimed your father to be all these years. But no one knew him like I did and as much as I loved him, I hated him, too. If for nothing more than dying and letting us to be stuck with each other."

I shake my head. "Don't worry, you're not 'stuck' with me anymore. You don't ever need to worry about me again. I'm good. After today, you don't even have to think about me anymore. I'll be gone in ten minutes."

I wheel back around and jog up the stairs to my room and slam and lock the door. Heading to my closet, I pull the banker's box off the top shelf. I'm not sure why I haven't taken it with me before now, other than I lived in the dorms and didn't have the space. But I have an apartment now. I have space. I'll have to figure out a way to get it in my carry-on, but that's an easier fix than ever coming back here again.

And when I descend the stairs and head toward the door, I don't even look over my shoulder at my mother before leaving.

As I'm taking my seat in my Power and Politics in America class, my phone vibrates in my back pocket and I pull it out to examine the screen.

> Flynn: Happy first day of spring semester.
> Kick ass, Crash.

I can't help but smile. Flynn's sent these texts to me every semester since I started at NYU. And despite his revelation the night of Jude's party, he's still the same steadfast, caring person he's always been. I should feel guilty for wanting to keep him tethered to me the same way we have been for the past three years. And a big chunk of me does. But having him in my corner, and occasionally in my bed, makes me happy. Shouldn't I be allowed to be happy?

I've always known I was never going to buy into the big American dream. I'm not maternal. I don't get all gooey around babies. I don't dream of waking up with the same person for the rest of my life. That's not to say I don't enjoy waking up with people. I do. But the idea of commitment or vows or anything denoting a future with one single person—even if that person was Flynn—it's not me.

> Brighten: You, too. BTW, did Sully tell you I ran into him? He has a girlfriend??? Did hell freeze over?

Flynn: Right?! Yeah, he said y'all got coffee. It's not fair that my two best friends get to possibly run into each other more than I get to run into either of them. I will be drafting a strongly worded email to the powers that be who put NYU and Harvard so far away from UT. It's a travesty.

Brighten: Don't even play like you don't prefer to not be in the frigid cold of the northeast. It's currently 15 outside. I checked my weather app. It's a balmy 45 in Knoxville. So with all the love I have for you in my heart, suck it.

A door at the front of the lecture hall bangs loudly and I shove my phone back in my bag and pull out and open my laptop, navigating to my copy of the syllabus. Looking down toward the podium from my seat almost dead center in the auditorium that seats just over two-fifty, I see a man in his early to mid-thirties, dressed in jeans, a button-down shirt, and a tie. He's white with blonde hair and glasses and appears to be fit.

As he putters around the podium, I give my syllabus one last look to ensure I have a firm grasp on the expectations. As this isn't my first semester, I know most of the time a syllabus isn't set in stone and slight deviations can occur, but I still try to memorize everything and not lose track of important details.

"Okay, we'll go ahead and get started. I'm Tanner Abernathy. You can call me Tanner, or Abernathy, or Teach, or Hey, you. I don't really care. This is Politics three hundred: Power and Politics in America. If you're not supposed to be here, now's your chance to escape. Otherwise, you will be subjected to my boring commentary on the current political landscape. Save yourself now."

A collective chuckle echos around the room, and I relax. Seems like Abernathy will be a decent lecturer from first impressions. He braces his hands on the podium and continues. "Alright, if you're still here, I'm going to assume it's because you're supposed to be. Let's go. This course was designed to give you an insight into American political institutions and their behavior.

"Now, within American politics, there are many different factions and facets that make up the powerhouse that is the public sector. And while you will have to listen to me drone on about the political parties, campaigning, elections, and interest groups, we'll also be doing some hands-on work that will make up a majority of your research project grade.

"You may ask, 'How will we be doing hands-on work? This is a lecture class, not a lab or practicum.' You would be correct; it's not. There is a method to my madness, I assure you. How many of you are familiar with market research?"

My interest instantly piqued, I, along with several others, raise their hands. Abernathy nods, his eyes scanning the room. "And can any of you tell me how market research and politics go hand in hand?"

Simply from conversations I've had with Flynn over the past few years about school and our internships, we've had discussions at length about how one influences the other and vice versa. So I keep my hand raised.

Looking around, there are only a few hands still raised, which surprises me, honestly. Shouldn't this be common knowledge for anyone hoping to delve into politics? Abernathy's eyes fall on me and he adjusts his glasses. "You. Who are you, and how would you say they're related?"

I drop my hand and clear my throat. "Brighten Dawes. Market research is integral to politics. Focus groups, polling—which really isn't used to determine coming trends, but gauge outcomes for current ones—and predicting outcomes are all earmarks of market research and politics. If you're waiting until halfway through an election cycle to start researching what your opponent is doing, you've already lost. Market research looks years—elections—ahead to help a candidate ten years from now have the information they need to get elected."

Abernathy nods. "That's all true. If any of you hope to have a future in politics; whether it's behind the scenes or even aspirations of someday living in the big house on Pennsylvania Avenue, market research will be necessary for your career. As interns, you'll be the ones expected to do the actual research. If you reach the upper echelons of politics, you will commission market research firms to do the research for you.

"And Miss Dawes is accurate. You cannot wait to see what your opponent is doing. You have to figure out five steps ahead what they're planning. Politics is the biggest chess match in existence and if you wait until you're in the endgame to start strategizing, you've lost.

"This semester, you'll have the unique opportunity to marry these two fields and some of you will have an even rarer opportunity to be in the room where things go down. You will see, firsthand, what it's like to figure out what steps a candidate or incumbent needs to take to see their goals come to fruition. I have the distinct pleasure to introduce you to someone today who hales from a market research background—some might even say he was born to it—and has recently become a state senator.

"I might be a little biased since we came up together and went to undergrad and grad school together, but if I didn't believe in what he says, I wouldn't bring him here to spout his political views or his plans to this class. But for a select few of you, you'll get to spend invaluable time picking his brain for information that will help you with your research project. And in your research, you will answer the question, 'How does a junior state senator become governor after only one term?' Is it possible? That is what you'll be strategizing. My friend has some lofty goals and we're going to help him achieve them.

"This isn't only for his benefit, though. Some of you also have big aspirations. Hell, one of you may end up being a future president of this country of ours. Through this process and your research, you'll be able to apply a lot of the things you learn to the future."

He glances at someone up front and nods, but I can't see who it is, other than a mop of light brown hair. "Before I bring him up, your first assignment. Two classes from now—so, in a week—you will hand in five thousand words on the role market research plays in elections. Three of you will be chosen, based on the papers you submit, to get individual time with our special guest and be able to gain knowledge his years in market research and, now, politics have afforded him."

Abernathy gestures to the guest and says, "Without further ado, I present one of my good friends and a man with a brilliant political future. Baker Roberts is a senior partner at Intuition market research firm out of Nashville, Tennessee and a state senator in his home state. Please welcome him."

I blink in surprise as the man who presented Flynn with his award the summer he did his internship in Nashville stands. He shakes Abernathy's hand and straightens his tie. He looks nearly the same as he did a few years ago, except he's grown a beard, and the watch on his wrist looks even more expensive than the last one he wore.

He smiles in the direction of the class and clears his throat. "Honestly, that was probably a nicer welcome than I expected. Part of me thought he'd drag out pictures from our days in undergrad where I had this terrible Justin Timberlake-inspired perm."

Everyone laughs and he continues as his eyes scan each row of seats. "As Tanner said, I am a senior partner with Intuition and I'm in my first term in the state senate of Tennessee for the twenty-first district. And he's also correct when he says I have lofty political goals. I truly appreciate Tanner for letting me commandeer some of your bright, young minds to help me achieve my goals.

"Regardless of whether you're left or right leaning, I don't care. I've learned over the years—." His speech falters for a beat when his gaze lands on me and recognition sparks in his eyes. Blinking, he continues his speech, his eyes moving past me. "I've learned over the years, regardless of differences in belief, there is common ground somewhere, even if it's only in how you like your steak cooked."

Another chuckle rises from the crowd and for the next twenty minutes, everyone—me included—hangs on every word Baker Roberts says.

CHAPTER SIXTEEN

FLYNN

I'm leaving my Regression Modeling class and climbing behind the wheel of my car to head to work when my phone vibrates. Seeing I've got a few minutes to spare, I check the screen.

> Crash: You will never guess who the guest lecturer was today.

> Flynn: Um, Bono? Britney Spears? The Queen of England? One of her corgis?

> Crash: You're such a smart ass. LOL. No. Baker Roberts from Intuition.

> Flynn: Wow, small world. What's he doing as a guest lecturer at NYU?

> Crash: He and my professor were in undergrad and grad together. Our research project marries market research and politics. Since Roberts recently won a seat in the state senate, he brought him in to consult. Seems pretty cool.

> Flynn: I remember reading about him getting elected. He's brilliant from what Elias says, not that I ever had much to do with him. Will you get to work with him, or was he just lecturing today?

> Crash: Possibly. Hinges on the five thousand words I'm about to write. I may call and pick your brain for a few extra little market research nuggets I can sprinkle in to make me sound better.

> Flynn: You've got this, Crash. I'm happy to help if you need me, you know that. I've got to go. Cole might only be a year older than us, but he's a scary boss. Don't wanna be late.

She shoots back a thumbs-up emoji and I shove my phone in my pocket as I peel out of the parking lot and off to the job site. As it's still winter, there aren't a lot of yards to mow, but apparently there are still landscaping things to be done and I'm lucky to have this job since Cole works around my class schedule.

It probably doesn't hurt he's still in college, too. He's graduating this year, but he's already got a successful landscape architecture company under his belt.

Tugging on my work boots and slipping on a hoodie and knit cap to keep the wind off my ears, I jog over to where Cole is standing with a clipboard with a few of the other workers, also college students. He gives me a smile. Dismissing the other workers, he turns to me. "First day's a bitch, huh?"

I laugh. "That obvious? Statistics ain't for the faint of heart. I bet you're ready to be done."

"Damn straight. Last semester. Of course, Ada still has another year, but we'll soon have it all behind us."

"Y'all have big plans for after she graduates? Getting a place together, putting a ring on it, popping out a couple little Campbells?"

His smile falters for a beat and I'm not sure how to read it. "Yeah, we'll get a place. But I don't want to get married or have kids. Not for me."

"Really? But you and Ada have been together for years. She doesn't want those things?"

Granted, I know some women—namely Brighten—who don't want families, but I always assumed Ada did.

Cole shakes his head. "She knows I don't want it and we're happy. It's just a piece of paper. It can't tell her or anyone else how much I love her, so it's not important. And Ada's not real sold on having kids, so I don't see that being an issue either."

I nod, knowing he's right about marriage not determining how much you love someone. My ability to go along with this less than traditional relationship with Brighten tells me that. The fact I'd be okay with only accepting what she's willing to give me also says that.

Bringing us back to the topic of landscaping, I gesture at the clipboard. "Sorry, didn't mean to run that rabbit. What's on the agenda for today?"

Two weeks later, as I'm sitting in the school library between classes, my phone vibrates next to my coffee mug. I reach to pick it up and bump my coffee, sending liquid flying right onto the torso of a passerby who yelps and drops all her things.

My eyes go wide in shock and embarrassment, and I jump up from my chair and bend to pick up her items. "Oh God, I'm sorry."

"No, it's fine. That'll teach me to wear a white shirt. I'm a magnet for stains, I swear." When I stand, I feel even worse when I see just how much coffee is on her shirt. The entire front of her white T-shirt is drenched in my French roast.

She gives me an understanding smile and tugs the shirt away from her body. I immediately set her stuff on the study table next to mine, pull off my hoodie, and extend it in her direction. "Here. I know you don't know me, but I'm not a weirdo and I won't come tracking it down. I don't smoke and it's clean." I glance down at her shirt, which is still clinging to a great set of tits. "Definitely cleaner than your shirt. Sorry."

She laughs, and it's a great laugh. And as I look closer, she seems a bit familiar. She's petite and slim with long blonde hair and brown eyes and yeah, totally great tits. A pang of guilt slams into me that I noticed how nice her rack was, but why? Brighten's made no secret of the fact she sleeps with other guys. And as much as I love her and want her all to myself, it's never going to happen. And there's no harm in looking anyway, right?

She takes my offered hoodie and slips it on. "Actually, I think we do know each other. Or, at least, we're in the same class. Regression Modeling?"

I nod. "Yeah. Right. Sorry, big class."

"It is. And you sit all the way in the front, so it's not like you'd see anyone, anyway. Are you some kind of overachiever or something?"

I shrug. "Something like that."

She puts her hand on her hip and looks up at me, an adorable smile on her face. "And since you, you know, maimed me and all, I think it's only fair you let me borrow your notes from today's lecture."

I huff a laugh. "That so? What, you make all the guys who spill coffee on you hand over their notes?"

She shakes her head. "No, just the cute ones who give me their hoodies." Extending her hand, she says, "Saylor."

I shake her offered hand. "Flynn. Saylor, huh? Your parents like boats?" I gesture to the seat across from mine. "I'll get you my notes."

Saylor drops into the chair and opens her book. "Mind if I study with you for a little while, too? None of the other tables are free and since you giving me your hoodie would probably constitute a marriage proposal in certain societies, that practically makes us family, wouldn't you say?"

I snort a laugh. "Sure." I dig around in my bag and find my notebook. Once I do, I pass it over, opened to the correct page.

"And no, to answer your question."

"What question?" I ask as I retake my seat.

"If my parents like boats. My aunts are named Sally and Taylor and because I'm the baby and the only girl, they thought it'd be neat or some shit to combine them. If you ask me, it feels like some sort of copout."

I shrug. "Nah, it's cute."

She blushes and bites her bottom lip. The gesture makes me think of Brighten and her lips and teeth and instances when she'd bite her lip. I now know with certainty I'm not the only man who gets to see her bite her lip. I'm not the only person she blushes for. I've suspected it since we became what we are, but didn't have it confirmed until I saw her tattoo.

I'm still so beyond hurt and angry at her for getting it. It's not the fact that she has a tattoo; I could give a shit about that. I like tattoos. It's that she'd cover up her scar simply to make it easier for other people to look at her. I'm fucking enraged. She shouldn't be sleeping with people who would look at her, scar and all, like she isn't the most beautiful person on this entire planet. She shouldn't be letting anyone put their hands on her who won't appreciate that scar. But she does.

"And where did you get your name?" Saylor asks.

I blink, bringing my attention back to her. "Oh, it's my

mom's maiden name. My brother got part of her middle name as his name and I got her maiden name."

"A brother? Y'all anything alike?"

"Not really. Other than the fact we're twins, we're nothing alike."

Her brows rise. "Twins? Does that mean there's another guy walking around looking as good as you?"

"Well, we are identical, so I guess that's a yes."

She taps her chin with her pencil and eyes me across the table. "Does he go to school here, too?" I shake my head. "Good. Then I won't have to worry about getting you mixed up." As she returns her attention to my notes, I drop my gaze back to my book. Ten minutes later, she makes a puzzled sound.

I look back up at her. "What?"

"I think you're missing something on these notes."

I frown, confused. "What? I don't think so."

She gives me a slow smile and taps the corner of the page. "It's alright, I fixed it. You were missing my number."

I blink. "Oh."

Her smile falters as she sees the surprised expression on my face. "Unless you have a girlfriend. Or boyfriend. In which case, your notes are perfect."

Even as Brighten's face flashes in my mind, I shake my head. "No. There's not anyone."

"Good." She closes my notebook and drops it on top of my other books and stands and plants her hands on the table in front of me and lowers her voice. "If you want your hoodie back, call me. We can work something out for you to get it. Until then, I'll probably be sleeping in it... and nothing else." As she walks away, she tosses me one last wink. "See ya, Flynn."

Brighten, she's not. She's not built the same, and she doesn't sound the same. But Brighten's not here and she doesn't want a commitment from me. She's made it very clear she has no plans for me being the only person she sees.

And in spite of the things I said to her after Dad's party about wanting to be all hers, I'm still so angry with her. And no, sleeping with someone else wouldn't punish her because we're not together. We'll never be together. But might I be able to work out some of this anger sexually? Possibly. I find myself shockingly close to considering it.

Since I started college, there have been instances where girls have smiled at me in a way that would make me think they're interested. Saylor's the first one who's actually come out and pretty much said she's a sure thing. Not to mention, she's fucking hot. Maybe I am a little like Jess after all.

CHAPTER SEVENTEEN

BRIGHTEN

I check my phone to see if I've missed a text or call from Flynn. I texted him a few days ago to let him know I was chosen to work with Baker Roberts, but he hasn't responded. It's not that we talk or text every single day; we're both busy people. But it's unusual for him not to respond to exciting news like this.

For some reason, I'm anxious about meeting with Baker. It's after midnight and I can't sleep because what if I only got picked because he recognized me? I know Flynn is still in touch with Elias Washington, so there's a chance Baker remembers Flynn and me being together and gave me this opportunity because of him. I know it's unlikely, but it still bothers me.

Sitting up in bed, I switch on the lamp after checking my phone one last time. When I still don't see anything from Flynn, I finally just call him. I know with his schedule this semester, his earliest class is at ten, so I don't feel as bad about it being this late.

"Hello? Crash?" He sounds like I woke him up, and a pang of guilt hits me.

"Hey, sorry. Did I wake you up?"

He yawns and I can picture him dragging his hand down his face. "Yeah, but it's fine. Everything okay?"

I open my mouth, but I hear a muffled voice in the background say something like, "Can you take that in the other room? I have an early class." It's a distinctly feminine voice, but I guess I could be wrong.

But then I hear Flynn's belt buckle and the sound of fabric rustling and he says, "Give me one second, Crash."

He must cover the mouthpiece, but I hear plain as day in that same feminine voice, "I'm holding your hoodie hostage. We now have joint custody, so I guess we'll have to work out a visitation schedule."

Flynn laughs, and a weight drops into the pit of my stomach. I've heard that laugh before. That's his post-sex, easy laugh. It's funny the things that you associate with people when you know them so well. He tells whoever it is, "See you later," and then a door shuts.

God, why does the mic on his phone have to be so good? I don't want to hear him tell another woman goodbye. He's never heard me telling another man goodbye. Not that it matters, I guess; it's just weird. Especially after everything he said the night of Jude's party. Maybe learning with certainty that I've slept with other people has given him the nudge to branch out as well?

"Okay, sorry. Is everything alright?"

I blink, shaking the thoughts from my mind. "Oh. Yeah, fine. I hadn't heard from you in a few days and you never responded to my text, so I wasn't sure if you got it."

"I did. Sorry. That's awesome about the Baker thing. I've been busy."

"Sounds like it. Didn't mean to interrupt your night."

"You didn't interrupt anything. So, are you excited about getting to work with him? It's a pretty big deal, it sounds like, right?"

I pull my knees up to my chest and wish he was here to actually talk to me in person and reassure me. "It is. Only three of us were chosen. The class has over a hundred and fifty people."

"That's awesome, Crash."

"It is. I know."

"Why are you anxious?"

His question reminds me that he knows me so well. It reminds me that he's my best friend and I relax a bit. "I think he recognized me the first day in class. From when I went with you to that intern party."

"Okay, but what's that matter?"

"What if he only picked me *because* he recognized me?"

"Crash, that would imply that you didn't get chosen on merit alone. Is that something you think could ever happen? Did you bomb the paper you submitted?"

"No, it was good. The notes you sent me helped a lot."

"Okay, then why would you think the fact he saw you once three years ago would be a reason he'd choose you for this amazing opportunity? I mean, I'd pick you if I saw you three years ago, but I'm pretty sure our motivations are very different."

Even knowing he probably just slept with someone else, I can't help but laugh at his suggestive comment. "Yeah, I know. I guess I just got in my head about it. What if, when I meet him, I completely forget what I'm going to say? What if I suck at this project and fail this class? What if—."

"What if you're great? What if he loves your ideas? What if something you tell him turns into some amazing thing he puts into some kind of stump speech someday when he runs for some other office? What's the worst-case scenario here?"

I sigh. "That I fail and look like an amateur."

"Okay, so you retake the class. Big deal. If you bomb it with Baker—and we both know you won't because you're Brighten Dawes and Brighten Dawes doesn't fail and she's sure as fuck no amateur—it's not like you'll ever work with him in the future. And if you do, it would be because you were paying his firm for market research purposes. In which case, he'd be working for you and he wouldn't be likely to bring up your failings if you're his client."

I huff a laugh. "Thank you."

"For what?"

"For being you. For talking me off the ledge and putting things into perspective."

"Always. You know that."

Despite the pep talk from Flynn, I'm still nervous about meeting with Baker and currently, I sit outside the small conference room he's booked for our meeting. Feeling my phone vibrate in my hand, I look at the screen.

> Flynn: You've got this. I'm not even going to wish you good luck because you don't need it. Make that meeting your bitch.

I laugh and immediately feel better. I take a deep breath and let it out, reminding myself I earned this. I deserve this. I'm going to do great.

"Miss Dawes?"

I snap my head up to see Baker Roberts standing at a door

to my right, and I get to my feet. "Brighten is fine." He smiles and ushers me into the room and I take the seat obviously meant for me, as there's only a folder at one chair next to the head of the massive table where he's set up shop. As he sits, I say, "And I want to thank you for this amazing opportunity, Mr. Roberts."

He flashes a smile that I'm sure makes women swoon and shakes his head, dismissing my formality. "Please, call me Baker. And you've earned this. Your paper was insightful and you have an impressive grasp on market research already."

Pride blooming in my chest, I smile. "Thank you. My best friend was a big help. He plans on going into the field after college. I don't know if you remember him from his internship at Intuition a few summers back. Flynn Tate? I was actually at the wrap-up party with him."

He nods. "I wondered where I recognized you from. Okay, yeah. Flynn's brilliant. Reminds me a lot of myself at his age."

I chuckle. "So, are you saying *you're* brilliant?"

He laughs and his smile widens with amusement. "I mean, I am, but I don't normally brag about it. So, I read your paper and already have some talking points to go over with you, but tell me a little about yourself. I want to make sure the things I'm thinking will be compatible with who you are as a person."

Somewhat surprised he'd want to know anything about me not related to the class, I rack my brain—gone suddenly blank— for anything I can tell him. "Well, I'm from Tennessee. Knoxville, actually. I want to be President someday."

He nods, impressed. "Well, alright. Ambitious. I like it. And are you a political science major?"

"Yes. And then I'll be going to law school after undergrad."

"At NYU, or somewhere else?"

I splay my hands. "Who knows? I love NYU and I love the

area, but since I want to get into politics, I'm thinking George-town or George Washington. That way, I can be in the thick of things while I'm in law school."

"Sounds like you've got everything figured out."

"I hope so," I agree.

He leans back in his chair, his posture relaxed. "And what made you want to get into politics?"

"My dad, actually."

"And how does he feel about you being all the way here in New York, away from home?"

I give him a smile, but I know it's a bit sad. "My dad passed when I was young. Cancer."

"Oh. I'm so sorry."

I wave off his apology and offer him a smile that's more genuine. "You're fine. It was a long time ago. But he was actually mayor of Knoxville for a period of time. I think he hoped to eventually be governor. I like the idea of making impactful change. Healthcare reform and getting more research funding in the hands of people trying to cure things we should already have cures for is something I'm passionate about."

He nods, his interest genuine and I'm honestly surprised he's still listening intently. "Wanting to take on healthcare, that because of you father, too?"

"Partly," I admit, "But Flynn's dad has multiple sclerosis, and watching him go from this vibrant, healthy, strong man to one whose body is slowly betraying him has had an effect on my life."

"I would imagine so," he agrees. "And what does your mother think?"

I huff a laugh. "You don't want to know."

He grins. "Not a fan of politics, huh?"

"No. She would've preferred I follow in her footsteps and

go into entertainment. She was rooting for Juilliard. Didn't speak to me for weeks when I refused the audition."

"Ballsy to turn down an audition at Juilliard. Your mother— musician, actor, writer, what?"

"Nothing anymore, but she used to be an actress."

"Anyone I would've heard of?"

I bite my lip. "Vanessa Eldridge," I say with a sigh.

Baker lifts a brow. "Oof, that was a loaded sigh. Vanessa Eldridge, huh?" Examining me a bit more closely, he nods. "Okay, I see the resemblance now. Maybe that's why I thought you were so striking that first time I saw you at the party."

Striking? That's a new one. I'm not sure what to make of his...compliment?

"So, can I ask you a question?" I start, my tone hopeful.

"Of course. I'm sure you'll have lots by the time we're done."

"Touché. What made you want to get into politics? And do you plan on stopping at the Governor's mansion?"

He's thoughtful for a moment and takes a sip from a bottle of water. "Well, I'm not sure if you remember what I said the night of the party, but my family started Intuition. I grew up around all the movers and shakers of Nashville. I saw deals being done in back rooms and at parties and maybe it's because I like to be the one who makes things happen, but shit like that fascinated me.

"How a business owner could have one conversation with a member of the general assembly and the next session, some- thing would happen. Politics in general is fascinating. I think there's a lot of bad shit and lots of people get their pockets lined by lobbyists and special interest groups, but there are people who are genuine about their desire to serve.

"And I think my background makes me uniquely qualified to run, simply because I have all the tools at my disposal to win.

Maybe, by the time you're done with your law degree, someone like me will be looking for a bright protégé to set up for their own run at the Hill."

"Your lips to God's ear," I say with a grin.

Opening a folder in front of him, he pulls out a pair of reading glasses and slides them on his face. "Okay, so on to my notes for you."

CHAPTER EIGHTEEN

FLYNN

When I wake up the Friday before spring break, it's with a blonde head on my chest. And as much as I like this particular blonde head, every time I see it, I wish it was red. Saylor snuggles closer and presses a kiss to my chest. "Morning." And even though her voice is sexy, it's wrong, too.

I smile down at her. "Morning."

"I was going to see if, when you get back from Vegas with your dad and brother, you wanted to come meet my parents?"

Something in my chest twists; guilt maybe? As much as I like Saylor—she's funny, she's beautiful, she's smart, the sex is... well, it's not sex with Brighten, but it's fine—I can't meet her parents. She's already been dropping hints about summer break, as if she thinks this is going somewhere. I know it isn't. And although I was clear when we started hooking up that this is casual, I haven't been seeing anyone else and neither has she, so she probably assumes it's more serious than it is.

I sit up and put on my glasses and reach for my boxers on the floor and rise to dress for my run. "I don't think I'll be able to do that."

Sitting up and pulling the covers up to her armpits and her knees up to her chest, she runs her hand down her face. "Oh. Okay. And have you given more thought to what I said about this summer? You're going to be at that internship in Atlanta and I'll be there anyway since it's where I'm from. If you wanted to get a place, we could split the rent. It's kinda expensive, so every little bit helps, you know?"

I slip on my running shorts and a T-shirt before sitting on the edge of the bed to pull on my socks. "I can't do that, Saylor."

She sighs and crawls to sit beside me. "Can I ask what your hesitation is to be in a real relationship with me? We've been having fun together. You're a great guy, Flynn, and I like you a lot. I'd like this to be more than just hooking up. You're smart and sweet and great in bed. Is there something...missing for you here? Something I could do that would tip the scales into a commitment? We've been seeing each other for a couple months, so it's not like it's been a week. I feel as though I've been patient."

I nod and give her my full attention. "You have been. But I told you I'm not looking for a relationship. It has nothing to do with you. You are great and we do have a good time. I don't want you to take this the wrong way, but a good time is all I can offer you."

She bites her lip and for a long moment, she's thoughtful before heaving a resigned sigh. "It's Crash, isn't it? Your best friend? Do y'all have a thing or something? You're hoping when you're both free during the summer, you'll spend time with her? Be with her?"

I give her a sad smile. "Crash—Brighten—is my best friend. Has been for almost ten years. Things are...complicated. When she and I are together, we're together. When we're not, we don't talk about who we're with at that time."

"Is it serious between you two but you just can't be together right now because you're at different schools? When you're together, is it like an actual relationship? I'm just confused."

"Like I said, it's complicated." I sigh, resigned. "I will always belong to Brighten. All of me. Body and soul. She won't ever belong to me; not fully. She loves me, but only as a friend."

"But y'all sleep together?" she confirms, her brow furrowing.

"Yes," I confirm.

"And she doesn't have feelings for you? Are you serious? Does she not know how amazing you are?"

I can't help but laugh. "Thanks for the ego boost, Say."

She shrugs. "I'm just saying, you're, like, the total package, man." After a beat, she sobers. "You love her, though, right? Like, *love* her?"

I nod, my chest beginning to ache. "Yeah."

"And you're okay with her sleeping with other guys? You don't get jealous? Does she get jealous? I mean, how long have y'all had this thing?"

"It started about three years ago. I purposely don't think about her with other people. I assume me being with other women doesn't bother her. Before now, that's never been something she's had to think about."

Saylor frowns. "What do you mean?"

"Before you, there wasn't anyone besides her."

"Well, don't I feel special," she says with a grin.

I drag my knuckle down her jaw. "You are special, Saylor. And you deserve someone who can give you all of themself. I'm sorry that can't be me."

She nods. "Well, you're nothing if not honest, I'll give you that." She considers something. "Will you see her before summer?"

"I'm not sure."

"Well, now that I know where I stand, I'm cool to keep

hanging out until the end of the semester or whatever. I enjoy hanging out with you and you're a good fuck, so you know, no hardship there." I huff a laugh. "I'm not going to lie, though. I hope someday, someone comes along who you let get past the Crash shield. That woman will be really lucky."

I rake my fingers through my hair. "I don't want to hurt you, Saylor. If you're looking for a commitment, I get that. You should have that. If you wanted to end things, I'd completely understand."

"I'm good with casual; I just wondered since neither of us had been seeing other people, if that's what we still were. I just needed to recalibrate my expectations. If you decide we're done, I'm good. If I decide we're done, I'll tell you. If you want to keep this up until the end of the semester, hey, great. If I find someone else I decide I'd prefer to spend time with, that's great, too, and I'll tell you. If we both have weekends where we see other people and then come back here to each other; whatever," she says with a wink.

Relieved that we're on the same page again, I smile and lean over and give her a kiss. She wraps her arms around me, the sheets falling down to reveal her naked breasts. "Come back to bed. I can be your cardio this morning." She straddles me, rolling her hips and what can I say? I'm a man. I'm an easy fuck, I guess, because in seconds, I'm hard.

Taking my glasses back off and tossing them on the night-stand, I wrap my arms around Saylor and stand and flip our position until she's below me. She looks up at me and smiles and she's beautiful. She's fun. She's fucking awesome. But she's not Brighten.

And even though she's not who I truly want, she's here and I've been honest and who am I to turn down willing pussy?

Even with my *cardio* with Saylor, I still head out for my run. And Sully was totally right; I crave it now. As I'm finishing the last mile of a ten-mile run, my phone rings in my earbuds, cutting through my running play list. Slowing to a manageable jog, I pull my phone out of my pocket and see that it's Brighten and I smile. "Hey. What's up?"

"A little late for your run today, isn't it?" she asks with a chuckle.

"Yeah. How are you? Are you getting ready for that spring break trip to San Diego you were telling me about? The one with your old roommate?"

"Well, that was the plan, but Lana went and got herself knocked up and is too sick to fly."

"Damn."

"Yeah, she's okay with it. They're getting married this summer anyway, so it's just a jump start, I guess. Personally, I can't imagine a kid period, let alone during college. Worst nightmare, if you ask me."

Not wanting to talk about kids, because Brighten will never have kids, and especially not with me, I clear my throat since there's no point in staying on the subject. "So, you're just cancelling your trip? That sucks."

"I don't have anything else to do, and I don't feel like going to San Diego alone. Too bad you're going to Vegas with your dad and Jess or you could come with me. We could sit on the beach, drink fruity cocktails, you could see me naked."

I let out a pained groan. "Damn, you trying to twist my arm? You could've led the part about you being naked, Crash. You could always meet me in Vegas. It's a trip for Dad, and you know he'd love to see you."

Thinking about Dad makes my chest ache and I clear my throat.

"How bad is it, Flynn?" Her voice is soft and I hear the slight edge of fear in her tone.

"He's not great. He had pneumonia last month. It was a rough couple of weeks. He's finally getting some of his strength back, but he's still pretty weak."

After a beat of silence, she clears her throat. "Okay. Yeah. Let me change my tickets. Will you have your own room, or do I need to book one?"

"You're covered."

"And when are y'all arriving?"

"Dad and Jess already left yesterday after he finished his last class. They're driving. Dad wants to see the sights. He and Mom took this same road trip when they first got married, so he wanted to do it again with us. Jess is driving down with him. I'm driving back."

"So, when are they arriving?"

Wanting time with her that's all my own, I throw out a suggestion. I'm more thrilled than I care to admit that I will have any time with her, let alone a few days. "They won't be there for a few days. I can bump up my flight by a couple days. Come hang out with me; just the two of us? I've missed you these past couple of months."

"Me, too. Alright, so tomorrow? Will that work?"

"Tomorrow. I'll send you the hotel info and call them to add your name to my room, in case you get there before I do."

"Perfect. See you soon."

"See you."

Arriving at the hotel and casino in Las Vegas a little after ten PM local time, I check in and upon finding out Brighten's already arrived, I practically sprint to the elevators with my room key. Thoughts of her face and hair and mouth and hands and pussy have my cock already lengthening in my jeans and I blow out a breath and will the elevator to move faster.

Entering the room, I find something I'm not expecting: Brighten, totally naked, with her hand between her legs. "Holy fuck, Crash," I breathe, dropping my bags to the floor and fishing condoms from the outside pocket of my backpack.

She gives me a wicked grin and doesn't stop moving her hand. "I had them call me when you were on your way up. I thought you might enjoy the view."

Toeing off my shoes and stripping naked in about ten seconds flat, I toss the condoms on the nightstand as I crawl onto the bed between her legs. Sitting up, she drags her fingers up her pussy and extends the hand in my direction. I grab it and suck her fingers between my lips, the taste of her flooding my mouth, making me groan. "Fuck, I've missed the way you taste."

She smiles and I grab the back of her neck and crush her to me, our mouths colliding in a hungry meeting of lips and tongue and teeth. I nip at her bottom lip as I kiss my way down her jaw and neck and she lets out a soft gasp as I move my mouth down toward her tits.

It's that sound that grounds me, reminds me that if only for tonight or the next few days, or however long we're together, I have her. I have all of her. I don't have to share her with anyone else. She is *mine*.

And now, having been with someone other than just Brighten, I can appreciate the differences—some subtle, some drastic—in their bodies; in their techniques. I could pick Brighten out of a sea of thousands, though. The way she feels under my hands, her distinct dips and curves. The difference in the way she kisses and the way her hands travel over my body, like she's reading a topographical map blindfolded, attempting to identify specific landmarks.

And even though I've only been with one other woman besides her, it will never feel as right with anyone as it does with her. There could a hundred willing women who would promise to love me forever and there would still only be her for me.

Her moans and the writhing of her hips against me has me shifting my dick away from her, lest I get any wild hairs about deciding to forget the condoms. Not that I wouldn't love to feel her with no barriers between us, but even if we were the only people either of us were currently fucking and we both had clean bills of health, I care about her dreams too much to put them in jeopardy by being reckless.

"Oh God, Flynn. Please. Fuck."

I pull back to look down at her and my heart squeezes with love for this woman who will never fully be mine, but is right now. And right now is enough. "You want something?" She snakes her hand between us to give my dick a rough stroke that makes me huff out a breath. "Jesus."

"I want your cock, Flynn."

I reach over and rip off a condom and tear the wrapper with my teeth. "Have you missed it, Crash?" She nods and I lift a brow. "Tell me."

She lifts her head to lick a line up my throat, and goose-bumps erupt down my arms. "I've missed your cock and your mouth and your hands. I've missed the filthy words you say and how well you fuck me." Dropping her head back to the pillow, she brings her eyes to mine. "Now, fuck me so I'll feel it tomorrow."

I huff a laugh as I yank her down the bed and brace the backs of her thighs on my biceps. "You talk about my filthy words. Damn, woman."

She opens her mouth to say something and I slam inside her, hard, and she screams, her eyes falling closed. I claim her mouth in an equally brutal kiss as I set a punishing rhythm and fuck; it's like coming home and Christmas morning and the finest drug on the planet. It's never going to be like this with anyone but her.

The women who come after or between times with her will only be filling a physical void, whereas Brighten fills the void that's in the shape of my heart. Because that's what she is: my heart.

For long moments, I completely lose myself in this animal-istic rutting; this need to reclaim her in a way that it sears her soul with my touch. It's not until she touches my face, gentle and imploring, that I bring my gaze back to hers. "Be here with me, Flynn."

I nod and slow my thrusts and turn my face to kiss her palm. I drop my forehead to hers. "I'm always with you. Even when I'm not." Brighten tilts her head until our lips meet and the kiss is tender and affectionate and makes my entire soul ache.

Knowing I can't look her in the eye and not feel the need to say the words I haven't said to her while she's awake, I trail my mouth down to her breast and tug her nipple between my teeth and feel her let go with a ragged sigh. It's only seconds before I piston my hips one final time, a guttural grunt falling from my mouth.

CHAPTER NINETEEN

BRIGHTEN

I look at Flynn as he pulls out. He shutters his emotions, the expression on his face morphing from open and elated to neutral.

I'm always with you. Even when I'm not.

The words slam into me like a fist. I know how he feels about me and I'm probably cruel for letting him keep coming to me, for agreeing to come to him.

God, why can't I be "normal"? It would be so much easier if I loved him as more than my best friend. It would be amazing if I saw myself waking up with him every morning. I don't. I don't see it with anyone.

He sits on the edge of the bed and disposes of the condom in the trashcan by the nightstand. He stares out the window, but I've seen him lost in thought enough to know he's not actually seeing anything. I crawl under the covers and pull them up to my chest, and wonder if I can keep doing this to him.

"Flynn?" He fixes a smile on his face and something in my chest twists painfully seeing him putting on a mask to look at me and tears well in my eyes.

"Yeah?" When he sees my face, his expression shifts to alarmed concern, and he scrambles over to me and takes my hand in his. "What is it? Did I hurt you? Was I too rough? Fuck, Crash. I'm sorry. I'm so sorry."

I shake my head. "No. It's not that. I'm fine. I promise." I swallow thickly. "Is this too much for you?"

He searches my eyes, his dark brows drawing down in confusion. "Is what too much?"

"This? Hooking up? Is it too much for you? Is it getting too hard for you?" The dam bursts and I sob and my words come out between shuddery breaths. "As your best friend, I-I can't want this for you. I can't want you to accept less than you deserve. If it were someone else you were doing this with who you had feelings for and they couldn't return them, I'd tell you to end it, Flynn. It's hypocritical of me to do the same thing and be okay with it."

Flynn climbs under the blankets with me and pulls me into his arms. I cling to him and cry into his bare chest, and he drops a kiss on the top of my head. "I'm alright. I told you I knew what I signed up for. I promise."

I pull back to look at him and he swipes his thumbs under my eyes and presses a soft kiss to my lips. "I'm okay, Crash. I told you I would tell you if it was too much. I told you I'm content with things. It just got a little intense for a minute. I'm sorry."

He sighs. "I don't want you to get upset every time we get together because I'll develop some kind of complex and I won't be able to get it up anymore. Then what good would I be to you?"

I scoff, sudden anger welling up in my chest and I open my mouth, but he puts a finger to my lips and gives me that lopsided grin. "There she is; I was fucking with you. I know you love me for more than my dick."

I bite my lip. "I do love you, you know."

He nods. "I know. And the way you're able to love me is perfect. I don't need more than you can give me."

"It's not enough for you."

"*You* are enough for me. Exactly the way you are. I'm never going to ask you to change, because how you are—how fiercely independent and driven and ambitious you are—is exactly why I love you."

I search his eyes. "Flynn, as your best friend, I should want what's best for you. Even if that's not me. I'm being selfish with you."

"And I told you I'm fine."

"What if you pass up a great opportunity with some wonderful woman who can marry you and give you babies and all the things you deserve? I don't know if I'd ever forgive myself."

"I don't see things like that in my future, so we're good."

His tone is neutral, as if he's telling me the time, and I don't understand his lack of emotion. "How are you so calm? I know you. This isn't everything you want for your life. You're not me."

He pinches the bridge of his nose and sighs. "No, I'm not. But I'm also only twenty-one, Crash. I'm still in college; I want my career. And I don't have any plans to marry or have kids, especially not anytime soon. I told you, if things change for me —the things I want or feel like I *have* to have to feel fulfilled—I will tell you. For now, the only thing I need is you; however I can have you."

Shifting in the bed, he rolls our bodies until I'm below him. His eyes are serious and full of hunger. He cages me in and presses a kiss to my lips. "As long as when you're with me— wherever we are, whenever we're together—you're mine, that's enough. I don't care how many men you fuck between visits with me. I honestly don't. As long as you're still *my* Crash and when we're together, we're together, I don't need more than that."

I bring my hand up to his face and trace the line of his jaw before running my thumb over his eyebrow. "You're such a good man, Flynn. I wish I—."

"Crash, stop. I don't want to keep hashing this out. It's a waste of precious time I already don't get enough of with you. I know who you are. I know the things you want and, more importantly, I know the things you don't. I know you better than anyone, and I care enough about your dreams to stand guard over them and make sure you have them. I will never get in the way of the things you want. I will never ask you to choose only me. I don't need to. No matter what, you will still be my best friend. No matter how old we get. No matter how many other people there are who come and go in our lives. You are my constant.

"And like I told you after Dad's party, if this part of things between us," he grinds himself against me and I feel him growing hard again and I gasp, "becomes something you no longer want, I will still be your best friend. I will still be in your corner and champion every one of your causes. I will come when you call and stand behind you while you slay your dragons."

A tear rolls out of my eye and down into the hair at my temple at the thought of how selfless he is and exactly how well he knows me, but I huff a laugh. "You mean you don't want to slay them for me?"

He smiles and shakes his head. "You don't need me to. You don't need anyone to take care of you or fight your battles. You are the most badass person I know. You are going to do so much in this life and I just want to be a part of it, in whatever capacity I can."

I nod. "Okay."

He reaches over for another condom and lowers his mouth to mine.

———

"Did you tell Jude I was coming?" I sip my glass of wine as we sit in the restaurant and wait for Jess and Jude to arrive for dinner.

Flynn shakes his head and takes a pull of his beer and runs his hand down his tie. "I told Jess. I wanted to surprise Dad."

"Does Jess know I've been here, or does he think I just happened to be in Vegas, or what?"

"Jess and I don't talk much anymore. He works or is in class all the time and when he's not working, he's busy. We live in the same city, but we might as well live in different countries for the amount of time we spend together. He doesn't know about you and me. He knows we're still close, of course, and he knows how close you and Dad have always been, so I told him you were on your way to San Diego and I asked you to make a stop."

My brows rise in surprise. "You lied to your brother? Your dad knows about us; I'm surprised you've never told Jess."

He sighs. "I omit from my brother. I just don't tell him. He doesn't need to know."

"So, he what, thinks you're celibate?"

Flynn snorts a laugh. "I'm not celibate. He knows that. He just doesn't know about how *not celibate* I am with you."

This is the closest we've ever come to talking about the other people we see. And after the night I called him and heard another woman's voice in the background, I've been curious. "Can I ask you something?"

He huffs another laugh and takes a drink of his beer. "Uh-oh, I know that tone. I'm not sure I want you to ask. It's going to be one of those questions that takes us down a road I'm not sure either of us really wants to go, Crash."

"No, I just wanted to ask—."

He sighs. "Her name is Saylor. We have a class together."

A bark of surprised laughter falls from my lips. "How did you know I was going to ask that?"

He rolls his eyes. "Crash, how long have we known each other? A long fucking time. Most of the time, I know exactly what you're going to say before you say it. And no, I don't want to know who you spend your time with."

"Can I ask about her, though? Is she nice at least?"

"Are we really going to have this conversation?"

I shrug. "I'm just curious. Is she the same girl who said she was going to hold your hoodie hostage? Which, for the record, good line on her part."

He chuckles. "Yeah, same girl. She's nice. We have fun. She wants more, but knows I don't."

I frown. "Doesn't that seem kind of ironic to you? She's you in this situation."

"No, she's not."

"How do you figure? You said she wants more."

He levels me with a gaze. "She wants more from me, but she doesn't really know me. We don't have that kind of relationship. We don't talk more than to share stats class notes and figure out a time for us to meet up. Sometimes, we have dinner. On rare occasions, we wake up together.

"I don't want more from you because I have exactly what I want. I have you as my best friend all the time. I have you as the woman I'd prefer to have in my bed all the time sometimes. It is enough for me.

"Saylor is great. She's smart and funny. I don't really care to know more about her than what gets her off. You're the only person I want to know every aspect of their soul, Crash. And I have that. She's just a good distraction."

Maybe I've been agonizing these past few days for nothing. Maybe Flynn does have a grasp on what our relationship is and I'm projecting because I feel guilty because I know he loves me, but I don't share his feelings. Maybe this weird relationship dynamic we've got going on can work for the long-term and I can trust him to be honest with me. I don't know why I'd question that; Flynn is honest to a fault with me. Always has been.

"Does she know about me?"

He nods. "Yeah." His eyes catch on something over my shoulder and he smiles. "They're here."

I turn in my chair, and sure enough, Jess and Jude are coming toward us. Jess looks the same as he always has, but Jude looks weaker than when I saw him a few months ago and my heart sinks. I paste a smile on my face and rise as they get closer.

I greet Jess with a quick hug before leaning down to drop a kiss on the top of Jude's head and wrapping my arms around his shrinking frame. "This is a good surprise, my girl," he says as I pull back to look at him.

"I couldn't resist. You going to let me blow your dice for good luck?"

He laughs and lifts a brow, his eyes—one clouded over in blindness—shining with mischief. "I'm not sure Flynn would like his old man stealing his luck."

I glance at Flynn, who is enthralled in a conversation with his brother, before returning my attention back to Jude. "I'm pretty sure Flynn makes his own luck."

He lifts a shaky hand—shakier than it was a few months ago —and touches my cheek, his smile softening. "He's lucky to have you, Brighten. I know whatever arrangement you and Flynn have is your business, and I'm not here to tell you how to live your life, but you're lucky to have him, too. I hope you know that."

I nod. "I know that."

"He loves you, you know. He'd kill me for interfering, but indulge me, huh?"

I nod again. "I know he does." I wish I didn't sound guilty when I said it.

"I know he says you think that you're not built for love. Someday, though, I think you'll learn what it means. You'll realize it. I have faith. As his dad, I hope it's with Flynn, but even if it's not, I'll just be happy if you know what it means to love someone with your whole heart." He huffs a laugh. "If you're anything like me, it'll take you completely by surprise and you'll wonder how you missed the signs."

Patting his hand, I shake my head, resigned. "I don't think so, Jude. I'm sorry."

"Don't apologize. I'm not judging or anything; just feeling sentimental. But I hope you'll still keep the promise you made me? You'll make sure he's okay?" He's quiet for a moment and blinks. "I'm tired, kid."

My breath catches and tears burn my eyes. I know Jude isn't saying he's tired right this second, even though I'm sure he is. He's tired of being in a body that no longer feels like his own. He's tired of living this reduced existence. Swiping a tear away before it rolls down my cheek, I nod. "I promise."

"Good. You know, I always wanted a daughter and you've been the best one I could've asked for."

Even knowing I'm in public and I'm about to start sobbing, I don't care. "And you've been a great dad to me. Thank you. And thank you for raising the best man I know. He's had a good example to follow."

"Crash, you okay?" Concern is evident in Flynn's tone and I try to quell my emotions.

Jude gives me a smile and a jerky nod. "She's alright. I just told her I didn't vote in the last election. You know how important that is to her."

I give his hand a squeeze and we join Flynn and Jess at the table. Flynn darts a glance between his father and me and gives my knee a squeeze under the table.

CHAPTER TWENTY

BRIGHTEN

A few weeks after spring break and the Vegas trip, I'm sitting with Baker, going over the last details of my research project. It's our final meeting and honestly, I'm surprised how much I've enjoyed working with him. I assumed with him being immensely wealthy and a borderline genius, he'd be pretentious or cocky, but he's not. He's funny and insightful and has helped me tremendously with my project.

He shuts his laptop and slides off his glasses. "I think that's going to do it. You've got this thing on lock."

I smile, happy to have it done. "I can't thank you enough for all your help. Truly. I have such a better understanding than I did at the beginning of the semester."

"So, what comes next? Internship during the summer, backpacking across Europe? Spending time with a boyfriend?"

I huff a laugh and, even as Flynn's face flashes in my mind, I shake my head. "No boyfriend. I'm not sure, honestly. I had put some feelers out for an internship in Nashville with the Governor's office, but I haven't heard back yet. I'm also scheduled to take my LSATs."

"So, not D.C.? Color me surprised."

I give him a sad smile. "My friend, Flynn? His dad's going downhill. I'd like to be closer to him so I can spend time with him."

"I take it you're close?"

I nod. "He really has been like a surrogate father to me. I lost my own dad really young, so I don't remember him much. I met Jude when I was twelve, and he's been such a big part of my life since Flynn and I are so close."

Baker examines my face and leans forward on his elbows, his expression curious. "Can I ask you something? And since we're no longer mentor and mentee, I don't think it would be considered inappropriate."

I frown, unsure how to answer. "Okay," I reply after a moment.

"You and Flynn? Are you two—? What I mean is, are you two linked romantically?" I huff a nervous laugh and Baker rushes forward. "Shit, I don't mean to sound nosy or anything like that. If you don't want to talk about it, you don't have to. I was curious how *close* you two are. Are you seeing him?"

I blink. How do I tell Baker what Flynn is to me? Especially when I don't know why he's asking. "Can I ask why you'd like to know?"

He blows out a breath and chuckles. "I'm totally blowing this. So, can I be frank?"

"Okay, so if you're Frank, then who will I be?" I ask, feigning seriousness.

He laughs and a lot of the tension of the moment breaks. "God, you're funny." His expression morphs into one that's a bit more hesitant and I'm at a loss as to why, since I've never seen him be anything other than confident and commanding. "I asked because if we're not working together anymore in this capacity, it would no longer be a conflict of interest if I were to take you on a date. But if you and Flynn are together, I don't want to step on any toes."

I blink in shock. *A date? With Baker?* "Oh."

He blanches. "Oof, that didn't sound like a good 'oh'."

I huff a surprised laugh and rush to explain. "You're fine. I just wasn't expecting that you'd ask me out. Sorry. Um, my relationship with Flynn is—. Well, you see—." I struggle to form words to explain Flynn. I've never had to explain who he is; what our arrangement is. I don't do more than one-night stands with people who aren't Flynn, so he's never come up.

Baker laughs. "Wow, did I ask an impossible question? I feel like you're glitching right now."

I nod. "I'm not sure I'm not. I don't usually have to talk about what Flynn and I are to other people," I reply and can't keep the blush off my face. "Flynn is my best friend. When Flynn and I see each other, we *see* each other. When we don't, we don't, if that makes sense. Flynn will always be a part of my life, but we're not committed."

A curious frown creases his face. "So, you're free to see other people when Flynn's not around. Is that what you're saying?"

"Yes," I confirm.

"So, if I were to ask you out, is that something you might be interested in?"

I'd be lying if I said Baker wasn't attractive. I thought it the night of the party in Nashville and he's only grown more handsome in the last three years. He's easy to talk to and we laugh a lot. He's also sophisticated and brilliant, and lord knows I find intelligence extremely sexy. I blame Flynn for that.

"What did you have in mind?" I finally ask.

He grins and looks like he's won a million bucks. "How about drinks? Friday night?"

As I'm picking through my closet trying to decide what to wear for my date with Baker, my phone rings. Seeing it's Lana, I swipe the screen to answer the call. "And how is my favorite pregnant lady this evening?"

"Still throwing up fourteen times a day. How are you? I haven't talked with you since you got back from Vegas. How was Flynn? More importantly, how was the sex? Please spare no details. I am too sick to even let Forrest look at me, let alone get me naked, so I'm dying here."

"It was good. It's always good with Flynn. His dad's not doing great, so that was really sad. But, overall, good trip." I tilt my head as I examine a dark green shift dress. "If you were going for drinks with a multimillionaire state senator, what would you wear?"

She lets out a choked sound through the phone. "I'm sorry. Back up. Who? Drinks? When?"

"Tonight. In an hour, actually. I'm standing in front of my clothes rack and nothing is sitting right with me. I'm supposed to meet Baker at the bar down from my apartment."

"Baker? As in, your mentor, Baker?"

"That's the one. Except he's not my mentor anymore. He asked me out."

"Didn't he work with Flynn before? Won't it be weird if Flynn finds out you hooked up with someone he knows?"

"Flynn and I don't talk about the people we see when we're not together. And he doesn't *know* Baker. He was just the senior partner at the firm he interned with. He and Flynn didn't interact at all. But what would you wear? It's just drinks."

"Yeah, I know what your 'just drinks' turns into. Keep it casual, but hot. Those dark skinny jeans that make your ass look fantastic, black lace camisole to give just a hint of cleavage and your tattoo, thin cardigan, and those red Manolo pumps."

I shake my head in amazement. "How do you do that? I've been staring at my clothes for twenty minutes and within thirty seconds, you have a perfect pick for me."

She sighs. "It's a gift. So, do you like Baker? I mean, he's obviously successful, but is he hot? Do you guys vibe?"

"Baker is handsome and sophisticated. He's mature. He's easy to talk to and got all nervous when he asked me out. It was adorable. He knows about Flynn, which was strange to explain since I never have to do that with the other people I see. But I've talked about him and his dad so much in passing and he saw Flynn and me together at that party, so he asked if we were together."

"And what did you tell him? I swear, I don't know how you keep Flynn on the back burner while you have all these other guys you spend time with when you're not with him."

I bristle, suddenly defensive. "Flynn isn't on the back burner. That would imply I'm waiting for something to happen that would warrant me to be committed to him. I'm not. Flynn and I know what we are. He's my best friend. And yes, we have amazing sex and our chemistry is off the charts. But I have no desire to settle down and he knows that. Baker knows that when Flynn and I are together, we're together, but that we see other people when we're not."

"And does Baker know you have no desire to change your status with Flynn or anyone else? He's in his thirties, right? You don't think he's looking for, like, a wife, do you?"

I snort a laugh. "He'll have to look somewhere else for that. But no, we haven't talked about any of that because this is a first date. For all I know, it'll be a last date. No sense in delving into all of that before I've even had a glass of wine."

As I step into the familiar bar in the West Village, I feel as though I'm transported back in time. The cozy bar has velvet-topped stools, exposed brick walls, and handcrafted wood details scattered throughout the space.

Weaving through the crowd, I spot Baker at a green leather booth toward the back of the bar. He stands as I approach and for the first time ever, he's out of a suit. Dressed in dark wash jeans and a light blue button-down shirt with the sleeves rolled to the elbows and white low-top sneakers, he somehow still manages to look more put together than most men in a suit. He's also traded his shiny Rolex for a more subdued, but still sophisticated, Tag Heuer.

He greets me with a smile and a kiss on the cheek and I get a whiff of expensive cologne. "Brighten, my God, you look gorgeous."

I blush and push my hair, currently styled in loose curls, behind my ears. "Thank you, Baker. You look very handsome. I've never seen you not in a suit."

"Gotta change it up every once in a while. I honestly can't remember the last time I wore jeans, though. I miss them." He glances around as we slide into the horseshoe-shaped booth. "This is a fantastic bar. Have you been here before?"

"It's been a while. But it's not too far from campus, so it's an occasional pit stop. Do you come to New York often? Aside from what you're doing this semester?"

He opens his mouth to answer, and a server steps up to take our drink orders. I land on a glass of rosé, while Baker orders an old fashioned. Once the server steps away, he continues our conversation. "I make it up this way occasion-ally. Mainly to see a show or visit friends. Since Tanner's here, and we're pretty close, I try to come up at least once a month. He's like a brother to me, so I like to see him as often as I can."

"It must be difficult to juggle work and your duties to the general assembly and this mentorship *and* maintain friendships. When do you sleep?"

He laughs. "I don't sleep much. And when I do, it's on planes and in the back of Town Cars, or when I crash on my office sofa."

"Sounds like you're too busy," I supply, my tone matter-of-fact.

Baker splays his hands. "What can I say? I'll sleep when I'm dead, I guess. But I like to think I make time for the things that matter." He gives me a slow smile. "I definitely make time for beautiful women."

Blushing, I huff a laugh. "Wow, does that line actually work on 'beautiful women'?"

Our drinks arrive and he eyes me over his tumbler. "You tell me, Brighten."

"I guess we'll have to see, won't we?"

Two hours later, I'm unlocking the door to my apartment and yanking Baker inside with me. He slams the door with his foot and grabs my face for a deep kiss, pushing my cardigan off my shoulders as his mouth travels down my neck. Heat shoots through my middle and I gasp.

Pressing my hands into his chest, I pant. "Wait."

He stops, dropping his hands. "What? Did you change your mind?"

I shake my head. "No, I just need to say something."

"Okay."

I lick my lips and try to breathe. I'm honestly shocked by

how much I want Baker. I don't normally feel this way with anyone but Flynn and it's got me a bit discombobulated because it's good. Not sure yet if it beats Flynn, but at first glance it's pretty damn close.

"The guys I see don't know about Flynn. You do. I know this is a terrible time to bring him up, but regardless of what happens between the two of us, he's still there. I need you to know that. If you've got it in your head that if we sleep together once—or a hundred times, for that matter—that I'll choose you over him, I won't. He doesn't—and won't—ask me to choose him, but Flynn is a permanent fixture in my life. I like you, but you'll have to respect what I have with him. If that's a deal-breaker for you, I understand, but this isn't something I bend on."

Baker chuckles. "I do like a woman who knows her own mind. I'm good with your terms." His eyes travel down my face and briefly stop at my lips and continue south before rising to meet mine. "Do you have any additional matters to discuss before I get you naked?"

I shake my head as he closes the distance between us and slides his hand along my jaw to grip the back of my neck. Tugging him with me toward the bed, I slip off my shoes as he claims my mouth.

Approximately twenty seconds after we start kissing, I'm somehow divested of all of my clothing and Baker's shirt and belt are somewhere in the vicinity of my nightstand. He grips my shoulders and turns me around. "Get on your hands and knees."

Okay, I guess he's not big on foreplay. As his zipper descends, I obey and reach over and open my nightstand drawer and pull out a condom and hand it over to him. He takes it and I watch as he rolls it down. He climbs up behind me on the bed and grips my hips and slams into me and I gasp in pain because I'm not nearly wet enough. "Holy shit, you're tight," he says with a groan.

No shit, it's tight. I'm not ready.

I give it a few seconds to see if my body catches up and after a moment, it's not any better and I'm about to stop him when he grunts and collapses on top of me.

In utter shock, I simply blink, my mouth hanging open. He gives me a slap on the ass as he pulls out. "Thanks. I needed that."

I'm at such a loss, I don't even know how to respond. I've had less than satisfactory sex before. Normally, I can predict it. Either, they're a bad kisser or not very engaging in conversation. And having had everything from mediocre to really phenomenal sex, I have a pretty good gauge these days. Baker wasn't just bad, he was *abysmal*.

Rising from the bed, I slip on my robe and start gathering up my clothes to put in the hamper. Baker returns from the bathroom a moment later, fully dressed. "You said you were trying to get an internship with the governor, right?" He taps away at his phone, not even bothering to look up as he speaks to me.

Reeling from just how bad the last two—if that—minutes were, I answer him. "Oh. I applied, but haven't heard back yet."

Eyes still glued to his phone, he says, "I can put in a good word for you, if you want. I play golf with the lieutenant governor pretty regularly."

Having just had—terrible—sex with Baker, asking him to use his connections to grease the wheels to get me a spot makes me feel dirty. I shake my head. "That's okay. I've got some other irons in the fire. I'll figure something out. Thanks though."

He finally looks up at me. "It's no problem. You could always come intern for me, if you want."

"I think that would be a bad idea."

His brow furrows in confusion. "Why, because we fucked?"

I wouldn't say "we" fucked. You fucked.

"Yeah. I don't sleep with people I work with; especially superiors."

He huffs a dismissive laugh. "You were happy to take me up on my offer of a date about three seconds after I was done being your mentor."

I scoff and put my hands on my hips. "You asked me. I had no intention of asking you. I was flattered, so I said yes."

My phone vibrates in my purse and I walk over to pick it up off the floor and dig it out. I instantly relax seeing Flynn's name on the screen and look back up at Baker. "I need to get this."

"So, what, I'm being dismissed?" he asks, his tone incredulous.

I frown, confused. "Was there something else you needed? It seems like you're ready to leave anyway. You didn't even take off your shoes." My phone stops ringing in my hand and now I'm even more annoyed because I missed Flynn's call.

Baker closes the distance between us. "Guess you don't need to get that anymore, huh? You want to watch a movie or something?"

I nearly laugh. I'm so far past the point of done I can't even see it in my rearview mirror anymore. "Actually, I can't. I need to return this call. Thank you for drinks, though; I enjoyed talking with you." It's not a lie. That part of the evening was exceptional. I'm still so perplexed as to how the conversation, flirting, and kissing could be so good and the actual sex fall apart. It boggles the mind.

He examines my face. "Yeah, it was fun. Maybe we can do it again sometime."

Not wanting to lie and also not wanting to bruise his ego, I give him a noncommittal shrug. "Maybe."

He reaches to lift my chin and smiles, and I have to force myself not to pull away. When he leans in to kiss me, I offer him my cheek and something like irritation flashes in his eyes, but it's gone just as quickly. "I'll call you."

I can't get the door shut and locked behind Baker fast enough once he's gone. As I return Flynn's call, I strip the bed, needing to rid myself of every part of Baker's presence. "Hey, Crash."

"Hey," I say with a smile. I only saw him a few weeks ago, but I miss him. "What's up?"

"Well, believe it or not, I'm headed your way."

I freeze, my heart lurching. "What? You're coming to New York? Since when? When are you coming?"

Flynn chuckles down the line. "It wasn't exactly planned. My Friday night class got cancelled and I'm finished with my Monday class, except for the final. I thought I'd surprise you. I mean, if you don't have plans. I probably should've checked. I had a wild hair and there was a flight and I had some credit card points so I cashed them in."

"Yes," I say automatically, excitement filling me at the thought of seeing him. "Get here."

He breathes a sigh of relief. "Thank God. I got on the plane and halfway here, I worried you might not be cool with me coming since I've never been to see you and I don't know what the protocol is. We normally have more notice than this when we're going to meet up, so I was just hoping I didn't ruin any plans for you."

Touched by his spontaneity, I can't keep the smile off my face. "Flynn, I would've changed my plans for you." It hits me in that moment that I would have dropped whatever I was doing when Flynn called. Would I have even kicked Baker out?

Yes. What if the sex had been good? Would I still have preferred to see Flynn? Always.

"But I didn't wreck anything? You're sure?"

I shake my head, even though he can't see me. "No. I promise. You've got my address, right?"

"Yeah. According to the taxi driver I should be there in about thirty minutes."

Happy I'll have time to shower and change my sheets, I move around the apartment, readying for his arrival. "Perfect. Just hit the buzzer when you get here?"

"You've got it."

CHAPTER TWENTY-ONE

FLYNN

I shove my phone in my pocket and tap my foot, willing the taxi to get me to Brighten faster. Showing up unexpectedly isn't something I would usually ever do, but I miss her and like I told her, I got a wild hair. I didn't even consider until the plane was already in the air that she may have had a date. That would've been awkward.

It's nearly ten PM when the taxi drops me off at Brighten's apartment on Bleecker Street in the West Village. I hoist my backpack higher on my shoulder and make my way over to the door of her apartment building. Her third-floor walk-up is situated above a little bike shop and between a pizzeria and a butcher shop.

Finding the button to ring her apartment, I hold it down and release it. A moment later, once she confirms it's me, the door buzzes and I take the stairs up to her place.

She must be standing at the peephole watching for me, because no sooner have I stepped in front of her door, does it open, revealing the woman I love, clad only in a silk bathrobe.

Her hair is damp and her face is free from makeup and she

pulls me into the apartment, slamming the door behind me and flipping the lock. I drop my bag and grip her shoulders and simply look at her for a moment. "I know it's only been a few weeks since I last saw you, but damn, Crash, I've missed you so fucking much."

She nods. "Me, too. We kept missing each other's calls and finishing up papers has been ridiculous. You have no idea what a nice surprise this is." Grabbing my hand, she tugs me farther into the apartment. "It's not much, but for now, it's home."

I look around at the tiny studio apartment. It has white walls and warm laminate floors. The kitchen consists of a stove, fridge, sink, and barely enough counter space for a coffee maker. Dining space consists of a bar large enough to seat two.

"No pink in sight," I say with a grin. "Not even a pink shirt."

She loops her arms around my waist. "There might be a pair of pink panties, but that's about it."

"I don't give a fuck what color your panties are."

Brighten laughs. "I know. You'd prefer me with no panties."

"Very true." I drop a kiss on her lips and she sighs contentedly. When I pull back, I ask, "Do you have plans for this weekend? Again, I should've verified. Sorry."

"No plans. It's great you're here. I can show you around the neighborhood and campus; there are some great bars. There's a ton of stuff right around my building."

I nod. "I noticed that. How's the pizza place next door?"

"Pretty good. We can go tomorrow, if you want."

"Definitely. First, though, I'm going to grab a shower if that's okay? Airplanes are gross."

"Sure, towels are below the sink."

I pick my bag up and take it into the bathroom with me, not bothering to close the door. The room is modern, with white tile floors and gray tile walls. After taking a five-minute shower,

I dry off and pull on some boxers and hang up my towel before heading back out to the bedroom.

Brighten is sitting on the bed reading with her legs folded, her robe loose and showing quite a lot of her cleavage and tattoo. "That is a nice sight," I say with a grin as I climb onto the bed with her. Leaning against the headboard of her simple black wooden bed, I stretch my legs out and reach over to tuck her hair behind her ear so I can see her face.

She smiles as she slides a bookmark into the autobiography she's reading and drops it to the floor beside her bed before rising to her knees and straddling me. I run my hands up her thighs. "Very nice, Crash."

"What, me naked under this robe, or my place?"

"Yes," I reply, making her laugh. She leans in and captures my bottom lip between her teeth and tugs before sweeping her tongue into my mouth and making me groan. I can't resist kneading the supple flesh of her thighs and ass as she rolls her hips above me. My dick springs to life and she smiles into our kiss.

I pull my mouth from hers and run the tip of my nose along her jaw. "You miss my cock?"

"You have no idea."

I huff a laugh. "What, the pickings less than exemplary these days?"

She frowns. "I thought you didn't want to hear about other guys."

Shaking my head, I shrug. "I only want to hear if I'm better than them. Not so much if there's someone else out there who rocks your world because, you know, ego."

Brighten bites her lip. "You are better than them. All of them."

I snort a laugh. "I don't need to be sold down the river, Crash. A simple, 'you're a good fuck' will do nicely."

She takes my face in her hands. "You are a good fuck. Excellent, actually. But you know you're more than just that to me. No one else knows me like you do. No one else is my best friend, Flynn."

Nodding, I turn my head to press a kiss to her palm. "I know. No one knows me like you do, either."

Brighten trails her fingers down my chest until her hands come level with the sash at her waist. "No one else knows I like a single onion ring with my burger." She works the knot loose and I watch as the robe falls open. "No one knows that I take the curves too fast and ride too close to the edge in *Mario Kart*." The robe slides down her shoulders and arms, revealing all of her tattoo. "No one else can tell I'm anxious simply by the sound of my voice and know exactly what to say to talk me down."

I can't resist bending to kiss and lick across where her scar is, and she sighs. "No one else knows what's under that feather." Threading her fingers through my hair, she holds me in place as she arches her back, her nipple brushing against my lips. I suck it into my mouth and she moans, the peak growing taut and stiff under my tongue.

Breathing in her clean, floral scent, I tug her closer, her pussy slotting right up against my dick, even through my boxers. She huffs a breath and I can feel the heat of her radiating through the fabric and it's all I can do to not simply take myself out and claim her. To remind her that no one will love her body as well as I do.

I also want to tell her no one will love her like I do, but I won't. Our last couple of visits have been overshadowed by our emotions and conversations that were necessary but definitely put a damper on things. I'm not here to do that this weekend. I just want to see my girl—who will never fully be mine—and enjoy whatever time I can with her. So I say nothing.

When I pull my mouth off her nipple, it's with an audible *pop* and Brighten gasps and writhes in my lap. I let out a soft laugh as I kiss my way back up to her mouth. "What's funny?" she asks, her voice breathy.

I shake my head and lick a line up her neck. "That wasn't a funny laugh. That was a contented one. Your sounds make me happy. Knowing that the things I do to you make you feel good makes me happy." I grip her chin in one hand and force her to look me in the eye while I drag a knuckle down her sternum and stomach with the other. "Your sounds are the things I dream about."

Parting her folds, I brush the pad of my middle finger over her clit and she inhales sharply, her eyes still locked on mine as I begin to work her already swollen clit. "That sound right there? I could come just thinking about it." I nip at her bottom lip. "I do a lot of times. When I get myself off, it's always with the thought of your face and those sounds."

Her mouth falls open on a sigh. "Oh God, Flynn."

I give her a slow smile. "And my name on your lips? Fucking hell, Crash. I could die."

She gives me an amused smile, even as she rolls her hips and moans. "You can't die. I need your dick too bad."

I laugh and slide my free hand around to the back of her neck and pull her mouth to mine for a deep kiss before breaking it to press my forehead to hers. "You want my dick now?"

"Yeah. Fuck."

"Come for me and you can have it."

Frantic, she claims my mouth and whines into our kiss before her lips part on a ragged huff and her body shudders in my arms.

I can't keep the smile off my face as she pulls back, her eyes nearly glazed. She blinks for a moment, letting her mind clear, before reaching over to her nightstand and pulling a condom out of the drawer and handing it over.

Taking it from her, I rip the wrapper with my teeth as I shuck my boxers with my other hand and lie down. Brighten drops her robe to the floor and no sooner have I rolled the condom down, does she straddle my lap again. Her eyes don't leave mine as she grips my cock and guides it past her entrance.

For a split second, something like pain flickers in her gaze and I'm worried. "You okay? Does it hurt?"

She shakes her head. "I'm alright."

Brighten begins to roll her hips, but I grab them to still her, despite my body's protests. I don't want to ask the question I'm about to, but I also don't want to make things worse if someone else was too rough with her and she doesn't need to do this. "Are you sore? Did something—. I mean, was another guy—."

She puts her finger to my lips to silence me. "I'm fine, Flynn. You always take care of me, you know that?" Confused by her question, even if it's true, I can only nod. "Okay, so take care of me now. Make love to me?"

And even though I know she doesn't mean it like, *I love you and want to share myself with you*, that's exactly what it is for me. So, I loosen my hold on her hips to free her movements and watch as she takes her pleasure, a look of relaxed enjoyment on her face.

Although she said she's fine, I've never seen her make a face anything like she did tonight and I'm not sure she was completely honest. The thought of anyone not treating her body with the reverence it deserves or simply using her and not taking the time to ensure things are good for her makes me want to tear someone limb from limb.

When she moans, I'm brought back to the moment and mindful of the fact she might be sore as I thrust my hips up, I keep my movements gentle. She drops her head forward, her hair following suit, and I push it off her face, needing to see her. There's no greater sight on the planet that watching Brighten Dawes get off.

Tonight is no exception. As she gets closer to her orgasm, a flush fills her cheeks and travels down her torso and her chest heaves with her labored breaths. Her fingers grip my sides, her nails digging in to my skin, heightening my awareness and making me groan with the tinge of pain mingling with my pleasure.

"Oh fuck, Flynn. God, I'm so close."

I huff a jagged exhale, my own climax bearing down on me. "I know, baby. I've got you. Shit, you feel so fucking good."

She throws her head back, and braces her hands on my chest as she seems to get lost in herself, her moans devolving into short, stilted pants. "Fuck. Oh, fuck. Sweet Jesus, Flynn." I grit my teeth and hold on for dear life as she lets go. "Fuck, yes. Oh, God," she whimpers as her pussy clenches down around my dick so hard I gasp.

"Fuck, Crash. Shit. You're going to to make me come."

She nods, even as she tries to breathe. "Give it to me. Fuck, I want you to come. Please." As if triggered by her words alone, electric heat sparks up my spine and down my limbs as I buck my hips one last time with a grunt.

Brighten collapses onto my chest and buries her face in my neck, and I wrap my arms around her and roll us on our sides. For a long moment, I simply hold her, relishing the feeling of her in my arms. She sighs contentedly and pulls back to look at me. "I don't want to give you a big head or anything, but damn."

I laugh and press a kiss to her lips. "You, too."

CHAPTER TWENTY-TWO

BRIGHTEN

As I roll over and stretch, I reach for Flynn, only to find his side of the bed cold. The sun is barely up, but I guess his runs don't wait. If I'm honest, I'm kinda sad he was gone when I woke up. I would've preferred to be able to snuggle up to him.

Thinking back on last night as I rise from the bed to go pee, I'm shocked he knew about me being sore. And I know if I had hesitated at all or decided I didn't want to have sex, he would've been fine with it. Even knowing he doesn't want to talk about the other people I'm with, the fact that he'd still ask to gauge how okay I was, makes something twist in my chest.

Flynn takes such good care of me and all I can give him is crumbs. He is my favorite person on the planet and I can only offer him a fraction of what he deserves? What is wrong with me?

After the experience with Baker and then Flynn directly after, I'm reminded that with most of the people I see, they've got good pregame but suck when it comes to the actual act. Or, they're strictly fun and can't stimulate me intellectually. I thought Baker might be good at both, considering our time at the bar and what a good kisser he was. But it was like flipping a switch.

No one is the entire package like Flynn. He's brilliant, honest, funny, kind, sweet, and God, is he good in bed. He's the person who knows me best and has never stopped putting me first. He is my best friend; the person who is my constant. What is that, if not the best I'm ever going to get?

Slipping on the T-shirt he was wearing last night, I pad over to my tiny kitchen to start a pot of coffee. I'm just pouring the water into the carafe when the buzzer sounds. Flynn huffs from the other end as I confirm it's him and I buzz him into the building.

I finish setting the coffee to brew and go wait at the door to let him in. He's sweaty and smells like himself and outside and I let my eyes drag down his body where his shirt clings to his torso. He gives me a quick kiss and chuckles. "You look at me like I didn't just fuck you senseless eight hours ago."

"What can I say, you're pretty addicting." I loop my arms around his shoulders. "I might need another fix."

"I'm all sweaty," he warns. "But I gotta say, I do love seeing you in my shirt."

"Me, too. I might have to keep this one."

Pleasant surprise flashes in his eyes and he shoots me that lopsided grin. "It's yours." He leans in and brushes a kiss down my neck. "On one condition."

I thread my fingers into his hair and tilt my head as he runs his hands down my sides and over my butt to lift me off the floor. "What's that?" I ask, wrapping my legs around his waist.

He begins walking toward the bathroom, peppering my face with kisses. "If you promise to wear it whenever you get yourself off."

I huff a laugh, desire shooting through my middle. He

drops me to the floor and starts the shower before tugging the shirt over my head. "I think I can do that," I agree.

Flynn strips out of his own clothes and pulls me under the spray with him. "It's a good thing you're not wearing it now."

"Why?"

He presses me against the shower wall and nudges his knee between my thighs. "Because it means I get to be the one to get you off."

I let out a sigh as he kisses his way down my neck, the warm water cascading down our bodies. "That's good, because you're a lot better at it than I am."

He laughs against my skin and for the next half-hour, proceeds to make me glad I'm not the one having to get myself off. And yeah, I totally wasn't lying. He's so much fucking better at it than I am. He's better at it than anyone else, too.

The next morning, when Flynn stirs, I'm already awake. As he sits up, I rise to my knees and wrap my arms around him. "Skip your run this morning. I want to snuggle."

He huffs a laugh. "I going to need some carbs and protein to *snuggle* with you."

I shake my head, brushing kisses across his shoulder blades. "No, I just want you to hold me," I admit.

He turns his face toward me, his eyes searching mine, his expression puzzled, but then he shutters it. I know he's confused because honestly, I am, too. I don't really cuddle, but today, I want it. "Okay, Crash," he says after a beat and lies back down and pulls me into his arms.

Burrowing deeper under the covers and into his chest, I tangle my legs with his and breathe him in. He sweeps the hair off my forehead and drops a kiss on the bare skin. I could go back to sleep like this, but I'd rather stay awake and talk to him.

"Are you excited about your internship?"

"Yeah, it should be alright. I would love to work with Elias again, because he is such a great mentor. But he's still giving me advice, so I guess, in a way, I am."

"He seemed really fond of you. I'm sure he'll be a good resource for you when you start looking for jobs."

He nods, dragging his fingers down my back. "He's dropping hints about staring his own firm, so that would be amazing. A little risky to get in with an upstart, but if anyone can do it, it's Elias. He's got more knowledge about the industry in his pinky than most analysts have in their whole body."

Changing the subject, he asks, "Are you nervous about taking your LSATs?"

After a moment to consider, I sigh. "Not really. I've got a study guide and I feel like, at this point, I've almost got it memorized. Pretty sure I've read through it about a thousand times."

"And are you still set on GW or Georgetown? Or have you been looking at other schools, too?"

"I figure I want to be in D.C., so might as well start there, right?"

"Right. And have you heard back about that internship with the governor?"

Thinking about that makes me think about Baker and I grimace, glad Flynn can't currently see my face. If I get it, I'm going to assume Baker had something to do with it. No way in hell I'd take it now. "I didn't get it."

"That sucks. I'm sorry. I know you were hoping for that one."

I shrug. "There will be others. If nothing else, I can work this summer and just focus on crushing my LSATs."

"You will. You'll score a hundred."

I snort a laugh. "Then I will have failed."

He laughs and turns my face up to his, his expression tender. "I know. I just really like to hear you laugh. It's my favorite one in the whole world." He presses a kiss to my lips. "*Mon endroit préféré c'est avec toi.*"

A bark of surprised laughter leaves my mouth. "When did you learn French? And what the hell did you say?"

He grins. "Mom's always wanted to go to France. Dad made me promise to take her. God knows I'm not going to go somewhere that I won't be able to understand the insults. I've been at it for a few months."

My mouth falls open. "How did I not know this?"

He shrugs. "Until recently, it was still pretty terrible."

"What did you say?" I ask, unsure of what I hope to hear. So far, this visit hasn't resulted in tears; which seems to be a bit out of the norm for us as of late. But I still want to know.

His eyes roam over my face and he drags the back of his index finger along my jaw. "My favorite place is with you."

I nod. "Mine, too," I admit.

He doesn't say anything, just tilts my head down to press his lips to my forehead. He releases a long exhale through his nose before pulling his mouth away and resting his chin on the top of my head.

———

For the second morning in a row, I'm awake before Flynn. And unlike yesterday, he's not stirring seconds after I do. This morning, I simply watch him sleep. It's not something I've ever really gotten to do whenever we've been together. Since his time in Nashville, he's gotten pretty accustomed to rising early, running, and beginning his day.

After spending all day playing tourists around the West Village and the NYU campus yesterday, it's no wonder he's tired. I am, too, but he leaves today, so subconsciously, I must be wanting a little more time with him.

He's currently still out cold and as I trace the plains and ridges of his face with my eyes, I think about the boy he was when we first started this thing. His brows are fuller, his jaw more chiseled, his acne, braces, and glasses all gone. He has two days of beard growth from where he's forgone his razor during his visit. He's still young—we both are—but he's a man.

However, if I squint, I can still see that sweet boy who witnessed my calamity and ran to help me. He stayed with me and kept me awake until the ambulance arrived to take me to the hospital. He made his parents bring him immediately and stayed in the waiting room until I could receive visitors. And when he was finally allowed into my room, he read to me.

Even now, he witnesses my calamities and anxieties and helps me work them out. He's my biggest cheerleader, and he's never doubted the things I want for myself. When I told him at age fourteen that I wanted to be President, he simply asked me if he could chill in the oval office with me. How did I get so lucky to have a best friend like him?

He says he doesn't need more than I can give him. He says he's content with our arrangement. Eventually, though, he's going to want a family, right? What if he didn't? What if he was content to only have me? And what if he was content to not cohabitate full-time? I know he loves me. I'm not sure I know what love is in the I-want-to-grow-old-with-you sort of way, but Flynn is the epitome of love. He's selfless, kind, generous, and thoughtful.

Could I possibly be content with only him? Lord knows no one satisfies me sexually or intellectually as much as he does. No one I've been with has ever come close.

Maybe I can see. Maybe if I figure out over the coming months what, if anything, I truly want, I can talk with Flynn about it. He says he's happy with anything I want. This is the twenty-first century, right? Who says you have to have marriage or "traditional" commitment to be with someone? Maybe we can chart our own path.

What if he's the only one I want? What if I asked him to let me be the only one he wants? I mean, I think I know how that interaction would go and thinking about the elated look on Flynn's face if I were to tell him I didn't want anyone else makes me smile.

PART 3

COLLEGE, SENIOR YEAR

14 YEARS AGO

CHAPTER TWENTY-THREE

BRIGHTEN

Two-and-a-half months. Seventy days. Ten weeks. That's how long it's been since I've had sex. Because I haven't seen Flynn. I've spoken with him, texted with him, sexted with him. I have not seen him. I have not jumped his bones. I haven't jumped anyone's bones except my own...while wearing Flynn's T-shirt.

And honestly, I'm finding it's not that hard to turn down other men. Even hot ones. So, maybe I can do this monogamy thing?

I purposely don't think about what Flynn's been up to in Atlanta during his internship this summer. I don't think about him kissing or sleeping with other women. I don't think about him falling in love with anyone else.

Five days. One hundred twenty hours. That's how long until I see him again. He's flying in to attend Lana's wedding with me and God, am I dying.

Unfortunately, that day isn't today, though. No, today is the day I rip everything off my clothes rack in an attempt to find something that fits. At the moment, nothing does. Apparently, lack of sex makes me want to eat my feelings, because everything is too small. Sighing, I look at all the dresses littering my bed and know I'll have to go shopping. And sighing again, I hang them back up.

A knock at the door makes me pause and for a brief second, I have a wild fantasy about Flynn surprising me and us spending the entire week together. The thought alone nearly makes me swoon. "One minute," I yell as I hurriedly put everything back on the rack. Jogging over to the door and looking through the peephole, my smile falls.

What the hell is Baker doing here?

I've intentionally avoided his calls and left his texts on delivered. I figured that was a pretty good indication I wanted nothing to do with him.

Arousal is quickly replaced with annoyance and I sigh for a third time and keep the chain on the door as I open it. He's wearing his standard suit and looks perfectly put together. I'm aware I'm currently in jogging shorts and Flynn's T-shirt and I haven't washed my hair in three days. I almost want to laugh. Maybe I really am going to be able to do the monogamy thing since I couldn't care less what Baker sees when he looks at me. Or maybe it's just Baker and my dislike of him that has me not giving a shit.

"Can I help you?" I'm aware I sound curt. Again, I don't give a shit.

"So you are alive. I assumed since you weren't answering my calls or texts, you'd perished in some horrible fashion." He chuckles as if he's laughing at his own joke.

"And I assumed if I didn't communicate with you, you'd get the hint that I wasn't interested. So, what can I do for you?"

"May I come in?"

"I'm not sure I'd like that."

"It's important. Please?"

I have no idea what Baker considers "important" that might

involve me, but I heave yet another sigh and unchain the door and open it to let him pass. He has an honest-to-God briefcase, and he's not alone. A slim white man, about his age, with jet black hair and blue eyes, carrying a small black bag, follows him in. I frown. "Who's he?"

"He will be explained."

I focus on trying to be patient, but I really don't like Baker and don't enjoy having him in my space. He doesn't look too thrilled to be here either, judging by the look of disdain on his face. "Brighten, come sit, please." He takes a seat on one of my bar stools and pats the other, and I reluctantly join him, wanting to get this over with.

He flips the latches on the briefcase where it sits on the bar, but makes no move to open it. The other man simply stands against the wall next to the bathroom and his expression remains neutral.

"What do you want, Baker?"

He taps his fingers on the top of his briefcase, rolling them from pinky to index finger in an annoying rhythm. I repeat my question and he stops drumming. "It's not really about what I want. It's about what *you* want. Or, more importantly, what you're going to do."

Confused, I blink. "What are you talking about?"

Not answering my question, he asks another one. "How are you feeling these days?"

I splay my hands, my annoyance growing by the minute. "Fine. Why?"

"So, no fatigue or nausea or increased urination or breast tenderness?"

"Excuse me? What the hell business is it of yours regarding the condition of my breasts? Last I checked, it's not."

He gives me a placid smile. "It is if you're pregnant with my child."

I snort a laugh. "Um, yeah, I think not. You wore a condom for the thirty seconds it took you to get off and I have an IUD."

He doesn't react to my barb about his ability in bed, even with his friend with him, and resumes tapping his fingers. He stops abruptly and grins. "Oh, the IUD you received on your last visit to see your gynecologist four months ago?"

I blink, unsure how he'd know that. "What's your point?"

He stands and paces, his fingers laced behind his back, as if he's getting ready to deliver a lecture. "I want to tell you a story, Brighten. Will you indulge me for a moment?"

I roll my eyes. "Do I have a choice?"

He grins, but there's no warmth in it. "Not really."

"Then proceed, I guess."

"Thank you," he replies, his tone even. "When I was nineteen, I was in love with a beautiful girl. We attended different colleges but had plans to someday get married and have a family. Unfortunately, she was killed by a drunk driver and everything I wanted for my life was stolen away because of someone who didn't even have the decency to call a taxi." His jaw clenches and apparently, fifteen years later, this is still a sore subject for him.

"I'm sorry to hear that, Baker." Because what else am I going to say?

"Yes, well, it gets worse. The person who killed my beautiful and vibrant Anna was never brought to justice. Because of their position in power—the friends and influence they possessed—it was ruled an accident with no one at fault. And I vowed that day that I would become powerful enough to change things in the future so no one else would have to lose someone they love to a reckless drunk."

I nod. "It seems as though you're on your way to being able to make the changes you want. I'm not sure what this has to do with me."

He turns his gaze on me. "The person who killed Anna was your mother, Brighten."

His tone is matter-of-fact and devoid of emotion, as if he's delivering a weather report. My heart pounds. I know—I've always known—my mother is an alcoholic. She normally doesn't even drive. Did she back then? I simply ask, "Do you have proof of this?"

He returns to the briefcase and lifts the lid and fishes out a folder and hands it over. I lay it on the counter and begin to open it and he lays his hand on top. "I'm warning you; it's graphic."

I nod and steel myself before flipping it open. On top, there's a police report listing the details of the two-car accident on a road not too far from our house in Knoxville. My eyes widen when I see my mother's name listed as one of the drivers, along with a remark about her blood alcohol content level being at zero-point-two-eight. I snap my head up. "Point-two-eight? How is that possible?"

He shrugs. "Keep reading."

Returning my eyes to the page, the report states that my mother was traveling at a high rate of speed and crossed the double yellow line and collided head-on with another vehicle, killing the other driver. The name of the other driver is listed as Anna Abernathy, age eighteen.

Flipping the page, I notice there are photos of the accident. My stomach drops when I see two hunks of metal, one red, one blue, practically in one large mass. If it weren't for the colors of the two cars, you'd never know they were separate entities. Further past the images of the cars themselves, there's a photo of the driver's seat of the smaller of the two vehicles, the blue one. All you see is a torso slumped against the steering wheel.

There is no head to speak of. Only blood. So much blood against the backdrop of the tan interior of what's left of the car.

Nausea roils in my belly, and I tamp down the urge to vomit and force myself to move to the next photo, terrified of what I'll find.

Sure enough, this one is so much worse. It's only a head, in what looks to be the back seat. Blood, glass, and blonde hair are all matted together, the face a gruesome mask of terror, blue eyes open but unseeing, mouth ajar. Was that the expression she wore when my mother killed her?

I scramble from the stool and run to the bathroom, barely making it to the toilet before I'm puking up everything I've eaten today. I'm sick until there's only bile and then dry heaving as tears stream down my face.

Sometime while I was losing my breakfast and lunch, Baker has joined me in the bathroom. He extends a damp washcloth in my direction and I take it and clean my face. He returns to the bar and flips to the end of the folder and brings something back to me. I eye it warily, unsure if I can handle another photo.

He shakes his head, seeing my unease. "It's not a picture. It's the report that eventually got put into evidence."

I get to my feet and flush the toilet and rinse my mouth at the sink before actually taking the document. As I walk back to my seat at the bar, I read the modified report. My mother's name is still on it, as is Anna's, but nothing about Vanessa's BAC or the speed being a factor. Cause of the accident is listed as vehicle malfunction; namely, the brakes failing. It was ruled an accident. My mouth falls open and I look back up at Baker, who now stands in my kitchen.

"It was covered up?" I ask, incredulous.

He helps himself to a cup of coffee and nods, sipping his mug. "Yes. By your father."

I shake my head automatically. "No way. My father was a good man. I can believe this is something Vanessa would do; she's a drunk. My dad was decent and served the people."

Baker sighs, resigned. He pulls the briefcase to the other side of the bar and lifts the lid again and plucks out a newspaper clipping. "Read the caption."

I take it from him and look at the image. It's old, dated from 1987, a year before I was born. Six months before I was born, to be more accurate. *Knox County mayoral hopeful Gregory Dawes says "I do" to actress Vanessa Eldridge in Las Vegas today. Witnesses to the happy affair were Dawes's longtime friends, Keith and Melissa Conners.*

After reading it, I hand it back and he taps the police report. "Look at who the reporting officer is." I pick it up and look it over, my eyes catching on a name: Keith Conners.

I still shake my head. "My father wouldn't do this. He wasn't corrupt. He was a good man." But even to my own ears, I sound unsure.

Baker takes the folder with the photos and reports and returns them to the briefcase. "Brighten, men will do almost anything for the woman they love. Your father covered it up to protect your mother. I can't say I wouldn't do the same thing for Anna or that Flynn wouldn't do the same sort of thing for you."

"Don't talk about him," I warn.

"He loves you, though, right? He'd do nearly anything for you."

I sigh. "Baker, I still don't know what any of this has to do with me. I'm very sorry for the role my parents played in your girlfriend's death, but my father's dead. My mother is...probably not far off, honestly."

"Well, you see, I can't exact revenge on the people I want, because yes, your father is dead. Conners is also dead. I had planned to ruin your mother, but she seems to be doing a fair job of that all on her own. Of course, a few calls to some studios didn't hurt. So, no, I can't fuck over my enemies, but I can and did fuck their daughter."

My cheeks heat. "If that's what you want to call it. Thirty seconds ain't much to brag about, pal."

His nostrils flare and his jaw clenches. "Do you think I wanted to fuck you? I had to take a Viagra to even get it up thinking about you. You look so much like your mother, it makes me almost physically ill to look at you."

"Then why? Why are you here telling me all of this? You want to take out my mother, have at it. I don't give a shit. Lock her up for all I care."

He doesn't say anything and opens the briefcase again. "Jesus Christ, just leave it open. Cut the dramatics, Baker," I spit out and fold my arms. He tosses a box onto the bar in front of me and my heart lurches, my mouth going dry. I don't touch it. I want to be about forty feet away from it. "What the fuck am I supposed to do with that?"

"You're going to march your ass into that bathroom and pee on that stick and confirm what I already know."

"I'm not fucking pregnant, Baker. You wore a condom. I have an IUD."

He grins, but this time, it's menacing and my heart rate spikes. "What IUD?"

"The one I got four months ago, like you said."

"Actually, you didn't. Amazing what you can convince people to do for money. Or, not do, as the case were."

Sudden anxiety grips me. "What? What are you talking about?"

"Brighten, this plan of mine has been in the works for a long time. Things have been expedited, but honestly, that's no real hardship to me. It's hard to run on a platform that values family if you're single at thirty-five. No one would accept that. They would speculate that I'm gay, even if I'm not. Regardless of the fact this is the twenty-first century, people like first families. They don't like governors who are bachelors. It makes them think something is wrong if a good looking, successful man can't find a woman or doesn't have children.

"Never-been-married single dads are also a no-go, since that gives the impression he's reckless and would be reckless with their tax dollars. Widowers earn a sympathy vote, but a single guy, unattached without kids? Go ahead and kill the campaign before it's even started.

"My original plan involved taking down your father and mother, but I can't do that. So, I'll do the next best thing and give myself a leg up in my career in the process. I'll marry their daughter in a whirlwind romance and pop out a campaign baby. Jesus, the headlines write themselves."

CHAPTER TWENTY-FOUR

BRIGHTEN

I laugh. Not because it's funny. None of this is anywhere close to funny. This is my nightmare come to life. "I can't marry you. I won't. I don't have any desire to ever get married. I'm also not having a baby. I don't give a shit what that test says. If I'm pregnant, I won't be for long, I can guarantee you that. I don't want to be a mother."

Baker's demeanor remains calm. "Well, I don't want to live in a world without Anna and yet, here we are. And you will marry me. You will have this baby."

"You can't make me. This is still a free country, last I checked. This is New York. I can walk into a clinic today and not be pregnant when I walk out."

He nods. "You know, I thought you might put up some resistance. I understand; it's a lot to absorb." He slides the pregnancy test to the side and lays another folder on the bar and I look at it like it will bite me. "You have political ambitions. I truly admire that about you. You're bright and driven; you've got the chops to succeed. But the public tends to frown on plagiarism. So do colleges. They also frown on students attempting to seduce their professors and mentors for grades."

My mouth falls open. "None of that is true and you know it."

He gives me an indulgent smile. "Yes, you are bright, but a bit naïve, it would seem." Flipping open the folder, he taps the papers inside. "It's not what's actually true, Brighten. It's what can be spun to be believed. A paper purchased online from your computer to turn in. Tanner has emails you sent him from your NYU email address that state you'd be willing to do 'just about anything' to ensure you pass his class.

"And God knows you pursued me. We went out, and you seduced me not two days following our professional relationship ending. Who's to say you hadn't been after me all semester? I'm only a weak man, after all. You're a beautiful young woman; who would turn you down?"

Fury courses through my veins. "This is bullshit."

"Maybe, but photos and emails don't lie. Tanner would be happy to, though. You see, Anna was his sister."

All the breath leaves my body. "This is blackmail," I say weakly.

"Yes, it is. I'm a businessman and politician, Brighten. You have no idea the lengths I will go to get what I want."

"I won't do it."

"You know, the public also typically frowns on sex work. And for the record, I personally have nothing against sex workers; oldest profession in the world and all that. But you really should be more discriminating about the people you let come home with you. Some of them have no qualms about taking money and signing an affidavit."

I reel, disbelief slowly giving way to abject terror.

Baker shrugs. "Like I said, I'll do what I have to do." He pulls out another folder. "And I'm sorry to say, photos of future presidential hopefuls performing sex acts? Oof, that's a really hard sell, I would think."

Tears spring to my eyes, nausea roiling in my guts again at the idea of this immense violation of my privacy. "Photos of me having sex?"

He nods. "So many," he says, his tone almost sounding impressed. "I mean, not any since the night Flynn and I were both here. What's up with that? Don't tell me you've finally decided he's the only one for you?"

He must see some sort of confirmation in my gaze because he offers me a sad chuckle. "Oh, that's sweet. And ill-timed, unfortunately." He taps the folder. "Don't believe me? See for yourself."

Not sure I'd ever want to see what I look like having sex, I still open the folder. It's thick. Baker's right, there are a lot of photos. There are a lot of men and even a few women. Some of the faces, I recognize from over a year ago. Something in my chest twists when I see the last ones. They're of Flynn and me. I don't even try to stop the tears as they roll down my face.

"You don't get to slut shame when you can't even classify yourself as a minute man, Baker. Convenient that there aren't any of you, wouldn't you say?" I ask angrily and push the folder away.

He shrugs. "I can't have that getting out. What would that do for my career?"

"Why, Baker? I'm sure there are a ton of women who will happily marry you and have your babies. Why me? I didn't have anything to do with Anna's death."

He blinks. "Actually, you did."

I frown. "How? I was six years old."

"Yes, but your mother was leaving your first piano recital. If you hadn't had a recital, she might've stayed home. Anna would still be alive. She'd be my wife and the mother of my children.

So yes, you did have something to do with her death, even if I don't hold you personally responsible. Which is why I'm giving you this choice.

"You can marry me, have the baby, and someday reach all of your goals. Once I'm Governor, we can amicably divorce. The public is much happier to accept a divorce rather than a single man. Such bullshit," he says, disgusted.

"That could be years. I'm not chaining myself to you for what could be a decade or longer; if you even get elected."

"Well then, you better get to campaigning." He picks up the pregnancy test and drops it back in front of me. "One more piece of incentive for you. If you don't do this, Flynn will never work in any capacity in market research. All his hard work, valedictorian of his high school, those grueling summer internships, being on track to graduate cum laude and have his pick of jobs; it's all for nothing."

His head tilts in consideration. "Actually, let's make it *any* industry. One word from me and he won't even be able to sling fries at McDonald's. And while we're at it, let's sprinkle in a little corporate espionage, shall we? I mean, there's no telling what sort of information he was privy to during his internship. Is that really what you want for him? Also, those pesky photos. *Tsk, tsk.*"

Thoughts of Flynn's future going down the drain and him possibly being prosecuted for something he didn't do flood my brain. After all his planning, I have no doubts that Baker could fabricate something to put Flynn behind bars for years. Not to mention, if those photos of us get out, that could damage not only his career, but his personal life. They're a private moment that should only be in our memories, not immortalized on paper.

Other thoughts of me planning to tell Flynn this weekend I wanted to be with only him swim through my mind. Me wanting to figure out what that looks like for us. Me wanting to tell him I want to be an *us*. Me finally telling him I love him as more than a friend. A sob wells up in my chest, tears flowing freely down my cheeks.

"Please," I plead. "Don't do this, Baker. I'm begging you. I will help you get elected. I will help you find a wife. I will do anything. Not this. Please. Flynn won't understand. I can't hurt him like this. I love him."

Baker's expression doesn't waver. "If you love him, then you want to keep him from losing his future, right? I'm not a heartless man. Well, not fully. You can tell him goodbye this weekend at the wedding. You can tell him—hell, I don't really give a shit what you tell him. Not the truth, obviously. You're a smart woman; you'll figure something out. Whatever you do, make it believable. It won't do to have him sniffing around after we're married.

"Monday, you'll move to Nashville. You can complete your senior year at Belmont, Vanderbilt, wherever. I'll make it happen. Of course, your last semester will be interrupted with the birth and all, so you'll have to work harder to finish early or you can go back once the baby's born. You can go to law school in Nashville. Like I said, once I'm elected Governor, after a year in office, we can divorce. I'll even help you when you're ready to pursue your political career. Really, it's a win-win. You scratch my back, I scratch yours."

"This isn't a back scratch, Baker. This is fucking extortion."

This is me losing my best friend and the man I love. If I do this, it will destroy him. It will destroy us. It would be an unspeakable betrayal of what we have; what we are to each other. It would be one thing for me to completely revert our relationship to what it was before we started sleeping together. It's a whole other thing to tell him I'm getting married and having a baby and it not be with him.

The thought alone nearly makes me sick.

"Yes, but you'll do it. If for no other reason than to protect Flynn. I also don't think he'd look too fondly on that visit to that abortion clinic you made shortly after returning from Nashville a few years ago. Even knowing that he supports you not wanting to have children, how do you think he'd feel if he knew you didn't even tell him you were pregnant?"

I've always heard or read the expression, "all the color drained from her face"; I now understand it. My entire body feels as though it's gone cold, the blood completely relocating to my heart to keep it pumping.

He nods. "I told you; I've been planning this for a long time. I didn't plan on doing it this soon. I was going to wait until you were out of law school because I'm sure trying to juggle law school and a baby are going to be hell. But imagine my surprise when you popped up on Tanner's roll for class this past semester. It was too good an opportunity to pass up. So, my timeline moved up.

"And if you think about it, it'll be seen as romantic. Sparks fly during a mentorship and a whirlwind romance ensues. Eloping in Vegas—you know, just like your parents did. Kinda poetic, really."

Resignation begins to creep in and I'm sure this must be what prisoners who await execution must feel when they know all their chances for appeal are gone. Grasping at straws, I ask, "What assurances do I have that you'll keep your word? That you won't hurt Flynn?"

Because protecting him would be the only reason I'd ever do this. To make sure his reputation and future are intact. To make sure he's safe.

Yet another folder emerges from the briefcase. "I have documents. A contract of sorts. Kinda like a prenup. It says that when you've fulfilled your end of the bargain—acted the part of the dutiful wife and mother until after I'm elected—I will give you a divorce and a generous settlement and destroy all the evidence I've compiled. You'll be free."

"What about the kid? That's assuming I'm actually pregnant. I don't feel pregnant. Not like last time."

"Trust me, you are. I've tracked your cycle and know with fairly good accuracy when you ovulated."

My mouth falls open. "Who the fuck are you? How would you even know that?"

"Your building isn't very secure, and I've had eyes and ears on you for a long time now. Haven't you been curious as to why you haven't had a period?"

"One of the symptoms of the IUD can be no period."

"Yes, except you don't have one. I made sure of that."

I blow out a breath, feeling sick and violated. "You wore a condom. Pretty sure those still work these days." My voice sounds thready and weak and I'm losing any hope that this is some sick joke.

"No, I didn't. Why do you think I fucked you from behind?"

"I saw you put it on."

"Yeah, you thought you did. And don't worry, I'm clean. We both are; I made sure before I did it. I'm not a total monster."

"Your definition of *monster* and mine must be vastly different. Again, what about the kid? I have no desire to be a mother."

"We'll have help. I won't leave you entirely on your own. And this is the only one I'll ever expect you to have."

I scoff. "You're fucking right it is. You don't get to come anywhere near me again."

"That's fine. You can even have your own room; I don't give a shit. But in public, you will be adoring and sweet and play the fucking part to a tee. I don't expect you to be celibate, but it can't be Flynn. There's no way he can be kept a secret; not with your history with him. We'll find someone suitable and discrete and they'll sign an NDA."

My mouth falls open. "Are you fucking hearing yourself? This is absurd."

"Maybe. But you'll still do it."

Movement out of the corner of my eye makes me snap my head to my right. The man who came in with Baker still stands against the wall, but he shifts his weight from one foot to the other. I'd completely forgotten he was there and my face flames with embarrassment at everything he's heard.

"He's cool and can be trusted. He's a doctor friend of mine and we go way back."

"Why is he here?"

Baker taps the pregnancy test. "First, we confirm you're pregnant. I mean, Bobby can do it with a blood test, but I want to make sure before we have him do the blood draw."

"Why do you need my blood? If I take that test, it's pretty accurate." Dear God, this is a conversation I never ever saw happening. Surely this is a nightmare and I will wake up and be able to tell Flynn about how wild it was.

"The blood draw is to confirm DNA. I'm sure it's mine, but I guess it could be Flynn's, even if he did always wear a condom. Y'all did fuck a lot that weekend. Damn, I'll give him this, dude's got stamina. Oh, to be twenty-one again."

"Shut up. You don't get to bring him up. What if it's not yours?"

"Then unfortunately, we'd have to terminate and start again."

I choke on air. "Fuck that. I'm not having sex with you ever again. Although, what you did hardly constitutes sex. Pretty sure the law might look at it as assault."

Struck with the thought that I can call the police and report Baker, I reach for my phone. He must be able to read my mind because he just snorts a laugh. "You think I'm not connected enough to make it so whatever report you file gets conveniently lost? And then, you'll still marry me and Flynn will end up in prison."

My hand is shaky as I will myself to dial the number just before Baker plucks the device from my hand and continues speaking as if he didn't just tell me he has the police in his pocket and I let out a shuddery, terrified breath.

"The contract does state a genetically-related child. Artificial insemination is always an option since I don't exactly relish the idea of fucking you again, either."

I rack my brain, scrambling for any way to get out of this and come up with nothing. I don't have a choice. If I want to protect Flynn, I have to do this. I have to break his heart. Hopefully, someday, he can forgive me. And hopefully, someday, I can forgive myself.

CHAPTER TWENTY-FIVE

FLYNN

The last couple of months with Brighten have seemed different. I'm not entirely sure what to make of it, but ever since I visited her in New York at the end of the semester, something's changed. I hope it's a good thing.

Guess I'll find out today.

I was surprised she'd ask me to attend the wedding, but happy to make the trip up since my internship in Atlanta wrapped up and the fall semester doesn't start for a couple more weeks.

Atlanta reminded me a lot of Nashville since Sully was there, so we hung out a lot. Not many nights out to speak of, because he's committed to his girlfriend and I'm not good at picking up women. Being picked up, I do alright with, but none of the women I brought back to my place even match up to Saylor, let alone Brighten, so after a couple hookups, I just stopped.

Anticipatory butterflies swarm in my gut as I climb out of the taxi and hit the button for her apartment. She buzzes me up and I jog up the stairs, hoping I have time to take her to bed before we have to get ready for tonight's wedding.

The door opens after the first knock and Brighten motions me inside, her expression making alarms go off in my brain the instant I see her face. "Hey, Crash." I also notice she looks tired and her face is puffy, as if she's been crying.

"Hey."

"Everything okay?" I ask, dropping my bag, something telling me there's a bomb about to be dropped. And in the nearly ten years we've been friends, I've never seen the distraught look she's wearing now.

"Can you sit? I need to talk to you."

Definitely a bomb. Maybe she's decided she doesn't want us sleeping together anymore. I can deal with that. It would suck, but she's my best friend over everything, so I can handle it.

"Okay. Are you alright, though? You seem off."

We sit on the edge of the bed and she rubs her hands down her thighs. I can't help but notice she's wearing my T-shirt and my heart lifts seeing her in it. But it's replaced with anxiety the longer she goes without speaking.

I take her hand in mine so she'll stop rubbing her legs. "What's going on? This is me. Talk to me."

She blows out a breath and turns her face toward me. "I didn't really bring you here for the wedding."

I frown, instantly confused. "What?"

She swallows thickly. "I brought you here to say goodbye."

I huff a laugh. "Goodbye? Are you going on a trip or something? Crash, just talk to me. Please. I'm so confused."

Pulling her hand from mine, she searches my eyes, and I have no clue how to read the emotion in hers. It's not one I've ever seen on her. I take her face in my hands and drop my forehead to hers. "Talk to me. What's got you acting so weird?"

"I'm pregnant, Flynn. Ten Weeks."

A weight drops into the pit of my stomach and all the breath in my lungs leaves my body in a whoosh and my heart pounds. "What?" She doesn't answer and simply gives me a moment to absorb her words. I pull back and that same unreadable emotion is still in her eyes. And doing the only thing I can, I push away the things I think or might want and switch into best friend mode because that's what she needs right now. "Okay. What do you want to do? Do you know yet? I know we never talked about what would happen in this situation, but you know I support whatever you—."

"Flynn, there's more."

I blink when she cuts me off. I briefly consider her telling me it's twins or something and my heart pounds even harder. "Okay," I say, my voice weak, even to my own ears.

"It's not yours."

A bittersweet mix of emotions flood my system. On the one hand, I'm not ready to be a father. On the other hand, Brighten got pregnant by someone else. If she didn't know who the father was but wanted to keep it, would I step up? I already know the answer, even if the outcome is unlikely. She doesn't want to be a mother. She's never wanted to be a mother. "Do you know who? Fuck, I'm sorry. It's none of my business."

She seems to steel herself to answer me and I'm not sure how to even prepare myself. "Baker Roberts."

I inhale sharply. I honestly shouldn't be surprised. They spent a ton of time together last semester. He's a smart, handsome, rich, successful guy. He's sophisticated and probably took her out to all the fancy places I can't afford yet. Even so, hearing she slept with someone I've actually met? It's a lot to take.

"Does he know?"

"Yes," she answers flatly.

"Alright, so what are you going to do?"

"Baker and I spent a lot of time together over the summer and of course, last semester. He's asked me to marry him."

I sputter, a stunned laugh falling from my mouth. "The fuck? You don't believe in marriage. You don't want kids. What the hell is going on?" I also can't resist asking, "You're sure it's not mine?"

She nods. "I had a DNA test done."

"Okay, but still, you don't want this. Do you?"

"Baker said he'll take care of me and help me in my career. He's a nice guy. I like him a lot."

"Do you hear yourself? 'He's a nice guy. I like him a lot.' And don't get me started on your fucking career. You don't have to do this to have a career. Even if you did have the baby, you can sign it over to him if you don't want to raise it and he does."

She laughs, but there's no humor in it. "Don't be naïve, Flynn. You know what that gets me? A female politician who abandons her child isn't electable. It would be career suicide. Regardless of the fact there are so many men who have children they don't parent and are still in Congress. It's such a fucking double standard, but that's the truth."

"Okay, so make an appointment. I'll go with you and hold your hand." There's no way this is something she wants. Not the Brighten Dawes I know. Never in a million years would this be something she'd ever consider.

"I've given this a lot of thought, Flynn."

"And what, you've had a brain transplant in the last few months? You've been replaced by someone who's content to marry someone she doesn't love all because she's pregnant? Who are you, your mother?" I spit out, rage filling my entire body.

Her cheeks flame and her nostrils flare. "I am not my mother. How dare you compare me to her."

"If the shoe fits. She did the same thing. I have no doubt that Baker could love you. God, you're you. But you don't love him. Please tell me you don't love him," I plead, the last words coming out strained, my throat tightening with the possibility that she might actually have feelings for him. She looks down, unable to hold my gaze and my heart lurches. "Do you love him?"

She stands and walks a few feet away. "I've made up my mind, and you always said you'd be my friend first. I need you to be my friend now, Flynn."

I jump up and close the distance between us and take her face in my hands, tears welling in my eyes. "I told you I would stand guard over your dreams. These aren't things you dreamed about."

"Dreams change," she says quietly.

I feel as though I've been punched in the stomach and tears roll down my face. "You always said if you could see a future with anyone, it'd be me. If you want a future, take mine. Please, don't do this. You don't love him. I love you."

She doesn't even react to my words and again, it's like I've been punched or stabbed, my guts spilling out onto the floor. "Like I said, dreams change. I can see a future with Baker and this will be a good jumping-off point for my career."

"You've got to be fucking kidding me right now," I choke out, a sob working its way up my throat. I drop my hands from her face, hurt and anger and confusion warring within me for place of prominence in my heart. "You're seriously going to sell yourself out for your fucking *ambition*? Wow, you must really be a politician."

"Flynn, I know you don't understand."

"You're fucking right I don't. This isn't you. I know you.

Something's going on and I don't know what it is, or why you'd agree to this." I take her face in my hands again and kiss her, but she pulls away and my heart plummets, a crack in my soul opening.

"I can't do this. Please don't make this harder than it is."

"It's supposed to be hard to break someone's heart, Brighten. But you sure make it look easy." Her eyes snap to mine when I say her name. It feels foreign to say it to her face, but she no longer feels like Crash to me. Not if she goes through with this.

"This isn't easy for me, Flynn. Please. I'm trying to do what's best."

"Best for who? For you? For me? Or for Baker? Seems like he's the only one who benefits in this. He gets a beautiful young wife he can trot out on the campaign trail and God knows the public loves a baby born in office. It'll make for killer headlines. Shit, it's publicity gold.

"What about law school? How are you going to do law school with a baby? And forget law school; what about senior year? Are you even going to be able to go?"

"I'm transferring to Belmont. They also have a law school."

I huff a ragged breath. "Jesus Christ. Is this for real? You've given this that much thought?"

"I've given it more thought than you can possibly imagine," she replies, her tone hushed.

"And did you think about what it would be like to watch me rip my heart out and hand it to you? If you need to marry someone to save face, marry me. If you need a father for your baby, I will do it. Don't marry him just because you're pregnant. He will never love you like I do. You will never love him. I know you love me; at least the best way you can. It's still more than you'll ever be able to give to him. Is that really fair to any of us?"

"Like I said, I've made up my mind. Please support me in this as my best friend. You always promised that would come first."

"That was before you changed everything you've ever believed, seemingly overnight. I promised to stand beside my best friend. Right now, you're not her. I'm not sure who this person is in front of me, but you're not Crash."

"I'm still me, Flynn. Please. I need you to please just—."

My chest aches and my throat grows so tight I struggle to draw breath. "Please just what, Brighten? Watch you marry someone else? Watch you have his baby? Watch you live this fancy life all so you can climb the political ladder? And all it will cost you is breaking my heart." A single tear slides down her cheek and she bats it away.

"I was content to live the rest of my life as second, third—last—choice for you. I was content to never ask you for more than you could give because I love you. And when you love someone, you put their dreams and needs and heart above your own. I've done that. I've done it for fucking years. And now, out of the blue, you've decided to choose someone for forever who's not me? This can't be real.

"Was this your plan all along? You string me along and keep me on the hook until you caught the big fish? God knows I'm never going to be him. I'm never going to have three hundred million dollars or drive a Maserati or live in a big mansion. I know I can never give you the things he can or catapult your career, but I can give you something he can't: my heart. You already have it. You've had it since I was eighteen, Brighten. Fuck. Please don't do this."

I'm aware I'm begging. I'm aware I sound pathetic. I'm aware I'm a blubbering mess. I don't have enough dignity left to care. Because if she does this, I might as well go ahead and drive my car off a fucking cliff. Who needs dignity when you'd rather be dead?

"It wasn't like that, Flynn. You are my best friend. You've always been my best friend. It's not about his money or a house or anything like that. I'm going to have this baby and I'm going to marry him. I understand if you can't support my decisions, but I still need you as my best friend."

I shake my head. "I can't do this. If you're really going to marry him, I can't look at you right now. This isn't a tattoo that you got to cover up your scar. This isn't you sleeping with countless other people and me just being okay with it because at least I still have you all to myself sometimes. This is you shitting on your own dreams; your own plans. As your best friend, I'm so fucking mad at you. As the man who loves you, I'm devastated and heartbroken."

Knowing I can't stay here and keep any part of myself intact, I head for the door. Brighten speaks, her voice low, but I don't turn around. "I'm so sorry, Flynn."

I grab my bag and walk out the door.

It's not until I pull the rental car in at the Intuition office that I even realize I'm there. I don't even remember getting off the plane in Nashville. I don't remember anything except Brighten telling me she's pregnant and it's not mine and she's marrying fucking Baker Roberts.

I don't know what's up with her, but I know something is wrong and he's responsible and I want to put my fist through his fucking throat to fix whatever he did.

I know I look disheveled. My clothes are rumpled, my face is puffy from crying the entire flight. But now, sadness has been replaced by rage and I want to commit murder. Elias is coming out of the building and has a huge grin on his face and I ignore him in favor of getting to Baker.

He steps in front of me and puts his hands on my chest. "Flynn, what's wrong?"

"I need to see Baker."

Elias frowns and examines my face and when I attempt to get past him, he stands his ground. He might have over thirty years on me, but the man is built like a Mack truck. "I think you need to tell me what's going on."

"I need to see Baker," I repeat.

"Flynn, I don't know what's happened, but something tells me if you go see Baker, I'm going to be answering questions to people in uniform and I'm too tired for that. Besides, Baker's not here. Come into my office and we'll talk."

"Do you know where he is?"

Elias scoffs. "Do I look like his keeper? Now, get your ass in here and talk to me."

He takes my arm and doesn't wait for a response and drags me inside. I vaguely register the elevator climbing up to the floor that houses the Intuition offices. I don't really *see* anything as Elias ushers me along. I know at some point we reach his office and he shoves me down onto the sofa. He makes a phone call, but I have no clue who he's speaking to. He puts a glass in my hand. "Drink this."

I don't even ask what it is, I just down it and cough as the stout liquor—whiskey, maybe—burns my throat. I don't really drink liquor. I'm strictly a beer guy. Watching Vanessa be mostly in the bag the entire time I've known Brighten, I don't really even get drunk. But at this moment, I want to find the bottle Elias just poured my drink from and turn it up. I want to numb this jagged wound I know will never close.

A sharp slap to my face brings me back to fully alert and I snap my eyes to him. "There you are," he says.

"Did you just slap me? What the hell, Elias?" I rub my cheek and blink.

"You had me worried. I thought I was going to have to call someone to take you to be evaluated for shock. You wouldn't even respond to your name."

I nod. "Pretty sure that would be an accurate term for what I am."

He refills my glass and when I go to guzzle it, he puts his hand over the top. "Sip it. I'm not carrying you out of here later." I nod again and he pulls over one of the chairs from in front of his desk and drops into it, unbuttoning his suit jacket. "Okay, want to tell me what the hell is going on and what Baker has to do with it? I've seen you stressed before. This isn't that. What is it?"

Even thinking about Brighten makes the tears start again and I wish I had my dad in this moment. He would know exactly what to say. But this would break his heart, too, and he's too sick for me to drop this in his lap.

"Flynn, what is it? You're scaring me."

And somehow, I get the story out. And not just about the baby and Baker; I start at the beginning and lay out our entire history from when I saw her crash her bike all the way to the moment I left her apartment, my heart in particles on the floor.

Once the telling is done, he doesn't speak for a moment. I'm not sure how much time has passed, but the sun has gone down and the lights of the Nashville skyline are bright outside his office window. I will never be bright again. My light has dimmed like the setting sun. Except mine won't come back up. Not ever again.

Elias leans forward and props his elbows on his knees and folds his hands and blows out a breath. "Wow. I'm sorry, Flynn. I'm sure losing your best friend and the woman you love in one fell swoop is devastating. I can't imagine what you're going through. But surely, if what you say about Brighten is true, she has a good reason for going through with this. Aside from the political advantage, I mean. Even with as ambitious as she is, does this seem like something she would do?"

I shake my head. "That's the thing; it's not. This isn't her. This is antithetical to everything Brighten is. Yes, she's driven and has political aspirations, but this is nothing she would ever do."

"She's a grown woman, Flynn. Regardless of what you think she would or wouldn't do and regardless of what might be her nature previously, when people are faced with the opportunity to have their dreams pretty much handed to them, they'll do things you'd never believe to get ahead."

"That's not her, though, Elias."

"Maybe she loves him."

"Bullshit," I spit out.

He sighs and gives me a sympathetic smile. "Is that you talking as her best friend or you as the man who loves her and is heartbroken?"

"Both. She doesn't love him. She couldn't even tell me she loved him. All she could say was that he's a nice guy, and she likes him a lot. She doesn't believe in love. At least, not soulmate kind of love. She loves me. It's not the kind of love where she'd ever want to marry me or anything like that, but she loves me the best way she knows how. And she doesn't love him. I will never believe that," I say firmly.

"People change, Flynn. Over the past few years, you and Brighten have been apart more than you've been together. She may have changed."

I shake my head. "I can't believe that. I won't. If that were true, and she's changed and wants him, it means that I was never going to be enough for her. No matter what. And if I believe that, I'm not sure I'll survive it. If she's doing this, I have to believe it's for something more than emotions that I'm not seeing. She didn't even fucking cry when she was telling me. She was like some kind of robot. If she wasn't pregnant, I might think she was drunk, but she wasn't. I refuse to believe this is about love. I can't and keep my sanity."

"Okay, well, if that's true, then as her best friend, shouldn't you support her the way she's asking you to?"

"I can't. I told her in the spring I would stand guard over her dreams. If I stand by and watch her do this, that's letting her dreams get trampled. Even if she finishes college and goes to law school like she's planning, I know her. Even if he gives her a career a jumpstart, she's never going to feel fulfilled because she didn't do it on her own. She's going to hate herself for this."

"All the more reason she needs someone in her corner who knows her like you do." I huff a sad laugh and he holds up his hands defensively. "I'm not saying today because I know you're in a shit ton of pain. But if you are the person she's counted on all these years, what's her life going to be like without you in it? What's that going to do to her? She's going to be in a completely new city trying to juggle marriage and motherhood and finishing school. All the while, Baker is running a campaign. It's going to be hell for her, I'm sure."

"I'm not sure I could do it. Stand idly by and simply watch her live this life I wouldn't let myself dream she'd ever want to have? I'm not a home wrecker, but I won't be able to respect any vows she makes to him. I won't be able to not still pursue her and want her and then, because she's her and despite a commitment she makes to him, she will eventually give in during a weak moment because our chemistry is that good. I'm not bragging; I'm just stating facts. It's not as good for either of us with anyone else, and we both know it. Then she's labeled as an adulteress and her career is put in jeopardy all over again. Then it will have all been for fucking nothing."

"Alright, so what do you want to do?"

"Get drunk and forget about this day. I want to rewind time. I want to never know about this. I want to still be oblivious to what this feels like." A choked sob works its way up my throat and tears flood my eyes. "I want to die."

Elias joins me on the couch and grabs me to him and I know it's probably not manly or brave or anything a tough, masculine guy is supposed to do, but I let my mentor hold me as I cry like a fucking baby into his shoulder.

CHAPTER TWENTY-SIX

FLYNN — SIX MONTHS LATER

It's amazing how, even without a heart, you can live. If that's want you want to call it. If you call walking the earth like some emotionless zombie who still somehow goes through the motions of daily life living. You eat, you sleep, you go to class, you still breathe. At this moment, I envy the tin man. At least he never knew what he was missing.

"Flynn? Did you hear me?" Dad's words come out slurred and I close my eyes from my position at the wall of windows in the sunroom at my parents' house. The slur's gotten worse, even over the past few days. His breathing is also labored from the aspirational pneumonia he's currently battling; has been battling for weeks.

I neutralize my expression and turn to walk over to his wheelchair and squat to look at him. "What, Dad? I'm sorry, I wasn't paying attention."

"I asked if you'd heard from Brighten lately. I haven't heard you talk about her. Y'all get in a fight?"

I haven't told my parents about Brighten getting married; which I only know for sure because I saw an online article that popped up about Baker. I haven't told them about the baby or the fact she's now living three hours away in Nashville and not fifteen in New York. I haven't told them she broke my heart and I'm a shell of a person.

"We're both really busy, Dad. It's senior year. We're getting ready to start our last semester of college. She's got lots of irons in the fire and I do, too."

"But she's okay? Y'all are okay?"

I don't want to lie to my father. I don't want to let him know the woman he looks at as a daughter has become this person I don't recognize. I don't want to give him another reason to stop fighting. He's so tired of living this diminished existence. He has been for years. Part of me fears the only reason he still hangs on is because he has hopes of Brighten coming home with me one day to say that we're in love and we'll get married. Even if that could never happen.

Especially now.

"Sure," I say, the dishonesty leaving a bitter taste in my mouth.

He smiles, but it's wobbly. The constant tremor he has now has spread not only to his extremities, but his face, and when he smiles, it almost looks as though his lips are quivering and he's on the verge of tears, even when he's happy.

"Good. I was worried something had happened. Can you call and tell her to come see me the next time she's in town?"

My heart lurches. I haven't spoken with Brighten in six months. It's killed me, but I can't do it. She's reached out and texted, but I'm just not in a place where I can put myself through hearing her voice or reading her words. "Like I said, Dad, she's really busy."

"I know, but I miss her. I miss seeing the two of you together. Please, Flynn." His eyes and tone are pleading and something in my chest twists. And even though he doesn't say the words, the implied *one last time* hangs heavy in the air. I'm pretty sure my dad loves Brighten almost as much as I do. They've always had this easy relationship and laugh at the same kinds of jokes; they love the same kinds of movies. She's his girl as much as she is mine. Except she's not *mine* anymore.

I guess she never really was.

I swallow thickly. I can do this for him. I can grant a dying man a last request, right? Even if it kills me? Well, sure. Apparently, heartbreak isn't fatal, just incurable.

"Okay. I'll ask her."

It takes me three days and four shots of Jack Daniels to work up the courage to call Brighten. I sit in the living room of my apartment and stare at my phone. I need to sack up and do this. Especially because Dad hasn't left his bed in the past couple of days and I'm terrified of letting him down. Of not letting him see her one last time. Because if I was on my deathbed, she's who I'd want there, no doubt. Even now.

Exhaling a deep breath, I click her name in my contacts. And even though I'm the one calling and should expect her to answer, the sound of her voice is like a knife to my heart all over again and I have to fight for breath. "Flynn? I honestly didn't think—."

I cut her off, needing to get this out so I can get back to my bottle of Jack and fall into bed. "Brighten, listen. I just called because Dad asked me to. He's asking for you and would very much like to see you." I keep my voice as level as possible, even as tears roll silently down my face.

She's quiet for a long moment before she speaks. "How bad is it?"

"Bad," is all I say.

"Okay. I'll make a trip. Do they know? I mean, about—."

"No. I'd prefer they didn't, if it's all the same to you. I don't really want to have to explain it all to them when I still don't fucking understand it." I roll my hand into a fist and try to breathe. I clear my throat. "Come while Mom's at work. Jess comes in the late afternoon. Dad's bedridden, so as long as he doesn't see you before you sit down, he won't know. I'm sure this seems like a silly request, but—."

"No, I get it. I'll move some things around and be there tomorrow."

"Will you be able to drive? You know, with...your condition? Is it safe?" I'm not sure why I even ask. She's not mine to worry about anymore. She's not mine to want or love or have.

"Yeah," she answers quietly. "I've got a few weeks left."

I blow out a breath. "Will you be alone?"

"Yes. Baker's in Albuquerque for the week."

Although I've steeled myself, hearing his name and her knowing his plans and all it implies feels like a hot poker through my guts. "Okay." After a beat, I ask, "Just text me before you get to the house so I can make sure the coast is clear?"

"Of course. Does he need anything?"

"Just you." *Same as me.* "He also asked if you'd play for him. I know it's probably been a while, but he's always loved to hear you play. If you can't, I get it, but you know him, and he'll probably browbeat you into it anyway."

"Alright. Any requests?"

How am I actually having this conversation? Like we've not had radio silence for months. Like this is normal. "No. He just asked you to play. I can have Mom's keyboard ready for you."

"Okay. Thank you for letting me see him." Again, the *one last time* is implied.

"I'm not going to punish him, Brighten. He doesn't deserve it. I'll see you tomorrow."

I don't wait for a response and disconnect the call. I squeeze the phone so tightly in my hand I think it will shatter. For a moment, I wish it would. I drop the phone on the coffee table and pick up the bottle of liquor. Forgoing the glass, I simply turn it up and hope to forget.

I'd give anything to be blackout drunk in this moment. I'd give anything to mainline any drug imaginable that would numb what this feels like. Knowing Brighten will be pulling in at any moment, there is nothing I can do to prepare myself. I simply stand like a prisoner awaiting execution. I already know it won't be humane.

Humane would be not having to see the love of my life climb from the car eight-and-a-half months pregnant with another man's child. Humane would be not having to get ready to bury my father soon. Humane would be to shoot me like the wounded, broken animal I am. Humane would be to put me out of my continued and unending misery.

But this is not humane. This is hell.

I don't wait for her to knock and as I open the door, in spite of my best efforts, I can't not look at her. She's Brighten and despite my life having no light, no color at present, she still lights up any room she enters.

She's done her best to disguise her large bump under a bulky black sweater she's paired with dark jeans. And looking at her head on, you might not notice. The moment she shifts to pull off her jacket and hang it on the hook by the door, her body turning a few degrees to the left, the full scope of just how close she is to delivery hits me and I nearly gasp. Her crimson hair is long and thick and shiny and her skin is glowing. Pregnancy has only made her more beautiful. So beautiful it hurts.

It hurts so fucking much.

"Is he awake?" she asks in greeting. Because really, how do best friends who turned into lovers who are now estranged because one of them got pregnant by another man and married him and broke the other's heart say hello?

I can't meet her eye because I don't want to see how green they look; how green they've always looked. I don't want to look into the eyes of the woman I love and not be able to act on it. Instead, I pick a spot an inch above her head and keep my eyes glued to it.

"Yeah, he was a few minutes ago. His nurse is with him. The keyboard is by the bed. I've asked the nurse when you're ready to play to move it for you. I've also asked him not to mention that you're pregnant. I suppose if you want Dad to know, that's your business."

"You're not going in with me?" She sounds surprised and maybe a bit hurt, but it's all I can do to stand upright, so I don't have enough energy to take how surprised or hurt she might be into consideration at this moment.

"No. I told him you were coming. He's setup in the sunroom. I'll be in the kitchen. If you need anything, ask the nurse."

"Flynn, I—."

Her words die as I pivot and walk into the other room, unable to be this close to her anymore. Unable to hear her talk to me.

CHAPTER TWENTY-SEVEN

BRIGHTEN

The last six months have been a blur. Literally. I don't remember most of the days that have passed. I don't remember the move or the wedding or even the first semester at Belmont, although my grades seem to say I did fine. I don't remember the first OB appointment or the ultrasound or hearing the heartbeat. I don't even remember the first time I felt the baby kick.

I have no recollection of all the fundraising dinners I've attended or the dresses I've worn or the publicity photos I've posed for. I don't remember the campaign stops where I've dutifully smiled like a perfect Stepford wife, pasting a radiant grin on my face as the parasite in my belly grows larger and larger and consumes all of my energy and changes my body into something I no longer recognize.

Somewhere in my mind, these things register, but I don't feel any connection to them.

I vividly remember the day Flynn came and I broke his heart. I remember despite the Valium I made Baker give me to simply be able to tell him the news. It made me numb enough that I could feel detached from the moment, but after he left and it wore off, I was a wreck. I nearly thought about ending it.

For weeks, I considered it. I would stare longingly at the razor on the side of my bathtub in the giant, sprawling home that belongs to my husband.

Husband.

I still have a hard time calling Baker that, even six months later. My jailer, more like.

It wasn't the fear that stopped me from dragging the razor up my arms and watching myself bleed out into the bathtub. It wasn't the thought of the pain. I knew aside from the initial cut, there would be very little pain. I'd simply fall asleep and that would be the end of it. As far as deaths go, it's relatively peaceful. It wasn't even the baby that stopped me.

Until recently, I've felt nearly nothing as my body grows and changes and my belly moves of its own accord. I watch with something akin to placid indifference as the proof of the thirty seconds of discomfort I felt with Baker squirms in my abdomen.

But not even the thought of keeping the baby—*him*—safe kept me from doing it. It wasn't the thought of what it might do to Baker's career if his young and beautiful pregnant wife killed herself. I could give two shits about his career.

It was the thought of Flynn and Jude and all the people I love. It was the thought of Flynn having to find out I was dead and then having to explain it to Jude and then probably bury him soon, too. I couldn't imagine breaking him even more. Not like that.

And it was in that one moment of weakness, when I did actually pick up the Bic and examine it with something like relief, that I realized I truly do love Flynn. And Jude's words came back to me like a punch to my solar plexus.

If you're anything like me, it'll take you completely by surprise and you'll wonder how you missed the signs.

I constantly wonder how I missed it. The fact that I'd call him before anyone else. The fact that he's almost always been the first thought I have when I wake in the morning. The fact that he's the only thing that actually made me do this whole thing; making sure his reputation and freedom and dreams stay intact. I know now, I've probably crushed a lot of his dreams, but they're still his for the taking if he wants them.

I think I could've eventually handled whatever Baker wanted to hurl at me. But like Flynn wanted to guard my dreams, I gladly stepped in front of the train that was barreling down the tracks to protect him.

My only hope in all this mess is that someday, once I've served my time and completed my deal with the devil, I can explain everything to Flynn. Hopefully, I won't have broken him beyond what the love we shared can mend and I can at least attempt to make amends.

It would be easier to hate Baker if he was actually cruel or mean to me. I do hate him, but it has nothing to do with how he treats me. I hate that he's shackled me to him for life with this person who will soon join the world. I hate that he's forced me to hurt the best person I've ever known. I hate that for the rest of my days, regardless of what trajectory my career takes, I'll question if any part of is because I earned it. I think my pride still hasn't recovered from that possible blow.

No, Baker's not cruel. He's indifferent to me. He's genuinely excited about the baby and stares at my belly when we're in the same room. He doesn't touch me unless we're in public and I'm playing my part. But when we are in public or at an OB visit, he'll splay his hand possessively over my abdomen and I mentally check out, even as I smile up at him.

In public, he's doting and sweet and I have to give it to him;

his acting chops are good. If it weren't me experiencing this, I would be fooled. I would've never imagined baby traps could be laid by men. I've heard of it happening by women, but never men. I know now, I'm as naïve as Baker accused me of being.

I wondered for the longest time if I'd ever hear from Flynn again, honestly. I gave him a month to process things before I began to reach out via call and text; all of them going unanswered and unread. But I'm not surprised he hasn't reached out before now. And if it weren't for Jude, I know he wouldn't have even done that. I wouldn't have been able to blame him.

Even though I'm here for Jude, there's this ache I have for Flynn. Not only as the man I love, but as my best friend. Until this, I haven't gone more than two days in the last ten years without some form of communication from him. It feels very much what I imagine a death feels like. I don't remember my father's death and he's the only person I've lost. But this is what it must feel like to lose the person you hold most dear in the world.

When I pull into the driveway, I immediately slip off the monstrosity of a ring Baker put on my finger. I carelessly leave it in the cupholder before thinking better of it and stowing it in my purse. If my car were somehow broken into, it could draw speculation. I'm constantly mindful of public scrutiny and perception. I want so badly to get Baker elected so I can get out.

And when I told him I was coming here, he was quick to point out it could be viewed as inappropriate. I told him to fuck off. I wouldn't budge on going to see Jude, and I would've liked to see him try to stop me from where he currently sits in a conference room in New Mexico.

As I walk in the door, I expected the rage and heartache and resignation I felt rolling off Flynn's body. I expected he'd be short with me, especially after the phone call. I expected he'd have a hard time looking me in the eye. I didn't expect him to not look me in the eye at all. I didn't expect to see the dead look in his eyes.

I should have. I know I'm essentially dead to him. I understand it; I truly do. Most days, I feel dead to myself. Most days, I'm moving through my life—if you can even call what I'm living a life—like one would move through waist-deep mud. It's a tedious and endlessly tiring slog.

I no longer recognize myself when I look in the mirror. My body is no longer mine. I have angry purple stretch marks, and my face is splotchy. It's massive and round and puffy and I can no longer see my feet—or my vagina, for that matter. Not that it does matter. Apparently, my libido is as dead as my heart.

But I also don't recognize Flynn. He's so gaunt, it's almost scary. I want to tell him he needs to eat a whole pizza and three burgers and a chocolate shake and oh, can I please have one of your onion rings? His hair is shaggy, and he's unshaved with what's probably a week's worth of beard growth. His clothes hang off him and he's gone back to wearing his glasses.

After our greeting—if you can call it that—he turns to leave the room and I stand rooted to the floor for a long moment and watch him go. Déjà vu of the day he left New York slams into me and I have to breathe through the tears already threatening to fall. I'm not prepared for this. I cry all the time these days. I know a lot of it is hormones, but it's also because I broke not only Flynn's heart, but my own.

A twinge in my low back and sharp kick to my ribs bring me back to myself and my feet carry me out to the bright room that does nothing to break the darkness I feel at present. A stocky man in scrubs sits in a chair in the corner and he raises his eyes to me as I enter and gives me a quick nod of acknowledgement. Jude appears to be sleeping and at least if he's asleep, he won't be able to see my massive belly and the betrayal that it is to the love his son had for me.

Molly's keyboard sits on its stand at the foot of the bed and I'm reminded of so many afternoons spent at this house where she and I bonded over pieces of music. I hadn't touched a piano in years until Flynn called me yesterday. Baker has one at home since, turns out, he plays, too. But last night, I sat down to practice and while rusty, muscle memory kicked in and apparently, the baby likes music because he was active the entire time I practiced.

I take the seat next to the right side of bed where Jude lies semi-prone in what looks to be a T-shirt and sweatpants under a sheet and scoot right up to the edge and debate whether to drop the rail on the hospital bed. I say fuck it and do it anyway. Jude is blind in his right eye now, so even if he turns his full gaze on me, he's not likely to really see my belly, especially if I'm leaning forward.

Reaching out a tentative hand, I take his hand in mine and even in his frail state, his larger one fully engulfs mine. He was such a strong, vibrant man and to see him stuck down in what should be the prime of his life makes me want to rail at the sky. He'll likely be gone before his sons marry or have children and their spouses and children will never know firsthand how amazing this man is.

He stirs, turning his head in my direction and his face lights up. Bringing our joined hands to his face, he presses a wobbly kiss to the back of mine before laying them on his chest. "How's my favorite girl?" His voice is slurred, but I can still make out what he says.

I huff a watery laugh as I shift in my chair and try to find a comfortable position. "I haven't seen Molly, but I'll be sure to ask if I do."

He chuckles. "I meant you, smart ass. We miss you around here." He coughs and the sound is jarring and wet and I glance at the nurse who doesn't look up from the book he's reading, so this must be normal.

Nodding, I swallow thickly. "I know. I'm sorry I haven't visited. School's a bitch." School, marriage, pregnancy, life. It's all a bitch right now. "You're looking well, though."

He shakes his head. "I'm looking like shit. But I appreciate your ability to lie; it was nearly convincing."

"I'll try to do better in the future."

Jude nods. "You'll have to if you're going to be a politician."

I used to think there might be some who didn't lie, but now I'm not so sure. Baker shocks me with how skilled a liar he is; how easily he turns his personality on and off. "Maybe," I admit, unsure if it's even what I want anymore.

Having been in the spotlight just these last six months has been daunting and the idea that I might be in for more of the same for years to come is nearly overwhelming.

"Eh, don't tell me you've finally turned into a typical college student and decided to change your future. I kept expecting it with Jess and Flynn. I didn't expect it from you, though. Of all my kids, you were the one I always saw sticking to their guns."

Hearing him call me his kid makes my heart ache. I've always felt like his daughter and I've not only missed Flynn so much I want to die almost daily, I've also missed this family and specifically, Jude.

"I'm trying to keep at it."

"You and Flynn make up yet?"

"What do you mean?" I try to keep my tone casual, but he's veering into dangerous territory and I'm not sure how much Flynn's told him or how much he wants him to know. I don't want to upset him and tell him things Flynn would rather he not know.

Jude heaves an exasperated sigh and raises one eyebrow.

"You really are going to have to step up your game, kiddo. Politician's wives are supposed to be better at hiding their emotions. You suck at it." Tears instantly blur my vision and I can no longer meet his gaze. I sniffle, and he squeezes my hand in his shaky one. "Look at me, Brighten."

Reluctantly, I bring my eyes to his and he wears no judgment or ridicule in his expression; only sympathy. "Did you have a good reason?" I nod quickly, unable to speak as sobs fight to break free. "Was it for more than just that baby?"

I nod again, and he brings my hand to his face and kisses it again. "Does he know why?" I shake my head. "I'm guessing you can't tell him?" I close my eyes for a long beat and shake my head again and Jude squeezes my hand. "But you did it because you love him?" I don't know if he means Flynn or Baker, but with the nurse here, I don't want to spill too much, lest it get out. Jude tugs me closer and keeps his eyes locked on mine. "And you know exactly who I mean," he says, his eyes widening slightly. I nod and he does, too. "That's what I figured."

"How did you know?" I ask quietly.

Jude huffs a laugh and it throws him into a coughing fit. The nurse still doesn't seem too alarmed, so I don't either. "I'm dying, Brighten. I have lots of time on my hands to read the news. I also know you. I know for you to have done this, you would've had to have a valid reason. You would've played out all the scenarios and weighed your options, and this was the only one that was feasible. He's too close to it, so he only sees things through the lens of his pain. I won't tell him I know, just because I'm sure it hurt not only his heart, but his pride."

I drop my head to the side of the bed and can no longer hold my tears at bay. I bury my face in the mattress in an attempt to muffle the sound so Flynn won't hear. Not that I think in this moment it will elicit much sympathy from him, but in the event he still cares but can't bring himself to check on me, I don't want him to feel any guilt for it.

Jude pats my hair and lets me weep until I'm all cried out. I've had no one to talk to about this since I don't talk to Baker at home. Flynn won't speak to me. Not even Lana understands since she knows I never wanted anything like this. I sure as hell don't speak to my mother. I'm in touch occasionally with Josie or Hensley, but this isn't something I can talk to either of them about. But knowing that Jude doesn't hate me, it breaks something in me because even in this moment, in spite of the pain I've caused his son, he's still treating me like a father treats a daughter and I don't deserve it.

I raise up and look at him and shake my head as I wipe my eyes. "I'm so sorry, Jude. I would understand if you hate me."

He reaches a shaky hand to swipe at my tears. "I don't hate you, Brighten. Flynn doesn't hate you, either. There's no way. My love for you isn't dependent on the things you do. You're my kid, too." His hand travels down to my belly. "So that makes this my grand baby."

I cover his hand with my own and nod. "You're going to be an amazing grandpa."

He coughs and smiles. "I prefer Pop-Pop."

I can't help but laugh, despite my tears. "You've got it."

"Do you know if it's a boy or girl?"

I nod. "It's a boy."

"And do you have a name picked out for this fella?"

I shake my head. "Not yet."

He leans his head from one side to the other as if considering and gives me a thoughtful frown. "You know, Jude's a pretty solid name."

I burst out laughing. "You're right; it is. I think they even wrote a song about it."

CHAPTER TWENTY-EIGHT

FLYNN

Although I'm within earshot from my spot at the kitchen table, I purposely don't listen to Dad and Brighten's conversation. At least, until she starts crying and then I do, too. I cry so hard I have to bite my fist to keep from sobbing. I have no clue what her tears are about, except they're full of anguish. I recognize the emotion as I'm intimately familiar with it these days. And then they're laughing and I want to cry again because I've missed her laugh so fucking much. I can't be upset that Dad is the one who gets to experience it, though, because he deserves to have a good visit with her.

The sound of the keyboard filters through the house and I hang my head as "Hey Jude" starts. And then they both laugh and she stops playing it. He's always hated that song and I know she only played it to get a rise out of him. A moment later, she begins to play a piece I recognize as Beethoven, but I can't name it.

It's one I've heard her play a thousand times while we were growing up, and I can almost imagine how she looks when she plays. When Brighten plays piano, she plays with her entire body and feels the music. She shuts her eyes and gets lost it in. And God, the facial expressions she makes are eerily similar to the ones she has when she's lost in the moment during sex. Great. Now I'm never going to be able to think about her playing piano again without getting hard.

Fuck, I wish I could've just left when she got here, but I think I secretly wanted to hear her play since I can pretend we're kids again. And honestly, aren't we still kids? We're twenty-two. This should not be happening. She shouldn't be having another man's baby. She shouldn't even be having a baby. She sure as fuck shouldn't be married. And she especially shouldn't be married to someone who isn't me.

I want to murder Baker. Like, legitimately put my hands around his throat and squeeze and watch the life leave his eyes. I want Brighten to still be mine, even if it means I have to share her. I want to never live in a world where she's not in my life anymore. I don't know how to do life without her, even now. Six months in and I'm no better off than I was that day I left her apartment. The pain is just as acute.

When the piano music stops, I mop my face and ensure I don't look as though I've been in tears for the last fifteen minutes. I don't know whether to stay where I am or see her off. How the fuck do I even do that? I just say, "bye, see ya" or "have a nice life" or "hey, did you remember to bring my heart with you when you came back"?

Her footsteps echo down the hall and I reluctantly rise from my spot and walk to stand just inside the living room. I lean against the wall and fold my arms, unsure how close I can be to her and not touch her. Doing my best to not watch her walk, I keep my gaze averted, but I still don't miss how even her gate has changed with her pregnancy. It's more sway than stride and I'm sure she can't be comfortable as big as she is. But

I'd never tell her she looks big, because who does that? Plus, she looks gorgeous.

As she passes me and faces away from me, I finally look at her. She has a hand braced on her lower back and she moves her torso as if she's trying to get comfortable. Picking up her jacket, she goes to put it on and struggles and knowing I'm not that big an asshole to let a pregnant woman suffer needlessly, I step up and hold her coat so it's easier for her to put on.

She looks over her shoulder at me and our eyes lock and I know instantly this was a terrible fucking mistake because she's close enough I could almost kiss her. But I don't look at her mouth, because her eyes are what have me so devastated. They're so sad. So sad and full of longing and I'm sure look an awful lot like the look in my own eyes.

But how can hers look like that when she's supposedly happily married? Is it only because she's visited with Dad and soon he'll be gone? That's what I have to tell myself; otherwise, I'll go insane thinking there's some other meaning I should interpret from how anguished her expression is.

"Thank you," she replies quietly and pulls her hair out of the top of her coat and lets it fall down her back as she turns to face me. The movement sends a familiar whiff of her shampoo in my direction and I'm instantly reminded of all the times I've simply breathed her in over the years.

"Sure," is all I can say as I take a couple of steps back, not trusting myself to be that close to her any longer than necessary.

"He fell asleep while I was playing, so I probably wore him out."

"Your playing was beautiful. As usual."

"Thanks. Pretty rusty these days. Apparently the baby likes it, though. He was turning somersaults last night while I practiced and today when I played for your dad."

The baby. He. Just go ahead and cut out what's left of my heart.

"Well, maybe he'll play piano like his mother."

"Maybe. Maybe he'll enjoy it more, too."

Neither of us says anything for a long moment and we're caught in this vacillation between staring and not and both of us opening our mouths to say something but quickly clamping them closed. I finally ask, "Are you going to be okay driving home?"

Home.

A place she shares with her husband.

Husband.

Brighten has a fucking husband. And it's not me.

"Yeah. I'll be fine." A look of pain flashes across her face, but it's gone just as quickly. "It's only a three-hour drive. I'll get out of your hair, though. Thank you for letting me come see him. It meant a lot to me."

I nod. "I'm sure it meant a lot to him, too."

And me.

"It was more than I deserved, Flynn, and I'll never be able to convey my gratitude for this. I understand what time with him costs, so thank you."

I want to tell her she deserves more than this, too. That in spite of how I feel, I want her to be happy, even if it's not with me. That I love her that much. But I simply nod.

She blows out a breath and turns to go. I want to tell her to stay. To talk to me. To catch me up on her life. To just talk. That I miss her voice so much, it's like missing a piece of myself. But I don't say any of that. I simply look down at my feet as she walks toward the door.

"Did you mean it?" Her voice is low, but I hear what she says.

"Did I mean what?" I don't look up for fear she'll be looking at me and I can't look into her eyes anymore right now; it hurts too much.

"What you said about coming when I call? Did you mean that?"

Tears well in my eyes and I nod, even though I don't know if she's facing me. "Yeah. Of course."

"Would you come right now?"

I snap my head up, and I'm sure I look utterly confused, because I am. My eyes widen when I see her face. It's lost all its color, and she looks terrified. "What is it?"

"My water just broke."

I blink, unsure I heard her correctly. "What?" And then I look down and see her jeans are soaked in the crotch and down the front. "Oh, fuck," I breathe, my entire body going cold with fear.

She nods. "Fuck is right. This cannot be happening." She pulls her purse over her shoulder and digs out her keys. "Okay, I've gotta go. Sorry about this. Bye."

On instinct and out of sheer disbelief that she'd try to drive herself anywhere while she's in labor, I step forward and grab her arm. "You can't drive yourself; you're in labor."

She rolls her eyes. "Thanks, I wasn't aware of that by the giant gush of wetness and the—*fuck*." She grits her teeth and rubs her lower back and blows out a breath. A moment later, she seems collected again. "I'll be fine. I just need to get myself to the hospital."

"I can take you."

She shakes her head. "I can't ask you to do that, Flynn. I'll call a taxi."

I scoff. "And you might be pushing this baby out by the time it gets here. Is that what you want? I'm not qualified for anything except practice making these things."

She blinks in surprise and laughs and, unable to help

myself, I do too. And it might be the most bittersweet laugh in the history of laughs. Brighten searches my face. "I really can't ask you to do this, Flynn. It's not fair to you."

I shrug, resigned. Because of course something like this would happen. "Life's not fair and you're kinda out of options. I hate to say it, but you're stuck with me." Grabbing my jacket, I usher her out the door. "Your car or mine?"

An hour later, they've got her admitted to the hospital and in a gown in one of the rooms on the labor and delivery floor. She's called Baker and given him the news and apparently, he's hopping a plane. I try my best not to listen to their conversation, but it's difficult and I'm not sure if her lack of emotion when she spoke with him was normal, or simply for my benefit.

Brighten is hooked up to all kinds of monitors and even through the gown she wears, I can make out how large and dark her nipples are and I'm probably going to hell for lusting over a woman in labor. "Flynn, you don't have to stay. You've already gone way above and beyond the call of duty today."

And even though she's given me this out and I'm emotionally exhausted from being in her vicinity and not touching or kissing her or hell, even hugging her, I still shake my head. Dad would kill me if he found out I left her like this. I also wouldn't be able to live with myself. What if Baker doesn't get here in time and she's forced to deliver this baby without someone who knows her? I can't do it. "I'm good. You call; I come."

She opens her mouth to say something and pain washes over her features and she groans and grips the rail on the bed as she tries to breathe. And despite how much I know this will kill me, I know I'll stay as long as I'm needed. I'll be exactly what she needs most in this moment: her best friend. Stepping forward, I pry her hand off the rail and loop mine in hers as if we're going to arm wrestle.

Brighten's gaze snaps to mine and tears fill her eyes as the contraction subsides. "I can't ask you for this, Flynn. It's not fair to you. I'll be okay."

Not dropping her hand, I grab a nearby stool and drag it over to sit next to her. "You call; I come. I made you a promise. I'm here as long as you need me."

For another three hours, she labors consistently, her contractions growing closer together and longer in duration. When she's offered an epidural, she turns it down and I can't help but laugh. "You know, if I was pushing something the size of a watermelon out a hole as big as my palm, I'd want all the drugs."

"I'm good. It's probably still early. If I get one now, it might wear off before I have to start pushing and then it won't matter anyway. I'm only doing this the once; might as well go all in with it."

"Well, you're pretty brave, so I'm sure you can make this thing your bitch."

She huffs a laugh. "Yeah, pretty sure I'm going to be its bitch." Her jaw clenches and she blows out a long, slow breath and I take her hand in mine again as she moans in pain.

I look to the monitor like the nurse showed me and I watch as the contraction peaks. "You're almost done. It's coming down now."

She sighs and drops her head back on the pillow as it subsides. A sheen of sweat glistens on her face and she looks tired.

"Do you think it was the playing that did it?"

"Did what?" she asks, a bit winded.

"The piano. You said the baby was doing somersaults while you were playing for Dad. You think that's what put you in labor?"

"I think I was in labor when I showed up. I was having these twinges in my low back and I didn't really feel them while I was with Jude, but once I started playing, I did."

She winces again and grunts, and I know they're getting a lot closer together now and I can't deny I'm scared shitless at the thought of being here. But there's also nowhere else I can make myself be at this moment. "Breathe, Brighten. They said you can't tense up." I grip her hand and brush my thumb across the back of hers.

When it lets up, she gasps in relief. "This sucks. Zero out of ten. Would not recommend."

I chuckle and rest my chin on our joined hands. "Nice."

Not even thirty seconds later, another contraction hits her and she curses under her breath and gasps again. "Shit, I want the drugs now. Can I have the drugs? Fuck." I push the call button and a nurse comes in to check on things. Brighten looks at her, fire in her eyes. "I want the drugs now. Epidural or laughing gas or fucking general anesthesia. I don't care. I want it."

I'm *this close* to shitting my pants with the fury in Brighten's voice. Meanwhile, the nurse simply nods, her demeanor calm and professional. "Okay. Well, let's check you out and see what we might be able to do."

I stand, readying to leave so they can check her, and Brighten grips my hand tighter. "Flynn, so help me, if you leave me right now, I will tell everyone in this place about the time you ripped your pants in gym class and showed everyone your *Golden Girls* boxers."

I don't move, and I try not to laugh at her threat. "Sorry, I don't think that's the big threat you think it is. I will happily share that story."

She blinks, fear replacing the indignation in her expression. "Please? Will you stay? I don't have any right to ask you for this." Her eyes well with tears and my heart aches. "But I can't do this alone. I won't make it, Flynn."

"I already wasn't going anywhere. I've got you."

She groans as another pain hits her and curses a blue streak impressive enough to make a sailor blush. "This hurts so bad."

The nurse, apparently having been examining Brighten while I've been focused on her, pulls herself to her full height and shakes her head. "Sorry, honey. You're already almost ten centimeters. It's just about showtime." She looks at me. "Dad, we need to get you gowned up."

I shake my head. "Not the dad. Just a friend." I'm shocked my words don't sound as bitter as they feel as they leave my mouth.

"Okay, so are you staying? We'll still need to get you in a gown."

I nod. "Yeah. I'm staying."

She walks over to a cabinet and pulls out a disposable thin yellow gown and helps me put it on. "Okay, I'll call the doctor, they should be here soon. Hang tight."

"I'd like to know where else I'm supposed to go," Brighten quips.

"Wow," I say, retaking my seat. "Labor makes you cranky."

"Well, maybe someday, you'll get a kidney stone and we can compare stories."

"Ouch, don't go wishing ill on my best feature now."

She huffs a breath and says, "We both know that's not your best feature. It's phenomenal to be sure, but nowhere near your best feature. That's your heart."

I sigh. "Not sure I have one of those anymore," I admit. "Pretty sure I left it on the floor in New York."

Brighten sobs. "I'm so sorry, Flynn. I told you this was too hard. Go; I'll be fine."

I shake my head, angry at myself for letting those words past my lips when I swore to myself I'd support her. Even if it kills me, apparently. "No. I'm sorry. I promise, I'm good. I told you, I'm here as long as you need me."

A doctor walks in, followed by a few nurses, and steps up to the end of the bed as they break it down to get ready for delivery. Brighten grips my hand as the doctor examines her and nods. "Yep, it's go time." She looks at me. "You're going to climb up behind Mom and straddle her back so you can support her. Team work makes the dream work. Let's go," she says with a smile.

I awkwardly climb up behind Brighten as she scoots down in the bed and I wish I could say it wasn't incredibly nice to have her in my arms, even like this. "Okay, Brighten, on the next contraction, you're going to bear down into your bottom. You're going to push for a count of ten, alright?" The doctor's eyes come to mine. "When she pushes, you're supporting her back, okay?" I nod, because right now, I'm terrified and have no words.

For several minutes, I completely blank. It's as if my soul and brain abandon my body and I have no concept of time or space or anything resembling real life. It's not until Brighten lets out a sharp cry that I snap out of my daze. The doctor is encouraging her to push, but Brighten is saying she can't, that she's not ready, that she doesn't want this.

My chest cracks open and despite my need to not watch the woman I love give birth to another man's baby, I draw on every emotional reserve I possess to simply be her best friend. I run my hands down her arms and grip her hands and tuck my chin into the crook of her neck. I push away how much I want to kiss her and smell her hair and simply tell her I love her in favor of helping her through this impossible moment.

"You've got this. You remember when you wrecked your bike, how brave you were? You were lying there with that hunk of metal sticking out of your chest and you wouldn't move because you'd read somewhere it could make it worse? Even when you were scared to death and in so much pain, you still were so smart and brave. It was the most badass thing I've ever seen.

"It's second only to this. You're going to help this little boy come into the world and you're going to be such a kick-ass mom, Crash. I know you think you can't, but I've never seen you unable to do something you set your mind to. You're going to be fucking amazing, and this kid is the luckiest kid on the planet because he's yours.

"You're going to show life what you're capable of. You're going to go to law school and someday, you're going to be the best fucking president this country's ever seen. You're going to do that *and* be the most amazing mother. Because you're Brighten fucking Dawes and you're a badass."

Brighten groans and it's a loud and painful keening sound that's nearly some sort of lament and in the next moment, there's a high-pitched wail that is the most beautiful and life-altering sound I've ever heard in my life.

They place the baby on her chest as he screams, and he's tiny and pink and has a headful of red hair. "Oh God, look at all that red hair. He's *so* going to get his ass kicked when he goes to school, Crash," I say with a watery laugh.

She laugh-cries and I press the only kiss I allow myself to her temple as tears steam down my cheeks. "You did so good. Look at him. You made that."

They swaddle him and place him more firmly in her arms,

and I extricate myself from the bed. Brighten looks down at him and the look on her face is so unreadable I'm not sure what words she needs in the moment. So instead, I drop my forehead to the side of her head. I don't say anything, I just stay and breathe her in, the smell signature only to her as well as this sweetness that must be the baby.

"So, do you have a name picked out?" the doctor asks.

Without hesitation, Brighten says, "Jude. Jude Maverick."

And it's in that moment, I shatter inside. Outwardly, I'm shocked I'm upright and able to breathe. Tears still slide down my face and yet, I don't sob or scream like I want. She looks up at me. "Is that okay?"

I nod and, with shaky hands, cup her face and break my rule and press a kiss to her forehead. "It's perfect."

Footsteps pound from the hall and instinctively, I drop my hands and back away. It's as if my body knows before he's even walked through the door that Baker's arrived. I give Brighten one last look, her face a mask of regret, and offer her a nod before walking around the bed.

I mop my face as I step toward the door and pass Baker as he enters. Surprise flashes in his eyes when he sees me and he slows to a stop and for some reason, I do, too. "Flynn. Thank you for being here for her. I'm sure—."

Pent up rage boils under my skin at the sight of him and my hands curl into fists. I take a step toward him and his eyes widen and I keep my voice low. "The only reason you're still breathing right now is because I don't want to take away from what she just did. You don't deserve either of them. I don't know what you did to get her to agree to all this, but someday, not even the love I have for her will keep me from kicking your ass, public official or no."

If he says anything, I don't hear him as I leave the room. I make it to the parking lot before I collapse onto a bench and feel as though I might actually die this time.

CHAPTER TWENTY-NINE

BRIGHTEN

I wish I could say that having Jude miraculously made me want four more kids, and that motherhood was all rainbows and butterflies and a dream I didn't know I wanted. It's not. It's no sleep and my body constantly being at the beck and call of a being who can't even hold its head up without support. It's a constant barrage of bodily fluids and tears—his and mine.

To Baker's credit, he's an attentive father. If I've pumped a bottle, he'll feed him and walk him around the house and he looks at Jude as though he's the best thing since sliced bread. He changes diapers and coos at him. I'm sure if I felt anything more than loathing for him, I'd swoon.

And when I look at Jude, all I can see is the man who should be his father. All I see are the things I would do differently and the man I've been forced to give up. A man who, even with a broken heart of my making, stayed with me and helped me in my lowest moment. He's better than anyone will ever deserve; least of all, me.

Jude is honestly an easy baby. He only cries when he's hungry or needs a diaper change. He latched instantly and has had no issues going from breast to bottle. And I can even appreciate how cute he is. He has a tiny cleft in his chin and long, elegant fingers and Flynn was right; he's got a headful of red hair. It's still too early to tell what color his eyes will be, but my bet is on brown, like his father's. Baker's parents think he looks like him. I can't say; maybe they're right.

They've been kind to me since marrying Baker. I'm sure they think I was the one who laid the trap considering my age and ambitions and I can't even blame them. Nonetheless, they're still kind to me and they adore Jude. And as is a requirement for my prison sentence, I paste on the smile and play the enamored mother in the presence of company.

I take care of Jude like I'm supposed to and don't leave him to cry and I don't resent him. I'm still not entirely sure I have any kind of maternal feelings, but I don't hate him. He's a baby. He didn't ask for this existence. I resent Baker and my parents and everyone who had a hand in the reason I'm in this mess.

Mostly, I hate myself.

True to his word, Baker got me help in the form of a live-in nanny so I can finish my last semester at Belmont. I'm pretty sure he's already sleeping with her and Jude's only three weeks old. Ask me if I care. I am markedly indifferent where they're concerned.

I'm swaying with Jude cradled in my arm as I make a pot of coffee when Baker climbs the stairs from the nanny's quarters dressed for the day, save his tie. I give him a dismissive glance as I finish scooping coffee into the filter. Baker has this super fancy espresso maker but I'm content to stick with my Bunn.

He steps up beside me to prepare his own coffee. "How'd he do last night?"

"Fine. Only woke up twice. You didn't keep the nanny up too late, did you? I have an early study group today."

"No. She can probably take him now if you want me to take him down."

I shake my head. "I need to feed him before I get ready. I don't want to get him off his schedule."

"Sure. If you've got any milk pumped, I can take him for tonight so you can get some real sleep. I don't have any meetings until late tomorrow morning, so I can get up with him."

I narrow my eyes. "Why are you being so nice?"

He huffs a laugh and rolls his eyes. "I'm his father and I enjoy it. I know you've been putting in a lot of long hours with classes and the baby, and you're not even released from your doctor yet. You really should take it easy."

"See, I don't know if you're just telling me I look like shit or if you're being genuine. I don't know if you have ulterior motives, Baker. Honestly, I'm afraid to take you up on any kindnesses because I don't know what it will cost me."

He frowns and nods. "I can see why you would be hesitant to believe my words considering our...arrangement."

"Oh, you mean the arrangement where you've highjacked my entire life and made me your puppet for the foreseeable future? You're right, I have no reason whatsoever to question your actions or words or anything else you might do concerning me," I answer, my tone dripping with sarcasm.

Jude rouses from sleep and roots for my breast, and Baker's eyes fall to the baby. "You want me to take him so you can fix yourself some coffee before you feed him?"

I'm past the point of modesty with Baker. God knows he's stripped me of my dignity and pride; my hope of any happiness in the future. What's a flash of breast? "I'm good." I unhook my nursing tank and get him latched on before pouring myself some coffee.

Baker makes quick work of knotting his tie and sighs. "No, you don't look like shit. You do look tired, only because I know you must be. We're in this together and for better and most likely, a lot worse, you are my wife and I've been trying to support you. I know ours will never be a 'real' marriage." He puts air quotes around *real* so I get his meaning. "But for however long we're in this, I don't want to live in a house where there's so much animosity. I'm not a monster, Brighten. I know you think I am. I hope in the coming days, you'll see I'm not.

"I gave you your entire pregnancy to grieve what you thought your life was going to be and come to terms with how things will be going forward. I gave you space. I understand how hard it must have been to see Flynn and have him at the hospital with you. Truly, I'm sure that was awful for the both of you. And I'm sorry for my part in your pain and Flynn's."

Tears well in my eyes, but I bat them away. I refuse to give him the satisfaction of seeing me cry.

"But since we're stuck together, I would like us to try to at least be civil. It won't be good for Jude to see us being hostile toward one another as he gets older. And I know I didn't say so at the hospital, but Jude is a great name and I understand why you picked it. Sort of fitting you'd name him after the man who was like a father to you."

I breathe through the tightness in my throat for the way I miss Jude. I don't know if he's already passed or if Flynn will even reach out when he does. I'm afraid to know which.

"Can I ask where you got Maverick? You a big *Top Gun* fan?"

Lifting my chin, I level him with a gaze. "It's Flynn's middle name," I answer with satisfaction and dare him to say anything about it. I'll take my victories where I can from here on out; small as they may be, I suppose. It's the least I can do for the man I love and who was such a big support to me as I was in labor.

He's quiet for a moment and a muscle tics in his jaw, but

after a beat, he nods. "Right. Well, when we're here at home, there isn't anyone to perform for. There aren't crowds we have to convince and you don't have to pretend to like me, but I think we could find some common ground if we really tried. I don't hate you, Brighten. I mean, God, you've given me this amazing little boy." He gently brushes the back of his index finger along the nape of Jude's neck.

"He's beautiful and half of him is you. I know you're still struggling with everything, but I don't want to be your enemy. I want you to have everything you want and I hope we can become, if not friends, then at least friendly."

The only thing I want is to go back in time. I want to never have accepted the offer of a date with him. I want to slap eighteen-year-old me across the face and tell her to wake up and realize that the love of her life was right in front of her the whole time. I want to run away in the middle of the night and find Flynn and convince him to take me back.

I let out a slow breath, knowing I can't take anything back, and that this is my life. This hell is my reality. Baker is still speaking and try as I might to tune him out, his words sink in.

"So, if I offer to help with Jude, it's simply me attempting to be a good father. If I offer to take him for the night, it's so I can spend time with him and give you a break. If it concerns Jude, there are no ulterior motives. If we're at home, I'm going to be straight with you. You're not the only one who has to play a part in public. It's exhausting and I'd prefer to drop the façade at home. I understand my word probably doesn't mean shit to you, but you have it."

He eyes my tattoo. He's never asked about it. I assume, if he's had eyes on me for as long as he claims, he knows exactly what it covers, but I've never offered up the information. "Why a feather? I know you got it to cover a scar, right?"

I nod. "Yeah. They have a lot of meanings, depending on

where you get your information. But I read somewhere they represent strength. I'd like to think I showed strength when I got hurt." I bring my eyes to his. "I'd like to think I'm showing tremendous strength right now."

Baker nods. "You are. You're doing great. I know you didn't want this, but you're a wonderful mother, Brighten. You're attentive and nurturing, even though I know you're not completely sold. I hope it gets easier for you."

What would've been easier would be if I had never been put in this position. But I don't say anything for a beat. I simply nod and pick up my coffee mug. "Yes, I would appreciate it if you kept him tonight."

"I'd be happy to. And anytime you need help, just tell me, okay? I'll check in with you, but if you get overwhelmed or anything and Anya's not around, call me. If I'm in the city, I'll make it work to come home. I don't plan on being an absent father in my own home. I know there will be some logistics we have to work out as he gets older and more cognizant of our living situation, but we'll figure it out."

I'm not sure at all if I can trust anything Baker is spouting. For all I know, he's going to make note of every instance I need additional help and use it against me later. For all I know, he's going to have me offed so he can get that widower sympathy vote he mentioned.

I nod and he sips his espresso. "There's a party next week. If you don't feel up to going, no one would blame you, but I wanted to give you the option. You don't get out of the house much except for class and political functions, but if you would rather skip the party, it's fine."

I shake my head and switch Jude to my other breast once he empties the first one and still seems hungry. "It's part of what I agreed to; I'll do it. I think some of my maternity dresses might still fit. What kind of party is it?"

"Elias Washington's retirement party. Work colleagues. At my parents' house."

My heart lurches hearing the name of Flynn's former mentor. If I don't go, it could be viewed as not supporting Baker and even though he's given me the out, it still feels like I can't take it. "Okay. So, will the dresses I have be alright?"

"Sure. But if you'd like to pick something out, you've got your credit card."

"You know I have my own money."

His jaw clenches. "I know you have the money your parents set aside for you, but I'd prefer you didn't spend their blood money while we're married. Anything I buy for you or you buy with my money is yours. I'm not going to suddenly take it back. Just like your car. It's in your name; it's yours. I take my responsibilities seriously and you and Jude are my responsibility."

We don't talk about my parents or what they did. We don't talk about my mother and the fact that she's been calling me. I understand him not wanting to bring them up. Probably for the same reasons I don't want him to ever bring up Flynn. They took away the person he loved without recourse. He did the same thing to me. This is the closest he's ever really come to mentioning them since we struck our bargain.

"Alright," I say. Because what else am I supposed to say?

Attending all these parties has gotten easier in the last several months. I'm apparently really good at turning it on and off. I suppose that's what makes a good politician's wife, right?

I didn't end up getting a new dress because despite what Baker said, I don't want to spend any more of his money than is necessary. I won't upset him by spending my parents' either, but I hate feeling like he's doing me a favor by letting me spend his.

So, instead, I throw on a simple black maternity dress that, while a little big, still fits pretty well considering how my body still isn't back to its pre-baby condition. Not sure it will ever be. Even as I was getting dressed, I hated to see the stretch marks and dark line that still travels down my stomach. I hate how loose my skin feels and how large my breasts are. I hate being in a body that doesn't feel like mine.

And yet, I get dressed. I fix my hair and put on makeup. I wear the ring and other jewelry Baker's given me since we got married. He plays the part of doting husband well, I'll give him that.

Normally, we have a driver who takes us to functions, but tonight, Baker's opted to drive and I simply look out the window as the city passes by. "Polling numbers are looking great."

"That's good." Because it is. The sooner he gets elected, the sooner I get out.

"You need to pick a cause."

I turn my head and give him my full attention. "I'm sorry?"

"You need a cause to advocate for. It won't only be me the public will vote for, you know. They'll vote for me because of you."

"How about bodily autonomy?" I deadpan. "That's something I've become very passionate about in recent months."

Baker nods, completely unbothered by my snark. "I'm sure. But pick another. One that doesn't have so much controversial connotation. Wield the big hammer after I get elected, okay?"

"Multiple sclerosis research," I answer immediately.

"That'll do. You've got stories about how the illness has impacted your life."

The idea that I would trot out stories about Jude simply

to garner public support nearly makes me ill. "I won't be sharing any of my stories. I won't use Jude Tate as political fodder, and neither will you. My family is off limits, Baker." He opens his mouth to speak and I press forward. "And yes, they are my family. Forever. Jude's name never comes up. Got it?"

"Yeah, I've got it. But for the record, that's the last time you ever dictate what I do or don't bring up."

Incensed, I ball my hands into fists in my lap. "Let's get something straight here, Baker. Just because this isn't and will never be a real marriage and I'm essentially your prisoner, I add value to your career; just like you said. I'm likable and charismatic and can reach a younger demographic than you can. I can relate to the new voters better than you can. So don't, for one second, think that I am someone you can just expect to be window dressing.

"You might have me over a barrel, but just know that someone who's lost everything has nothing left to lose. You start trying to tell me what I will and won't have an opinion about and things might start getting interesting. It'd be a real shame if, when someone asked what your motivation is behind fighting for harsher drunk driving charges, Anna's name got dropped. It might make certain people curious. And then the connection to Vanessa and my father gets brought to light and then, oh my, you married the daughter of the woman who killed your girlfriend? Yeah, that's not suspicious at all. I'll play nice as long as you do."

Baker nods and offers me a half-smile. "I wondered if you were still in there. Let's hope you bring that kind of passion to the campaign."

"Fuck off, Baker."

He laughs. "I'll give you this, Brighten; you've got the fire. Let's see what you do with it."

As we arrive at the party and enter his parents' house—mansion is a better term as it makes the house Baker owns look like a dollhouse—I'm really wishing I could drink. I'm wishing, as we mingle with the same crowd at all of Baker's work and political functions, that I had stayed home. I'm so fucking tired, and after only a few minutes of small talk, I'm exhausted.

I stick close to Baker's side until I have to excuse myself to go pump. I slip into the study and breathe and try not to think about Flynn. I'm not sure if I should consider it a blessing that he's not here. My guess is, if he received an invitation, he declined to come since he knew I'd probably be here. Even so, I swipe away the tear that slides down my cheek, hating that he didn't feel like he could come for the same reason. He admired Elias and looked up to him, and under any other circumstances, he'd probably be in attendance.

After I tuck away the two bottles I've pumped into my cooler bag, I step into the adjoining powder room to check my appearance and apply some fresh lipstick before rejoining the party. As I step out into the hall, my eyes are downcast and I run into a tall, solid form. "Oh, I'm so sorry," I say automatically and snap my head up. "I wasn't loo—. Sully?" My stomach drops at the sight of him.

He blinks, obviously shocked to see me. "Brighten," he says curtly after his brain catches up.

"Excuse me," I say and attempt to go past him. I can't even look at him because Flynn is one of his best friends and I hurt his best friend. And I have no defense to anything he could say to me. And when he grabs my arm to stop me, his expression livid, I shouldn't be surprised. Nevertheless, I give a little yelp of shock.

His eyes drill into mine as he releases me and I'm frozen by the look of near hatred in his face. "You know, I told Flynn that first summer that he was going to get hurt. He said you'd never want anyone—not even him—so he was content with the way things were between you two. But you go and marry fucking Baker Roberts? I never pictured you as a gold digger or someone who'd hurt the best man either of us has ever known for the sake of your fucking ambition, Brighten. What the hell?"

Tears burn my eyes with the venom that laces his tone. I open my mouth to speak, but he shakes his head. "Save it. Just know you were never good enough for him anyway. This just proves it. What was it you said about your mother? Opportunistic, fake, vapid? Sound familiar? Guess the apple really doesn't fall that far from the tree."

He doesn't give me another opportunity to speak because he steps past me, leaving me to absorb his words and try not to sob. And because I have no choice but to carry on, I blow out a shaky breath and paste a smile on my face while I die a little more inside.

PART 4

THE DARK DAYS

3-13 YEARS AGO

CHAPTER THIRTY

FLYNN

Dear Crash,

Dad died today. Nearly five months to the day after you gave birth. I know he was tired. He was so fucking tired of his body betraying him. But even with having MS, he was young; too young to be so weak and gasping for air. I know many would say that death is a mercy in a situation where the person is in pain and no longer has the willpower to fight. Death would be a mercy for me anymore, too.

He went peacefully and the doctors say he most likely didn't feel it. So, that's something to be thankful for, I suppose. It wasn't even the aspirational pneumonia that did it. It was a massive heart attack in the middle of the night. Who could've seen that coming? Not me.

But the night he died, I was playing checkers with him. I know, checkers is a kids' game, but I was his kid, so I guess it's okay, right? As I crowned his first king, he asked me again if I'd spoken with you and I gave him the same "we're both busy" bullshit I'd been feeding him for the past eleven months. He finally got fed up with that answer and asked if I knew what you'd named your baby. I think it was then I knew he really thought his time was short.

Of course, that led to the inevitable conversation of our "breakup"—although, can we even call it that? I'm not too proud to admit that I cried like a baby on my father's chest and he held me as I relived my pain. But when I told him you'd named him Jude, I think that was the proudest moment of his life. I'm not sure he was even that proud when I graduated cum laude.

By the way, I graduated cum laude. Apparently, without a heart, I've become a mindless workaholic. I guess I should thank you for all the job offers pouring in. The only one I'm interested in is the one that takes me far enough away that I don't have to see Baker's face on the TV with you and Jude by his side as he campaigns. I don't want to see him hold your hand or kiss your cheek or smile down at you as he makes promises to voters.

I'm proud of you, though, for how vocal you've been about MS. I may or may not have donated to the charity you're sponsoring as part of your platform. And although I know you could use Dad in your message, I'm thankful you don't. Not that I ever worry you will, because that's not something you'd do. You love him too much to ever allow him to be used as a token for your ambition.

But, I guess I could be wrong about that anymore. It seems like you're a lot more devoted to your ambition these days, so someday I might read the name Jude Tate in conjunction with your platform. If that day ever comes, I really will feel like you're not you.

Sully said he ran into you at Elias's retirement party. I gave him hell for not treating you with the respect you deserved. I'm sorry for the things he said. I think he was just being protective of me. He's a good friend. You know me; those are hard for me to come by. Even so, you didn't deserve for him to tell you how I was too good for you. That could never be true. There's more goodness in you than anyone realizes.

Jude is adorable. You definitely make cute babies, Crash. And since you'll never read this—you'll never read any of these letters I write you—I can admit that I dream about what a child of our making might look like. Obviously, green eyes, but hopefully more like yours. Yours have those darker rings around the outside of the iris that make them look like pools you can step down into.

And as much as I said Jude might get shit for having all that red hair, he's fucking precious. So, red hair would be just fine with me. Really, as far as I'm concerned, they could basically be a copy and paste of you and I'd be content. As long as they were ours. That would be my only requirement. And to prevent any confusion about my meaning, Jude would've been mine, too. DNA doesn't mean shit to me.

Back to the job. I've decided to take a job in Paris, as they need someone who is fluent in French and English. Apparently not having you around also made it so I can easily learn a different language. Who knew? Mom is thrilled since she is planning to come visit when I move. Jess is at a loss as to why I'd want to move to France. Of course, he's only ever lived in Knoxville and is content, so he doesn't get it. I would've been content to live wherever you were. I can no longer say that, though.

I'm not sure there's a place I can go on this planet—possibly, this galaxy—that would be far enough away that I still didn't feel your presence. But especially in Tennessee. Not with Baker's face plastered on every other commercial and all the memories of the places we used to go; the things we used to do.

I'm sure I'll be forced to come back to the states occasionally, since Jess already said he won't come to me. So I guess Christmas will be the only time I will have to steel myself to possibly see the reminders of us. At least until you run for president. I'll have to come back just to vote for you.

That, I'll make a special trip for. Because I know you'll make it. You've got the ruthless part down. Pretty sure that might be the number one quality of a good candidate.

Sorry, I don't mean to get bitter. That's not what these letters are for. They're really just to vent and update you. Even though you'll never read them, it still feels like I get to update my best friend on my life.

I still wish I could understand. I wish there was a plausible explanation that could explain why you've done this. I know things changed that weekend I came to visit you in New York. You seemed more open, if that makes sense. I felt like you might've been starting to come around to the idea of there actually being an us. I didn't dare hope for it, but that's the way it seemed. Maybe I'm just projecting. Someday, I hope it makes sense.

I'll never be sorry for loving you. I'd never take it back, even if it meant taking away my pain. Because then I'd have to give up the joy loving you brought me.

I'm still yours and will always come when you call.

-Flynn

Crash,

It amazes me how even after three years and the countless—literally, because I have no idea how many—women I've used in an attempt to forget the way you feel under my hands and lips and wrapped around my cock, there's still only you. I fucking hate it.

I can't bring myself to sleep with redheads or women with green eyes, so it does make the task of finding a nameless body to bury myself in simply to scratch an itch a bit more taxing. But this is Paris, so there's always someone willing to follow me to a bar bathroom or even the alley outside the bar. Sometimes multiple someones. I don't bring them home or even ask them their names anymore.

I was sorry to hear Baker didn't win his bid for governor. I'm sure that was a tough loss for you both, what with all the hard work you put into the campaign. Maybe he'll get 'em next time.

Jude is looking more like you by the day. Except for the eyes and chin, he's your twin. Does he play piano like we predicted? If so, does he love it? I mean, he's only three, so maybe it's too early to tell with stuff like that.

Sully got married last week. I flew into Miami for the weekend and stood as his best man. I'm glad to see him get his happy ending, even if I'll never get mine.

I recently moved into a new apartment. You would love it. It reminds me a lot of your place in New York. It's only about a ten-minute walk to the Musée Marmottan Monet and I can be to the Seine and the Statue of Liberty in less than a half-hour on foot.

I finally upgraded to a two bedroom so Mom would have her own room when she visits. She's taken to staying a month at a time and fancies herself this adorable French lady. She's made a friend down the way and they walk the neighborhood while Mom speaks broken French and her friend, an elderly lady named Elodie, speaks broken English. It's exactly as cute as you'd imagine.

By my calculations, you should be about to finish up law school. Was it as much a bitch as you thought it'd be? You nailed your LSATs, so I can't imagine you wouldn't ace law, too. Just one more stop on the Brighten Dawes Success Train.

I'm sure you're already working on Baker's next campaign, but don't lose your own trajectory while you're helping him climb. He wouldn't be anywhere without you. I don't even have to be there to know that. He would do well to listen to your ideas. I'm sure, even against his will.

I dreamed about us last night. It was that day we walked the West Village and we stopped into that little clothes shop on Bleecker. You'd pulled a dress off the rack to try on and I ended up coming into the dressing room with you and going down on you. Do you remember that? God, I thought for sure we'd get caught when you started moaning. You tasted so fucking good that day, Crash. When I woke up, I could smell and taste you. Fuck, the human memory is a cruel thing.

Sometimes I wonder if you ever wear my T-shirt. Selfishly, I hope when Baker's away on business or whatever it is that takes him away from you that you wear it and think back on us together. I don't have a shirt to wear, but I still remember so vividly I could swear you were with me.

You're looking as stunning as always and motherhood suits you. Try as I might, I can't keep from checking the local Nashville news and social media. I limit it to once a month since the whole next day, I'm typically hungover. It's the one day a month I allow myself to get shitfaced. But I know how you feel about drunks, so I don't let myself get to that point otherwise. I'd never want alcohol to ever be a reason for you to not take me back. Is it wrong that on the day of each month I read about you, I'll hope to read that you and Baker have decided to divorce?

Would you come to me if that were the case? I know I said some hurtful things to you and as your best friend, I should've reacted better. But the moment I fell in love with you, the best friend in me hopped into the backseat and the lover took the wheel. He was really bitter. I'm sorry.

I still miss you like my next breath. I wish there was a way I could come to you and be in your life right now and it not physi-

cally end me. It wouldn't take much these days. I'm still barely hanging on. I'm sorry I can't be the kind of friend you deserve.

-Flynn

Crash,

Has it really been eight years since Jude was born? He's gotten so big. Is he as stubborn and assertive as his mother? Does he like chocolate shakes and a single onion ring with his burger? Or, do y'all subscribe to one of those fancy vegan or paleo diets that I'm not sure I could ever abide by? The wine and bread alone in Paris is enough to keep me planted squarely in the category of never dieting. Of course, you know me; I get my run in. Pretty sure running is the only thing keeping me sane these days.

I could've sworn I saw you last week. It was only a flash of red hair and a general shape, but I had such a visceral reaction to seeing who I thought was you, I chased the woman down. It wasn't you, of course. I wasn't sure if I was happy about that or sad.

I'm not sure if, given the opportunity, I'd be able to resist dragging you into the nearest dark alleyway and making up for lost time. Sometimes, I imagine what would happen if you happened to be traveling to Paris and we ran into one another.

I told Elias the day I found out about your pregnancy and I flew straight to Nashville ready to murder Baker that I wouldn't be able to honor your vows. That because our chemistry is so good, neither of us would be able to keep our hands off the other. I imagine we'd get so caught up in the moment, it wouldn't matter if Baker was standing right there. I'd remind you who you really belong to. It will always be you and me, Crash.

I've given up looking for anything close to what we had; not that I actually look. I keep hoping somewhere deep inside, one of these other women will spark something in me that makes me feel alive again, but no one does.

Maybe I'm not really alive. Maybe I've done something so terrible in my life that this is the hell I've been assigned. Maybe my punishment is such that I'm forced to be separated from the life we should've had together.

I know it wouldn't have looked anything like yours does now, but it still would've been ours and it would have been perfect.

It's hard to believe Cole's gone. God, it just seems so surreal. He was one of the nicest guys ever. I can't imagine what Ada, Silas, Josie, and their parents must be going through. Well, I guess I can kind of imagine what things are like for Ada. I'd never tell her that, because losing someone through a death is nowhere near the same thing as someone leaving you for a man you're sure they can't love. But I guess you've proven me wrong about that, huh?

I'm crossing my fingers that Baker gets elected this time. He's got some great plans for the state. I especially like his plan to work with prosecutors to implement harsher punishments for drunk drivers.

I can't wait to see you be First Lady of Tennessee. You're going to kick ass at it.

-Flynn

Crash,

It's been a shitty year, huh? I was really sorry to hear about Vanessa's passing. Of course, I don't know if y'all ever made up, but I'm sure it's still difficult to lose your mother.

You're doing an amazing job as First Lady and looking spec-

tacular in the process. Your ass is still top-notch, by the way. Shit, Crash, sometimes I swear I can feel that ass in my hands. Jesus.

I'm really sorry to hear about Baker's diagnosis. Cancer sucks ass. How's Jude holding up? If I know you, at this point, you know more than the doctors, huh? You've probably scoured all corners of the internet for every piece of information you can on prostate cancer. I'm sure he's going to pull through just fine. With you by his side, how can he not?

Jess said Ada and Silas got married. How wild is that? I always knew he had a thing for her and I say, if they can make some happiness from all they've lost, they should.

Speaking of Jess, you will be shocked to find out he has a girl-friend. Like, a legit girlfriend. Some travel blogger or something, so maybe the fact she's not home all the time keeps things alive for them. I seem to recall the distance only making us want each other more.

Apparently, distance still does that. Apparently, a decade can pass and I can still vividly recall the sound you make when my cock slides into your pussy. I can still vividly recall how your fingers feel in my hair and the way you feel in my arms. I can remember the way your breath smells in the morning. Even that is something I miss. I miss every molecule of your being.

I miss the way I was when I was with you. I miss the boy who would watch you play Mario Kart and remind you to slow down on those curves and laugh when you didn't listen and went over the edge. I miss the way you'd look at me, even with my braces, glasses, acne, stretch marks and soft middle, like I was perfect exactly the way I was.

Kinda like how I looked at you before your tattoo. I'd be lying if I still didn't miss looking at your scar. Those mornings we woke up together before you got it, I would trace it with my eyes while you were still asleep. Not that your tattoo isn't perfect for you, because it is. I miss it, too. Hell, Crash, I just fucking miss you. I miss my best friend.

Sully's going to be a dad, if you can believe it. He's going to have a little girl. God, he's going to be so wrapped around her finger. I can't wait to be Uncle Flynn. He and his wife visit a couple weeks a year and I make a yearly pilgrimage to Miami, simply so I can get some beach time and American food.

You know, a lot of times, I look at all these notebooks I filled with letters I'll never send and you'll never read and I have the urge to just throw them all in the river or burn them in the fireplace. But I won't. I occasionally look back at earlier entries and see how much I was hurting; how lost and betrayed I felt. I still hurt, to be sure, but it's more for the loss of our friendship than the loss of your love.

And even if you didn't ever love me the same way I loved you, what we had was still love. It was the best love I've ever known—the only love.

I wonder if I will ever move on from the want of you. I wonder if any woman will be enough to fill the crater you left where my heart used to be. So far, no. But that's okay. I hope you're happy, Crash; both as your best friend and the man who still loves you.

-Flynn

PART 5

PRESENT DAY

CHAPTER THIRTY-ONE

BRIGHTEN

"Is that all, Shane?" I ask my assistant as I sign the last form I will ever sign as Tennessee's First Lady.

"Yes, ma'am. And if I may say, it's been an honor working with you."

"Thank you. It was a wild ride, that's for sure."

He nods and gives me a small smile. "And I wanted to express my condolences as well. Governor Roberts will be greatly missed."

"Thank you." I rise from my desk and place the last item in the banker's box to carry out to my car. "If there's nothing else, I should be going. Jude has a piano recital and if he doesn't get to drink his customary pre-recital Yoo-hoo, he never feels like he performs as well."

"Of course. Would you like someone to carry that out for you?"

I huff a laugh. "I'm good. The day I get to thinking I'm too good to carry my shit is the day I should be knocked off my high horse. Thank you, though."

"And is there anything else you need from us?"

"No, Shane, you've done plenty. You've gone above and beyond. Truly. Organizing the movers was already more than you needed to do. Don't get me wrong, I appreciate it; you have no idea. But I'll be fine."

I walk around my desk and give my assistant, who's been with me since I became a title instead of simply a person, a hug. "If you don't get out of here, Gunnar is going to break down my door for holding you one second longer than is contractually obligated. He's been a patient man these last four years. You should get home at a decent hour for once, huh?"

He laughs and returns my embrace. "He'll be fine. I'm sure he's already popped open that celebratory bottle of champagne you sent us."

I step back and grip his shoulders. "Well, becoming dads is a huge thing. I'm so happy for you two. There is nothing like parenthood. Make sure you send me pictures when that little nugget arrives."

"We will. What will we do with you all the way in Knoxville?"

I shrug. "It's a mystery. Just going home to figure out my next move. As soon as I decide what that is, you're one of my first calls, okay?"

"I better be. You know no one handles you like me."

I laugh. "You're right about that. I don't know what I would've done without you."

"You just remember that."

As I bid the rest of my staff goodbye and carry the box out to my car and slide behind the wheel, thankful to finally be rid of the protection detail, I breathe a heavy sigh. I start the car and point it in the direction of the home Baker and I shared until he became governor and then subsequently returned to when his cancer progressed and he needed more full-time care.

To say that moving back to Knoxville isn't bittersweet would be a lie. On one hand, I'm finally fucking free. Free. Free. Free. Free. *Free.* I'm no longer beholden to anyone but myself and Jude. I'm no longer afraid of things coming to bite me—or Flynn—in the ass. Mainly because there will be no reason for anything to come to light.

After more than thirteen years in the public sector and having to navigate life in politics, I learned with brutal speed that all that glitters isn't gold and I don't want it. The public scrutiny and ridicule, the having to talk out of both sides of your mouth, the lack of basic privacy.

On the other hand, though, as wild as it sounds, I'll miss Baker. Ours was far from a loving relationship, but we did develop a sort of friendship over the years and although contractually, I could've left him when he was diagnosed with cancer since it was right about the time he'd been governor for a year, I couldn't bring myself to do it.

It wasn't only the bad press I was concerned with, although I'd be lying if that didn't play into my reasoning. It was the fact that he was Jude's dad and if my son saw me abandon his father in the midst of the fight for his life, I couldn't have lived with myself. Also, his mistress abandoned him when he got sick and he was heartbroken along with dying and in spite of it being the perfect opportunity to gloat, I didn't.

I stayed. I stayed and thought of Flynn every fucking day for the past fourteen years. Even having someone to occupy my time in the form of a "pilates instructor" for ten of those years did nothing to make me miss him less. Thankfully, he wasn't clingy and other than our weekly "sessions", never even spoke to me. It was a great arrangement, I suppose, as it scratched an itch. Also, thankfully, he didn't pitch a fit when I ended things. I suspect he had other "clients".

When I pull in at the house, I don't bother parking in the

garage and honk the horn. Thirty seconds later, Jude comes running out the door with his folder of sheet music, dressed in his recital suit.

He pushes his glasses up his nose as he climbs into the passenger seat and pulls the visor down to check his teeth in the mirror. He is fastidious about keeping his braces clean. And Flynn's kid he may not be, but damn if a lot of his mannerisms don't take me back to when we were kids.

Reaching over to ruffle his hair, I smile. "You look good. Which piece did you decide to go with?" I ask as I put the car back into gear and take off.

"'Clair de Lune'."

I nod. "That's a really good one."

"We're going to have time to get my Yoo-hoo before, though, right?"

"Of course. We'll stop at that gas station before we get to the church."

"Alright."

"Are you nervous?" I ask.

"No. I just wish Dad was here to see. I kept messing up on that one part and I finally got it right and really wanted him to hear it played perfectly."

My heart aches for my son. As much as I didn't want to be a mother, Jude has been the biggest blessing of my life. Some days, he was the only thing keeping me moving. He most likely literally saved my life a lot during those early months.

Baker was an exceptional father, that I can say with the utmost confidence. And although we were never romantic after we married, we bonded over our mutual love for our son. And we were—sometimes acrimonious—friends.

"I know. But I'm sure he knew you'd get it. You're going to do great."

"Will I have recitals in Knoxville? Do they play piano there?"

I can't help but laugh. "Yes. Believe it or not, Knox County has indoor plumbing and everything."

"And what's our new house like?"

"It's the house I grew up in. Your room will be exactly the same as it is here, down to the paint colors. It's a great room. And you're lucky, because I'm never going to tell you what colors you can and can't paint it or how you can decorate."

"How come we've never been there?"

"Well, my mother died a few years back, remember?"

He nods. "Yeah, but how come we never went to see her? How come I never met her?"

"Just because someone shares your DNA doesn't make them family, and it doesn't mean you should have anything to do with them. My mother wasn't a nice person. She was an alcoholic."

"Is that one of the reasons Dad was so big on taking down drunk drivers? Because of your mom?"

"Yeah," I answer honestly. "One of the reasons. It's also one of the reasons I don't drink much. Children of alcoholics are far more likely to be alcoholics themselves."

"There's the gas station," Jude says, pointing up ahead on the right.

I pull in and we hop out of the car and he runs into the store. "Jude, slow down. We've got time." Watching him run to the back cooler, I stay where I am so we can jump in line to pay and as he comes back toward me, I make my way over to the register and freeze in my tracks, my breath catching and heart rate spiking.

Flynn.

But when he turns, it's not Flynn. It's Jess. I know instantly, based on the warm smile he gives me. It's not lopsided and his eyes are devoid of things like betrayal and hurt and longing.

"Brighten?"

I huff a breath, willing myself not to cry. "Hey, Jess."

"Mom, I've got my Yoo-hoo."

I shake the thoughts from my head about Flynn and look at Jude. "Oh, right." I pull some cash out of my back pocket and hand it over to him before returning my attention to Jess. "So, how are you?"

"Great. How are you? You have a kid? How did I not know that?" His rapid-fire questions and friendly smile make me remember how personable Jess is.

I almost laugh. "You been under a rock or something?"

"Yeah, I guess I have. I saw when you got married, but that was it."

I nod, and Jude comes to stand beside me. "Well, this is Jude. Jude, can you say hi to my old friend Jess?"

Jess and Jude greet one another and Jess's eyes slide back to mine, his gaze questioning.

"Mom, we've gotta go. I want to warm up before the recital," my son says, growing impatient.

I look down at him. "Okay." Glancing back at Jess, I offer him a smile. "Good to see you, Jess."

"Do you have plans later? I'd love to catch up. I'm headed back home, but I've got a little time. I know Mom would kill me if I didn't at least let you catch me up."

"Well, we're on our way to a recital. You're welcome to join us. I can't promise it'll all be good, but Jude is."

He considers and nods. "Sure. Let me call my wife and let her know I'll be later than expected."

My mouth falls open in shock. "You have a wife? Mister Player?"

He nods and laughs. "Right?"

After the recital wraps up, Jude begs to hang out with a friend for the evening since we're moving, and who am I to deny him? Jess and I end up at The Pharmacy and I'm reminded every time I step into this place of that night I had burgers with Flynn and Sully.

Once we're seated and our server has dropped off some beers, Jess eyes me over his drink. "So, Jude, huh?"

I nod. "You know how close your dad and I were. It was only right. He was more a father to me than my own. He was a better man than my father."

"And how old is he?"

"He's thirteen going on twenty-five. They say teenagers know everything, but damn. I don't know how your mom handled having two of you going through puberty at the same time. Shit's exhausting."

Jess huffs a laugh and his eyes fall to my wedding ring. "So, how's married life?"

"Seriously, have you been living under a rock? Do you know who I married?"

"Not really," he admits. "Wasn't he like some rich white guy? A lot older than us?"

"Yes, to all the above. And governor for the past four years."

He blinks in shock. "Jesus. Really? Oh, and he just passed, right? I do remember seeing that. I'm so sorry."

I nod, giving him a tight smile. "Thank you. It was a long illness. So, tell me about this wife of yours," I prompt, not wanting to talk about Baker.

"Her name is Ophelia. She answered an ad I'd placed

when I needed a roommate. After a few months, we were no longer roommates," he says with a sheepish smile. "She's beautiful and funny and a lot smarter than I am."

I laugh. "It's always better to marry someone smarter than you. And how is everyone else back at home? I haven't been to Knoxville since the campaign almost five years ago and I didn't have time to look anyone up."

"Everyone seems to be good. You know about Cole Campbell?"

I nod. "I saw that on social media. And then Ada and Silas got together, right?"

"Yeah. They've got a couple of kids. Named their youngest Cole. And Josie got married last year to a former NHL player."

"Wow. And Hensley?"

"Still unattached. You know her, the person who catches her is going to have to really be worth it."

"And how's Molly? Antsy for grandkids since you've put a ring on it and all that?"

"Pretty much. Hopefully, that'll be coming soon. I can't believe you're a mom, Brighten. That's wild."

Nodding, I sip my beer. "That it is. He's the best kid, though. And brilliant. Jesus, I'm in so much trouble. He's already memorized the entire periodic table and knows pi to over a hundred places. He's also kind and kicks my ass at *Mario Kart*."

Jess's brows rise. "Wow, sounds like my kinda kid. He's good looking. Looks just like you."

"That's what they tell me. He has so many mannerisms that aren't mine, though, most of the time I don't even see the resemblance."

Our burgers are delivered and we dig in and Jess eyes me. I'm not sure if he wonders that I don't ask about Flynn because he assumes I know how Flynn is or because he knows I don't know. I have no clue what Flynn told him. I'm guessing not a ton, since Jess didn't even know about Jude and he's not treating like I broke his brother's heart.

"And I'm guessing you know about Dad?"

"Yeah. I went to see him a few months before he died and then after I heard, I took Jude to his grave and we had a nice chat."

"He loved you."

I swallow thickly. Even though Jude's been gone thirteen years, I still miss him terribly and wish I could get his advice regularly. "I know. Like I said, he was more a father to me than my own. He was one of the best men I ever met."

"And I suppose you know about Flynn?"

I blink, unsure how to answer. "What about him?" I ask tentatively.

"That he's getting married?"

A weight drops into the pit of my stomach and all the breath leaves my entire body and I will the floor to open up beneath me. I clear my throat. "I wasn't aware of that. When?"

"Two weeks. I've successfully avoided traveling out of the state except the twice I've been to Vegas and I now I have to go to Miami. It's bullshit. I don't know why they couldn't do it here."

"Miami?"

Jess chews his burger and takes a sip of his beer and explains. "Yeah, his fiancé's family is from there. His friend, Sully?" When I nod, he says, "His sister-in-law."

"Wow."

"Yeah. Kinda sudden, but I guess when you know, you know."

"Right." It's the only word I can say. Flynn is getting married. In two weeks. I only let myself look him up once a year and the last time was months ago. Last I saw, he was still single. And I still had hope.

Honestly, though, I shouldn't be surprised. Of course he's getting married. He's an amazing man and deserves all the best things. He deserves someone who loves him without needing to lose him to see it. He deserves someone who can see from the get-go what a catch he is and do something about it. Now, I guess he'll have it.

"And what comes next for you?"

I push away conjured fantasies of what I thought would happen once I returned to Knoxville. Thoughts of tracking Flynn down—even all the way in France, if needed—explaining everything to him and begging him on my knees to forgive me. Thoughts of us finally being together. Thoughts of him being a part of Jude's life. Thoughts of us being the family we should've always been.

I try to keep my voice even and not break down into tears at this table. "Well, at present, we're moving back to Knoxville later this week. Back to my old house. I'm going to rest for a while and then figure out my next moves. Get Jude settled in a new school, maybe start my own law practice, continue my charity work. I'm not sure, honestly."

"Wow, I'm not sure I've ever seen you without a concrete plan."

Well, my plan just got blown to hell, so I think it's safe to say I'm scrambling.

"The last fourteen years of my life were scheduled almost to the minute, so I'd just like to breathe a little."

Once we finish supper and say our goodbyes, I drive home and

I'm so thankful Jude's not here because I barely make it in the door before I collapse on the floor in racking sobs.

I served my fucking time. I paid my dues. I suffered enough. This was supposed to be when I could finally try to go after the man I love and make amends. I suppose this is my penance for hurting Flynn and God knows I deserve it. God knows I deserve to have to watch him be happy. God knows happiness is the least of what he deserves. He deserves every good thing.

CHAPTER THIRTY-TWO

FLYNN

"Babe, we need to make a decision here." Cleo holds up two roses that look identical to me and I tilt my head, trying to see anything different about them.

"Are they different?"

She chuckles. "Yes, this one," she says, holding up the rose in her right hand, "is cream. This other one is white."

"I'm sorry; I can't see it. I'm good with either, you know that." I check my watch. "I'm going to have to get on the road or I'm going to miss my flight. Why don't you and all your girls decide? Y'all are a lot better at it than me. I'm really only good at three things: picking a suit, picking a bottle of wine, and fucking."

Cleo laughs. "That you are." Standing from the sofa, she walks over to where I'm shoving my glasses case into my bag. She wraps her arms around my neck and I give her a smile and pull her in for a kiss. "No strippers, right?"

I shrug. "Only if Sully gets smashed. He does enjoy being naked. It's a wonder your sister allows him to drink in public at all anymore."

"Well, you know if he gets naked, and it ends up online, she'll blame you because you never get drunk."

"I'll try to keep him in line."

"You better. Kara will have your ass if you don't and you know how ruthless she can be."

Nodding, I take her face in my hands. "We'll be good. It's just a poker game at Hensley's. Trust me, not much is going to go down there. Well, not unless Ford decides to bring moonshine." I search her blue eyes and give her another kiss. "I'll call you if I can. For all I know, they'll confiscate my phone."

"Have fun and then come back to me. After next weekend, you're stuck with me, so live it up while you can, mister."

"I will." After one last kiss, I grab my bag and dart out the door.

When Sully's and my plane lands in Knoxville, we're greeted by Jess and Ford and after a moment to say our hellos, we head out to Ford's SUV. Jess nudges me as we get closer. "Sit in back with me?"

"Okay."

Once we're headed down the road and Sully finds some music he deems acceptable, Jess leans over to me and keeps his voice low. "I ran into an old friend of ours in Nashville a few days ago."

I blink, my stomach dropping, knowing without even having to ask who he's referring to. "Yeah?"

"I also met Jude."

"Yeah?"

Surprise flashes in his eyes. Probably the fact that I'm not confused hearing the name Jude shocks him. "Anything you want to tell me about that?"

I turn to look at him, giving him my full attention. "Like what?"

Jess raises a brow. "He's thirteen. You and Brighten spent time together in Vegas that year we took Dad."

"Your point?"

His jaw clenches and his nostrils flare, and he lowers his voice even more. "Are you telling me y'all didn't sleep together?"

"Yeah, we did. So what?"

"So you don't find the timing suspicious? You're not even surprised she has a kid?"

"I was there the day he was born."

"What the fuck?" he booms, all ability to keep his voice low gone in his shock.

Ford glances at us in the rearview mirror. "Everything okay?"

I nod. "Fine."

Jess splays his hands and widens his eyes, lowering his voice again. "What the fuck do you mean you were there when he was born? How did I not know about this?"

I sigh. "I'm not talking about this right now. This is supposed to be a fun day. Those memories aren't fun for me. Drop it, Jess."

My brother rolls his hands into fists. "Ford, pull the car over."

"What?" Ford asks in confusion. "Dude, we're kinda on the highway here. There's nowhere to pull over."

"Don't pull over, Ford; it's fine."

Jess shoves my shoulder. "It's not fucking fine, Flynn. Ford, stop at a fucking gas station for all I care."

Sully turns in his seat. "What's going on?"

"Nothing. We're good," I reply.

Jess scoffs. "We're not fucking good."

Ford looks torn about what to do. "Am I pulling over?"

"No," I say.

"Yes," Jess responds at the same time.

"No. We'll be at Hensley's in twenty minutes. Don't pull over." I glare at my twin. "Drop it, Jess."

Except he doesn't drop it. No sooner have we parked at Hensley's estate and walked in the front door with our bags, does Jess drag me into a room off of the foyer, slamming the door behind us. I attempt to get past him and he pushes me away. "Don't act like I can't kick your ass. I'm sure you've got a shit ton of stamina, but I'm stronger than you and will beat your ass if you don't talk right the fuck now."

I throw my hands up in frustration. The last thing I want to do is hash all this out when I'm getting married. There's no fucking point. "About what?"

"Is he yours? Or, do you even know?"

"No. He's not mine."

"How do you know? Did y'all only sleep together that once? I mean, I know about senior year in high school, but was Vegas the only other time?"

I shake my head. "No. We slept together on and off throughout college until she got pregnant and decided to marry Baker."

"And you're sure he's not yours?"

I nod, folding my arms across my chest. "Yes. There was a DNA test."

His eyes widen in shock. "So, there was a chance he could've been? She was sleeping with other guys while y'all were together?"

I sigh and drag my hands through my hair, *so* not ready to

drag all this out again. But since Jess is obviously not going to let it go, I try to break it down to its most basic parts and hope he doesn't ask any follow-up questions. "We weren't together unless we were together. It was casual, except it wasn't. It was a shit show, Jess. I don't want to talk about it. She's married. I'm getting married. None if matters anymore."

Jess frowns. "So, y'all don't talk at all anymore?"

Just go ahead and fucking kill me. Even after all this time, I can't stop the ache that settles into my chest at the thought of how long it's been since I last saw Brighten in person; last spoke to her. I've accepted it will be something I live with for the rest of my life. But at some point, you have to move on, right? You have to try to build a life with the rubble that remains from how broken you are.

That's what I'm doing now. With Cleo. And Jess bringing up Brighten just reminds me how much that chapter of my life hurts; how damaged I still am. How much I still wish things would've gone differently. How much I still love her. Even now. Even after how much she hurt me. I will never escape her.

But Cleo's a wonderful woman and is everything I should want. She loves me and wants a future with me; a family with me. And I can be happy with her. Well, as happy as someone who doesn't have a heart can be, at any rate. At this point, that's the best I can hope for.

I roll my shoulders and swallow against the tightness in my throat. "Not since the day Jude was born. She came to see Dad a few months before he died. She went into labor at the house and I took her to the hospital and stayed while she gave birth because Baker was on a business trip across the country. He conveniently arrived about ten minutes after Jude was born."

"So, why don't you talk anymore?"

"Why do you think, Jess? She broke my fucking heart. Like

I said, none of it matters anymore. She's in Nashville and married to the governor."

He blinks. "When did you get into town?"

"What do you mean? You know exactly when I got into town. You picked me up at the fucking airport."

"Fuck," he grits out, frustrated. "I mean, how long have you been back in the States?"

I shrug. "About a week. Cleo wanted to look at houses and we had time to make up for and wedding shit to do. Why?"

"Her husband died, Flynn. She's back in Knoxville. Like, as of yesterday, I think."

My breath catches. *Baker's dead? Brighten's in Knoxville?* "What?"

His eyes widen. "Oh, shit. You're still in love with her."

I blink, on the verge of hyperventilating. "What?"

"Oh, shit. What are you going to do?"

I swallow. "What do you mean?"

His eyes widen even more. "Fuck, Flynn. You have to go to her. Like, now. Tonight."

"I can't do that. This is my bachelor party. I'm getting married," I argue.

"Why?"

Splaying my hands, I scoff. "What the fuck do you mean, *why*?"

A knock sounds at the door. "Everything alright, fellas?" Sully asks through the wood.

"Not now," Jess and I say in unison.

"Why are you marrying Cleo?" he asks again.

"Because she's perfect."

"*That's* your answer? Seriously?"

"What? She is," I respond, unsure why he's so incensed.

"Ask me why I married Ophelia."

"I know why you married her. You love her."

He nods. "Exactly. So why was your answer 'she's perfect'?"

I heave a resigned sigh. "Because Cleo is the closest thing I've found to love. I don't love anymore, Jess. But she's great; she wants kids. Mom loves her. Her sister is married to my best friend. There are a lot of pluses."

"Yeah, and there's a huge fucking negative, Flynn. She's not Brighten, who you apparently *do* love, don't you?"

"It doesn't matter. I'm not sure I'm good for her anymore. I'm...pretty fucked up, Jess. Cleo is the closest thing to normal I've had since Brighten. Thirteen fucking years; I was in a hole. She's the only remotely bright spot in my life since then.

"You asked me all those years ago why I moved to France. It was so I could get away from the constant reminder of Brighten being married to someone else. So, like I said, it doesn't matter. She made her choice all those years ago, and it wasn't me. It was her ambition and a life I never, in a million years, would've imagined her choosing.

"I begged her to choose me. I cracked my fucking chest open and presented my heart to her and she threw it on the ground. And then, I watched her give birth to a baby that wasn't mine. I held her hand and talked her through it and God, she was such a fucking badass. And she named him after Dad and I shattered, Jess." Tears fill my eyes and I swipe them away.

"So go to her, man. Don't fuck up your life and Cleo's when you'll always wonder. I know you; it will eat you alive. She's single; you're technically still single. You're in the same city. What are the fucking chances, man? You're never going to get another opportunity. If you go and she doesn't still have feelings for you, then at least you tried. Which, I gotta tell you, when I told her you were getting married, it was like she'd been punched in the stomach. I thought it was just because y'all had grown apart or whatever and she was surprised to hear the news from someone else. I didn't realize there was substantial history."

My heart rate triples. "You told her?"

He nods. "And she looked devastated. She also didn't seem too tore up about her husband being dead."

Baker's dead. Brighten's here in town. I'm here in town. I'm not married yet. Can I do this? Would it matter? Is there enough left of the man she knew to salvage anything we had or am I too broken for her to still see any good in me?

Would she even still want me after all this time after how we left things?

Do I even want to know?

"Ford," Jess hollers and opens the door to the study. "Get your ass in here."

I stand, rooted to my spot, racked with indecision.

"What do you want, Jess? I'm trying to catch a buzz here."

"I need your keys."

"What's going on, guys? Isn't the party in the other room?" Sully asks, jerking his thumb over his shoulder.

"Ford, I need your keys," my brother repeats and extends his hand toward Ford in a *gimme* motion.

He hands them over to Jess and Sully steps farther into the room. "What's happening here?"

My brother doesn't answer him and instead turns to me and jingles the keys in front of my face. "Are you doing this? Don't you owe it to yourself to at least find out? If you had one extra seat in your lifeboat, who's getting it? Who is in that bed with you when you're a hundred years old?"

Brighten's face immediately flashes in my mind, but I still don't move.

Sully frowns. "What am I missing?"

RACHAEL OGLE

Jess doesn't take his eyes off mine. "Brighten's here in town. She's single. Flynn's still single."

"Fuck," Sully says, and runs his hands through his hair.

"Who's Brighten?" Ford asks.

Sully sighs. "The girl who got knocked up by a millionaire douchebag in college. She married him and smashed Flynn's heart into a billion pieces, all in the name of her ambition."

Ford blinks. "Okay, so I'm guessing Sully's not a fan?"

"Yeah, but before that, they were best friends since they were twelve when he rescued her after a terrible bike wreck. They were each other's first kiss and lost their virginities to each other. He's still in love with her."

"Okay, and Jess is a fan."

Sully steps up in front of me, his expression incredulous. "Dude, are you seriously considering ditching Cleo? After how Brighten did you? You've gotta be fucking kidding me."

Jess shakes his head. "No, he's just going to go talk to her. They might not even still have any feelings. But is it fair to any of them if he marries Cleo and he spends the rest of his life wondering 'what if'? Wouldn't it be better to know for sure?" He shoves the keys in my hand and closes my fist around them. "What's it going to be, bro?"

CHAPTER THIRTY-THREE

BRIGHTEN

It's surreal to be back in this house. It looks the same and at the same time, doesn't. The stark white walls have been replaced with grays and pops of rich color throughout the entire house. The white carpet has been replaced with warm hardwoods. And there's not a damn thing in the entire house that's pink.

Currently, we're living out of boxes and everything is everywhere and I'm about to lose my damn mind. I should've hired a professional organizer to get things in order because two days of unpacking is about to drive me up a wall.

"Mom, have you seen my Nintendo? It's not in any of the boxes in my room."

"I'm not sure. Check the ones in the living room. Maybe it got put in with the books and movies and stuff."

"Okay. Did you order the pizza yet? I'm starving."

"Yeah, it should be here any minute. Listen for the doorbell?"

Jude nods and heads back toward the living room as I open yet another box of dishes to put away and try not to think about the fact Flynn is getting married in a week. I constantly have to remind myself not to reach out to him. If he's getting married, it must be because he loves her. And if that's true, I should be happy for him. I should be happy that he's found someone. But in truth, it feels like the day fourteen years ago when he walked out of my apartment in New York all over again after I decimated both of our existences.

I open a drawer to put away some utensils and freeze. There's supposed to be something written in Sharpie in the bottom of this drawer. It's supposed to say *Crash + Flynn were here.* It was under an organizer tray, so I never worried Vanessa would find it because she didn't ever clean out the drawers to deep clean. We had a housekeeper who came in once a week and I bribed her with my allowance to not get rid of it because we wanted to see how long it would take Vanessa to find it. Flynn and I even had bets on how long it would take. His guess? Never.

But it's not here. I open all the other drawers, thinking maybe when they painted the cabinets, they put the drawer back in a different slot, but it's not here. I know they must've cleaned it or painted over it or something, but I immediately feel this sinking loss. Because now it's as if "Crash and Flynn" were never here. And maybe that would have been the least painful thing. If Flynn and I had never met.

My hand reflexively comes to my scar inside my tank top under the loose, thin cardigan I wear, and I run my fingers over the ridges and puckered skin. Even under the ink, I know exactly what it looks like.

How different would my life be if Flynn hadn't found me? Would I have died that day? Would I have had other friends and because they didn't believe me when I said I wanted to be President, would I have lost confidence in myself and veered down another path? Would I still have Jude?

This scar is responsible for so much. I think back to the

night Flynn and I made love the first time and how he looked at my scar like it was beautiful. I was so concerned about needing people to not flinch when they saw it, I just covered it up.

Don't hate on something that means so much to me.

As the words roll through my mind, tears burn my eyes. I've done an exceptional job of keeping it together during the day. Granted, it's only been less than a week since I learned the man I love is about to marry someone else. At night, though, I sob uncontrollably for hours.

This must've been what it was like for him to know I was going to marry Baker. At least he loves her. He should have that. He should have all the things he's always wanted. He should have them with someone who can be what he deserves. He should have someone who will choose him first.

"Mom?" Jude calls from the direction of the front door, but his tone is confused.

I heave a sigh. "I've already paid for the pizza, honey. They should just hand it over."

"Mom, can you come here, please?"

"What is it? I've got my hands full."

"Mom, it's not the damn pizza. Jeez."

I drop the utensils back into the box and walk, angry, to the door. "Jude, language." *Can't I have a fucking moment to wallow in my—.* I nearly choke on air when I see who's at the door.

"Mom, he says he's not that Jess guy, but he looks like Jess."

I swallow and try to breathe. "That's Jess's twin brother, Flynn."

Jude gives me his full attention. "Mom, are you alright? You look like you're about to pass out."

I blink rapidly. "Yeah. I'm good." Movement over Flynn's shoulder catches my eye and the pizza delivery driver walks up onto the porch. Oblivious to the tsunami of emotions washing through me, Jude steps up to accept the pizzas and takes off toward the kitchen.

"Do we have plates yet?" he calls over his shoulder and I still can't take my eyes off Flynn.

"Uh, yeah, in the cabinet."

"Can I take mine into my room? I want to finish organizing my music."

"Sure."

Flynn is still on the porch and I'm standing at the door gripping the side of it and I have no clue what to even say. The last time I saw him, he was so heartbroken, the look on his face so anguished that day in the hospital when he said whatever he said to Baker. Baker never told me. The expression on his face has haunted me for over thirteen years.

Flynn's eyes follow Jude's movements up the stairs and when he's out of sight, his gaze slides back to mine, one brow raised. "I figured governor's wives were more gracious hosts, Crash."

A rush of air leaves me hearing him call me Crash. Ever since the day I ended things, he's only called me by my name except for when I was laboring and wanted to give up, and his pep talk got me through those last agonizing minutes.

I huff a weak laugh. "Shit. You're right. Please, come in."

He steps inside and I take him in as I shut the door behind him. Expensive dark wash jeans and a black button down, casual shoes, expensive watch. Fit, runner's body. Stylish hair, cut short, and intentional scruff on his jaw. Glasses very similar to the simple black plastic frames he used to wear. Still no wedding ring. He looks so fucking perfect I can't stand it.

I look down at myself and immediately feel frumpy and grimy in the leggings, tank top, and cardigan I'm wearing. My hair is up in a messy bun and I'm not wearing any makeup, all my age spots and splotchiness on full display. I can't even remember when I last shaved my legs. Not that it matters, it just serves to remind me how sloppy I must look at present.

Flynn shoves his hands in his pockets as he looks around the room, cataloging all the changes. "You let him eat in his room? Vanessa would shit a brick."

It's the most normal thing I've heard him say in longer than I can remember and I laugh out of the sheer joy of hearing him sound like himself. I blink back my tears at the happiness I feel at getting to see him. Even if he's here to tell me himself that he's getting married to a wonderful, beautiful woman who actually deserves him.

Maybe that's why he's come here today. Maybe he wants to watch my heart break the same way I broke his. I couldn't blame him. It would truly be the least that I deserve.

"I love what you've done with the place. It actually looks like somewhere people want to live and not just visit. I'm guessing no pink?"

I can't help but smile. "Fucking right."

He huffs a laugh. "Nice to see politics hasn't taken away your eloquence."

I shrug. "What can I say? You can put the girl in the spotlight, but when it's off, she's still her."

He nods and we both stand several feet apart for a long moment, neither of us speaking. Flynn's eyes travel down my frame and I nearly want to cringe because of how disheveled I look when he looks so amazing. "You look good, Brighten."

My heart sinks when he says my name. "You're one to talk," I reply quietly. "You still run?"

He nods. "Every day. Sometimes twice." He glances around again. "Honestly, this would be the last place I would ever expect to find you again. I figured you would've sold it after Vanessa died."

I sigh. "She wanted to sell, but since my father left it in

both of our names, she couldn't sell it without my permission. I made her keep it out of spite. And honestly, it's a good house and the school district is great, so it made sense." Turning the subject back to him, I ask, "You've gone back to wearing your glasses?"

He shrugs. "My eyes dry out when I fly. I forgot to take out my contacts before I left Paris and by the time I got to Miami, they were killing me. I'm giving my eyes a few days' rest."

"Right. Paris. I think I knew that. How long have you been there?"

He blinks, surprised that I would know where he's been living. "Since right after Dad died." At his mention of Jude, my chest tightens. Flynn looks toward the stairs. "He's huge. Damn."

"I know," I say with a laugh. "Probably going to end up being six-four, or so they tell me."

"He's beautiful."

"He is," I agree.

My stomach rumbles, reminding me I've not had anything since toast this morning before I started unpacking. Flynn gestures toward the front door. "I'm sorry I showed up right at suppertime. I can go."

I step forward. "No," I say immediately. "I mean, I have plenty of pizza; have you eaten?"

"I don't want to impose."

"You're not. Please?" I plead. I almost don't care if he's here to tell me it's too late for us. Just getting to look at him is like finding an oasis after walking through the desert for weeks without a drop of water.

"If you're sure."

I latch onto his words like a life preserver and nod quickly. "I am. We're still sorta living out boxes, but the kitchen's been my priority today, so we should be good." I head toward the kitchen and hear his footsteps behind me, thankful he's following.

I pull a couple of plates down from the cabinet and hand one to him. "Beer?"

He nods. "Sure."

I grab us each a bottle from the fridge and when I turn around, he's looking down at the two pizzas, a look of horror on his face, and I can't help but laugh. "I don't claim that. That's all Jude."

"Pineapple? Really? What are you teaching that kid? Does he not know the best pizza is just pepperoni?"

"Thus the pepperoni that's all mine. And yours, I guess."

He nods. "Perfect. Want me to just take the box over? I'd really like to not be anywhere near that pineapple monstrosity ever again."

I laugh again and I think it might be the most I've laughed since that day in New York. "Sure."

Flynn hands me his plate and picks up the box and carries it over to the table and sets it down. We each pull a slice onto our plates and for a few minutes, we're both quiet; simply eating and watching each other eat and drink. It should feel awkward, but it's never been awkward with him. Tense and heartbreaking sometimes, but never awkward.

After a single slice, I'm too amped up to eat any more, needing to know why he's here. "How are you here?"

He blinks, as if surprised I've finally broached the subject of his presence. "I was at Hensley's with Jess, Sully, and Ford. She's hosting us for my bachelor party. She's out of town, but she offered us the house for a poker game."

"Ford?" I ask, not recognizing the name and not wanting to linger of the "bachelor party" bit.

"Josie's husband," he supplies. "Former hockey player. Fucking giant. Biggest guy I think I've ever seen."

RACHAEL OGLE

"When did you get into town?"

"Today. Sully and I came in from Miami."

Thinking about Sully takes me back to the day he confronted me at Elias's retirement party. I deserved everything he said to me; I hurt his best friend. It still stings, though, the things he said.

"He shouldn't have said the stuff he did to you at Elias's party."

I shake my head. "Yeah, he should've. I would've done the same thing in his position. I'm sure he wanted to say a lot worse than he actually did. I've never felt like he was in the wrong."

"He was still disrespectful. I'm sorry."

To hear him apologize for anything at all makes me feel about an inch tall. "You don't need to apologize for anything, Flynn. Ever, where I'm concerned." I look up at the ceiling to the approximate location of Jude's room—my old room—and sigh. "There's so much I wish I could tell you."

"So tell me," he replies, his tone even.

How would I even begin? How do I explain myself after all this time? Is it even possible? Not with Jude here. I can't do that, I know. I'd never break my son's heart. Baker was his father, and he was a great one. Regardless of my feelings about him, I'd never do that to Jude.

"When would be a better time?"

I blink and return my gaze to his. "What?"

His eyes dart to the ceiling before looking back at me and repeating himself with more meaning. "When would be a better time? Or is it that you can't tell me at all?"

I blow out a breath, marveling after all these years at how he can still know exactly what I'm going to say. "He's got an early morning lesson with his new piano teacher, so he'll probably turn in soon. He's had a busy day, so I wouldn't be surprised if he passes out after pizza and a round of *Mario Kart*.

Can you hang around? We can talk after he's in bed. I can't have him overhear any of it," I say meaningfully.

Flynn nods. "I can understand that." After a beat, he gives me a genuine smile and my heart nearly stops. "So, piano and *Mario Kart*? Damn, he really is your kid."

I huff a small laugh out of my nose. "He's better at both than I ever was. He'd give you a run for your money on Rainbow Road. Beat me when he was eight."

Flynn laughs. "Wow. That's pretty good. Maybe I'll get to challenge him to a game."

I don't give myself permission to hope his words mean anything, regardless how badly my heart is aching for exactly that. "So, Jess said—."

"Yeah," he confirms. "That's the plan."

"How do you do that?" I ask, incredulous.

He shrugs. "You're you. I'm me. Some things don't change, even when everything changes, I guess." Leaning back in his chair, he sips his beer. "Is it weird being back?"

"Fucking surreal," I admit. "I keep expecting Vanessa to pop up from around the corner and choke me with that god-awful canopy that was on my bed."

He laughs. "Yeah, that room was atrocious."

"Damn straight."

His eyes roam over my face and his smile morphs into something softer that makes my chest ache. "A lot of good memories, though."

I nod. "Definitely. Some of the best."

"Mom?"

Both our heads snap toward the stairs where Jude stands holding his plate. As he walks into the kitchen and puts his dishes in the dishwasher, he eyes Flynn and me. "I'm going to go practice for a while before bed. Is there anything you need help with unpacking before I do?"

I stand and walk over to him and smile and drop a kiss onto his cheek. He's too tall for me to put one on the top of his head anymore. "I'm good, kiddo. I'll get everything unpacked. You've been a huge help today. Will you wear your headphones while you practice? I might watch some TV in a bit."

"Sure. Night, Mom. Nice to meet you, Flynn."

"You, too, Jude. See you later." Again, I don't give myself permission to let hope take root. It's a simple, normal way to say goodbye. Nothing more. Flynn waits until Jude's bedroom door opens and closes again before he speaks. "Will you be able to get it all unpacked?"

CHAPTER THIRTY-FOUR

FLYNN

"Will you be able to get it all unpacked?" I ask the back of her head as her eyes are still trained on the stairs. She knows I'm not talking about the boxes that are stacked all around the house. She knows I'm referring to us and what the fuck happened with Baker and why she's back in town and in this house.

I haven't really been able to take my eyes off her since I came inside. I stopped giving myself permission to look her up after ten years went by and she was still married to him and he was diagnosed. It was causing me more damage than even the joy the glimpses of her gave me could overcome.

But now I'm here and she's here and her kid is the spitting image of her and polite and cares about his mother and offers to help her unpack. He's not a shit. Not that I really thought he would be; Brighten wouldn't stand for it. But I don't know; maybe I thought since he was Baker's he would be this pretentious little snot who I'd want to throttle at first sight. And other than his annoyed curse about the pizza when I showed up—and if I'm honest, I get it, so I cut him some slack about that—he seems perfect.

And God, Brighten is fucking magnificent. She's aged, of course, but it's done nothing but made her even more beautiful. Her hair is up in a mass on the top of her head, but is still that brilliant, shiny, coppery red that I used to thread my fingers through. Her face is free of makeup and I'm reminded of all the mornings I was privileged enough to wake up beside her. Her hips are wider and breasts fuller and it's all I can do to not reach out and run my finger along her tattoo simply to feel her scar.

It's so fucking unfair that I still want her like this. Like a blind man who's lost his sight, so he remembers what things and people look like, but over time, the acuteness of those memories fades and you only have the dimmed images in your mind. I've suddenly been given my sight back and everything is in brilliant technicolor and almost too much to look at.

I should hate her. I shouldn't give a shit what explanation she has for everything she put me through. I shouldn't want to hear her finally tell me she loves me, even after all these years. I shouldn't want her to want to drag me to her room and beg me to fuck her. I shouldn't want her to tell me the last fourteen years were the worst years of her life. I shouldn't want her to ask me to never leave. And yet, those are all the things I want.

She turns to face me and she's kept her expression mostly neutral since I arrived. I expect she's afraid to show any emotion since she's unsure why I'm here. I want answers more than anything right now, so that's all I'm hoping for tonight. Or, at least, the start of answers. Fourteen years is a shit ton to unpack. Regardless of what my heart—or what's left of it— wants, I'm not sure I can let it call the shots. Logically, I shouldn't be here. It's dangerous. But Jess is right, it will eat me

CRASH INTO ME 331

up if I don't at least know once and for all if we're done. I owe it to myself and my possible future with Cleo to get closure.

Even if closure is the last thing I truly want. Closure would mean that Brighten and I are a finished book and not just at the end of a painful chapter. Closure would mean that I would finally have to lay my heart to rest. Closure would mean that the flicker of hope I've tried to keep locked away will never be able to burn bright again. Closure would mean that the way I feel right now—the half a man I've been since I left that day in New York—is the best I'll ever feel.

"I hope so," she finally says, yanking me out of my thoughts. She seems to come to some sort of conclusion and nods, but it's not directed at me, so I simply wait. "Did you drive over here?"

I frown. "Yeah. Why?"

"Because I can't have this conversation in the house. Can we sit in your car and talk?"

"Sure."

Picking up her phone from the counter, she walks into the living room and turns the TV on and glances up the stairs one last time before motioning for me to follow her. I almost want to laugh at the lengths she's going to simply so Jude doesn't overhear, but I also understand it. If I were her, I wouldn't want to my kid to overhear me talking about my past. God knows I never want my future children to know about it. Especially not the past fourteen years and all the nameless, faceless women. All the anger and self-loathing. All the times I eyed a bottle of gin beside my antidepressants and wondered how much it would take to go to sleep and never wake up again. So I follow her outside.

I click the fob on Ford's SUV, and she automatically climbs in the backseat. I'm not sure what to make of it, but I just walk around to the other side and get in with her. It's cool enough outside that in the car it's not too hot, so I don't start the engine and sit back and shove the keys back into my pocket and watch her.

She sits facing forward, her posture stiff, her hands rubbing over the tops of her thighs exactly like she did the day she told me she was pregnant. And I just wait.

An eternity goes by, but I'm thinking it's really only about five minutes. She darts occasional glances up to the window where Jude's room is located and, even through the blinds, you can make out his form over a piano or keyboard.

"What did you say to him? That day at the hospital?"

Her voice piercing the silence is nearly jarring and I almost startle. "Who, Baker?"

"Yeah. What did you say to him?"

"He didn't tell you?"

"No. I've always been curious. I mean, if you can remember. I know it was a long time ago, and there was a lot going on that day."

"I remember," I confirm. "I remember everything. Everything before and after and things I wish I didn't." Her eyes fall to her lap and in the light spilling into the vehicle from the full moon, I see her close her eyes as if in pain and bite her lip.

In spite of the urge to simply take her in my arms and say, "fuck the past, let's start over and be us again," I'm not sure that's what I want. I still have Cleo to consider and despite how much my heart and body still react to this woman, I'm not sure if what she's about to tell me will be enough to make me want to have to break Cleo's heart and blow up my life.

"I told him the only reason he was still breathing was because I didn't want to take away from what you'd just done. I said he didn't deserve either of you and that someday, not even the love I had for you would be enough to prevent me from kicking his ass."

"Looks like cancer beat you to the ass kicking. Sorry."

"No, I'm sorry. I'm sure that was a lot to deal with. Are you and Jude holding up okay? I know that's such a stupid question considering he died, and no one's okay after a death."

"I'm fine," she says automatically. "Jude's coping. He's got a counselor. Plus, Baker was sick for a long time."

"Still, I'm sorry. No kid should have to lose their dad."

She sighs and looks back up at his window. "No, they shouldn't. I'm sorry I didn't come to Jude's funeral. I didn't want to make it harder for you and I'd already said my good-byes to him, but I've always regretted I didn't come to pay my respects to your mom and you and Jess."

I nod. "I understood. Not sure Mom would've remembered you being there, anyway; she was a wreck. She still has that tree you sent, though. She planted it in the backyard and it's gotten pretty big."

"I'm glad. I'm guessing you can see it from the sunroom?"

"Yeah."

"Good. I hoped you could. I went to his grave when Jude was about a year old and even though I knew he wouldn't remember, I wanted him to know where he got his name."

"He was tickled pink when I told him what you named him," I say with a sad smile.

Her eyes snap to mine and they're wet with unshed tears and my chest aches. "You told him?"

"Yeah. He got fed up with my bullshit the night before he died and came out and asked me if I knew what name you'd picked. I didn't know he knew and then that led to me telling him everything."

"I'm sorry you had to go through that; to relive it."

"Brighten, I relived it almost daily for ten years."

She wipes under her eyes, swiping her tears. "I'm so sorry, Flynn. God, I've had this conversation in my mind so many times since that day in New York. I imagined what I'd say if I ever got to see you again. I was going to track you down and try to make it right and finally tell you everything."

"So tell me now," I plead.

"Will it matter?" Her voice cracks and even through the obvious anguish in her tone, there's hope, too.

Anger swells in my chest to think that she'd only tell me if the outcome might make me toss a grenade into my life; even if I already know it may do just that.

"You don't get to ask me if it will matter. What comes after you tell me shouldn't fucking matter. I've racked my brain for years trying to figure out why you would've done it. I deserve the truth, Brighten, and you don't get to tell me I don't."

She nods quickly. "I know. I'm sorry. You do deserve the truth. I only ask if it will matter because if you're happy and in love, I don't want to step on any toes. I don't want to derail any of your plans. After everything I did to you, all I want is for you to be happy. You have no idea how badly I want that. I will gladly live the rest of my life watching you be happy if you are. I don't want what I tell you to change what you've already decided."

I scoff, annoyed. "There you go again, telling me what's best for me. You've never given me enough fucking credit. Why don't you let me decide for myself, huh? Why don't you tell me why the fuck you married Baker? I know it wasn't for fucking love. I mean, for all I know, you grew to love him, but there is nothing you can say to ever make me believe it started out that way.

"And I'm sure you don't regret Jude. I can see it on your face how much you love him; you're an amazing mom. But you never wanted it. So explain it to me. Explain to me why you're back here and not in Nashville blazing a path to fucking D.C.."

"Because I don't want it anymore."

I choke on air with my shock at her words. "You don't fucking *want it*? You mean to tell me you did all this for your fucking ambition and you don't even want it anymore? That's bullshit. You cannot be serious. You were made for it. I watched how you were during the campaign; how you were with the public. And as much as I hate hearing myself saying this, you looked happy doing it. You and Baker looked happy."

Brighten lets out this sputtering sob and shakes her head vehemently. "It was a fucking act, Flynn. Every bit of it. I've been playing a part for almost fourteen fucking years and I'm tired. I'm done. That's why I don't want it. I've had my fill of pandering and public opinions and protective details and not even being able to take a shit without someone knowing about it.

"And no, I never loved Baker. For years, I barely tolerated him. Toward the end, we were something like friends, but it was probably more begrudging respect than anything. I respected him as a businessman and political leader. I respected him as a father. I detested him as a man for years.

"And I hated him so fucking much when he got sick. I was finally going to be free and I was going to come find you. And then he got sick and Briana left him and he didn't have anyone else to take care of him. And in the event I ever did decide I wanted to run, I'd never outlive the bad press of a wife who left her dying husband. So I stayed. Three years longer than I was required to."

I blink, so confused, and have no clue where to start. "Okay, I'm going to need way more to go on. Who's Briana, and what do you mean 'required'?"

She sighs. "Briana was his mistress. For eight years. She was great. We were friends. But she couldn't deal with the chemo and radiation and the side effects and watching him wither away, so she broke things off with him. And my deal with Baker was that I would stay until he'd been in office as Governor for one year or ten years of marriage, whichever came first."

"What deal? And he had a mistress? He cheated on you? What the fuck? I'm so fucking confused." And I am. I am reeling from this. She made some sort of deal with Baker and bargained away ten years of her life? "Can you just please start from the beginning?"

"Yes. But please know I don't expect you to understand and if you hate me after I'm done, it would be justified. Most days, I still can't believe I actually agreed to it, but I did it because I love you."

I love you.

Her words hit me like a physical blow to my diaphragm and I huff out a breath and nod, because I have no words in this moment.

"That night you surprised me in New York?" I nod and she takes a bracing breath. "I'd been on a date with Baker earlier that evening. It was fun, and we had a nice time. It was the first date we'd been on because he'd been my mentor up to that point, but the day we wrapped up our last meeting, he asked me out. He was smart and charming and I agreed to meet him for drinks.

"We had a good time and went back to my place after. And the kissing was good, and I was happy to take things further, but I told him that regardless of what happened between him and me that you were always going to be there and I'd never choose him over you if that's what he was thinking."

Except she did choose him. And knowing she was with Baker the same night as me? I'm not sure how I'm supposed to feel about that.

She blows out another breath before continuing. "He said he understood, and I got naked and it was the worst thirty seconds of my life. He didn't even take off his shoes. There was no foreplay, and I wasn't even wet enough. And by the time I was about to stop him, he was finished. It was abysmal.

"I was so shocked by how bad it was, I just wanted him to leave. After a few minutes of small talk, my phone rang and it was you and suddenly, I just wanted him gone, and I wanted to talk to you and I missed you so much. So I got rid of him and called you back."

Her eyes close and she bites her lip. "And then you came. It was the best surprise ever. You have no idea how much that weekend meant to me, Flynn."

I can't help but ask, thinking back on that first night I was in New York. "So, when I asked if you were sore, you were, weren't you? Because of him?" She nods and I've never wanted to bring someone back to life just to kill them all over again until now. "Fuck," I breathe, my jaw clenched.

Continuing her story, she swipes a thumb along her lashes. "That weekend, it finally hit me that you were the absolute best out there for me. And I don't just mean sexually, although, I think we both know you're that, too. I realized no one challenges me or stimulates me intellectually like you. No one knows me like you do. No one else is you.

"I started to think that maybe I could choose only you. That we could figure out what a future could look like. That maybe even if I never wanted to get married or have kids, we could still be together. Without other people. I even went that entire time after our weekend together without anyone else just to see if I could.

"And thinking about the prospect of having you all to myself made it easy to turn other people down. I knew then I could do it. I was going to tell you the weekend of the wedding that I wanted *us*. I was going to tell you that I loved you." Her voice breaks at the end and tears spill down her cheeks. My breath catches and wetness immediately fills my eyes.

I clear my throat to loosen the tightness that's settled in. "So what changed? What did Baker do? You told me y'all spent time together over the summer. You said you liked him a lot. What the fuck happened?"

She sniffles. "You have to promise to let me get through it all before you react. Please?"

"I'll try." Even though I'm not sure how I'll keep that kind of promise.

She nods and opens her mouth to speak. What comes out is a fantastical tale of Vanessa and her father and an old girlfriend of Baker's. When she tells me about him sabotaging her birth control and purposely getting her pregnant, I'm nearly sick with rage. And then she tells me about his threats to ruin any future she hoped to have with lies of plagiarism and sex work and photos of all her sexual exploits—ones including the two of us—and it's all I can do to not come out of my skin and put my fist through the window of this fucking car.

And when she tells me about his threats to my career and freedom and finishes with him planning to reveal that she had an abortion after she left Nashville the summer of my internship, my heart aches; even if I can understand why she'd do it. We were eighteen. Neither of us would've been ready for that, but I would've gone with her and held her hand so she wouldn't have had to be alone.

"And I didn't see a way out. It was me or both of us, so I fell on the sword. I know it broke you and I figured I loved you enough to give you up so you could at least have your dreams. And I couldn't tell you the whole truth because he had cameras in my apartment, so I lied, and I had to take a fucking Valium to even get through breaking things off with you and not be a blubbering mess.

"Originally, the deal stated that we would stay married until he was Governor and a year later, I'd be released and he'd destroy any of the things he was holding over us. I demanded he amend the agreement to say governor or ten years, whichever came first. I think my hope was, even after ten years, you might still have enough memory of the good times we shared that I could explain it all and we could heal. If not to be together, at least to be friends again. Because fuck, I've missed your friendship.

"And I was about to walk out the door to the lawyer's office when he came home and told me about his cancer. It was like I was losing you all over again because I knew I couldn't leave him. Not and keep my son's respect or any hope of a political future if that's what I wanted someday. So I stayed and prayed I'd still be able to explain it all to you. I knew there was probably no way you'd be unattached in some way because you're you, but I at least wanted to make amends.

"Not because I ever hoped to be forgiven, because I don't deserve it. But simply so you could have closure. I know you've always wondered and I couldn't tell you then.

"And no, I didn't want to be a mother. Even after Jude was born, I hated that I'd been put in the position I was. I didn't resent him or hate him and I didn't mistreat him, but motherhood didn't come naturally to me. It wasn't until he was nursing one day when he was about three months old and he reached up and touched my face and his eyes locked with mine that I actually felt anything. I think it was the first day I breathed in almost a year. Since the day I hurt you.

"And Jude is the only thing that kept me going most days. I'd put on this mask whenever we were in public and even in front of Jude, and I was so exhausted all the time. But he's honestly the best thing in my life. I'd lost the only man I ever loved, so I put the love I realized I'd probably always had for you into Jude and my charity duties and carved out an existence from what was left of the shell that remained when I destroyed *us*.

"Thirty seconds changed our entire lives and I've hated myself for it every single day for almost fourteen years, Flynn. There were even days when I'd think about what it might be like if I wasn't here anymore. And I wish I could say it was the thought of Jude that kept me around, but it wasn't. It was the thought of you finding out I'd killed myself and you never knowing why I did what I did. I couldn't handle the thought of what that would do to you. So I made myself live despite that being the last thing I wanted to do most days.

"And it would have been easier to hate Baker if he was cruel or treated me badly, but he didn't. He didn't love me and I didn't love him and we only ever had sex the one terrible time. We slept in separate beds our entire marriage.

"But he was a good father. He loved Jude, and he was attentive and a good co-parent. He was a villain, but I didn't hate him. And other than when we struck our deal, he wasn't ever heartless. I even understood his reasoning behind everything. I hated my parents for what they did. I never spoke to Vanessa again after I found out what she did except through the lawyers.

"I'd taken this box of things that belonged to my father; some photos and a journal of his. I was so angry, I just burned everything. I'd always thought of my father as this great man and I wanted to be like him and follow in his footsteps. He covered up a murder that my mother committed. I don't want to be anything like him anymore.

"And maybe that's why I don't care about politics much anymore. Besides being tired of living my life—and Jude's life—under a microscope, I no longer want to follow in his footsteps. I want a normal life for Jude. He's never known what it's like to just be a normal kid. He's only ever been Senator Roberts's or Governor Roberts's son. I want him to figure out who he is without that identity.

"I want him to find a friend who will call him on his bullshit and challenge him and believe in his dreams. I don't want him to question if he only got where to he is because of who his father was. I want him to feel that sense of accomplishment I never will. Even if I ever go into office, I'll always be the widow of Governor Roberts. I won't ever just be candidate Dawes or anything all on my own again.

"I'll never regret my time in Nashville, aside from Baker, because I got to bring awareness to the disease that killed one of the best men I ever knew. So if for nothing more than having Jude and doing something to help in the fight against MS, I think I'd have to say I'd do it all over again. But I'd give anything short of my son's life to take back the pain I caused you and the time we lost."

Her lip quivers and she swallows thickly and clears her throat. "I know you're getting married and I want you to know I'm so happy you've found someone who will love you the way you deserve to be loved. That you've found someone who can choose you without reservation and didn't have to lose you to see exactly how much you meant to her. As your once best friend, I cannot convey how elated I am that you will have everything you've ever wanted.

"I know when we were together you said you didn't need a family or marriage, but I know you've always wanted those things. You want to be a dad like your dad. And really, who can blame you? He was the best dad ever. And you want a marriage like your parents had. You should have those things. Even if it's not with me."

Throughout the telling, her eyes have remained mostly dry, and I wonder if that's because she's played this out in her head so many times over the past several years. I have no clue what I expected to feel when she finally came clean. I'm not even sure how to process it. It's honestly more than I ever imagined was possible and I'm not even sure I'm angry with her, even if I know I have the right to be.

"I need you to get out of this car," I say before I explode.

CHAPTER THIRTY-FIVE

BRIGHTEN

"I need you to get out of this car."

Entirely emotionally spent from the telling, his words are like a jolt to my system. "What?"

"Crash, get out of this car. Please. I need a minute alone and I can't be outside because you have neighbors and Jude and I need this. Get out."

I scramble from the SUV, still a bit rattled, but as soon as I close the door, he lets out an ungodly anguished scream that even through the glass and metal of the car sounds like he's standing right in front of me and I start in surprise. He repeatedly pounds his fists against the seat beside him and releases a string of curses that were this not such a serious moment, I might find comical.

But nothing about this is funny and I want so badly to be the one receiving those blows, because at least I'd have visible proof of the pain I caused him. And even if he can't forgive me and doesn't still love me, I've cleared my conscious and told him that I love him.

And even if I still love him, I don't deserve him now; if I

ever did to begin with. I genuinely don't want to cause another woman the pain of losing him by asking him to choose me. Regardless of how badly I want to do exactly that. I know how badly it hurts to lose him and I won't do it to someone else.

The sounds from inside the vehicle grow softer until it's only those of him crying, with his head in his hands. And I'm not sure if he'll allow me to comfort him, but it's all I want to do in this moment. I open the door, the sound of his wailing growing markedly louder when I do. I climb back into the car and wrap my arms around him and hold him as tight as I possibly can as he attempts to absorb the past fourteen years.

He lets me hold him and buries his face in my neck and clutches me to him and tears fill my own eyes. He feels so familiar, even after all this time, and he still smells the same, even with the scent of the cologne he now wears. But underneath it, I can smell the boy he was before I broke him.

I think back to the day I told him we should have sex simply to get it over with. I recall his obvious reservations and then the care he took our first time. He loved me even then, and I was so oblivious and couldn't see it and thought I needed anything more than him. God, if I could go back and talk to my younger self, I'd tell her that Flynn is the only thing I'd ever need.

But you can't go back, no matter how much you want to. And even now, as he lets me console him, I don't dare hope it's anything more than him needing some sort of tether. I don't hope that after everything I've done—everything I've cost us—I can ever think he'd still love me.

It could be two minutes or six hours as we both cry and hold on to one another until we're spent and unable to even make any more tears. He pulls back and I take his face in my hands and drag my thumbs across his cheeks. Somehow in his rage and subsequent tears, his glasses have gone missing and even only illuminated by the moon filtering through the windows, I can see the gold ring around his pupil as his eyes search mine. "I'm so—."

My words are cut off by his lips against mine, and I gasp in surprise as he kisses me. His tongue sweeps into my mouth and desire like I haven't felt since the last time we were together floods my entire body and I can't help but moan and thread my fingers into his hair and yank him closer and deepen the kiss.

He lifts me onto his lap, and I straddle him as he kisses his way down my neck. "Fuck, Crash." His words come out pained and desperate and all I can do is revel in the way his lips feel on my skin after all this time.

"Oh God, Flynn," I moan and drag his mouth back to mine. Both of our hands are everywhere and I have his shirt unbuttoned and my cardigan is somewhere in the floor and he shifts us so I'm lying on the backseat and he's above me, my knees bracketing his hips.

He looks down at me and smiles and my heart fills, and there are no words to describe how impossibly blissful this moment feels. It's not anything I ever expected to have again, and I want to weep with joy to have it now. He drops his mouth back to mine and grinds himself against me, and I gasp with feeling him hard and perfect behind the zipper of his jeans.

"Jesus Christ, those sounds," he says and huffs a laugh into my neck and I'm in the process of pushing his shirt off his shoulders when a shrill ringing blasts from his pocket and we both freeze.

He yanks his head up, his eyes locking with mine, and we both know without him even having to look who it is. Because of course it is. All the color drains from his face and a weight drops into the pit of my stomach as I extricate myself from under him and open the door. Flynn grabs my hand. "I have to go."

Blinking in shock, I simply nod. "Okay. Be safe." I'm afraid to say more than that for fear I break down and beg him to stay. But I already told myself I didn't expect anything from him after the telling. And if that's the last kiss I ever get from him, I know I will love him until the day I die.

Retrieving my cardigan from the floor and picking my phone up from the seat, I hop out of the car and watch as he steps out and climbs behind the wheel and starts the engine. I can't bring myself to look at him out of fear I'll see regret for the kiss we just shared. It would be understandable. He has a fiancé. He's getting married. I am his terrible past. She is his wonderful future. She will be the mother of his children.

I step into the house and lean back against the door and hang my head and sigh.

"Mom?"

Jude's voice makes me snap my head up. "Yeah, honey?"

"Who was that guy?"

I frown and slip my cardigan back on and scrub my hands down my face to clear away any stray tears. "Who, Flynn?"

"Yeah. Who was he?"

"He's an old friend."

"You were outside with him."

"We were just talking. I haven't seen him in a long time and we were catching up."

"Did he know Dad?"

I nod. "Yeah. A little."

"Was that him screaming? Why was he yelling?"

"Yeah. It's fine. Why don't you go back to bed, okay?"

Jude examines my face as if he wants to ask me or tell me something else. "How long have you known that guy?"

"Since I was twelve."

He nods. "And when was the last time you saw him?"

I cross to the sofa and sit and turn off the TV and Jude

comes to sit beside me. "I last saw Flynn the day you were born."

His eyebrows rise. "Really?"

Nodding, I roll my shoulders. "Yeah. I'd gone to see Flynn's dad—the man you're named after—because he was really sick and he asked me to come play piano for him. I went into labor while I was at their house. Your dad was in New Mexico, I think. Flynn took me to the hospital and stayed with me until your dad got there. I gave you his middle name as yours."

"Is he going to be around a lot?"

"What do you mean?"

"Like...Briana. Is he going to be around a lot?"

My heart rate spikes and I swallow. "Briana and I were friends. Flynn and I were friends a long time ago. I'm not sure what we are now. I'm not sure if he'll be back," I admit.

"Do you want him to come back?"

"I would like us to be friends again," I confirm.

Jude's brow pinches in concentration. "Can I ask you something?"

I reach up to run my fingers through his hair, smoothing the top from where the band of his headphones has left an indentation. "Of course."

"Did Dad like Flynn?"

I splay my hands. "They didn't know each other very well. They only met a few times."

"And did you and Flynn stop being friends because you married Dad?"

"What's with the twenty questions, kid?"

His eyebrows rise again. "That's a yes. You answered a question with a question. That's dodging and you always say if you answer a question with a question, it's because you don't want to answer the question you've been asked."

"You're too smart for your own good, you know," I say with a laugh.

"I know. But you and Dad were pretty smart, so I guess it's your fault. So, Flynn? Is he cool?"

I nod, a small smile pulling at the corners of my lips. "He's the coolest. To this day, I've never beat him at *Mario Kart*."

"Sorry, Mom, but you suck at *Mario Kart*."

I scoff. "Ouch. Harsh."

"Just being honest." Thinking for a moment, he pushes his glasses up his nose. "So, if Flynn comes back again—and why wouldn't he come back, anyway? But if he comes back, will you be happy about that?"

I don't give myself permission to get my hopes up, but answer Jude honestly. "I'd be elated."

"You didn't look at Flynn like you did his twin brother." Blinking, I open my mouth to say something and Jude tilts his head. "Did you and Flynn like each other? Before Dad? Like, was he your boyfriend?"

"Flynn and I loved each other," I admit.

"But you met Dad? That's why you didn't stay with Flynn?" I nod because it's true. "Do you still like Flynn? Like, love-like him?"

I huff a laugh at his wording. "Fourteen years is a long time and people change."

"That's really vague, Mom."

"It's all I've got, kid."

Jude looks down at his hands. "If you were friends with Flynn again, would you still cry at night?"

I blow out a breath, feeling as though I've been punched. "Sometimes people get sad, Jude. Your dad was sick; I was stressed. Lots of things make people cry."

"Yeah, but you cried a lot before Dad got sick."

My stomach drops. I never wanted him to know how hard

things were for me in that house; how miserable I was. "Like I said, people cry for lots of different reasons." Patting his hand, I give him a tight smile. "You should go on to bed. It's late and you've got an early morning tomorrow."

He sighs. "Fine." Standing, he walks over to the steps and stops, his hand on the railing. "For the record, if you and Flynn became friends again, I'd be okay with it. He made you laugh, Mom. It was nice."

My heart squeezes with emotion and I give him a more genuine smile. "Goodnight, Jude."

CHAPTER THIRTY-SIX

FLYNN

As I pull back in at Hensley's, I've yet to return Cleo's call. I can't, since I know if I have her talking, I'll spill everything and this isn't a conversation I can have over the phone. Even knowing what I'm going to do and having no regrets about the decision, it still sucks that someone will get hurt. Even worse, that I'll be the one causing the pain.

I walk in the door and as soon as I enter the living room, three sets of eyes snap to my face, the movie they're watching forgotten. Ford is indifferent because he has no clue what's really going on. Sully looks resigned, as if he already has an idea. And it sucks, because this will impact him, too. Jess looks hopeful. Falling in love with Ophelia has made him such a fucking romantic.

"Well," my brother says, "did you talk? You were gone for hours."

I nod. "We talked. Well, she talked. I listened."

He leans forward and rests his forearms on his knees. "And did you get the answers you were hoping for?"

I blow out a breath. I got so many answers and so much more rage and hate for Baker than I even had before. I have forgiveness for Brighten and hope for the future. I also have regret for the pain I'm about to cause. "It wasn't anything I thought it would be," I admit.

Three sets of brows draw down in confusion. "What does that mean? Are you getting married or not?" Jess asks.

"Not," I answer, no joy in my tone. Because I don't relish having to tell Cleo the wedding's off. She knows little about Brighten except that we broke up in college and I was a wreck.

"Fuck," Sully groans. "Kara's going to kick my ass. Thanks a lot, man."

Jess jumps up. "So, what happened? Why did she marry him? Did she love him?"

"It's not my story to tell, Jess. I just know she had her reasons and I understand why she did it. It sucks, but it is what it is."

Bringing my gaze to Sully's, I offer him an apologetic smile. "I'm really sorry, Sully. I know a lot of this fallout is going to land on you. I'm so, so sorry. I will buy Esme a pony to make up for this."

He huffs a laugh. "The fuck you will. Where am I going to put a pony?" Standing, he walks over to me. "So, I'm guessing we go back to Miami? And can I please be there when you break the news to Cleo so I can watch her go apeshit on you? I'll take that instead of a pony."

I roll my eyes. "Fuck off."

He laughs before his expression sobers. "I know how much you loved Brighten, man. If you think you still have a shot at the two of you making it work, I say you grab that shit while you can. Kara and Cleo will be fine. Cleo will find some other rich guy to give her babies."

"Thanks, Sully."

He nods. "Just know that you will be on the shit list for a good long time and Kara will probably ban you from your goddaughter's birthday parties for the foreseeable future."

"Understood. Get me on a plane?"

I nearly knock before I remember I have a key. Blowing out a deep breath, I slot the key into the lock and turn the doorknob. As it's only eight AM, I'm not surprised that Cleo would still be in bed. I make my way to the bedroom, knowing this is a terrible way to wake up, but I don't have a choice. I already have a return flight to Knoxville booked for this afternoon.

I take a seat on the edge of the bed and gently brush Cleo's blonde hair off her shoulder and shake her. "Cleo? Can you wake up for me?"

She rouses and rolls over and blinks in surprise. "Flynn? What are you doing here? Did something happen? Why aren't you in Knoxville?"

"Sit up. I need to talk to you."

She drags herself up to a seated position and yawns, rubbing the sleep from her eyes. "What's going on? You look tired; did you not sleep at all?" Reaching up to touch my face, she brushes her thumbs over my cheeks. "What's wrong?"

I gently squeeze her wrists and pull her hands from my face. "There's no easy way to say this, Cleo."

Her eyes widen and she blinks rapidly, her breath catching. "Did you cheat? You flew home not even twenty-four hours after you left to tell me you cheated?"

I shake my head. "No. I didn't cheat."

"Then what is it?" she asks, her tone wary.

"I'm sorry, but I can't marry you."

All the air leaves her chest, her expression morphing into one of shock and disbelief and pain, and I imagine this must've been the face Brighten saw when she told me about the pregnancy and Baker. "What?"

"I said—."

"Jesus, Flynn. I heard what you said. Why? We're supposed to get married next week. Is it cold feet? Is it moving back to the States? I know I wasn't sold on living in France, but I could probably come around to the idea."

I give her shoulders a gentle squeeze. "It's none of that. It doesn't have anything to do with you. I can't marry you because I'm in love with someone else."

The color drains from her face and she swallows before her eyes turn flinty. "Let me guess, Brighten or Crash or whatever the fuck you called her?"

I nod. "Yeah. I'm really sorry."

"You said she broke your heart. How can you still love her if she hurt you as badly as she did? You were miserable for years, Flynn."

I nod again. "I know. I saw her last night."

Her jaw clenches. "So you did cheat."

"No. We talked and I kissed her. That's it." Tears fill Cleo's eyes and something in my gut twists knowing I'm causing her pain. "But when we talked, she told me stuff she couldn't tell me all those years ago; the reason for our breakup."

"What kind of stuff? It must've been pretty monumental for you to just up and forgive her and want to get back with her after one fucking conversation."

"It's not my place to share her business, Cleo. But if I marry you, I'll always wonder and that's not fair to you. You deserve someone who won't have doubts. You're amazing and I know there is a man out there who is the perfect guy for you. I'm sorry it's not me."

"This isn't fair, Flynn. I love you. Please don't do this." Cleo's full-blown sobbing now and guilt stabs through me knowing I'm the root of her pain.

"I'm so sorry, Cleo." Even through her tears, her expression turns stony and before I know it, she's ripped my glasses off my face and snapped them in half. My mouth falls open in shock and I start to say something just before her fist lands squarely in my left eye. Electric pain radiates through my brow, cheek, and nose and I grunt with the blow. My hand flies to my face to cradle my eye. "What the fuck?"

"You're lucky that's all I hit you with. Get your ass out." She scrambles from the bed and grabs the vase on the nightstand, and it shatters against the wall beside my head as I run out of the bedroom.

Thankful I don't have anything here yet except my laptop and messenger bag, I grab them and bolt out of the house as Cleo's footsteps pound down the hall toward me.

I'm gasping for breath when I climb back into Sully's car. "Dude, what the hell happened? Your eye looks like shit. And where are your glasses?"

"Don't ask, just go."

Despite the pain in my face and how tired I am, I put in my contacts in the airport bathroom after I land in Knoxville. It seems strange I only left twelve hours ago. I realized while I was waiting for my return flight, I didn't have Brighten's number anymore. She must've changed it after she moved to Nashville, because when I texted her old number, I was informed someone else had it now.

I guess I shouldn't be surprised and my number's different, too, since I've been out of the country for thirteen years, but I hoped hers would still be the same.

But now, I have no choice but to just show up at her house. And it hits me as I knock on the door that I could've checked social media and I feel like an idiot. Too late to back out now, I guess.

Footfalls signal that someone is coming to the door and my heart rate spikes and I take a deep breath, hoping this wasn't all for nothing. I'm inclined to think not since Brighten kissed me and we were on our way to getting naked when Cleo called last night.

The door opens, and it's her and all the breath leaves my body. Yesterday, she looked amazing in leggings and a tank top and a messy bun. Today she's dressed like she stepped out of an ad for Banana Republic in dark jeans, a tucked-in white button-down blouse, and patterned flats. Her red hair falls in loose curls over her shoulders, her makeup tasteful and natural and she's a vision.

Her eyes light up, but then she shutters it and swallows. "Hi."

"Hey. Is this a bad time?"

She shakes her head and opens the door wider for me to enter. "Come on in."

I look around. "Where's Jude?"

Her hand flies to my chin, and she tilts my head down. "What the hell happened to your eye?"

"Hell hath no fury and all that."

Her eyes go wide. "Your fiancé did this?"

I reach up and take her hand off my face and wrap it in my own. "*Ex*-fiancé, Crash."

Brighten's breath catches as her eyes search mine. "Flynn, I didn't want to break up your engagement."

"I know, but it couldn't be helped. Where's Jude?" I ask again.

"Piano practice. He didn't click with the teacher from this morning, so the music school let him try another instructor. Why?"

"And when is he done?"

"Two hours. I just dropped him off. Why?"

I drop her hands and grip the back of her neck. "Because if I didn't have time to fuck you properly, I was going to have to leave and come back. I can't be here with you alone and not get you naked and I'm not going to do it unless I can give myself ample time."

Her eyes widen in surprise and I lean in and capture her lips with mine and she gasps. I smile into our kiss and sweep my tongue into her mouth and she returns my fervor with a hunger of her own and for a long moment, I simply relish getting to kiss her.

Brighten's fingers skim under the hem of my T-shirt and having her hands on my bare skin has my dick rock hard in seconds. She pulls back to look up at me, her eyes seeking. "Is this for real?"

I nod. Running my hands over her body, I give her soft, gentle squeezes at intervals. "Feels pretty real to me."

Her eyes well with tears. "And we can be together?"

Her voice is filled with so much hope and longing it makes my chest ache. I nod and reach up to swipe away a tear off her cheek. "Yes." I drop my forehead to hers. "And this time, you're all mine, Crash."

She huffs a watery laugh. "Thank God." We kiss as she shuffles us toward what I'm hoping is her bedroom. I'm sure as hell not making love to her in anything but a bed the first time I take her in almost fourteen years.

When we turn into a bedroom, I smile. "First-floor

bedroom, huh? Easier for me to sneak in and out of. I like it. Not that I wouldn't have climbed the downspout just to be able to sleep with you, but I'm glad I won't have to."

Brighten laughs and reaches around me to shut the bedroom door. "I think we're past the point of needing to be sneaky, don't you?"

"Not when your husband *just* died and you have a teenager who adored him. I'm not going to jeopardize my ability to get him to warm up to me by letting him think I didn't give you enough of a mourning period. I want him to accept me, but I know it's not going to be like flipping a switch. So, no, we're not past the point of being sneaky. I'm not going to fuck this up and have it cause problems between you and Jude."

She drops her forehead to my chest. "Still such a good man. I don't deserve you. Not sure I ever did."

I grip her jaw and lift her face to look at me. "I am a good man. And as far as *deserve?* Well, I think we've both paid for our separation. I thought it was only me who'd been suffering all these years, but I know the cost was steep for you, too. Pretty sure we deserve each other. We deserve to finally be happy, Crash. Don't get me wrong, I want to talk. I want to talk about everything and nothing for the rest of forever. But right the fuck now, I need you naked more. Can we do *that*, please?"

Nodding, she takes a step back and toes off her shoes and leaves them by the closet door. I do the same, never taking my eyes off of her. Tugging her shirt from her jeans, she takes a moment to work the buttons free and I just watch until she shrugs it off her shoulders and the fabric falls to the floor, revealing a camisole over her bra. She unbuckles the thin belt she wears and, as her fingers hovers over the button, I step forward and drop to my knees, batting her hands away.

For a beat, I simply let my forehead fall to her stomach as I run my hands up her calves, the backs of her knees, her hamstrings, over her butt. I can't bite back the near growl of satisfaction that leaves my mouth as I knead her ass. Brighten brings her hand to my scalp and threads her fingers through my hair and I'm transported to all the times she'd fist my hair while I fucked her or went down on her. It feels so surreal to know I'll get to have it again.

Somewhat reluctantly, I drag my hands around to the front of her pants and look up at her as I undo the button and zipper of her jeans. Still not taking my eyes off hers, I silently work the denim over her hips and down her legs and help her step out of them. Jeans discarded, I let my eyes travel up her body, starting at her toes, and I lick my lips in anticipation.

"You know," I say, running my hands up her now bare legs, "that first time, when we went up to your room, I just stood in the doorway and watched you shove all ninety-seven of those pillows off the bed." Brighten chuckles, her fingers still moving through my hair. "But I wanted to memorize what you looked like in that moment. I knew everything was about to change, and I wanted to remember exactly what you looked like."

I lean in and run the tip of my nose along the hem of her camisole, nudging up the fabric to reveal a sliver of skin above the waistband of her panties. As I brush soft kisses along the exposed skin, her breathing grows more shallow and my heart is already pounding behind my ribs. Just being here with her, knowing I can touch and taste and fuck her to my satisfaction is an almost heady feeling after so long without her.

Gripping her hips, I begin walking her toward the bed a few feet away, my hands and mouth never leaving her skin. I'm struck with the realization that this is the first time I've ever crawled for a woman and I'd happily do it for Brighten for the rest of my life. The backs of her knees hit the edge of the mattress, and I look up at her eyes as I hook my index finger into the sides of her panties. "How long has it been since anyone touched you, Crash?"

"A little over a year."

"Let's remedy that, shall we?" I tug her underwear down her legs and she steps out of them. "Sit and lie back for me." As she drops onto the edge of the bed and reclines on her elbows, I step between her legs and plant my hands on the insides of her knees. "Open up for me. I need to see what's mine."

Her chest heaves and she swallows as she spreads her legs wider apart and I finally give myself permission to look at her. "Sweet Jesus, I've missed that sight," I say on an exhale as I, too, struggle for breath.

She bites her lip and lifts one brow. "And are you just going to look at it, or are you planning on doing something with your mouth besides talk?"

I huff a laugh and bend to kiss and lick my way up her inner thighs. "Still so mouthy. Glad to see some things don't change." I can smell her as I get closer and it evokes such visceral sense memories for me that my mouth nearly waters and my dick jerks in my jeans with what I'm about to do.

Hooking her knees over my shoulders, she releases a shuddery breath as I slide my hands up her thighs. I'll never, for as long as I live, get used to hearing the sounds she makes and I can't help but smile. And when my tongue sweeps up her pussy and I groan with the taste and feel of her, she gasps, her thighs squeezing against my head. As I suck her clit into my mouth, her hips buck and I chuckle and hear her mutter a soft *fuck*, as she threads her fingers through my hair.

For several moments, I simply revel in the knowledge that she's mine. Wholly, and without reservation, she's made the choice to only be with me. It's a nearly overwhelming feeling that anchors and grounds me and isn't something I ever thought I'd have.

It's so overwhelming, in fact, I'm nearly in tears as her moans turn into stilted pants and she begins to lose herself in her pleasure. She holds me in place and grinds her hips and I suck and lick until her entire body shudders and my name falls from her lips and I nearly lose it, my heart so full in this moment, the tears threatening to spill finally roll down my cheeks.

CHAPTER THIRTY-SEVEN

BRIGHTEN

Best. Orgasm. Ever. My head is lolled back as I attempt to breathe and come down when I feel Flynn turn his head to press kisses into my inner thigh and he sniffles.

I bring my head up to look at him and he has tears in his eyes. Alarm immediately fills me and I drop my legs off his shoulders and sit up and take his face in my hands. Thoughts of him having regrets about ending his engagement and coming to me flood my mind and I swallow nervously. "What's wrong? Are you having regrets? About—."

"No," he says forcefully, cutting me off. His eyes find mine and they're full of so much love and joy and not even a flicker of doubt that I breathe a sigh of relief.

"Then what?"

He wraps his arms around my waist as he continues to kneel on the floor and pulls me closer. "I never thought I'd have this again, Crash. And not just you—even though I never imagined I'd actually have you, either—but the way I feel when I make love to you. I'd forgotten how it is. I'd gotten so used to the diminished feelings of simply scratching an itch, I forgot how good it is when you love the person you're with."

I nod, knowing exactly what he means. "I know." I lower my mouth to within inches of his. "And we'll never have to be without that feeling again." I press a kiss to his lips and lean back to tug my camisole over my head. "Now, get naked and come fuck me properly."

He huffs a laugh and gives me a kiss as he stands. "Yes, ma'am."

I unhook my bra and drop it to the floor and his eyes fall to my breasts and appreciation and hunger vie for top emotion in his gaze. I scoot back toward the headboard and settle in to watch him shed his clothes.

He unbuckles his belt and then the button and fly of his jeans before dropping them to the floor and stepping out. He tugs his shirt over his head and it's not the muscular physique of his lean runner's body that catches my eye, although it's quite something. It's something else entirely that my vision hones in on and I scramble to my knees and over to the edge of the bed, my heart pounding.

Tears instantly spring to my eyes. I hadn't noticed it last night in the dark interior of the car, but I see it clearly now. Bringing my hand up to his right pectoral, I run my fingertips lightly over the tattoo that spans from his sternum to just under his armpit. It's a near exact replica of my scar. I almost expect to feel the puckering of the skin beneath my fingers, but it's only ink. "Flynn," I breathe, my voice filled with awe as tears roll down my face.

He lifts my chin so our eyes meet. "I could draw it from memory and I did. I got it about ten years ago. I allowed myself one day a month to wallow and look up stuff about you. This particular day, you'd been to some sort of benefit, I think, and you were wearing a strapless dress and just a tiny bit of your tattoo was visible. I got really sad and missed your scar. I know it sounds stupid to miss a scar, but I did. The tattoo artist didn't want to do it because I was really drunk, but I kept throwing money at him until he agreed."

I nod. "It's not stupid. Sometimes I miss my scar, too. I wish I'd been more comfortable in my own skin and could've taken your advice about anyone who was worthy of me not flinching. I was so insecure about it, I just wanted it gone."

"I know. It's still there. I know it's there. You know it's there." He bends his head and presses a kiss to the center of where my scar would be. "And now, it's like this private thing only we know about. I kinda like the idea of that, too."

I loop my arms around his shoulders and smile. "I like that idea, too. It's probably as much your scar as mine, anyway. It's kinda what makes us *us* and it's the whole reason we met, so it's nice to see it again after all these years."

Flynn runs his hands up my sides to cup my breasts and his eyes drop back to my chest. "I've gotta say, these are nice to see again after all these years, too, Crash. Shit."

I can't help but laugh until his thumbs brush over my nipples and desire scorches through my middle and my inhale is sharp. I slide my hand to his jaw and bring his face to mine for a deep kiss. And he's so right. It's vastly different when it's with someone you love. Perhaps that's why it's always been better with him than anyone else. My body recognized what my mind and heart couldn't; even all those years ago. I'm just thankful I don't ever have to give it up again.

Trailing my hands down his sides, I feel the plains and ridges of his torso and the muscles under his skin. I run my fingertips along the waistband of his boxers and he huffs a breath when I dip my hand inside and wrap my fingers around his cock and give him a long, slow stroke. "Oh, fuck," he groans into our kiss and I pull back and watch his face as I pump my fist over him.

"Is this for me?" I ask, my tone teasing.

"Always. Whenever you want it."

"I want it right now."

He pulls my hand away from his body and gives me a slow smile. "You've got it. Lie down."

Heart beginning to pound, I open my nightstand and pull out a condom and hand it over to him and lie on my back. I watch, my skin beginning to prickle with anticipation, as he shucks his underwear. I nearly moan at the sight of his cock. "That's nice to see after all these years, too."

He rolls down the condom and crawls onto the bed between my legs. "You're going to do a whole lot more than see it; don't worry." Hooking my leg around his hip, he slots himself against my entrance. "Have you missed my cock, Crash?"

I bring my hands up to his face. "Yes. But I've missed your heart more."

He smiles and drops his forehead to mine as he enters me. It's slow and perfect and feels as though I've come home after the longest absence ever. I have the strange thought that this must be what prisoners feel like when their sentence is commuted and they have a second chance at life again.

We both let out a moan and, for a moment, he doesn't move. "Jesus, you feel good." I tilt my hips and he grabs my waist to still me as he huffs a breath. "Wait. Fuck. I need a second. It's too good. Shit." Nodding, I grin and shift my head so I can capture his lips with mine and simply kiss him, our bodies joined together.

When he finally begins to move, he lets out a low, possessive growl in his throat that makes my breath catch and goosebumps scatter across my skin. He continues to kiss me, his easy thrusts claiming not only my body, but my soul, and in this moment, a sense of utter completeness floods my entire being.

Flynn skims his fingertips down my arm until our hands meet. He intertwines our fingers and lifts our linked hands to place above my head. I huff an exhale and he smiles against my lips. "You remember the night before I left for Nashville?"

I nod. "When I came in through your bedroom window?"

"Yeah," he replies, bringing my free hand up to join the other one, pinning it under his. "You said you were there to give me a proper goodbye."

I huff a laugh and gasp as Flynn rolls his hips at the same time I tilt mine, changing up the angle of his movements and hitting a deep, sweet spot. He smiles and runs his free hand over my breast, rolling the nipple between his thumb and fingers, and I let my head fall back onto the pillow as I moan.

"As far as goodbyes go, it was pretty great." He kisses down my jaw and neck. "But I think I'm more interested in giving you a proper hello."

Without my hands and sense of touch, it seems as though my other senses are heightened and my pleasure begins to mount. "Fuck," I breathe. "I think you're saying hello pretty well. Shit, Flynn."

He huffs a laugh and braces the back of my leg on his free arm and presses my knee back. "Yeah, because this time, there is no goodbye, Crash." He slams into me harder and I gasp, nearly coming from the impact alone and my eyes fall closed. "No. Look at me."

I open my eyes and find his and I whimper as I grow closer and closer, my heart jackhammering in my chest. "Tell me there's no goodbye this time. Tell me you're mine."

"Fuck," I gasp.

"Say it, Brighten." He exhales a groan and I can barely think, let alone speak. "Fucking say it. I need to hear you say it."

"Yours. All yours. Forever." I reply between ragged breaths. "Fuck, Flynn. God, please."

He releases my hands and claims my mouth in a punishing kiss. I reach down between us to work my clit and a moment later, I cry out, my moans swallowed by our kiss as wave after wave of intense sensation crash over me.

Flynn pulls his mouth from mine in a gasp. "Fuck, Crash. Jesus, baby. So fucking good. Shit." His forehead drops to my chest as he pumps his hips one final time, a low grunt working its way up his throat.

He laughs as he raises his head, his expression content and relaxed, even with the black eye, and peppers my face with kisses, making me chuckle. Rolling to face him as he pulls out and lies beside me, as cheesy as it is, I can't help but feel as though today is the first day of the rest of my life.

I reach down to the foot of the bed and pull up the throw blanket and drape it over us and pick up Flynn's wrist to look at his watch. He leans in and presses a kiss to my forehead. "Are we okay on time?"

I nod and snuggle into his chest. "I've got about forty-five minutes before I have to leave." We simply lie in each other's arms for a few minutes until I tilt my head back to look at him. "Does your eye hurt?"

"Nah, just tender. I'm just glad Cleo was alone. If her sister or any their friends had been there, I would've probably left in a body bag."

I sigh. "I'm sure that was a hard thing for you to do. Breaking something off with someone you care about is hard."

He looks down at me, his smile soft. "I'd already decided before I even came over here yesterday that if your explanation was at all plausible and you still cared, I was going to do whatever I could so we could be together. When Jess told me you were in town and I found out you were single, I was shocked. And even knowing it was you, I was terrified you might not still have feelings for me after all this time. Especially considering how long you were married to Baker. But he asked me if I was on a lifeboat and I had one extra seat, who would be in it. It was a no brainer."

My heart lifts with his words and my throat grows tight as I try not to cry. "I'm glad you came. I was never going to come for you, simply because I'd already had my chance with you and I fucked it up so bad. And if you were happy, I didn't want to blow up your life."

Flynn sighs. "Not sure I was ever happy, sorry to say. Even after Cleo and I got together. She was sweet and beautiful and wanted kids, but she still isn't you, Crash. No one is you. Anyone else would just be me settling. I knew when I asked her to marry me I was setting. And honestly, none of it was probably fair to her. She's young, though. She'll find someone who can love her like she deserves."

I bite my lip. "Are kids of your own something you'd still like to have?"

He sweeps a stray hair off my forehead. "Like to have? Not going to lie, yeah. Have to have to feel fulfilled? No." I nod and he smiles. "And I don't need to be married, either, before you ask. I told you when we were kids and I'll tell you now, all I need it you."

I press a kiss to his lips. "Still such a good, selfless man. You know," I say nonchalantly, "I didn't mind being married so much. If it hadn't been to Baker, I might've even liked it. Turns out, combining lives with someone isn't that hard and the tax advantages are pretty substantial. And Jude's turned out pretty great. I imagine if I was having a child with someone I actually loved, I would look forward to it."

Excitement flashes in Flynn's eyes, but he pushes it down

and swallows. "I'll keep that in mind." Changing the subject, he asks, "So, what are you going to do for work?"

I shrug. "No clue. I don't *have* to work if I don't want to. As awful as Baker was, he set us up for life. Jude has a substantial trust he'll gain access to when he turns twenty-five and just from the contract I setup with him alone, I'm a very wealthy woman, believe it or not. And, I don't know, maybe when he got sick, he grew a heart, because he left me everything. Including a majority stake in Intuition."

His mouth falls open, the color draining from his face in his shock. "Holy fuck. That's—."

I nod. "I know. I could pretty much do anything I want. Part of me thinks I want to devote my time and resources to continuing my charity work. Another part of me thinks I might like to do pro-bono law. It won't be politics, I know that."

"And you're okay with that?"

"Yeah. I've made peace with it. Like I said, I'm tired of the public life. I just want a quiet life with my kid and the man I love, and that's all I need. For now," I say with a grin.

CHAPTER THIRTY-EIGHT

FLYNN

Reluctant as I am to leave this bed, let alone let Brighten out of my sight, I know she has obligations. And so do I. After leaving Cleo's, I'd been single-minded about getting back to Knoxville and telling Brighten about breaking my engagement and us finally being together after a lifetime of misery.

But as I kiss her goodbye with a promise to come see her again soon, as well as us exchanging numbers, I dig out my phone to return a call I'd received as I'd landed in Knoxville. I'm dreading it, but it's got to be done.

When I call my mother as I make the drive to her house, she answers by saying my full name in lieu of any kind of actual greeting. And although I'm a grown man, successful and wealthy in my own right, when my mother pulls out the full "Flynn Maverick Tate", I'm pretty sure my balls retreat a good six inches.

"Hey, Mom. You got a minute?"

She scoffs. "Looks like I have lots of time now. Care to explain why Cleo called me sobbing? What's going on, son?"

"I'm about to pull into the driveway; can we discuss it in a minute? I just wanted to make sure you were home."

"Of course I'm home."

"Okay, then why don't you put on a pot of coffee and I'll be there in a few minutes."

She's quiet for a moment. "I'm thinking alcohol might be a better idea." My mother doesn't wait for a response and disconnects the call. And as resolute in my decision as I am, especially given that there aren't any more secrets between Brighten and me, my mom loves Cleo and I know this is going to be hard for her. Also, Mom's not blind. She knows I've been different since I got back from New York that spring and even more after the day Jude was born; even if she doesn't know exactly why. And I'm sure watching your child suffer makes your parental defenses rise.

As I walk up the path toward the porch, I see my mom through the living room window, sitting at the kitchen table with a bottle of liquor and two glasses. She doesn't rise or even look up at me as I enter the house, and she's already pouring us both a drink when I drop into the chair next to hers. It's not until she slides the glass of gin in my direction does she even bring her eyes to mine and when she does, she blinks rapidly, her jaw going slack.

"What, Mom?"

"Dear God, it really is true."

I pick up my glass. "What's true?"

A single tear rolls down her cheek. "Right before he died, your father said that someday, when you and Brighten worked everything out—because he always believed you would—you'd come back to yourself. That the light would come back into your eyes. I chalked it up to how much he loved her and the two of you together and how much of a hopeless romantic he was. But he was right."

My throat tightens at the mention of Dad and I blink and look down into my glass. "Sentimental bastard," I say with a watery laugh.

Ice clinks in her tumbler as she lifts it to her mouth for a long drink. "I was prepared to read you the riot act and tell you not to throw away a good thing, but I can't do that anymore. Not when I don't even have to ask if you truly love Brighten."

I shake my head and raise my gaze to hers. "I never stopped, Mom."

Tears well more fully in her eyes. "I know. And I hated it so much for you. To watch you be this shell of the sweet—if solitary—boy I raised and loved. So, I take it you and she have talked and cleared the air?"

Nodding, I sip my gin. "Yes. And I know you love Cleo and I never wanted to hurt her, but if I had gone through with things, it wouldn't have been fair to anyone. Least of all, Brighten and me. She and I have both suffered enough. I wasn't alone in my misery, even if I didn't know it."

"But you do now? And her reasoning was worth breaking your heart?"

"Yes. She did what she thought was best at the time and as much as I hate that we lost all that time, I forgive her. And I'm not wasting any more of my life not having the life I want. Life with her—and Jude—is what I want."

Mom's breath hitches at the sound of his name. "What's he like? Have you met him yet?"

I nod and offer her a soft smile. "He's perfect. I kept waiting for him to be this snotty little shit, but he's a sweet kid. He looks just like her."

"And you're sure he's not yours?"

"Yeah. I'm sorry if you've wondered all these years."

She shrugs. "I think part of me hoped he wasn't because then I would've had to give thought to the fact that another man was raising your child and how you must be feeling about that. And I knew if you thought he was yours, you would've done everything in your power to be a part of his life. I know you've always wanted to be a father. You were going to have that with Cleo."

"I have always wanted to be a dad," I confirm. "But I always wanted Brighten more. Even now."

My mother drains her glass and pushes it away. "So, what comes next for you?"

I huff a laugh. "Hell if I know. I've got some calls about the wedding I need to make and I've got to find a new job locally, I guess. And I hope you'll let me crash in the basement for a while. I don't want to buy a house if things with Brighten are going to progress quickly, but I also don't see me moving in with her and Jude anytime soon. I can look into getting an apartment if I need to."

She dismisses that thought with a wave. "Please, you gave me the opportunity to be a Parisian lady for at least a month a year for the last decade. The basement's yours. What about you and Brighten? And...Jude?"

"I don't know that either. I know Brighten and I are together, but we have to be careful, for Jude's sake. I don't want to move too quickly and him end up resenting her. From what she says, Baker was a good dad and as much as I hate the man—dead or not—I don't want to hurt Jude when none of what happened is his fault. I hope I get to build a relationship with him, but I know it'll take time."

———————

"And he's cool with me coming for supper?" I ask, shifting the phone from one ear to the other. It's been several days since Brighten and I reconciled, and due to scheduling conflicts, we haven't been able to see each other. And like some drug addict who's fallen off the wagon after more than a decade of sobriety, I'm majorly jonesing for a taste of my favorite drug. The drug in question simply happens to be a certain gorgeous redhead.

As eager as I am to become part of Jude's life, I'd be lying if I said I wouldn't prefer to spend the evening in bed with his mother instead of across a dinner table. But knowing this is important for our relationship and our future as a family, I focus on what Brighten is saying. "Yes, he and I have talked a lot about you. He knows the reason we broke up was because of Baker."

I blink in shock. "What?"

She sighs. "Of course, I couldn't and won't tell him the entire story of things, but he knows that you and I were in love and that I want to have you as a part of my life again. We'll still have to take things slow, but I don't think Baker and I did as good a job as we assumed hiding his relationship with Briana. But since he's not asking questions about that, I'm not touching it with a ten-foot pole. At least, not right now."

I nod, even though I know she can't see me. "Okay. Well, he's your kid, Crash. You know I want to spend time with him and get to know him, but I'm not going to lie; I'm scared shitless."

She huffs a laugh. "You'll be fine. I hope you've brushed up on your Nintendo skills. Jude is well aware you're the guy to beat on Rainbow Road." Brighten's quiet for a beat. "I'm glad you're coming over. I've been so antsy to see you."

I chuckle, so far beyond happy that this is now my life. A life that includes Brighten. "Me, too. How's the unpacking going?"

"It's going. You want to help me unpack my bedroom later?"

"Would that be some sort of euphemism?"

"Most definitely. Jude's made a friend down the street. They've got a pickup basketball game scheduled for after supper." Even through the phone, I can hear the smile in her voice.

"Then limber up, because I can help you *unpack* as long as you need me to."

"Perfect. Listen, I've gotta go. Jude's coming in from school. I'll see you at six. Love you."

I'm still not used to hearing her say it, and my heart swells hearing it now. "Love you, too, Crash. See you soon."

When I show up for dinner, I'm dressed casually in jeans and a T-shirt, and it nearly elicits some sort of déjà vu. It brings back memories of me as a kid, dressed much the same way, when I'd come to hang out with Brighten. But neither of us are kids anymore. Hell, she has a kid who's a teenager. I almost want to hold my breath as I knock on the door, but I simply shove my hands into my pockets and watch through the wavy panes of glass as Jude runs to answer the door.

As he opens it, he wears a big, braces-filled smile and pushes his glasses up higher on his nose as he waves me in. "Hey, Flynn."

"Hey, Jude. How's it going?"

"Pretty good. Mom said you might play some *Mario Kart* with me so I can beat you before supper."

I huff a laugh. "That so? Well, let me go see if she needs any help and then I'd be happy to dust you."

He eyes me skeptically, and the look is so familiar to one Brighten used to give me when we were kids, it makes my heart ache. "You sure you remember how? I know it might be different than it was back in the old days."

I feign insult. "Ouch, kid. I'm not *that* old." I hold my hands up and wiggle my fingers. "Muscle memory. Just like riding a bike, I'm sure."

"I'm going to head on up. You know where my room is? Mom said it's her old bedroom."

"I remember exactly where it is," I say with a nod. "I'll be up soon."

He flashes me a warm smile and jogs up the stairs. I round the corner into the kitchen and see Brighten standing at the stove, stirring a deep skillet, a large pot steaming on another eye. I walk up behind her and slip my arms around her waist and pull her against me and bury my face in the crook of her neck and simply breathe her in. "You always did like to live dangerously," she says and leans back into me.

"I made sure he went upstairs. I even heard the door shut. You can't expect me not to put my hands on you, especially since I'm allowed now. Smells great."

She chuckles and sets the wooden spoon on the stove and turns in my arms. "What, supper or me?"

"Both," I reply, dropping a kiss on her lips and I have to make myself keep it a light peck. All I really want to do in this moment is drag her into the walk-in pantry and push her against a wall and remind myself that she's actually mine. That this is a thing I get to do now. That I'm the only one who gets to do it.

"You need any help? Jude wants me to beat him before supper."

She laughs. "I'm good. And I'm very sure he phrased it like that, too."

I shrug, giving her a wide grin. "Maybe not in so many words." She blinks and her eyes roam over my face, her expression morphing into one of awe. I frown, confused. "What is it?"

She swallows thickly and brings her hand up to my face.

"That smile. Your lopsided one you give me when you're play-ful. I didn't realize how much it would affect me to see it again."

I press my forehead to hers. "You can see it anytime you want. For the rest of forever."

She nods. "Thank God."

After one final kiss, I drop my hands and back away. "Just holler when food's ready."

Brighten smiles and hands me two bottles of water. "Go play."

I turn and jog up the stairs and knock on Jude's bedroom door and when he gives me permission, I enter. I expect to feel a lot of the same things I did when I was last in this room before I left for Nashville that first time, but it's not the same room.

The walls are now a soft gray, the ultra-feminine, white furniture replaced with simple, but high quality, black wood pieces. The bedding is gray and black versus the white lace and frilly pink of Brighten's youth, and the entire energy of the room reminds me of my own room as a teen. His bookshelf is full of binders of sheet music and graphic novels, along with your standard Tolkien, some John Green novels and a few Shusterman dystopian books I remember reading when I was in middle and high school. Against a far wall, next to the window, is his keyboard, a pair of expensive headphones resting on top. The wall opposite his bed contains a wall-mounted tele-vision and entertainment center with a blu-ray player, several movies, and a Nintendo Switch, along with games and accessories.

"This is a great room. Ready to lose, kid?"

He narrows his eyes good-naturedly. "Not likely. Just because you're better than Mom doesn't mean you can take me."

I huff a laugh. "Hate to break it to you, but your mom has

never been good at *Mario Kart*, so that's really not the flex you think it is."

He grins. "Right? She's terrible." He extends a controller up to me and I drop to the floor next to him and lean against the footboard of his bed.

For the next half-hour, we play in companionable silence with occasional smack talk sprinkled in. He's good, but my skills aren't as rusty as I feared and for the entire time, all our races are pretty close. We're about to start another when Jude puts his controller down. "Can I ask you something?"

I turn my head to give him my full attention. "Sure."

"It's about you and my mom."

Not at all sure what I'm allowed to tell him, I simply nod. "Okay. I'll answer if I can."

He considers my words and is quiet for a beat. "You and Mom were together before her and my dad, right?"

"Yeah," I confirm.

"And you and Mom loved each other?"

I blow out a breath. "It's complicated, Jude." I pick up my nearly empty bottle of water and take a sip.

"Is there a chance you're my dad?"

I choke on my water and he simply waits as I attempt to breathe. Coughing, I shake my head. As I clear my throat, I set my water back on the floor. "No, Baker was your dad. You have his eyes, you know."

"Did you know my dad?"

"Not well. I met him a few times." I don't want to insult Jude's memories of his father, so I stick with facts. "He was a very smart man; driven."

The boy looks down at his hands. "I'm not sure he and my

mom liked each other very much." When I don't say anything, he brings his eyes back to mine. "But she likes you. She smiles when you're around and when she's on the phone with you." He chews his bottom lip, his braces flashing in the light. "She doesn't cry anymore. Not since the day you came. Do you like her?"

I look him in the eye when I speak. "I love your mom. I have since we were kids."

He smiles, but it's a little sad. "I'm not sure my mom and dad loved each other."

"They both loved you very much. You are the most important thing in the world to your mom."

"She said you were there the day I was born."

I nod. "I was."

"My dad wasn't," he says matter-of-factly.

"He got there right after you were born."

"And she named me after your dad?"

I nod again, my chest feeling tight. "Yeah. She had just visited him when she went into labor. They were very close, and he treated her like a daughter. He loved her and was overjoyed when he found out she named you after him. It gave him a really big head," I say with a laugh.

"Am I a good Jude? Would he like me?"

I blink rapidly, trying not to tear up. "Wow, kid. Your mom said you ask a lot of questions." I clear my throat. "He would've loved you."

I would've loved you.

"Are you going to marry my mom? I mean, someday?"

"That's up to her. I'd be honored to be married to your mom. You'd have to be okay with it, though. It's not just our decision."

He rises and walks over to his desk and opens a drawer and pulls out a binder. Or, at least I think it's a binder until he brings it over and I see it's a photo album. He hands it over to me. "I found this when I was unpacking. I think these are of you and Mom."

I take the book and flip it open and a bark of surprised laughter falls from my mouth. "Wow. I forgot we even took a lot of these." He points to one of the first images. It's of Brighten and me while she's still in the hospital. She's in a gown, her red hair in braided pigtails, a bottle of Mountain Dew in her hand. I'm sitting in the bed beside her and we have school books spread out on our laps. "You look so much like your mom. It's wild."

"This was right after her accident, right? When y'all met?"

I nod. "Yeah."

"And that's why you call her Crash?"

I nod again. "Well, she crashed. It made sense. But she's the bravest person I know. Most people wouldn't have survived what she did." And even if he doesn't know I'm speaking about more than simply her bike wreck, I do.

He flips ahead a few pages. "You had braces and glasses like me."

"Yeah. I still have glasses; I just wear contacts most of the time. I felt like I was never going to get my braces off, though. I hated them so much."

"Me, too."

A few more pages forward has me blowing out a breath. My going away dinner before I left for Nashville. Immediately, it makes me think of the night she crawled in my bedroom window. Then the half-marathon and internship wrap-up dinner. Vegas. New York. All our greatest hits.

Jude's quiet for a moment. "She's happy in these." He stands again and goes over to the bookshelf and pulls down another album and flips through it. Baby photos and family portraits. News clippings and promo shots. Very few images of just Brighten and Baker. Many of Brighten and her son, along with several of Baker and Jude. "She's not happy in any of the ones with my dad. And he's not happy in the ones with her," he says bitterly.

And I don't know what to tell him. It's not my place, first of all, to tell him anything about his parents' relationship. It's not my place to rip apart his innocence.

"But she's happy now. With you."

"I hope she is."

"And are you happy with her?"

I nod. "I am."

"Okay," he replies with finality, and I almost want to breathe a sigh of relief as he rises again to put away the albums. "Can I ask you one more thing?"

Why not? "Sure."

"If you and my mom get married, can I have a brother or sister?"

A shocked laugh falls from my mouth. "Wow. Now that, I can't answer. Your mom and I would have to discuss it. She might not want any more kids."

"Do you want kids? I mean, you'd kinda be stuck with me since I'm already here, but do you want to be a dad?"

I nod and when I speak, my tone is serious. "First of all, I wouldn't be *stuck* with you. I'd be proud to be part of your family and I would've been proud to be your dad when you were born if you'd been mine. When you came out and you cried, it was the most amazing sound I'd ever heard in my life. I couldn't forget it if I tried. But whatever your mom wants, I'd be up for it."

"Okay." He hands me my controller. "Can you show me how you take that one curve without falling off the edge?"

I give him a smile and accept the device. "I'd be happy to."

CHAPTER THIRTY-NINE

BRIGHTEN

I was about to go into the bedroom to tell Flynn and Jude that supper was ready, but I heard them talking, so I decided to listen for a minute. Jude asks Flynn if he thinks Jude Tate would've liked him; if he's a "good Jude". I couldn't stop the tears if I tried. And as they continue to roll down my cheeks, I listen to their conversation and hurt so badly for my son and all the things he's realized as of late.

As his mother, it breaks my heart that he can see by simply looking at photos that Baker and I weren't happy. Despite all our acting, we couldn't fool our son and I hate it.

I expect at any time, Flynn will grow tired of answering Jude's questions, but he doesn't. He answers them honestly and with patience, and I nearly fall over when Jude asks if he can have a sibling. It's definitely not the first time he's requested a younger brother or sister, but Baker and I both always played off his question by telling him we didn't need another kid since we already had the closest thing to perfect we were ever going to get.

But then Flynn tells him about the day he was born and

how he felt and my heart does this little flip and floods with love for this man, who, even now, still wants to put my needs and wants first. He's never stopped trying to do that, not since we were twelve years old. Even when I couldn't let him stand guard over my dreams anymore, he still wanted to.

What about his dreams and all the things he's always wanted? All the things I couldn't give him all those years ago, I can now. I can give him myself and my dreams *and* his. I can make sure he has everything he's ever wanted or needed.

I'm quiet during supper, opting to let Jude and Flynn dominate the conversation. And they talk like two people who've known each other for years, not only a few hours. They discuss books and school and it's just extraordinarily nice. And although our dinners with Baker in Nashville carried on in much the same way this one has, there's an ease to this one I never once felt with Baker. I don't even have to analyze why that is. I don't resent Flynn or blame him for having to sit here. I simply get to enjoy watching my two favorite people in existence carry on an intelligent and fun conversation.

Jude doesn't have his phone out on the table, but he keeps glancing at the clock, and I know he's anxious to go meet up with his new friend. "Jude, if you're done, you can go hang out with Hazel."

His eyes light up. "Really?"

I nod. "Sure. Just be home by nine, okay?"

He jumps up from the table and starts to run off before coming back and taking his dirty plate to the kitchen and dropping it into the sink and practically sprinting out the door. "Bye Mom. Bye Flynn."

Flynn laughs as the front door slams. "Wow. He's not excited or anything."

I shrug. "I'm just glad he's made a friend."

"A friend who's a girl? Those kinds of friendships can get complicated."

Rising from my chair, I extend my hand in his direction. "Yeah. She's a lot better at basketball than him, though, so it should keep him humble."

He stands and takes my hand and pulls me toward him. "Humble is good. If he's anything like his mother, he'll need humbling from time to time. I did a pretty good job kicking his butt at Nintendo, but I'm old, so I guess that doesn't count."

I wrap my arms around his waist and begin shuffling him back toward my bedroom. "You know, you might have to help me get these dishes done so it doesn't look like we abandoned them right after he left."

He grins and drops a kiss on my mouth. "Deal. We've made this sort of timeline work plenty of times before."

I nod and turn us into my room and shut the door. "We have. You know, there are a lot worse things in this world than friends falling in love."

He sobers and nods and takes my face in his hands. "I'm glad we don't have to experience those worse things anymore, though, Crash; not going to lie."

I drop my eyes to his chest. "Me, too."

Flynn lifts my face until my eyes meet his again. "But that's all done now. We're going to put it behind us and look forward to only good things." He drops onto the bed and pulls me into his lap. "Jude and I talked while we gamed."

"Oh?"

He gives me a soft smile. "He's a smart kid."

"He is," I agree.

"He asked if there was a chance he could be mine."

My eyes go wide and my breath catches. "What?"

"He said you told him you and I were together right before you and Baker got together. Who knows, maybe he did some math about your anniversary and knows you were pregnant when you got married. I told him that he wasn't, of course. But I did tell him that I would've been happy if he had been."

He swallows thickly and his eyes well with tears. "He asked me if he was a 'good Jude' and if my dad would've liked him. God, Crash, talk about a heartache. I had to try so hard not to cry, but I wanted to. Dad would've loved him."

Wetness fills my own eyes and I sniff. "I know." I chew my lip. "That day I came to see your dad, he knew about Baker and the baby already. Because he always knew things. But I felt so guilty for everything that had happened and I hadn't had anyone to talk to, and then I felt even worse because Jude still called me his girl. I wanted to die, Flynn. This man, who'd raised the best man I'd ever known and hurt more than anyone ever could deserve, still loved me.

"He said that if I was his kid, that made my baby his grand-kid. I told him he was going to be the best grandpa ever. He said, 'I prefer Pop-Pop'. Just like that. And he held me while I cried. I'd hurt his son and broken his heart, and he still loved me. I've wished so many times I could show your dad what an impact he had on my life. That so much of who I am is because of who he was. That when I think about the kind of man I want my son to be, it's a man like him. And a man like you, Flynn."

We're both crying in earnest, and I run my hand along his jaw and drop my forehead to his. "For the rest of my life, I'll never be good enough for you. Even now, after everything you've ever done for me and how I've hurt you, you still put me first; my wants and needs and dreams. I want to do that for you and I want to spend whatever time we have left trying to earn you. Marry me, Flynn."

He yanks his face back and searches my eyes. "Crash, I told you, I don't need that. I only need you and Jude. I don't need a piece of paper to tell me you love me. I know you do. I don't need anything but to have you for myself."

I nod. "I know. But I want it. With you. And I don't care if it's improper or would be frowned upon if we did it soon. It's clear Jude already loves you. God, y'all are so much alike, you'd think he really was your kid. I want to show him what a good marriage looks like; what a happy, loving relationship should be. Will you help me do that?"

"Marriage? Really?" he asks, his voice shaky, as if he's unsure he can actually believe what he's heard.

"Really. I don't have a ring to offer you, only what's left of my heart. Flynn Maverick Tate, will you marry me?"

"Name the day," he says with a watery laugh and a radiant smile. He presses his lips to mine, and it's sweet and tender and our tears mingle with our kisses. But then, it's decidedly less sweet and tender and much more frantic and greedy as I tug his shirt up his torso and we're forced to break our kiss for it to come over his head.

I take a moment to drag off my own shirt and rise from the bed to shuck my jeans before dropping to my knees in front of Flynn, much the same way he did the day he showed up after he broke his engagement. His eyes track my movement and his lips part on an exhale as I run my hands up his thighs. "Have you thought about this, Flynn? What you might do if you had me to yourself again?"

His chest rises and falls as I work the buckle of his belt. "Every day since New York." He lifts his hips to assist me in removing his jeans and boxers and as his dick springs free, I can't keep my eyes off of it. His was the first and I'm so glad it'll also be the last one I ever see. "And now that you've got me, what do you plan on doing with me?" he asks with a slow smile.

I kiss my way up his thigh, the coarse hairs on his legs tickling my lips. "Oh, so much, my love. For the rest of my life. Do you remember the first time I gave you head?"

He huffs a laugh. "I remember everything. I thought I was going to die."

"We were only kids then."

"Yeah," he agrees, running his hand along my jaw.

"But even back then, it was good."

"Yeah, it was." I begin to drop my mouth to the head of his dick, and he threads his fingers into my hair and tugs to get my attention. "Don't get too overzealous there; I don't plan on coming anywhere but inside your pussy. I'm not as young as I used to be and my recovery time is nowhere near as short as it was back then," he says with a chuckle.

"Good to know. No worries, I don't want to get you off; I just want a taste." He opens his mouth to say something else, but my tongue skating up the underside of his shaft and around the flared crown of his cock makes him forget whatever it was he was about to say in favor of a sharp inhale. The taste and feel of him in my mouth is so familiar, it's as if I did this yesterday and not fourteen years ago. In this moment, I'm transported back to a time before my life changed and I became someone completely different than the girl I was back then.

Flynn slowly beginning to thrust brings me back and I relish his groans and the feel of his hand fisting my hair. I bring my eyes to his and his gaze is heated and full of love and affection and God, how I love this man. How I ever thought I could never love anyone—especially him—I'll never be able to understand.

He drags the thumb of his free hand under my eye, swiping away a tear, and his chest heaves as he looks down at me. "Fuck, you're perfect, Crash." I hollow out my cheeks to focus suction on the head and he grunts, his hips bucking. "Shit. You're going to have to stop. It's too good. I want inside you." He pulls me off him and drags me to my feet as he leans down to capture my mouth with his. His kiss is claiming and nearly steals my breath and somehow, in the next second, I'm completely naked, my bra and panties seemingly disappeared, and I'm on my back, his cock poised at my entrance.

Time seems to slow and all it would take would be for me to shift a half inch and he'd sink into me. I meet his eyes, my breathing ragged. "I'm clean."

He nods. "Me, too. Got my results back this morning."

I blink and huff a laugh. "Really?"

Flynn takes my face in one hand and grips my hip with the other as he slowly enters me and I gasp. This is not something I've ever let myself do, not even with Flynn, but knowing we're forever? It's all I want to do; to share myself with him like this. "Okay?" he asks.

Giving him a jerky nod, I pull his mouth down to mine. "Perfect." I tilt my hips and he makes a low sound of appreciation as we begin to move together. Even knowing we're up against the clock, he doesn't let me hurry us up, even though I'm already on a razor's edge from how badly I've wanted him all day.

Anytime I try to speed up, he intentionally slows down and shakes his head. "You don't get to rush me. You think I'm not going to to savor the first time I get to have you raw? Fucking hell, woman."

"It's good, right?" I ask and grip his shoulders.

He drops his forehead to the crook of my neck as he slowly drives in and out in a maddeningly perfect rhythm. "Fucking heaven," he says with a huff.

"Careful, you'll give me a big head." He shifts his hips abruptly and hits a deep, sweet spot, and I let out a low moan.

He raises his head, his eyes searching mine as he brings a

hand to my breast to tease my nipple. "You make noises like that and you're liable to give me one."

"Keep that up and you'll have earned it. Fuck, Flynn."

He kisses me deeply and I thread my fingers through his hair, needing to hold him closer as my pleasure builds. He breaks his mouth from mine and licks and sucks his way up my jaw to my ear. "Those fucking sounds you make, Crash. Jesus. And the way this pussy feels? Holy fuck. No one feels like you. Because no one is you. It didn't matter who I was with; they were all you. Every single one. But this? Knowing I get to have you all to myself? Christ, baby, I love you so fucking much. You feel so fucking good."

I pull his mouth back to mine as my heart squeezes with love for him. "God, Flynn, please. I'm so close."

He smiles into our kiss. "I know. Don't I always take care of you?"

"Yes. Fuck."

Flynn pulls my hand from his hair and brings it to his lips and sucks my two middle fingers into his mouth, swirling his tongue around the fingertips, making me moan, before guiding it between our bodies. "Get there for me. I want to feel you come on my cock." He nips at my bottom lip. "Then, I'm going to fill you up so good, my cum's going to drip down your thighs for hours."

His words make my need build even more and as I strum my clit, I'm so close I can taste it. And when he tugs my nipple gently between his teeth, I cry out, my orgasm crashing into me so suddenly tears spring to my eyes. He groans, "Fuck yes. Jesus, so good." Shifting our bodies, he braces the back of my knee on his bicep and increases the momentum of his thrust, making me gasp.

"Fuck," I cry. "Oh God, Flynn."

His breathing grows even more labored and a bead of sweat

trickles down the side of his face as he pounds into me so deliciously, another climax is swiftly building. I heave ragged breaths and Flynn looks down at me. "You got one more in you?" I give him a jerky nod and he huffs a laugh. "That's my girl. Fucking give it to me."

I pull his mouth down to mine and kiss him deeply as I let go a second time with a soft sigh. He groans into our kiss and with a few final pumps, his body goes rigged, a deep grunt working its way up his throat as his cock jerks inside me.

For the few minutes it takes him to drop to the mattress beside me and pull me into his arms, we both simply try to breathe. I check his watch and see we still have almost an hour before Jude comes home. Flynn peppers my face with slow kisses, his hand dragging lazily down my back.

"Careful, you'll get me all riled up again."

He huffs a laugh. "What a shame that would be." Tilting my chin up so our gazes meet, he gives me a soft smile. "You're really going to marry me?"

I grin. "Well, technically, since I asked you, I think that would mean you're going to marry me. But yeah."

He heaves a contented sigh. "Pinch me." I laugh and pinch the skin above his hip, and he yelps and yanks my hand away. "Ouch. It's a figure of speech. I didn't mean to literally pinch me, Crash. Damn."

I snort in amusement. "Just following instructions. Next time, be more specific."

He smiles wickedly and rolls me on my back again and settles between my legs. "Next time, I'll give you better instructions. Too bad we don't have time now."

Shaking my head, I bring my hand up to trace his brows with my fingertip. "No, we don't. But we do have time for you to come help me with the dishes."

He drops a kiss onto my lips and rolls off the bed. "Not

even married yet and already nagging me about housework. Wow."

I give him a playful slap on the ass. "Listen, I'm a powerful woman now; I'm used to getting my way these days."

He slips into his boxers and jeans. "You've always been a powerful woman. Especially when it comes to me. And there's nowhere else I'd rather be than under your power."

I go up onto my toes after tugging my shirt over my head to give him a kiss. "Such a sweet talker."

Over the next several weeks, as we settle into a routine, Flynn joins us most nights for supper and we spend time as a family either watching TV or playing video games. Sometimes, Jude will go over to Hazel's or she'll come over and we'll give them the living room to watch television and Flynn and I will go for a walk or sit on the back patio on the swing and talk about the future.

Tonight, though, he's away for work, so it's just Jude and me. Which, honestly, it's good, because, as we've all settled into this wonderful family dynamic, I've been giving a lot of thought to when Flynn and I should get married. Since I've given myself permission to want it with him, it's all I want. I want to be able to fall asleep next to him and wake up with him and for the three of us to be a real family.

Over burgers and shakes and a shared order of onion rings from our favorite diner, I bring up Flynn. "You like Flynn okay?"

Jude rolls his eyes, as if he can see through my question. "Yeah, Mom, I like Flynn. You love him, though, right?"

Hearing my son say this with nothing but genuine interest makes my heart skip a beat. I nod. "I do."

"So, when are you getting married?"

I can't hide my surprise at his question. "What?"

He rolls his eyes again and heaves a sigh, as if he's bored. "Seriously? You think I don't know you're going to marry him? I'm not stupid, Mom. Flynn practically lives with us. I know he goes home at night, but he's always at the house and you two are all gross around each other."

I frown. "What? We're not affectionate in front of you."

Jude scoffs. "You don't have to be. You look at him like he's the biggest piece of cake on the planet."

A surprised laugh escapes me as my cheeks heat. "Sorry. I'll try to be more discreet with the way I look at him."

My son sobers. "No, you shouldn't. It's good, Mom. Can I ask you something?"

Unsure where this conversation could possibly go and not at all confident that his question won't leave me reeling from how intuitive and wise beyond his years he is, I still find myself nodding. I only hope it's a question I can answer without much difficulty.

He looks down at the tabletop. "If you hadn't had me, would you and Flynn have stayed together? Is it my fault you broke up and married Dad?" His tone is hesitant and vulnerable and makes my chest ache. "Because you're happy with Flynn. You weren't happy with Dad. You never laughed with him. I used to think you just didn't laugh at stuff because you would smile, but you never laughed. Not like you do now. You and Flynn laugh all the time."

"Oh, Jude," I say, my voice thick with emotion. "I wouldn't trade you for anything in this world. And I could never wish to take back any moment in my life, because it would mean I'd have to change the way things have turned out and I can't say I'd ever want that. Being your mother has been the best thing I never knew I ever wanted.

"If I'm honest, becoming a mother wasn't ever something I thought I would want. Looking back, though, I think it had more to do with my relationship with my own mother and how dysfunctional it was. And I had a really hard time after you were born, because I was sad.

"None of that was your fault, honey. Most days, you were my only happiness. I was sad because I had all these plans for my life and they changed. But even more than that, because of the changes, I hurt my best friend and lost him. And that's why I'm happy now. I have you and I have my best friend back. Flynn has always felt like this huge part of me and without him in my life, I didn't feel like I was whole."

"But you feel whole now?" he asks.

I nod. "I do."

"Were you and Dad ever happy? I mean, if you always loved Flynn, why did you and Dad even get married?"

I'm not about to tell him that Baker blackmailed me and practically held me captive for ten years. He would never understand, even if he knew everything. And as someone who's had their image of their father completely demolished, I can't bring myself to do that to my son. So I simply say, "People get married for a lot of reasons."

He narrows his eyes. "That's really vague, Mom."

I shrug. "It's all I've got, kiddo."

"But that's the same answer you gave me when Flynn left that first night."

I nod and give him an apologetic smile. "Sorry."

"Will you tell me the truth someday? All of it?"

"I can't promise that," I admit.

Jude sighs again, and this time it sounds resigned. "Okay." After a beat, he asks, "But are you and Flynn getting married?"

"Is that something you'd be okay with?"

He nods. "Flynn's cool. He's really smart; like Dad."

I huff a laugh. "I've always had a thing for smart guys."

"And if y'all get married, will I finally get a brother or sister?"

I shrug. "Flynn and I would have to talk about it."

His eyes widen. "That's not a no."

I shake my head, a small smile pulling at the corners of my mouth. "No, it's not a no."

CHAPTER FORTY

FLYNN

"I shouldn't be nervous; it's not even my recital," I say sheepishly.

Brighten looks over at me from her seat and grins. "Aww, that's adorable. You'll get used to that. His first recital, when he was six, I felt like I was going to throw up. I was so nervous for him. But he just walked to the piano and rocked it out."

Jess turns in his seat and whispers over his shoulder. "Plus, it doesn't hurt that he's really good." He taps his program. "'Moonlight Sonata' is a great choice. Ophelia plays a lot of Beethoven for the baby, now that he or she can hear—from what the OB says," he remarks. "Maybe we can get a recording and play it the next time she puts her headphones on her belly."

Brighten beams with maternal pride and I put my arm around her and pull her into my side and drop a kiss onto the top of her head. Mom, Jess and Ophelia, along with Baker's parents, are here at the recital.

They're both in their seventies. His father is an older version of Baker; stocky with olive skin and silver hair, his eyes the same brown as Jude's. His mother is the epitome of a life-long corporate wife; sleek and posh and slim, with her dark hair styled in a neat bob. They're both dressed as if they're ready for an evening at a country club; him in a dark suit and her in a navy shift dress and low heels and a set of pearls.

I was nervous to meet them, considering it's only been a few months since Baker died and I'm in a serious relationship with their only son's widow. But it is what it is, right? And the fact that Jude is the one who introduced me to them made me feel a bit better about things. They're being civil, at least. I also have no clue how they feel about Baker leaving his controlling shares of Intuition to Brighten, either. I would imagine she'll tell me after the shareholders' meeting tomorrow.

But tonight, I watch as—exactly as Brighten described—Jude strides confidently to the grand piano in the auditorium of the church where the recital is being held. He takes a seat on the bench and readies his sheet music. Just before he begins, he takes a deep breath and flexes his fingers over the keys.

And although he has the sheet music, he never once glances at it as he plays. When he does, I'm immediately transported to the day he was born and goosebumps erupt all along my skin as the notes float through the room. It's the same song Brighten played for Dad and I'm forced to close my eyes for a beat and try to breathe as the bittersweetness of it washes over me.

As I'm no pianist, I can't be sure, but it seemed as though his playing is flawless. And to watch him, his mannerisms while he plays are very similar to that of his mother. When he finishes and stands, the crowd cheering, it's all I can do to not shoot to my feet and whistle for him. But I assume that wouldn't exactly be proper, so I keep my seat. He scans the crowd and when he finds our group, his grin widens.

The next student takes the stage and I turn to Brighten.

"Did you know he was going to play that?" She nods. "You played that the day you came to see Dad."

She smiles, and it's a bit sad. "I know. Jude asked me what I played that day and when I told him, he wanted that to be the first song you heard him play in public."

My breath hitches, my heart kicking over in my chest. "What?"

Her grin widens. "That was for you, Flynn. As a welcome to the family gift." She leans closer and lowers her voice. "I told him we were getting married."

My mouth falls open in shock and a bark of laughter escapes me that I try to disguise as a cough. "What? Really?"

She nods. "Yeah. He said, and I quote, 'Flynn's cool'."

And I suppose, for a thirteen-year-old, that's as ringing an endorsement as one is likely to get. I peer up at the ceiling, still fighting off my emotions. *You hear that, Dad? Jude thinks I'm cool. Not sure I'll ever be as cool as you, though. You can bet your ass I'm going to try.*

As the recital participants stream out to the auditorium, our small group waits for Jude. And after a quick round of "great job" from my mom, brother, and sister-in-law, they all depart. Baker's parents wait patiently and his grandfather, whom I remember in passing from my internship at Intuition, claps Jude on the shoulder and offers him stoic praise. His grandmother is a bit more effusive, but still holds back some bigger emotions you can feel radiating off her. They make plans for the upcoming spring break and Brighten confirms that we'll bring him with us to Nashville to drop him off when we come for the shareholders' meeting tomorrow.

"Flynn, may I speak with you for a moment?" Baker's

father, Hayden, asks as we're exiting the building. He doesn't give me an opportunity to answer before he turns to Brighten and his wife, Dottie. "Why don't y'all go on to the restaurant? Brighten, can Dottie ride with you? Flynn and I will be along shortly."

Brighten looks like she wants to object, and although I have no clue what this man has in store for me, I'm not afraid of him and I give her a quick nod to let her know it's okay. "Sure," she replies, only a hint of uncertainty in her tone.

Jude steps forward and looks up at me. And considering how tall he is already, it's not a chore for him. "Can I ride with you guys?" he asks me.

I shake my head, not even needing confirmation from Hayden that he'd prefer our conversation be private. "Not this time. We'll be right behind you, okay?" I ruffle his hair playfully. "I'm proud of you. Save me a seat at the restaurant?"

He pushes my hand away, but has a smile on his face. "Okay."

I shoot Brighten a smile and climb into the passenger seat of Hayden's Mercedes. He wastes no time before beginning to speak as he reverses out of the parking spot. "I understand you and Brighten will be getting married."

"Yes, sir." I offer no further explanation because it's not really his business, but I steel myself for him to tell me the timing is tasteless or that I'll never be a good enough father to his grandson. Because whatever vitriol he could spew—if that's his aim—doesn't matter, because Brighten is mine. Jude is mine. But he's still a grieving father, so I'm prepared to hear whatever it is he feels the need to say.

His grip tightens on the steering wheel and he sighs. "I'm glad."

I blink in shock. "I'm sorry?" The words leave my mouth before I can bite them back.

He switches on his blinker and turns into a shopping center a few miles away from the restaurant. Pulling into an empty spot, he parks and turns to give me his full attention. "Baker and I had a conversation before he died. I believe he was trying to clear his conscious. I'm assuming you're aware of Baker and Brighten's origins? I don't need to explain all that?"

"No, sir, you don't," I say, unable to keep the bitterness out of my tone.

Hayden nods. "Good." He licks his lips nervously and clears his throat. "I make no excuses for the actions of my son. Hearing him tell me the things he did—and the reasons why—it wasn't easy to absorb those words. His mother and I raised him to be an honorable man. We also raised him to be ambitious and driven, but I always hoped he would be a good man. I want to say that he was, but learning what he did to Brighten—and by extension, you—even as his father, it's difficult to reconcile.

"He told me as soon as he died, he knew she would try to find you. That if he hadn't gotten sick, they would've divorced and he knew you'd be her first call. He said I didn't need to worry about Jude, because you were a good man who would finish the job he started and make sure that his son turned out to be a better man than his father was."

I'm not sure if I want to cry or scream with the warring emotions within myself. For fourteen years, I've hated Baker and now I'm not sure if I can anymore.

Hayden looks down, and he's quiet for a moment. "I understand that my son hurt you with his actions. And I'm sure since you can't retaliate against him, it would be easy for you and Brighten to keep Jude from us or expose his father's sins. Man to man—father to father—I beg you not to do that." His voice thickens with emotion and my chest grows tight. "He's all I have left of *my* son."

I shake my head. "You have nothing to worry about, sir. I've never had plans to tell Jude what Baker did. I know he was a good father and provider, even if I hated him—no offense intended. But my love for Brighten and Jude has tempered the majority of my anger. And if it's up to me, you and your wife will always have access to Jude. You're his grandparents; I can't hold your son's actions against you."

He breathes a sigh of relief. "Thank you. And for what it's worth, I can see that you love them. I understand Jude is named for your father; is that right? And you?"

"Yes, sir. Brighten and my dad were very close. The song Jude played tonight was the song she played for my father the last time she visited him before he passed."

"I'm sorry he's not here to see his namesake, but it's obvious he raised you to be a good man. I'm glad my grandson will have a fine example to follow."

"Thank you," I reply. My voice comes out gruff because I'm trying so hard not to cry. First Jude's recital piece and now Baker's father subverting every expectation I could've had for how this conversation would go? Damn.

He puts the car into gear but seems to think better of it and returns it to park. "One more thing. From what Baker said, you interned at Intuition several years ago?"

I nod. "Yes, sir. Right out of high school. Elias Washington was my mentor."

He smiles. "Good man, that Elias."

"Yes, sir," I agree.

"Well, then, that makes this next part even easier. I'd like to offer you a job, Flynn."

I blink. "I'm sorry?"

"We're expanding operations and we need someone to oversee and manage the new location. The plans will be finalized at the shareholders' meeting tomorrow, but it's merely a formality at this point, since Brighten has a controlling share and she's already placed her support behind the idea. We're opening a branch here in Knoxville and I'd like you to consider running it. Your professional reputation is impressive and really, we'd be a fool to let you continue with any other firm; especially considering your soon-to-be wife controls Intuition. What kind of message does that send to our shareholders and clients if you're with a competitor?

"And before you suggest this is some sort of payoff or bribe to incentivize you to continue letting us have a relationship with Jude, I can assure you it's not. The plans for this expansion have been in the works for several years; even before Baker's diagnosis. The timing just happens to be unfortunate. Like I said, your reputation is impressive and this would be a well-earned position for you."

I'm floored by this turn of events. "I'm flattered by this offer, Mr. Roberts. May I have the night to think it over and discuss it with Brighten?"

He nods. "Of course. And please, call me Hayden. I hope, going forward, we can be friendly. If for nothing other than the love we all have for Jude."

"I'd like that."

As we take the elevator up to the conference room for the shareholders' meeting—for which I will remain in the adjacent room as I am not a shareholder—Brighten asks, "So, have you made your mind up about the job offer?"

"I have to take it, right? It's the only thing that makes sense. Career-wise, it's a no-brainer. And my opinion about Baker notwithstanding, Intuition is a great firm. I thought so when I was eighteen, I still think that. And the fact that we wouldn't have to move for me to work there, it's appealing, not going to lie."

Her brows lift, a hopeful expression lighting her eyes. "So, is that a yes?"

I huff a laugh. "Yeah, Crash, it's a yes."

She grins. "Great. I'll inform the board." Just before the elevator doors open, she blows out a breath and rolls her shoulders. She looks like a kick-ass ballbuster in a pair of slim black pants, a dark green silk blouse that makes her eyes look even more rich, black stilettos, and her red hair in loose curls.

"You look like you're ready to take your place on the throne."

She nods, but keeps her eyes forward as the lift comes to a stop. "I'm so nervous, I could throw up."

I give her hand a supportive squeeze. "You got this." The doors open and we step out. Brighten sways on her heels and I take a more firm hold of her hand to steady her. "You alright?" I ask, unable to hide my concern.

She nods and takes a deep breath and looks up at me. "Yeah. Just got a little dizzy for a second. That was weird. Maybe too much caffeine and all the nerves?"

"Okay. After we get done here, we'll go get a bite to eat."

As we reach the conference room doors, I give her a quick kiss and step into the next room. Because all the Intuition offices have glass walls, I can still see into the conference room as I pour myself a cup of coffee and sit in an office eerily similar to the one Elias had all those years ago. Same style leather sofas, just a bar and coffee area to replace the massive wood and metal desk.

I take a seat on the sofa facing the conference room and pull out my phone to compose my letter of resignation to my current company. Glancing up as the meeting gets underway, I watch as

Hayden takes the seat at the head of the table and everyone flips to a page in a folder as he begins speaking. But as I start to look back down at my phone, movement out of the corner of my eye has me standing to walk out into the hall. "Elias?" I call, surprised.

The man turns, a look of delighted shock on his face. A face I haven't seen in person in over a decade, but have kept up with via phone and email sporadically. "Flynn? I'll be damned." We embrace for a quick hug and he claps me on the shoulders. "What are you doing here? Last we spoke, you were moving to Miami to get married."

I huff a laugh. "Wow, I have a lot to catch you up on." I give him the rundown of everything that's happened over the last few months and gesture to the conference room. "And I'm getting married, but not to Cleo," I say, and I know my grin must look like that of the goofball teenager I was when we first met.

His face morphs into a warm smile. "How about that? You got your girl back."

"That I did. What are you doing here? You're supposed to be retired."

Elias nods. "I am. I like to show up every once in a while and remind everyone what a big shot I used to be," he replies with a wink. After we share a quick laugh, he splays his hands. "Actually, I'm going to step in to do another mentorship this summer. Retirement's a little boring for me. I promised Camille I'd keep it strictly to the summers so we can still travel through the year and visit with the grandkids. But I miss it, so here I am."

"Wow. That's great."

"So, how's family life treating you? Jude's what, thirteen now?"

"Yep. Instant family is pretty great, I gotta say. He's a good kid."

He lifts a brow. "Think you'll have any more?"

I shrug. "It's a regular topic of discussion. If it's up to Jude, we will, but even if we don't, I'm a happy man."

My mentor beams. "Happy is a good place to be."

Facing the conference room, I nod. "Doesn't hurt when it looks like her, that's for sure." Elias chuckles. Brighten fans her face with a folded sheet of paper and even from here, I can see a sheen of sweat on her forehead. I frown in confusion, but she's not looking at me. Her attention is firmly focused on Hayden as he says something and then gestures to her at the opposite end of the table.

She nods and rolls her chair back, making to stand. As she gets to her feet, she sways and my body is moving before my brain even registers she's going down. I'm through the conference room door and manage to catch her before she hits the ground. Collective sounds of concern filter through the members of the board, but I don't hear them as I attempt to rouse her. "Crash? Can you hear me?"

It vaguely registers that someone calls for an ambulance, but a few seconds after she's fainted, her eyes flutter open. "Flynn?" Her tone is confused, but I only feel relieved.

"Yeah, I'm here. Where'd you go?" I try to keep the fear out of my voice, but it's been an emotional couple of days and I'm not sure I succeed. She blinks in confusion and tries to sit up. "We need to get you checked out, Crash."

Brighten shakes her head. "I'm okay, I think. Maybe I just need something to eat."

"Are you sure?"

"Yeah. I'm fine." I help her to her feet and Hayden is standing by, concern etched into his features.

"Brighten, someone will be up to check you out." He extends a bottle of water toward her and gestures to her chair. "Please sit so we can make sure you're alright."

She obeys and takes the water, but waves her hand dismissively. "I'm fine. Just too much caffeine this morning, I think."

I squat to look her in the eye. "You don't get dizzy and caffeine hasn't ever affected you before. I want you to get checked out."

"Flynn, I'm fine."

Taking her hands in mine, I can't ignore how clammy they feel, but I know if I point that out to her, she'll just dismiss it, too. "For me?" I plead. "It'll be like old times and I'll go with you to the hospital. You're beautiful, but you're not looking so good. It would make me feel a lot better if you get checked out."

She heaves a resigned sigh. "Fine."

CHAPTER FORTY-ONE

BRIGHTEN

Although I agree to get checked out, I refuse to take an ambulance and opt for urgent care over the emergency room since it doesn't appear to be an actual emergency. Yet, as we walk in, Flynn hovers as though I might faint again at any moment.

"I'm fine, Flynn. Please stop treating me like I'm some fragile thing. I'm getting checked out—per your request—but I refuse to be coddled and fussed over simply because I got a little lightheaded."

"You fainted, Crash. That's not insignificant."

I gesture to the papers I'm filling out. "And I'm getting checked out. But you're going to have to chill. I promise, I'm okay."

He clenches his jaw. "Listen, no one knows how much of a badass you are more than me, but you are not a medical professional. So until *they* tell me you're fine, I'm going to believe otherwise."

I huff in annoyance and hurriedly fill out the papers and

return them to the reception desk. As I return to my seat, I fold my arms. "Some first impression to the board I made."

Flynn shakes his head. "Like anyone is going to say anything to you about it. Ever. You're the boss. You could probably attend all your meetings in a meat dress like Gaga and they'd pretend you were wearing a designer suit."

I snort in amusement. "I guess power does come with certain privileges."

He sobers and takes my hand in his, intertwining our fingers. "You scared me, Crash."

"I'm sorry. But I promise, I feel fine."

"I'm sure. But humor me?"

I level him with a gaze. "I'm here, aren't I?"

He leans over and presses a soft kiss to my lips. "Thank you," he says when he pulls back. He's about to say something else, but the door leading to the exam rooms opens and my name is called. "You want me to stay out here?"

Shaking my head, I tug his hand. "No, you dragged me in here, so you get to endure this, too."

"Yes, ma'am," he replies, standing to follow me.

We're led down a hallway and the nurse gestures to a room and looks at Flynn. "If you'd like to wait in there, I'm going to get some basic medical history and take her vitals. She'll be in shortly."

He gives my hand a squeeze and nods to the nurse before stepping into the exam room. After having me step onto a scale, the nurse gestures for me to sit and proceeds to take my blood pressure, pulse, blood oxygen level, and temperature. Once she's recorded all of my pertinent medical history, she asks, "And when was your last period?"

I think back and my stomach drops when I realize I haven't had one since I moved back to Knoxville—over four months ago —but I'm on the pill, so I immediately laugh off the thought.

"I'm on the pill and I take them straight through so I don't have one."

She nods. "Okay, and do you always use a backup method of contraception?"

"No, my fiancé and I are monogamous."

"So, there's no chance you think you could be pregnant?"

I splay my hands. "I mean, I know it's not a hundred percent effective, so I suppose there's always a chance, but I've been on the pill the whole time we've been together and was celibate for a year before that."

She nods again and taps some keys on her computer. "According to your medical records, you've had your current prescription for the last four months?"

"Yes," I confirm. "I've had two IUDs since my son was born, but when I got the last one removed, I wasn't sexually active. My fiancé and I are considering having children, so I didn't want to go through with another IUD if we were going to attempt to conceive in the near future. The pill seemed easier."

She offers me a warm smile. "Sure; I get that. Just to be on the safe side, we'll run a pregnancy test just to rule it out. That way, if it's not that, we'll know we need to dig a little deeper." Extending a small paper cup in my direction, she gestures across the hall. "Just place it in the door in the wall once you've provided your sample and then you can go on in with your fiancé and the doctor will be in soon, okay?"

I blow out a nervous breath and nod, accepting the cup. As I go through the process of "providing my sample", I think back to the last time I took a pregnancy test. Baker practically stood guard as I peed on the stick. Bobby took my blood. I felt like it was the worst day of my life. Granted, the actual worst day of my life came later that week when I broke Flynn's heart, but it was still a rough day.

And if you'd told me when I first woke up this morning that

this would be something I would be doing, I would've assumed I'd break out in a cold sweat. But faced with the reality of possibly going through this again, I know if it's positive, I won't fall apart this time.

Motherhood no longer terrifies or repulses me. Jude is a blessing I never would have asked for but could never wish to take back. This would very much be a blessing. This time, I have a partner I love with my whole heart and as I place the cup in the designated door, I'm not scared of the outcome.

I wash my hands and step across the hall and into the exam room. Flynn's head snaps up, his expression concerned. "That took a while."

I nod. "They just had to go over everything. I'm sure I'm fine." At this point and after my conversation with the nurse, I have a suspicion I know what caused me to faint, but I'm not going to give Flynn a reason to suspect or freak out until I know without a doubt. And at least this way, we'll find out together, right?

"I still expect you to take me to eat after this. I'm starving."

He huffs a laugh. "Sure thing. Pharmacy?"

"You know it." I take a seat on the exam table. "Did Jess tell you that's where we went to eat when we ran into each other?"

"No. I didn't know that."

"Of course, all I could think of was that first time we went with Sully and us coming back to your apartment after."

His eyes slide up and away as if he's remembering. "That was a good night."

His arm currently lays on the end of the table, so I scoot over and take his hand in mine. "That it was. All the nights with you were good."

He rises and comes to stand in front of me and plants his hands on either side of my hips. "You're not wrong." Flynn's eyes search mine before he leans in to press a kiss to the side of my neck. "And can I tell you how excited I am that I get to fall asleep with you all this week while Jude is spending time with his grandparents?"

I run my hands up his arms and loop them around his shoulders. "I'm excited to wake up with you. And I'm thinking we can get a lot of wedding planning done this week"

He grins. "I like the sound of that. And will this be naked wedding planning?"

"I'm amenable to that request," I reply with a smile of my own. Bringing my hands to his face, I look into his eyes. "I love you, you know that?"

He nods, giving my wrist an affectionate squeeze. "I do. You know—." His words are cut off by a knock on the door and he steps back and moves to stand beside me as the doctor enters.

His expression is neutral as he introduces himself and washes his hands. He takes a seat on a stool and rolls it over next to us. Flynn shifts nervously from foot to foot. "Well, do we need to worry?"

The doctor, a Hispanic man about our age named Dr. Martinez, glances at me for confirmation that he's free to speak with Flynn in the room, and I give him a reassuring smile and nod. He answers Flynn's question. "No, sir. Things like this usually resolve on their own." He turns his gaze to me. "In about nine months. Or, in your case, probably about five or six, given the dates you provided us," he says meaningfully. "You'll need bloodwork and an ultrasound to confirm that, though."

My heart kicks over and a huff of shocked laughter falls from my mouth. "Really?" I ask, realizing I'm hopeful and excited.

Dr. Martinez nods, and Flynn blinks, confused. "Wait, so what's wrong with her?" my beautiful, intelligent, oblivious fiancé asks.

I snort a delighted laugh and the doctor stands. "Absolutely nothing." He looks at me. "Would you like to do the honors?"

Nodding, I swipe away a tear and turn to Flynn. "I'm pregnant, Flynn."

His mouth falls open and all the color drains from his face before a huge grin takes over his entire countenance. "R-r-really?" he stammers, looking from me to the doctor and back to me.

Dr. Martinez extends his hand to Flynn and they shake, Flynn still in blatant shock. "Congrats, Dad." Flynn inhales sharply and my chest tightens with emotion as his shock turns into joyful awe. The doctor looks to me. "You'll want to follow up with an obstetrician soon, but other than that, you're good to go. Y'all have a great day, okay? And good luck."

He steps out and Flynn turns to me. "Is this real?" And immediately after he says it, he shutters his excitement, sobering so quickly, I nearly have emotional whiplash. "And is this what you want? I told you I didn't need this, and I meant it. So forget my initial reaction. This is your decision, Crash. You know I'll support whatever you want to do."

His words make my heart ache because I know he's being completely honest. Regardless of how badly he wants this, he would give it up if I didn't. Tears well in my eyes and I take his face in my hands. "I want it, Flynn. I promise. I love you so much and can't wait to do this with you. You're going to be a dad."

He barks a watery laugh, his own eyes growing wet. "I'm already a dad, Crash. But thank you for the opportunity to become one again." He sniffs, wiping his eyes. "Jude's going to fall over."

I nod, an amused chuckle falling from my mouth. "Probably."

If you had told me when I was eighteen—you know, when my life was entirely planned out—that I would be getting married not just once pregnant, but twice, I would've informed you that, surely, you were mistaken. And moreover, if you had told me it was exactly the life I'd be thrilled to have at thirty-five, I would've laughed in your face.

And yet, here I stand with Flynn, Jude, Jess, and an even more pregnant Ophelia at the Knox County courthouse, vowing—this time, with all my heart—to love, honor, and cherish my husband until death parts us. It's also nowhere near the bitter experience it was the first time I went through this. And to hear Jude tell it, it was all his great idea. Especially the baby sister who will join us in the next few months.

While we could've held out for a big wedding with all our friends and family, we both wanted to be married more than we wanted a wedding. And I have no regrets. Much like I told Flynn, I'd give up everything short of Jude to save us all the heartache we've both faced in the past fourteen years, but we can't. I'm simply thankful the heartaches will all be in the past. We have only hope to look forward to, and I cannot wait.

When I was twelve, I crashed my bike and changed the entire trajectory of my life. Little did I know, the love of my life would crash into me—and my heart—that same day.

EPILOGUE

FLYNN — FIVE YEARS LATER

"Daddy, where's Jude? Do you see him?" Mila asks and goes up on her tiptoes and attempts to look through the crowd.

I try to see over the throng of people leaving the airport. "Not yet. He should be here soon." Glancing over to Brighten, she offers me an excited grin. Looking past her to Hazel, she only appears to have eyes for the exit door.

And sure enough, she spots him before all of us and stands up straighter, picking a piece of lint off her sweater. Brighten leans over to her. "You look great. Do y'all have plans after we all go eat?"

I nudge my wife and whisper in her ear. "Probably the same things we did when we were eighteen, Crash. Damn."

She huffs a laugh and Hazel tucks her blonde hair behind her ears. "We're just going to hang out, I guess."

"I'm sure y'all will have a lot to catch up on," I offer.

A beat later, Mila squeals with delight as Jude walks out of the airport, his large frame taking up nearly half the sidewalk as he makes his way over to us. My daughter breaks free from my grasp, but as her big brother is only ten feet away, I don't immediately panic. He swings her up into his arms and gives her a big squeeze. All the while, his gaze lands on Hazel and it's like they only have eyes for each other. The look of affection and *more* he obviously has for his friend is blatant.

He sets Mila back on the ground and takes Hazel's face in his hands and presses a kiss to her lips. She's shocked for a second before wrapping her arms around his waist. Brighten and I share knowing smiles and a surprised giggle falls from Mila's mouth.

"Daddy, they're kissing. Eww. Boys are—." Brighten covers our daughter's mouth, cutting off her words, but unfortunately it's enough to get Jude and Hazel's attention. Jude pulls back and Hazel's face is a mask of confusion, mixed with hope.

Neither of them look at us, and I start to get the feeling we're intruding. "Sorry," Jude says, brushing a hair off her forehead. "I've wanted to do that for five years."

She bites her bottom lip, a blush coloring her cheeks. "Me, too."

He grins. "And I figured, it worked for them," he remarks, tilting his head in our direction, "it might work for us, too. Life's too short not to at least try, right?"

Hazel nods. "Right."

"So, how's Juilliard?" Mila asks suddenly. "And did you bring me anything?"

As if a spell is broken, Hazel and Jude turn our direction and Hazel swings our daughter up into her arms like the surrogate big sister she is and they all begin walking toward the parking lot. Our son takes Hazel's hand in his and looks over his shoulder at me, a big grin on his face. I offer him an approving nod and take Brighten's hand in mine to follow behind them.

My wife takes our linked hands and drapes my arm around her shoulder and leans into me. "Told you."

I roll my eyes. "You didn't tell me anything. I told you when he left for school in August this would happen by the time they were back home for winter break. Absence makes the heart grow fonder and all that. Especially after Jude said Hazel broke up with her boyfriend. I knew he'd shoot his shot."

"Looks like it panned out."

I nod and drop a kiss on the top of her head. "Hopefully, if it works for them, they won't have as many roadblocks as we did."

"Seriously," she says with a huffed laugh. "They look happy, though, right?"

"Yeah. So happy that we didn't even warrant a hello."

Brighten chuckles. "Last I checked, anytime we were their age, we didn't have much use for the parents, either."

"True. We were kinda wrapped up in each other, weren't we?" I give her a squeeze. "You were one of the only people I actually liked. Thank goodness you were able to look past all my asshole."

She stops and turns to look up at me. "Thank God for that. And now look at us. It's a pretty sweet life you've got here, Tate. You're wealthy and successful, have a beautiful family. You've got everything you could ever want, right? Imagine if all I saw was the asshole back in the day."

I nod. "Yeah, and imagine if I hadn't been walking past that construction site at the same time you came flying by on your bike."

Shaking her head, she loops her arms around my shoulders. "Now that, I'd never want to imagine. That was the best day of my life."

I lean down and brush a soft kiss across her lips. "And here I thought it was the first time you saw me naked."

She laughs. "A definite close second."

"You realize we can hear you, right?" Jude asks, annoyed, a few feet away.

Brighten snorts a laugh. "Sorry, kids."

He rolls his eyes, but isn't able to keep his smile hidden. "No, you're not."

"What can I say? I think my husband's hot," she says with a grin.

"Can we go eat now?" Mila asks with a pout. "I'm starving."

Jude's eyes widen and he leans over to tickle his little sister. "Me, too. I'm thinking your tummy would make a good snack."

She squeals and squirms in Hazel's arms, who laughs and whispers something in Mila's ear before setting her down. They both go after Jude, cornering him against the side of the car and retaliating with tickles of their own. They all laugh and my heart lifts to see how happy they are.

God, I love my life. No matter what it cost me to get here, I wouldn't trade any of it. Even through all the immense pain, knowing it got me *this*? How could I ever wish to take any of it back? I can't, because Brighten's right. Everything we've been through has brought me to this point in my life where, yes, I have everything I could ever want and it is most definitely the sweetest life.

ALSO BY RACHAEL OGLE

Until Duet

Until August and onto Forever (Until Books 1 & 2)

Summer Lovin' Series

Fake it to Forever (Summer Lovin' Books 1 & 2)

Knox County Series

My Ada Mae (Knox County Book 1)

Not Your Girl (Knox County Book 2)

Change My Life (Knox County Book 3)

ABOUT THE AUTHOR

For as long as she can remember, Rachael has been a voracious reader. At the age of eleven, she discovered her grandmother's stash of clench-cover romance novels and she was forever changed. A lover of many, many fictional men and one very non-fictional one, she strives to write real and emotional characters who always get their happily ever after. Rachael lives in East Tennessee with her husband and two sons on their family farm. When she's not tackling her endless TBR, she can be found drinking all the coffee in existence.